The

Empire Rising Book 1

D. J. Holmes

https://www.facebook.com/Author.D.J.Holmes

d.j.holmess@hotmail.com

Comments welcome!

This is a work of fiction. Names, characters, places, and incidents either are the product of the author's imagination or are used fictitiously and any resemblance to any persons living or dead, business establishments, events or locales are entirely coincidental.

To all my friends and family who made this first novel a reality.

Table of Contents

Prologue

July 11th 2456, Near Earth Orbit.

HMS *Vulcan* floated in high geosynchronous orbit over the British Midlands. With minimal maneuvering thrusters she wasn't really a spaceship, yet her designers hadn't wished to break with tradition when naming her. If anyone asked, the explanation was that S stood for Shipyard.

Construction bay twenty seven was a hive of activity. For a number of months construction workers had been expanding its capacity to accommodate the latest designs for a new class of ship, the first British battlecruiser. A few thousand meters higher up in orbit, work was being completed on two identical giant structures, soon to be attached to *Vulcan* and designated bays twenty eight and twenty nine. Likewise, they too would be focused on churning out the new battlecruisers for the Royal Space Navy.

Once completed this retrofit and extension would simply become one more in a long list of alterations in *Vulcan's* history. Initially constructed when Britain decided to invest heavily in interstellar expansion, *Vulcan* had been serving the RSN for over 200 years as its main shipyard. Once the shift drive had been discovered and the stars opened to humanity, interstellar exploration had taken off. Britain had banked a substantial percentage of her GDP on gaining a lead over the other space faring nations and *Vulcan* was the result.

With the discovery of Britannia this investment had paid off eighty years later. HMS *Vulcan* had hastily dispatched her third colony ship full of handpicked volunteers from all over Great Britain as well as her Moon, Mars and asteroid colonies. Britannia contained one of the rarest metals yet known to man. Named after its discoverer, valstronium was almost as revolutionary as the shift drive.

Officially classed as a metal, though the designation was still debated in the universities, it showed a remarkable ability to protect a spaceship from the wear and tear of space travel while blocking harmful cosmic radiation from injuring a ship's crew. And, once fixed by a combination of electrical and thermal treatments, the metal actually flowed like a liquid in an effort to retain its original shape when damaged. This was a ship designer's dream as it provided the perfect armor. With traditional armors, when a thermonuclear missile or a plasma bolt hit a ship it would have to return to a shipyard in order to have the damaged armor sections replaced. Armored with valstronium, a ship could take a number of hits and keep on fighting. These attributes, combined with its lightweight and the resultant gains in shift drive velocities meant that valstronium revolutionized spaceship design.

With the discovery of valstronium on Britannia, Britain gained a monopoly almost overnight. Along with this monopoly came the military power and diplomatic capital that allowed Britain to fuel its expansion beyond the Sol system and become one of the dominant space faring nations.

Despite over one hundred and fifty years having passed since the discovery of Britannia, and two hundred since the discovery of the shift drive, the exploration and colonization race between the major space faring nations showed no sign of letting up. Paid for through valstronium sales HMS *Vulcan* continued to churn out all kinds of civilian and military craft to further Britain's interstellar empire. With the new construction bays about to be finalized, battlecruisers would soon be added to that list.

Almost unnoticed among the hustle and bustle over bays twenty-seven, eight and nine a small ship slipped out of construction bay thirteen. Encased within its own valstronium armor, HMS *Drake* made her way out into space for the first time. She was one of an ever-increasing number of RSN Survey Ships. With almost one hundred and fifty in commission they served the RSN by mapping the dark matter between the stars.

*

May 7th 2464. Beijing, China.

Almost eight years later Na Zhong turned from the large holographic display to face the other politburo members. As the minister for Exploration he was a junior member in the politburo and so tried to keep his head down in these meetings. Today, that was impossible.

"And so you see," Na concluded. "There are four habitable worlds and over fifty two other systems with varying degrees of resources. This is the find of the century."

Most of the other members were still looking over his shoulders at the sphere the holographic projector was displaying. Within the sphere there were fifty-six white dots, four of which were flashing red.

Na looked over his fellow politburo members and started when he saw Chang staring at him. "Minister Na, what did your scout determine about the likeness of a shift passage into British space?" Chang Lei asked.

"As you know our scout vessel did not deem it wise to spend time investigating all the systems before coming back with this news. However, they did spend two weeks surveying the perimeter of the sphere in order to identify any passages that may lead to British space," Na replied to the minister of Defense. "There is at least one passage leading off in the rough direction of British space, though of course, without exploring it extensively we can't know where, if anywhere, it goes." This brought all eyes back to Zhong.

"Two weeks! You mean your Commander knew about this sphere of space for two weeks and didn't think to come straight back to us?" Shouted the Minister for Foreign Affairs.

"I'm afraid not, but in his defense his mission was to seek out potential shift passages into British space," Zhong said as meekly as possible, hoping to placate Fen's anger.

"Calm down Fen," the Intelligence Minister said as he lifted his hand towards the Minister for Foreign Affairs to stop any further outbursts. "This is useful, it may be a little later than we would have liked but at least we know the British may want to join our party. So what are our options?" he asked the room at large.

Chang Lei was the Intelligence Minister for the Chinese Communist Party and currently the power behind the President. Everyone knew he would make the final decision regarding this new discovery.

Fen was the first to speak, "Well we all know what we are expected to do. Those swine at the UN will want us to publicly declare this discovery first thing tomorrow."

Smiling Chang shook his head, "You all know our attempts to grow our space empire have been falling behind the other major powers. This is not an opportunity we are just going to let pass us by. We only have six habitable planets colonized so far; this is our chance to almost double that. What other options do we have? Options that will ensure China benefits from this discovery and not those lackeys at the UN."

"Well, we could send elements of third fleet into this new area of space," began the Minister of Defense. "Once we establish military bases on each of the habitable worlds we can declare our discovery and present them with a *fait accompli*. No power would dare go to war with us over these planets then."

"Ha," interjected the Minister for Development, Wen Xiang, "and how long do you think it would take the British to figure out where our ships were going. It seems that we can't keep anything from them."

Chang tried to hide a grimace. The Minister of Development was his closet rival and so did not fear his wrath. Whilst Chang prided himself in the power of his intelligence services both at home and abroad, it was undeniable that the British had managed to penetrate their government and military. Not that Chang liked being reminded of that of course.

"And don't think the British won't fight for what they think is theirs." Wen continued. "Our military might out-mass theirs but whoever controls this new discovery will become the dominant power in our area of space, there can be no doubt about that. We need to present them with a *fait accompli* true, but one that cannot lead to war. As you all know, we have one colony ship sitting in orbit waiting for just this kind of opportunity. We also have another two under construction. I suggest we rush their completion and get civilians on the ground as soon as possible. We can colonize three of the habitable planets and offer one to the UN. That way when the British demand it from the UN or us they will look like the bad guys. Plus there is no way the British will start a war over a planet already occupied by zealous Chinese nationals – even if they could win a planet from us they wouldn't want to deal with the occupation." Sitting back Wen looked over at Chang for his response.

Chang bowed his head in a begrudging sign of respect. "I think this will work. We will need a cover story for when we ask for colonial volunteers. I'm sure Minister Zhong and I can come up with something before your colony ships are ready to depart. How long until those under construction will be ready?

Wen picked up his datapad and quickly scanned through some documents. "Thirteen months," he replied. "However, we can have the *Henna,* which is in orbit at the moment, prepped and ready to go in five. I suggest we load her up and send her off as soon as possible. If we can establish a colony on one of the planets then we can quickly move more people onto each of the others."

"Very well," Chang said as he stood and brought both his hands to rest on the table everyone sat around. "This is the discovery we need to ensure we overshadow Britain and Germany. If we can colonize and industrialize this cluster of systems we will be able to out produce anyone else."

Everyone took this as a sign that the meeting was over and so began to stand up and leave. Chang then continued more quietly, "Minister Quin," he said to the Minister of Defense, as he was about to leave. "Please remain behind, we need to discuss some other scenarios in case Britain doesn't dance to our tune."

Outside Na exchanged a glance with Wen-Chong, another junior member of the Politburo. It seemed their worst fears were coming true. When he had expressed an interest in going into politics his father had warned him that things weren't quite as they seemed. The political minds of the upper echelons of the Community Part were changing, he had said. Over the last several years Na had been able to see this for himself. As many of the Politburo members and leading Communist Party officials felt backed further and further into a corner by British and German expansion, there had been a growing sense of isolation and hostility. China and her interests were of paramount importance. The rest of humanity could be dammed for all they cared.

This had been expressing itself in the growing border tensions with Britain and Germany, which, in turn, had spilled over into the public domain. Na knew that the Minister of the Interior spent many millions of credits each year on propaganda aimed at encouraging the general populace to see Britain and Germany as China's natural enemies. Worse, the feelings of resentment and hostility held by the leading communists had also led to successive waves of military expansion. Even though the British economy was valued at roughly one hundred and thirty percent of the Chinese, the Politburo had thrown far more credits into building up its naval forces. Of course the Politburo had also ensured that only lieutenants who agreed with the party line concerning Britain and Germany gained advancement to the rank of Captain and beyond. Every time there was a border incident Na feared that it would erupt into war for the Chinese navy now had too many trigger happy Captains who were just waiting for the chance to fire a shot at the British.

Yet Na knew there were many who did not share this view, even within the leadership of the Party. Wen-Chong was one of them. When Na had first expressed his concern to him Wen-Chong had revealed his own fears. Even so, they were both junior members of the Politburo. Actually doing something to avert the self-destructive path their leaders were taking them on had seemed impossible. Now, thought Na, it didn't matter, there was no turning back, they had already travelled too far.

Chapter 1 – Loose the Dogs of War

The First Interstellar Expansion Era began in 2203 with the discovery of the shift drive. Throughout the era tensions between the space faring powers were always strained and often frayed as one power sought to cut off exploration routes from another.

-Excerpt from Empire Rising, 3002 AD

15th November 2464, HMS *Surprise*, the Damang system.

Commander Lightfoot sat in the command chair of *HMS Surprise* as his ship exited shift space. As an Archer class frigate *Surprise* was just a baby among the fighting ships of the RSN, which meant she was assigned all sorts of menial tasks. Lightfoot had already tired of his current mission on the outward journey to their destination. Now that they were finally heading back to Earth, he was beginning to look forward to his next assignment with a bit more hope.

As the sensors began to update the holo-display Lightfoot could see that almost all the ships in the convoy had exited shift space in formation. *Surprise*, along with the Lancer class frigate *Renown* and the light cruiser *Resolution* were escorting a convoy of nine freighters. They had made the five week journey to the British mining colony in the Reading system and were now on their way back home. Typically, freighters would make their own way to their various destinations but Admiralty regulations stipulated that all freighters had to be escorted to and from Reading.

Thanks to a quirk in the UN Planetary Allocation Act, Britain had been awarded the mining rights to the Reading system even though it was only accessible by passing through Chinese territory. Given the past scuffles between China and Britain and the rising border tensions, the Admiralty had set up a convoy every three months to Reading in order to deliver supplies and pick up processed ore from the system. As a commander of a frigate in the RSN these kinds of tasks always seemed to fall to him.

Sub Lieutenant Samson, who was manning the communications console of the bridge, turned to speak to his Commander. "Sir, Captain Turner is hailing us from the *Resolution*."

As Lightfoot nodded Samson put the feed onto the main holo-display. Impeccable as ever Lightfoot thought, as the Captain appeared in front of him, though he was careful to keep his face impassive. Captain Turner was from a wealthy noble family back on Earth and he always seemed to be immaculately dressed and turned out no matter what the occasion or hour.

"Commander," he began, "it seems we have lost one of our charges again. The Captain of the freighter *Jackson* has signaled to say that he picked up a shift space exit off his port bow. I'm sending you the coordinates now. No doubt someone made a miss calculation. I'm sure the freighter will start radiating heat as soon as they bring up their main drives so it won't take you long to find them. We'll wait here with the rest of the convoy until you return."

Lightfoot replied with a simple, "Yes sir," before switching off the feed from *Resolution* and turning to his navigation officer. "Avery, do you have the coordinates?"

"They're coming through now," Avery replied without turning round to directly address his commander.

"Very well, take us there at eighty percent thrust," Lightfoot ordered.

Two hours later *Surprise* had opened up a distance of twenty light minutes from the rest of the convoy. They had just picked up the freighter on their thermal scanners and sent her a message ordering her to make for the convoy when a message arrived from *Resolution*.

Sub Lieutenant Samson scanned over it before addressing his commander. "Sir, *Resolution* has just picked up a fleet dropping out of shift space. Based on the readings they obtained from the re-entry patterns they think they are Chinese. *Resolution* estimates there is a battleship, a battlecruiser, three heavy cruisers and at least thirty other ships that they can't make out yet, though they think some are freighters. They are reporting one more large vessel that they can't identify. It isn't a battleship but it seems to be in the same mass range."

Lightfoot grimaced. Ordinarily the opportunity to see a Chinese fleet maneuvering would provide priceless intel. Yet, ideally, he would like to get the information while lying in stealth, not while escorting a convoy that would be lighting up every sensor within a light day. Britain and China might be at peace but being out in the open so far from home made him feel a little nervous. Not to mention the battleship. The Chinese only had one of the mammoth ships in their fleet. What was it doing out here?

"Tactical orientate our optical and heat sensors towards these new comers. Let's see what our Chinese friends are doing with themselves out here in the back end of nowhere."

It would take over fifty minutes for the heat and optical data to travel from the Chinese fleet to *Surprise*, twenty more than it would take to reach the convoy. Yet getting so much information back to the Admiralty and the Royal Space Navy Intelligence would be priceless.

*

Aboard the Chinese medium cruiser *Yang Wei* Captain Zu was just receiving a communication stream from his admiral. "Captain, you know the importance of our mission and the importance of secrecy. Those British ships cannot be allowed back to Earth. You command our fastest ship, I'm detaching the *Yang Wei* and her sister ship the *Chao Yung*. I want you and Captain Kuang to destroy that convoy. Don't leave a single ship alive. I know you didn't sign up for these kinds of missions but it is essential that the British do not learn our fleet was here. No word can be allowed to get back to Earth. I'm going to jump on to our next destination once we have charged our jump drives. You are to follow once you have finished here. Understood?"

"Yes sir, they will all be turned into space debris."

The Admiral smiled as he clicked off the communication. He had handpicked his Captains for this mission because he knew they would follow him no matter what. He had just ordered his subordinate to fire on friendly naval vessels and unarmored freighters and he hadn't even blinked! Fifty years ago such an order would have been unthinkable but the British were about to find out that things had changed in China. He knew the ultimate responsibility would fall on him for what was about to happen but he did not care. That, he suspected, was why he had been chosen for this mission. His superiors knew he would do whatever it took to ensure China acquired the four habitable worlds they had discovered.

*

"Sir," Sub Lieutenant Erickson said with alarm from his tactical station aboard *Surprise*, "two of the Chinese ships have gone to full acceleration. They are heading straight for the convoy."

Ordinarily ships could only be detected by the radiation they vented into space. They, therefore, did everything they could to prevent any radiation escaping but when it came to heat radiation it was almost impossible. With fusion reactors and impulse drives operating at even sixty percent a ship lit up in the cold dark expanse of space like a firework in the night's sky back on Earth.

However, as radiation only travels at the speed of light, ships were effectively limited to looking into the past. Over short distances this didn't cause a problem but for anything over a light minute away it meant that a Commander was always reacting to what his opponent had done in the past.

The only exception is when a ship wants to use anything close to its full acceleration. The impulse drives human vessels use for traveling through normal space produce huge levels of acceleration. Yet, in doing so, they create gravimetric disturbances that could be picked up instantaneously over long distances.

Cursing, Lightfoot brought up the feed from the gravimetric sensors on his own console. Erickson was right; the Chinese were heading straight for the convoy. He transferred the data to the main holo-display and let the computer crunch the numbers.

Lightfoot swore even louder. The convoy had been slowly heading into the mass shadow of the Damang system as they waited for *Surprise* to locate the stray freighter. A system's mass shadow was the area of space where the combined mass of the system's star and planets produced enough of a gravimetric disturbance to prevent ships using their shift drives. The Chinese had come out of shift space right on the edge of the mass shadow; almost exactly at the same position the convoy had entered the system. Even if the freighters went full burn on their drives they couldn't reach a safe place to enter shift space before the Chinese ships got within missile range. Knowing Captain Turner he guessed what was about to happen next.

"Sir," Erickson called excitedly, "*Resolution* and *Renown* have gone to full military acceleration, they are heading straight for the two Chinese vessels."

Nodding, Lightfoot had to push down the urge to rebuke Erickson for his enthusiasm. The boy really needs to grow up, he thought to himself. Battle was never a thing to get excited about!

Instead he asked, "and what are our charges doing?"

"They are beginning to accelerate now, wait, from their acceleration patterns it looks like they are scattering. Some are going for the mass shadow, others are diving into the system," Erickson answered.

"Have you been able to identify the two Chinese ships?"

"The computer has a positive match now. Their acceleration rates are higher than anything we have ever seen from a Chinese ship before. They must be the new Yang Wei class. Only three have left the construction yards according to intelligence. One of them is bound to be the *Yang Wei* herself. "

Lightfoot ran the numbers in his head. *Resolution* and *Renown* could only put out a combined salvo of nine missiles. RNI estimated that the British missiles had better ECM capabilities than the Chinese but that wouldn't make up for the disparity in numbers. The Chinese medium cruisers had thicker armor than *Resolution*, and combined, had a throw weight of twenty-two missiles.

Turner was no fool. He must know the odds too. Lightfoot guessed he was hopping that *Renown's* armament would cause enough of a surprise to allow *Resolution* to get in close. All human warships were equipped with plasma cannons. Short ranged weapons, they shot out super-heated plasma bolts that could shred even valstronium armor. If *Resolution* could get into plasma range she could cripple both Chinese cruisers with a single salvo allowing the rest of the convoy to escape. *Resolution* would never survive the return fire but she would go down fighting.

Turning to First Lieutenant Cromwell, Lightfoot sought his opinion, "what do you make of all this?"

"Well sir," he began, "it seems the Chinese don't want us in this system, or at least they didn't want us seeing that fleet of theirs. We're too far away to come to *Resolution's* aid but if those two ships blow through *Resolution* and *Renown* they'll be coming straight for us. I'm sure they will have picked up our gravimetric signature too."

Lightfoot nodded solemnly. "Agreed. Unless there has been a declaration of war since we left Earth those ships don't want us reporting back what we've seen. There's no good reason for them to have a fleet all the way out here, even if we are at war. We can't help *Resolution* so we're going to have to think only of ourselves, as hard as that is. Getting this information back to the Admiralty could be more important than all the ships in our little convoy. Given how far into the system's mass shadow we are I don't think they're going to let us get to use our jump drive, I do have a few ideas though."

Cromwell leaned in closer to his Commander to hear him outline his plan.

*

Aboard the *Yang Wei*, Zu was struggling to contain his anticipation. Both of the British warships were coming right for him. It would allow him to quickly dispatch them before the freighters and the other frigate could make their escape. "Hold fire until we enter optimal missile range," he commanded.

Zu knew the British had a slight advantage in missile range but he was gambling they would not want to fire the first shot. There was no way his opponents could know what their fleet was doing out here and as there had been no declaration of war there was no reason for the British ships to risk a diplomatic incident by opening fire first. That said, it was obvious the two British combat ships knew their business. They were putting themselves right between his two cruisers and the freighters they had been escorting.

Speaking to his bridge crew Zu began to bark out orders. "Contact the *Chao Yung*, I want them to prepare to fire on my mark. Spread the missiles between both ships."

Zu watched the range gradually drop. "Prepare to fire....Fire, missiles away."

As shouted the command to fire, Zu found himself sitting at the edge of his command chair. It would take over five minutes for the gunners to reload the missile tubes but he hoped that their first salvo would be enough to obliterate the British ships. With both pairs of ships accelerating towards each other it would only take another fifteen minutes for them to enter plasma cannon range. He smiled, he knew both British vessels would be space dust before then.

"Impact in sixty seconds," his weapons officer announced. "They still haven't opened fire."

Dismissing his concern Zu leaned closer to the holo-display. At forty seconds out both British ships began to fire off counter missiles.

Zu frowned. The frigate was putting out more than twice the amount of counter missiles intelligence said its class could. His twenty-two missiles had been reduced to ten. Then, in disbelief, Zu watched as the missiles entered the range of the close point defense batteries and all but one of his missiles disappeared off the gravimetric sensor screen before they reached their targets. The final missile detonated close to the British light cruiser but its gravimetric signal continued on strong.

After a string of Chinese curse words Zu brought up the imagery of the battle. The two pairs of ships were so close now that he could almost watch the British counter missiles fire in real time. When the missiles were twenty seconds out, space around the both British ships lit up as they fired off their point defense plasma cannons. Zu's frown deepened. Along with the bursts from the plasma cannons there were other explosions. They looked like, like, flak explosions he had seen from 20th century war films. Quickly Zu zoomed in on the frigate and let out a final curse. The frigate only had a single missile tube down its flank. Instead of the customary second one it had two large railguns mounted fore and aft.

"A flak ship," he shouted. "That frigate is a dedicated flak ship! They are firing some kind of exploding shell! Order the next salvo to be targeted on the frigate and fire immediately." Flak ships hadn't been used in hundreds of years of warfare, not since wet navies had duked it out with airplanes back on Earth. It had been deemed that space was just too big and the velocities involved just too great for exploding flak rounds to actually hit an incoming missile. The British had obviously found a way to bring the concept into space warfare and they had managed to keep it a secret too!

Looking down Zu saw that they were just waiting for number three tube to report target locked. Moments later *Yang Wei* Zu shuddered as she fired her second salvo at the British.

Almost as soon as the twenty-two Chinese missiles appeared on the gravimetric plot nine more appeared from the two British ships as they eventually returned fire.

Zu almost didn't notice as he was checking the distances between the two pairs of closing ships. He would have time for one more salvo before they entered plasma range. "Navigation, reduce us to ten percent thrust, we can't let them use their plasma cannons."

Reducing their closing speed would give him time for another salvo before the British would get too close. With luck one extra salvo would do it. Zhu sat back and watched his missiles approach the enemy ships. He left defending his own to his subordinates. A *Yang Wei* class cruiser was designed to defend itself against incoming salvos of ten missiles; his two cruisers should handle the British missiles easily.

One by one his missiles began to drop off the plot as British counter missiles intercepted them. Twelve made it through into close point defense range. Again they began to explode quicker than should have been possible yet not quickly enough. The frigate didn't seem to be doing as good a job of destroying the missiles when they were headed straight for it.

Two made it through and as they both dropped off the plot showing they had exploded, the British frigate dropped off as well. Looking quickly over to the visual sensors Zu was able to see both missiles penetrate the frigate before they turned it into an expanding ball of particles.

Zu's smile was immediately replaced with a startled snarl as the bridge shook violently. "What was that?" he demanded.

His first officer, who was responsible for the point defense, replied in a concerned tone. "The British must have had a dedicated ECM missile in that salvo. Just before we began to fire counter missiles it activated and suddenly our sensors thought we were facing fifteen missiles rather than nine. The targeting computer didn't have time to distinguish between them so it targeted them all. One got through and got a proximity hit."

"Damage report?" Zu snapped.

Again the first officer had to speak up as no one else wanted to take responsibility. "We have lost some sensor blisters on our port side along with one missile tube and a counter missile emplacement. Engineering is reporting a fluctuation in engine number three; they have had to shut it down for now. Everything is at full functionality."

"We'll soon have our revenge. Target the light cruiser and fire our next salvo when ready." Zu growled in anger.

Just then the gravimetric plot beeped to announce new contacts. Zu had to blink to make sure what he was seeing was real. The British had fired another salvo, only three minutes after their first.

"Weapons, what's going on?" Zu demanded.

"Sir, I'm not sure. Wait, we're getting active radar seekers from all nine missiles. I think they have gone into a rapid-fire mode. At this close range they aren't trying to upload targeting data from their ship's sensors. They are just pointing and firing them, letting the missiles lock on to us themselves."

Cursing Zu finally realized what the British had intended all along. They had never thought that they could make it to plasma cannon range. They had banked on their flak frigate getting them close enough to shift to their rapid-fire mode. One or both of his cruisers was about to take a hammering.

Zu watched dispassionately as the British missiles zeroed in on his sister ship. *Chao Yung* managed to get off another coordinated salvo before the British missiles reached her. Again they seemed to magically multiply on the sensors just before they entered counter missile range. All but two were destroyed however both proved to be real missiles not ECM illusions.

Neither managed to directly hit the *Chao Yung* but both got proximity detonations. The blast waves washed over her and she visibly shook on the holo-display as Zu watched. Moments later damage reports came across from the other ship. She had lost most of her external sensor nodes and sixty percent of her point defense capability. Her stabilizing thrusters were in disarray and Zu watched as she began to roll slowly.

His weapons officer brought his mind back to the fight. "Sir, our missile salvo is about to enter counter missile range."

Zu looked back to the main holo-display showing the progress of his missiles. There was no sign of any counter missile fire. Then the plot erupted with eight more contacts. The British had managed to get off another salvo!

Just as he released a sigh of relief when he saw the missiles were going for *Chao Yung* and not his ship, the British light cruiser erupted into a fireball. In delaying their counter missile fire to fire their own salvo of anti-ship missiles they had sealed their fate. The light cruiser had only knocked out seven missiles before the rest of his third salvo vaporized it. Yet she would have the last say in this engagement. Reluctantly Zu forced himself to watch as eight missiles closed in on the damaged *Chao Yung*.

*

Back on board *Surprise* there was a groan as first one and then both of the gravimetric readings from *Resolution* and *Renown* dropped off the plot. There was a muted cheer when one of the Chinese medium cruisers quickly followed but as the final cruiser re-orientated itself towards *Surprise* all eyes turned towards Lightfoot.

"You all know my plan by now. We can't hope to stand up to a single medium cruiser even if she took some damage from *Resolution*. Cromwell, signal the freighter and tell them we are going ahead with the plan.

As Lightfoot turned back to the main holo-display he watched as one by one the other freighters that had been with *Resolution* dropped off the plot, a clear sign that missiles from the Chinese cruiser had caught each of them.

On cue the remaining freighter, the one they had been sent to find, dumped all its cargo and went to full burn on its engines. They were heading towards the mass shadow at an angle that would give them the best chance of escaping into shift space. The plot on the holo-display updated to show that the Chinese cruiser would still catch the freighter before she could make her jump. Yet there would only be minutes to spare. Clearly the cruiser had taken some damage in the skirmish with *Resolution* as she was only producing ninety percent of the acceleration she had before.

If *Surprise* could delay the cruiser, even just for a couple of minutes, it might give the freighter time to escape. At least that was what Lightfoot wanted the Chinese Captain to think. In reality there was no way the freighter could sneak all the way back to Earth through Chinese space. It was just not designed with the stealth capabilities required for such a task.

As soon as the cruiser entered maximum range *Surprise* opened fire. Unlike the *Renown* she was not a flak frigate and so could bring two missile tubes to bear on the enemy cruiser. Her slight missile range advantage allowed her to get off three salvos before the cruiser was able to open fire. *Surprise* only carried one of the new advanced ECM missiles. The crew had whooped for joy when it managed to confuse the cruiser enough to let the second missile of the first salvo score a proximity hit. However, the joy was short lived as the cruiser flew through the explosion and relentlessly kept on coming. With *Surprise* now running at full speed away from the cruiser she was almost able to keep the range open enough to stay ahead of her pursuer, however, even damaged the cruiser had a slightly greater acceleration rate and, eventually, was able to get into attack range.

As the Chinese ship opened fire Commander Lightfoot turned to his first lieutenant. "Is everything in place?"

"Engineering has just reported in sir." Cromwell confirmed, "The warheads on all the missiles are keyed to detonate on your command."

"Very good. We're going to have to cut this very close so tell everyone to secure themselves into the emergency harnesses."

Lightfoot looked away from the lieutenant, trusting him to ready the crew. They hadn't been idle as *Resolution* and *Renown* had fought for their lives. From the destruction of *Resolution* it had taken the Chinese cruiser over four hours to catch up with *Surprise*. In that time Lightfoot had ordered the cargo bay and some of the surrounding superstructure to be cut away from the rest of the hull. Only a few key struts were still holding it in place.

All the missiles but those needed for the mock engagement with the cruiser had been removed from their magazines and were now being towed behind *Surprise*. They were all set to detonate simultaneously. With any luck the Chinese would mistake the explosion for their fusion reactors overloading. That was the plan at least.

As the Chinese ship entered range, ten missiles shot out towards *Surprise*. Lightfoot returned fire moments later to keep up the pretense of trying to land a knockout blow. The missiles were timed to reach the Chinese cruiser just as *Surprise* was going to detonate her towed missiles. Not for the first time Lightfoot prayed their missiles would disrupt the Chinese sensors enough for them to buy the fake reactor overload.

As the Chinese missiles entered counter missile range Lightfoot keyed the ship wide communications. "Everyone hold on, this is going to be a rough ride."

He watched the holo-display as one, two, three and then four missiles were knocked out by the counter missiles. Then the point defense plasma cannons opened up. Two more missiles exploded taking direct hits. Four more still bore down on *Surprise*.

Five seconds from impact the missiles accelerated to attack velocity. Just as they went into overdrive Lightfoot hit the switch, telling the towed missiles to detonate. At the same time the charges on the remaining struts holding the cargo bay in place detonated and the ventral maneuvering thrusters went full burn for one second.

Behind *Surprise* a massive fireball erupted as fifteen thermonuclear warheads exploded. Everything on the bridge went dark as the explosion disrupted power across the ship. Two of the Chinese missiles dived straight into the expanding fireball and exploded, adding their nuclear power to the detonation. The other two had their seeker heads fried by the intense radiation given off and shot off into space tracking nothing.

Lightfoot had been knocked momentarily unconscious by the g-forces caused as the explosion shook *Surprise*. As he came to he immediately looked around him to see if his crew was all right. Everyone looked more than a little shaken up but they were all in one piece.

"Tactical," he began, trying to keep the shaking he felt inside him from reaching his voice. "What is our status?"

It took the Sub Lieutenant almost a minute to get his console up and running again and to find all the relevant information. "Sir, it appears your plan worked. We are on a ballistic trajectory with a twelve degree rotation. All our engines are shut down and all nonessential equipment has been turned off. Our valstronium armor has been seriously fried by that explosion but most of the engines seem to be in working order. We won't know for sure until we try to fire them back up."

"Very good Lieutenant," Lightfoot said with a smile. "And what is our Chinese friend doing?"

Again the sub lieutenant spent over a minute checking his console before replying. "Sir, most of our passive sensors have been badly damaged but it looks like he's still heading for the freighter."

"Even better," Lightfoot said as his smile grew into a grin.

*

Zu finally allowed himself to relax. He had been worried that this second frigate would be a flak frigate like the first. If he had been forced to spend too long hammering another flak frigate into submission the last freighter might have managed to escape. Now his sensor officer assured him that the frigate was a tumbling ball of wreckage.

After reading through the damage reports from the last near miss he stared at the holo-display watching the distance count down to the remaining freighter. Ten minutes and he would be able to blow it to pieces. He was already beginning to compose his report to the Admiral, focusing on the successes of the mission and all the valuable intel he had managed to get about British battle tactics. Hopefully that would be enough to gloss over the loss of his sister ship.

Suddenly the sensors officer brought him back to reality. "Captain Zu!" she frantically called, "I'm picking up an energy spike from the wreckage of the frigate."

"Show me the visuals immediately." Zu demanded. He had a sinking feeling as the wreckage came up on the holo-display. The frigate was slowly rotating and even as he watched its main plasma cannon came into view. Quicker than he imagined possible it traversed to track his cruiser and opened fire.

Before Zu could call out any orders the twin plasma bolts covered the distance between the two ships and blew through the valstronium armor of his cruiser. By chance they managed to knock out the communication links between the bridge and the central firing control for the cruiser's plasma cannons. The order to return fire never made it to *Yang Wei's* weapons officer.

Within seconds two more plasma bolts ravaged the *Yang Wei* and then two more burst right through the ship causing her to explode in one more dramatic fireball.

Chapter 2 – Command

Some say the roots of our Empire date back to the English Monarchy that arose after 1066. Whilst this is disputed, certainly the Empire can trace its development back to the rise of the English nobility after the period in Earth history known as The Troubles.

-Excerpt from Empire Rising, 3002 AD

21st November 2464. HMS *Drake,* in shift space beyond the Cambridge system.

Commander James Somerville sat in a dark mahogany desk chair. He was in his private office adjacent to his sleeping quarters. His feet were resting upon the matching desk with little regard for its age or quality. With a stretch he pushed on the desk and tilted his chair unto its back legs as he turned the page of the old-style book he was reading.

To anyone not associated with the pomp of the British nobility the scene would have seemed comical. On one hand the archaic *wooden* furniture and *paper* book sharply contrasted with both the modern styling of the Captain's quarters and the modern synthetic Royal Space Navy uniform. Pure black boots met tightly fitted white trousers, which ran up to be overlapped by the blue tunic James wore. The tunic had two lines of decorative buttons up the middle, both sets were yellow, identifying James as a Captain of a starship. On his right shoulder was a single yellow star displaying James's rank as that of Commander in the RSN.

Both the desk and collection of old style books had been a gift from his uncle upon his posting to command HMS *Drake*. Whilst he had little respect for the value of the desk and matching chairs, either financial or sentimental, the old style paper books had grown on him.

After a year of the monotony of deep space exploration, James had turned to the books as a last desperate attempt to hold back the depression he felt creeping upon him. Commanding a survey ship in the RSN was not the constant high paced life of discovery and excitement the news reports and novels on the datanet made out. The books had at least been an escape for the last year.

Ever since the discovery of the shift drive, the spacefaring powers had been rushing to explore and map the dark matter that hung between the stars. The shift drive gave a vessel the ability to create a gravimetric anomaly around itself that allowed it to enter shift space. Entering shift space catapulted a vessel to speeds greatly exceeding the speed of light and so opened up the stars to humanity, with one catch.

The anomaly couldn't be opened in close proximity to other large gravimetric sources. Stars, planets, asteroids and of course dark matter, prevented the formation of the gravimetric anomaly or caused vessels already in shift space to revert to real space, often with catastrophic results. Scientists estimated that upwards of eighty four point five percent of the galaxy's mass consisted of dark matter. Thus this dark matter, strewn between the stars in nebula like formations, limited the scope of humanity's expansion into space. It was the job of HMS *Drake* and the one hundred and fifty other survey craft in the RSN to survey the dark matter nebulas and map out potential shift drive passages.

After taking command of HMS *Drake* Commander Somerville had been tasked with exploring deep space around Cambridge. One of the most recently settled colonies of the growing British colonial empire, Cambridge bordered Chinese space. As a result there was a likely chance that a shift drive passage could be found linking British controlled space and Chinese. If such a passage could be found then the opportunities for trade would explode exponentially, both for the British Merchant Navy and for independent corporations.

On the face of it, James realized his posting was a prestigious one. At twenty-seven he was the youngest Commander in the RSN, he had been given one of the newest survey ships in the navy and assigned to a key sector that could shape the future of the British colonies over the coming decades. However, he knew better and this knowledge, coupled with the monotony of deep space exploration had slowly been wearing him down.

Back on Earth the British nobility was a focal point for the general population. Their surge in power after the Meccan Incident and the subsequent Solar Expansion Period had thrust them back into the political and economic limelight. Despite over three hundred years having passed this relationship had not changed. The general populace looked to the nobility as a spring of hope for the future and yet also as a source of entertainment and even a punching bag when things went wrong. When once the monarchy had largely been the sole focus of the media's attention now the entire nobility shared that privilege. Their business transactions, marriages, affairs, births and countless other activities had become the drama that the British populace loved.

The result was that the nobility themselves had embraced their role as the custodians of the values and hopes of the British population. What had started out, as a patriotic opportunity to increase their power and wealth, became the altruistic fixation of the British nobility. The vast majority of the nobility had followed King William VI's call to invest in solar real estate. In droves they had sold off their Earth holdings in order to finance Britain's expansion into space, believing William rightly saw the future of the British nation in space. If the future was there then so too were the profits.

However, they also followed William's example in giving fair wages to all workers and fast promotion tracks to those who excelled in their various responsibilities. As a result the nobility provided the means for vast numbers of the British population to drag themselves out of poverty and into space. In this way the nobility contributed significantly to the reestablishment of the British identity after the Meccan incident. This in turn led to the nobility becoming the focus of the public eye and over time an uneasy relationship developed.

The nobility knew they needed the popular support of the British people. Both to keep parliament on their side and to ensure there was a constant stream of patriotic volunteers for the RSN, its merchant fleet or for the various space and planetary colonies and industrial nodes the nobility had significant financial stakes in. As a result the nobility had to present a patriotic idealized face to the public if their position in society was to remain and so James Patrick William Somerville, Duke of Beaufort, found himself commanding a RSN survey ship over 60 light years from Earth.

Banishing thoughts of London's high life James turned another page of his book. He enjoyed the rough feeling of the paper under his fingers and the weight of the book in his hand. Letting out a sigh he savored the moment. He allowed his free hand to return to twirling the long sideburns he had grown to match the latest trends in London. At least it was the latest trend when he had left two years ago!

When he had turned to the old style books as a distraction he had raced through the first couple, flicking the pages in annoyance at the hassle but now each moment was precious. Turning the page allowed his mind to take in what he had just read or to just wonder aimlessly depending on his mood. This book was the last in the collection his uncle had given him.

His uncle he knew had a vast array of ancient paper books, possibly the largest outside the British Library. Giving James thirty of them had been a major gift. Smirking, James knew that the term gift was too generous for his uncles' actions. All the books had been 20th century novels depicting the life and times of British naval officers. The colonial wars of the 17th and 18th Century between Britain, France and Spain and the subsequent Napoleonic war had made for an exciting time in the navy.

Generous may have been going too far but manipulative may not. Idealized and overblown the characters and feats of some of the hero's couldn't possibly have been realistic. Yet James had to concede that the novels might have at least partially had their intended effect. After a year engrossed in the novels James wanted to be a hero. He wanted to emulate the men in his fantasies - if for no other reason than to allow him a route back into the high life of the nobility. For if the public embraced him as a hero, he would have to be readmitted into the inner circles of the nobility and once there his real desire would be within grasp.

Secretly James had to admit his desires had widened just a little. He wanted to be a hero in his own right. The characters from his uncle's novels *were* inspiring, even if they were all fictitious.

Yet being a hero or returning to London just seemed to be a pipe dream. Command of a survey ship wasn't the place to cover oneself in a cloud of glory nor had there been a shooting war between the major space faring nations in over twenty five years. James could feel the old depression welling up inside him. This was the last novel in his collection and his source of escape was about to end.

Before he could begin the next page his COM unit beeped. Tapping the control panel James's annoyance at being interrupted showed in his sharp, "Yes?"

"Commander," Sub Lieutenant Fisher began after a pause that showed her nervousness about disturbing her Commander, "we seem to have reached the end of this shift passage, it's a dead end sir."

"Ok, I'll be out momentarily"

James tapped the COM unit rather aggressively before he stood to make his way to the bridge. Lieutenant Fisher's nervousness irritated him. He had been on the ship for over two years now and she still had not gotten used to being round a member of the nobility. The RSN was one of the few places where the nobility and commoners interacted freely on equal terms. Acceptance into the RSN lunar academy was solely on ability and at least theoretically, advancement worked along the same lines.

Yet after two years Lieutenant Fisher still hadn't overcome her awe at his presence. He knew he couldn't entirely blame her of course. For a greater part of her childhood his family had been making the headlines in the British news outlets and reporters had been the bane of his life. As a commoner from a poor family he knew Fisher had grown up fixated on the nobility. Now, in many ways she had found herself face to face with a larger than life character.

On top of that he couldn't be the easiest Commander to serve under. He was the Duke of Beaufort after all, he should be spending his time among the most powerful of the nobility not skulking around in unexplored space in a small tin can. His irritability and occasional outbursts of anger may just as easily been the source of her nervousness he conceded, as he walked from his private quarters onto the bridge.

Upon entering the bridge James walked over to the sensors station where Sub Lieutenant Fisher sat in front of a large holographic display. Currently it was displaying a large worm like protrusion through space. The minor shift passage they had been exploring for the last week. The display said that it was just under half a light year long as it wound its way through the dark matter twisting and turning as it went. James grimaced. It would take a considerable amount of time to work their way back to the main passage they had been exploring for the last six months.

Reaching over Fisher's shoulders James shifted the view of the display to zoom out. The main passage came into view. Like the minor passage they had just explored it twisted and turned through space. However, unlike their minor passage it had many offshoots. Civilians often likened such a display to the roots of a tree. Typically when they occurred, main passages through the dark matter between the stars were large and somewhat like a cylinder in shape. Each of these main passages had numerous smaller minor passages snaking off them.

More often than not both the minor passages and main passages led to dead ends but occasionally they intersected with the dark matter vacuums created by stars. Within these vacuums, sometimes up to a light week in radius, no dark matter existed. Where the passages through the dark matter in deep space intersect with these bubbles a starship could enter shift space and traverse through the passage to a new star. One end of the main passage James was looking at led back to the Cambridge system. For the other end, the navigational data ended near the minor passage they were currently located in - still waiting to be explored.

Switching the display back to where Fisher had set it, James studied their minor passage more closely. "How long will it take us to get back to the main passage?" he asked Fisher.

"Four hours forty seven minutes, sir," Fisher replied as she looked up at him.

James had to repress a smile. It was a fact he liked to keep quiet back on Earth but he had done quite well in his RSN lunar academy exams, being seen as a swat among his nobility friends would have badly damaged his reputation. His subsequent postings as a sub lieutenant and as a third lieutenant aboard HMS *Prestige* had further enhanced his talents.

Obviously the last two years of boredom had not completely dulled his wits. With just a visual inspection he had estimated it would take at least four hours and thirty five minutes to get back to the main passage. Not bad for a commander who had spent the last two years skirting the thin line into alcoholism. Strictly banned from the RSN it wasn't hard for a ship's commander to rewrite his personal food processing unit to create various beverages and then delete the records from its core. Twelve minutes off wasn't a bad estimate from a solely visual inspection.

Theoretically the shift drive greatly reduced the time to travel through space. Yet this was only true where the passages through the dark matter were straight. Entering shift space catapulted a vessel at great speeds in a single direction. However, once in shift space this direction couldn't be changed. To change direction a ship had to leave shift space, re-orientate itself and re-enter shift space. To traverse back down the minor passage they were in HMS *Drake* would have to make four directional adjustments to compensate for the various twists in the passage. Between jumps it would take 30 minutes to charge the capacitors on the shift drive, thus to cover a distance that would take approximately two hours and forty five minutes in shift space would instead take the four hours and forty seven minutes Fisher had reported.

"Ok, send your data over to the navigational station," James said as he strolled over to Sub Lieutenant Hanson. Determined to start to break down some of the walls he had allowed to build between himself and his crew, after all that is what the hero's in his books did wasn't it? James placed his hand on Sub Lieutenant Hanson's shoulder. To his credit the sub lieutenant didn't jump when he felt a hand on his shoulder.

"Lieutenant Hanson, I want you to plot Fisher's course back to the main passage and as soon as the capacitors finish charging from our last jump take us out of here."

"Yes sir," Hanson eagerly replied.

Looking over to Sub Lieutenant Graham, James called to him. "Prepare a communication drone to send back to Cambridge. Once we revert back to the main passage you can dispatch it with the details of this latest dead end we have discovered, and prepare a message to send to Lieutenant Gupta, I want her on the bridge when we reach the main passage. I'm going to retire for the night."

Sub Lieutenant Graham nodded to show he understood. Typically a RSN ship had five Sub Lieutenant positions, communications, sensors, navigation, tactical and defense. This meant the larger starships had upwards of fifteen sub lieutenants onboard, five for each of the three watches.

However, *Drake* had only nine, one for each watch in communications, sensors and navigation. Tactical and defense were not deemed worth wasting a sub lieutenant on for a survey ship that was not designed to see action.

As a result, posting to a survey ship was highly sought after by sub lieutenants. Regulations stated that a sub lieutenant couldn't be considered for promotion until they had served at each station for at least a year. The lack of a dedicated tactical and defense watch meant that the other sub lieutenants could fill in on these positions on their off hours and so increase their clocked station hours.

In reality though simply clocking the required five years was a minimum requirement for promotion into the senior lieutenant ranks. The RSN largest ships were the *Reliant* class battlecruisers and regulations stipulated there be a maximum of five senior lieutenants. With up to fifteen sub lieutenants per ship throughout all the classes in the RSN there was a tight bottleneck that ensured only the stand out sub lieutenants progressed up the command tree.

And this turned James' thoughts back to HMS *Drake's* second lieutenant, Georgia Ashan Gupta. A second-generation emigrant from India, Lieutenant Gupta had served on HMS *Drake* since she was commissioned 8 years ago. From his files and from slightly illegal searches of the datanet James had done before they left Earth, he had found out that Gupta's family had left New India to escape the strictly enforced caste system. When the previous Captain of *Drake* had been promoted two years ago Gupta had been his natural successor to take over command. James knew that his whirlwind promotion from third lieutenant to commander must smack of favoritism and the caste system Gupta's family emigrated to escape.

Under the circumstances Gupta's barely hidden hatred of James was understandable and James certainly hadn't done anything to ease the situation. When he had first assumed command James had been too caught up in his own troubles to care for a subordinate's misunderstandings about the inner workings of the nobility. As a result their relationship had only soured as the months had rolled on.

A solution had dawned on James a few months ago and his mood brightened up as he considered it again. *Drake* was scheduled for a maintenance cycle in three months and this would hopefully take them either to Britannia or Earth. Either way he could write a glowing recommendation of Gupta's abilities and with luck get her reassigned before the end of the cycle. Nodding to himself James turned to walk off the bridge to his quarters. In mid step he turned back to Sub Lieutenant Hanson.

"Lieutenant, as you are plotting our course back to the main passage you have the bridge, so take care of my ship."

This time James was unable to hide a smile from the bridge crew. Typically the sub lieutenant in charge of sensors took command of the bridge in a survey ship if the commander or the second lieutenant wasn't present. The look of shock on Hansen's face had been worth the slight risk to his ship. Hanson was the least experienced sub lieutenant on board and this would be his first time commanding the ship. But James knew Fisher would be double checking everything Hanson did so there wasn't really a risk – and everyone had to start somewhere.

As he walked out of the bridge James couldn't help adding, "Oh and Lieutenant, I want you to plan out the next few jumps further into the main passage. You and Lieutenant Gupta can go over the details when she arrives on the bridge."

Chapter 3 - Discovery

Analysis of the available records indicates that it took an average of twenty million hours of exploration to discover a new habitable world. Given the available survey ships each major power had during the first expansion era it meant that on average one planet was being discovered every five years. Anything more than that usually brought a dramatic shift in the delicate balance that was the First Interstellar Expansion Era.

-Excerpt from Empire Rising, 3002 AD

22nd November 2464. HMS *Drake*, the Void.

James woke to a loud beeping noise coming from directly above his head. Groggily he reached up and banged around on the wall until he hit the COM unit built in above his bed.

"Yes," he stuttered as he shaded his eyes from the COM unit's display with his free hand, "what is it?"

"Sir," Lieutenant Gupta's voice came across the speaker with no hint of remorse for waking her commander, "I think you better get up here."

"Ok, I'll be there in a minute," James replied as he swung his legs out of the bed. It was strange. Gupta usually avoided him at all costs, which meant that any communications came through a Sub Lieutenant. Why was Gupta waking him up personally? Did she just take a strange delight in knowing she had disturbed her commander's rest or was there a real problem?

Two minutes later James strode onto the bridge in his hastily donned uniform. After glancing at the clock he reckoned he had gotten four hours of sleep. He had finished his novel before turning in, *Drake* must have made it back to the main passage and Sub Lieutenant Hanson's planned exploration jumps should have been well underway.

"So, what's going on this fine morning?" James addressed the bridge crew on watch. Looking around, he noticed that Gupta had ordered tactical and defense manned by Sub Lieutenants. Something was obviously up so he turned to Gupta and waited expectantly.

Meeting her commander's eye Gupta began. "Once we got back to the main passage we began a series of micro jumps further into the passage as you ordered."

James nodded. A micro jump typically lasted no more than two minutes. It was standard practice for a survey ship to survey and map out the dark matter within sensor range then micro jump to the edge of its sensor range. There it would survey and map the new dark matter in range before completing another jump. Exploring shift passages was a simple, yet tedious and time consuming, combination of micro jumps and sensor sweeps.

"After the fourth jump our sensors could only detect dark matter out to a range of point zero zero five of a light-year. We thought you might want to be on the bridge for this," Gupta said with a rare smile.

"A galactic bubble?" James asked with a strong hint of sarcasm.

Scientists had theorized that bubbles should exist in the dark matter. If all of the Milkyway was as full of dark matter as the space humanity had explored then the galaxy should mass 20% more than it did. The upshot of this was that there should be significantly large pockets of space completely devoid of dark matter. But the galaxy was a big place and finding one was a dream more than an expectation. For all humanity knew, these bubbles wouldn't intersect shift passages and so would never be discovered anyway.

"Show me on the holo-display," James commanded as he sat in the command chair Gupta had just vacated.

In front of him a large 3D projection of the main passage they had been exploring appeared. The passage now extended point zero three of a light-year beyond the minor passage they had found to be a dead end. *Drake's* sensors could detect and map dark matter up to point zero one of a light-year and so four micro jumps typically revealed just under point zero four of a light-year's worth of shift passage. Where the passage should have continued along in its cylinder like shape the edges instead tapered off, curving out away from the center of the main passage. Its shape certainly looked like the outer edge of a roughly oval bubble.

"Navigation, how long until we can make our next jump?" James asked.

"Fourteen minutes sir," Sub Lieutenant Becket replied. She was a petite blonde who seemed to love all things to do with *Drake's* engines. When she wasn't on duty on the bridge she seemed to spend as much time with the chief engineer as on her studies.

"Ok, navigation, plot us a course right to the end of the shift passage, put us right at the edge of whatever this is. If we still can't detect anything then we really may have a dark matter bubble on our hands ladies and gentlemen," James said with a grin.

The next fourteen minutes were spent in near total silence as everyone on the bridge watched the clock count down on the capacitors for the jump drive. When the clock hit zero Hansen looked over at his commander. James nodded and Hanson initiated the jump.

The jump would take them a further zero point zero one light-year along the passage and would take two minutes to complete at their current velocity through shift space. Theoretically they could reach greater speeds as the velocity attained was a simple equation of the energy discharged into the shift drive from the capacitors divided by the mass of the ship. *Drake* couldn't reduce her mass but the capacitors were designed to hold twenty percent more energy than was necessary to make the slowest jump into shift space. But, as it took longer to charge the extra 20% than it did to complete the current jump, there was no need to waste time waiting for the extra charge from the fusion engines.

Exactly two minutes later the shift drive shut down, dumping HMS *Drake* back into normal space. Immediately the sensors began to update the map of the dark matter around the ship.

Sub Lieutenant Fisher gasped, a few seconds later James saw why. When the holo-display in front of him updated with the same data Fisher was already seeing he too almost gasped. As far as the *Drake's* sensors could see, the dark matter continued to curve away from the apparent end of the shift passage. What's more, its curvature seemed to be consistent, implying that the dark matter continued to curve out, forming a bubble like shape.

James thought to himself that the scientists might be right after all. But before everyone on the bridge got carried away he spoke up. "Let's not get ahead of ourselves just yet. Navigation, I want to make a couple of jumps along the edge of the dark matter and see how far this curvature continues. We don't know yet if it is uniform all the way around or if this is only a small abnormality."

"Aye sir," Hanson replied and began to input the new commands.

"Gupta, I want you and Fisher to estimate the size of the dark matter bubble based on extending our current projections. Work out how many systems fall into the bubble and begin long range scans of them. Cross reference your data with the interstellar data we have from Earth."

From Earth it was possible to detect planets orbiting distant stars but the science was imprecise. Small planets could be missed and estimations of the detected planet's orbital paths were just that, estimations. *Drake* would be able to pick up much more information on the nearby systems but only a survey from within each system would reveal all its secrets.

As Gupta and Hanson began to whisper together, James settled deeper into his command chair to wait. This was the life of a Captain of a survey ship. A few short bursts of orders followed by long periods of tedious waiting. Realistically, a student back at the RSN lunar academy could do his job. In a main or minor passage all he did was order *Drake* to micro jump along the center of the passage. Navigation and sensors would do the rest as they worked together to map out the passages and keep *Drake* in the center of the twisting turning tunnels through the dark matter. Even here, on the edge of one of humanity's most exciting discoveries, all he really had to do was sit around waiting and watching as others worked.

One hour forty-five minutes and three micro jumps later James gathered all his commissioned officers into the tactical room. The tactical room was simply a large holo-display with a series of seats arranged around it. Each seat was fitted with the same command and control functions as the tactical stations on the bridge. This way all the participants in a briefing could manipulate the holo-display and project their plans and tactics for all to see.

"I've brought you all here because I want input from everyone,"

James began, "this is the first time we have ever encountered a dark matter bubble and so all your thoughts will be useful."

"Lieutenant Fisher, talk us through your findings so far," James said as he sat down in his seat. His sitting was a cue for everyone else to sit and so eight of the Sub Lieutenants and Second Lieutenant Gupta took their seats. Gupta was the only senior officer on board as survey frigates were only appointed a Second Lieutenant and a commander to oversee the rest of the crew.

Fisher remained on her feet as she manipulated the main input for the holo-display. "At the moment we have called the dark matter bubble the Void for lack of any other suggestions. From our micro-jumps around the edge of the Void it does seem that it forms an almost perfect sphere."

On the holo-display a large sphere appeared in front of her audience. This was followed by the main shift passage they had been exploring and a data point indicating that it would take just under three days to travel back along the shift passage to the Cambridge system. Next, a series of black and yellow dots appeared, interspaced throughout the Void. Finally, a dotted line started at the point where the shift passage to Cambridge began, it passed through the center of the Void and ended at the opposite end. The data projected along the line indicated that the Void had a diameter of approximately twelve light-years.

"As you can see there are fifty-six solar systems within the void. Initial scans from Earth indicated that five of these systems contained planets within the goldilocks range. Lieutenant Gupta and I are pleased to confirm that four of these systems do indeed contain such planets." At this point Fisher could no longer maintain her professionalism. "We have really done it," she said with a beaming smile, "we have actually found four habitable systems!"

This was met with cheers and whoops from the other Sub Lieutenants. So far the British survey fleet had only found eight habitable worlds in over two hundred years of exploration. It was an explorers dream to find a colonizable world. It was pure fantasy to imagine finding four!

Added to this was the prospect of prize money. The Admiralty offered a prize of a million credits per crew member to any ship that discovered a habitable world that resulted in a British colony. For two of the Sub Lieutenants this wasn't a great sum of money. Sub Lieutenant Hanson came from a rich shipping family whilst Sub Lieutenant Robson was from a noble family who had a considerable stake in the Oxford colony. But for the rest of the Sub Lieutenants, a million credits was a sum to balk at. Fifty years on a Sub Lieutenant's pay wouldn't even stretch to a million credits and the Admiralty didn't skimp when it came to salaries; they wanted to attract the best.

Shouting over the cheers James attempted to bring the meeting back on track. "How have you labeled each of the planets Lieutenant Fisher?"

Fisher blushed at her earlier exuberance but a single tap at her console brought up a list of numbers beside each of the black and yellow dots. "We have designated each of the systems V1 through to V56. As you can see the four yellow dots represent the systems with colonizable worlds; V2, V17, V31 and V48 respectively."

Nodding James continued his questioning. "Assuming your projection about the Void being a sphere is correct how long would it take us to survey the Voids outer edges and confirm them?"

Fisher looked back down at her command console as she typed a number of keys. "Just over three months sir," she answered.

"And how long would it take us to survey all the solar systems, assuming we can reach them all?"

Again Fisher looked down at her console. "Approximately sixty four days sir."

"Ok," James looked around the briefing room, "Suggestions anyone?"

Becket was the first to speak up. "Surely we can't spend the next three and a half months out here surveying the entire Void. Anything could happen to us in here and if it did it could take the admiralty months or even a year or two to send another survey ship up the shift passage from Cambridge."

Sub Lieutenant O'Rourke countered her argument. "But if we go back to the Admiralty now what are we supposed to tell them? We *think* this Void is real? We *think* there are four colonizable worlds out here?"

Becket looked as if she was about respond but instead she folded her arms and began to look around the room, happy to let someone else speak up.

Fisher chimed in with her thoughts. "Whatever we do, surely telling the Admiralty has to be our priority. What we have discovered is a game changer. Four habitable worlds, all within a few hours travel of each other, not to mention another 52 systems that may provide all sorts of useful resources. The Admiralty will want to know about this as soon as possible so that they can factor it into their long term plans."

James slowly eyed each Sub Lieutenant. Tapping his fingers on the armrest of his seat he was happy to let the open conversation continue.

___

48

Hanson was staring at the ground but as James looked at him he brought his head up. "What about the territorial borders. How close is the Void to British and Chinese space?"

Gupta smiled and reached over to the controls on her seat. After a second, two colored bands ran across the holo-display. Each band dissected the Void, splitting it into three.

James watched Gupta's smile and wondered if she had caught onto what he was doing. After reviewing Gupta and Fisher's data James had already decided what his next course of action was. This meeting was simply an opportunity to let the Sub Lieutenants flex their wits and decision making abilities in a real situation.

Sub Lieutenant Hansen had just asked the million dollar question. What would the Chinese do if they found out about the Void? Or maybe they had already discovered it! The red band on the display representing space that fell under Chinese influence covered roughly one tenth of the Void. Only two of the solar systems fell into the band, neither of which contained a habitable world. The blue band representing British controlled space covered about fifteen percent of the Void. However, twenty-three systems fell into the band two of which contained planets within the goldilocks zone.

When the two bands appeared on the holo-display Hanson nodded his head. "I'm not an expert in Chinese relations but the longer we take to report this to the UN's Interplanetary Committee the more of an uproar the Chinese will make. If they even suspect we tried to keep this from them there'll be trouble."

Nodding, James stood up to take over the briefing. As he did so Fisher sat down. "He's right, you all know there has been no love lost between us and the Chinese over the last few decades. Getting this information back to the Admiralty is of paramount importance.

They can decide if and when they want to tell the UN but we should at least give them the opportunity to do so as soon as possible."

Looking over at O'Rourke, James lifted his fingers in recognition. "Of course we want to be able to actually report some concrete findings to the Admiralty so here is what I purpose."

Stepping over to the main control station James tapped a single command to upload the plan he had already formulated. "We will survey the four habitable planets and bring back a full report on each to the Admiralty. They'll need that much data if they are going to register the planets with the UN. So we'll start with V2 then jump to V17. Once we have finished there I propose we jump out to the predicted edge of the Void that is diametrically opposite the shift passage back to Cambridge. If the Void is a perfect sphere confirming its other end should be enough for the Admiralty for now. Then we'll work our way back, surveying V31 and V48 before we head for home."

James looked over to his second in command. "Lieutenant Gupta, do you have anything you think we should add?"

"Yes sir," Gupta began. "I would suggest we enter each system under stealth. If the Chinese have already found a shift passage that leads to the Void there're not likely to take kindly to visitors. Especially if they have neglected to inform anyone else about their discovery," she responded.

"Agreed," James replied, begrudgingly he had to acknowledge Gupta had a point. "You, Hanson and Thirlwall plot our next jumps and prepare the ship for stealth mode." Thirlwall was scheduled to take over navigation from Hanson for the next watch. With long thick curly brown hair she always seemed to be attracting the stares of the male Sub Lieutenants. Yet their attention never seemed to register with her. Instead, like Fisher, she seemed to have a little too much interest in her commander – in James' humble opinion at least.

"And I want tactical and defense fully manned until we are back in the shift passage heading for Cambridge."

Strolling out of the tactical briefing room James made his way to his quarters. The capacitors would have another handful of minutes before they fully charged. That and the hour it would take to reach V2 would give him time to start his report to the Admiralty.

Minutes later at his mahogany desk James felt the subtle shift in the internal compensators indicating *Drake* had jumped into shift space. Accessing his cerebral implant he set his personal timer to inform him when they should be approaching V2.

Chapter 4 - Second Place

Whilst many of the tactics and weapons of naval warfare employed during the rise of the Empire were crude by our standards one tactic remains the same - stealth. If a ship can sneak up on an opponent or, better yet, lie in wait for it, then the ship has a decisive advantage. Missiles and plasma bolts fired from close range are almost impossible to defend against.

-Excerpt from Empire Rising, 3002 AD

22nd November 2464. HMS *Drake*, the Void.

Just under an hour later James walked onto the bridge. His personal COM unit beeped once and then went quiet. Seeing Gupta removing her hand from her own unit James smiled. He had set his personal timer to allow him to make it to the bridge before Gupta should be informing him they were approaching V2. It was never a bad thing to keep your subordinates guessing as to your whereabouts.

"Status report?" James queried.

Gupta vacated the command chair for James. "Two minutes until we reach the outer detection range of V2 sir," she replied. "The ship is in stealth mode. All non-essential electronics are switched off. The fusion reactors are at minimal output and our active sensors have been powered down."

"Good," James said. "Now the fun begins."

Entering and exiting shift space created a gravimetric pulse that was detectable out to one light hour away, at least by known human sensors. Standard stealth practice was to exit shift space one point five light hours from the mass shadow of a star so that no ships patrolling the shift limit could detect their arrival. Stealth mode also meant that most of the ship's heat signature was being directed away from their angle of approach. Whilst it was almost impossible to mask a ship's heat signature the RSN survey ships were designed to double as surveillance ships in times of war and so *Drake* had sophisticated stealth capabilities, allowing her to vent her excess heat in any given direction.

Immediately after feeling the subtle shift in the internal compensators from returning to normal space, James looked at the holo-display. Within a few seconds the display began to update itself with information on the system. When she was built *Drake* had had the most powerful sensor system in the RSN. Eight years later it was still better than anything outside the survey fleet. However, in stealth mode it counted for nothing. *Drake's* active sensors would immediately alert anyone in the system to her presence and so she had to rely on passive sensors.

"Propulsion, how long until the shift drive capacitors are charged enough for us to jump out?"

Sub Lieutenant Julia Shannon who had taken over navigation whilst *Drake* had been in shift space, replied, "approximately three hours at current rates sir."

Drumming his command chair with his fingers, James considered his options. The problem with being in stealth mode was that *Drake's* two fusion reactors had to be almost switched off. It meant that if they ran into trouble they couldn't escape in a hurry. Jumping into the system under full power would have allowed them to jump out again in thirty minutes. Of course anyone who would intend them harm would eventually learn of their presence. With both fusion power plants at full *Drake* would light up like a mini star even with her stealth capabilities. Whilst it would take two and a half hours for their heat signature to reach the planet, if there was someone in the system they would eventually know of their arrival. "Fisher, any sign of anyone else in the system?"

James had allowed Fisher to continue manning sensors despite her watch having ended. He wanted her to have the privilege of carrying out the first scans of what was sure to become one of the newest British colonies.

"No sir," she replied. "There's no signals or sign of industrialization from any of the planets in the system. I'm also not picking up any ship drives or reactors."

Nodding, James continued to sit in silence. No signs of a ship just meant there were no ships in the system several hours ago. The infrared signals the ships sensors were currently picking up had left the system hours ago and, traveling at the speed of light, had only reached *Drake's* position now. A ship could have entered the system in the last few hours and they wouldn't know about it. Also, anyone in the system lying in stealth wouldn't be giving off much heat radiation in the first place. They could be in stealth mode just as *Drake* was. And that was the dilemma. All RSN ships were designed to operate under stealth for prolonged periods, if they had too. Even the missile and plasma cannons were designed with energy cells that would allow them to operate for two minutes without drawing on any energy from the reactors. Combined with the passive sensors' ability to easily track ships with their reactors and drives lit up, it meant that a ship in stealth mode could cause a real problem. From a good starting position a ship in stealth could maneuver close to their target and unleash a volley of missiles or even rake their target with plasma cannons before anyone even knew they were there.

Drake had almost come straight to V2 from the shift passage to Cambridge. If a Chinese or even an alien ship knew about the Cambridge passage then *Drake's* current position would be the most logical one for a British ship to exit shift space. The next logical move would be to head straight for the habitable planet. James silently berated himself for not thinking of this sooner. If he were a Chinese Captain tasked with keeping the Void a secret he would position his ship between where a British ship would enter the system and the habitable planet. Lying in stealth he could wait for the British ship to move into the system and then fire a spread of missiles as they passed. He should have taken *Drake* to the far end of the system and entered it on a completely unpredictable route! The Void made such a maneuver easy for there was no dark matter to limit where he could go with the shift drive. The tactics book would have to rewritten if war ever broke out here.

"Navigation, plot us a course that will round the fifth planet in the system and then take us in toward the habitable world. And take us there with 20% thrust."

In her space trials *Drake* had been able to reach 25% of her maximum thrust before the heat radiating off the ship was detectable. James didn't want to take any chances.

"Sensors, dispatch two stealth recon drones. The first one is to go on a direct path to the habitable planet. The second is to follow the path we're going to take into the system, use the fifth planet's gravity to sling it towards the third planet," James ordered.

The habitable planet was the third planet in the system. With luck a detour around the fifth would keep them from being detected by any ships expecting them to head straight for V2.

"Yes sir," Fisher replied.

Normal recon drones were fitted with small impulse engines similar to the missiles *Drake* carried. Outfitted with their own active and passive sensors they allowed starships to scout a system without entering the mass shadow of a star. Any astronomical body with a gravimetrical field created a mass shadow within which the shift drive couldn't be engaged. Since the invention of the shift drive spacers had been calling these gravimetric fields the star's 'mass shadow.'

James didn't want to take any chances though. If there was another ship out there, he didn't want to warn them of their presence. Like normal drones stealth drones were fitted with passive and active sensors. However, their engines had been removed, by default their active sensors were switched off and additional passive sensors were loaded in the extra space left by the engines.

They were fired from *Drake's* single forward missile tube. Essentially a long railgun, it allowed missiles to be accelerated to high velocities before they had to engage their own engines. The stealth drones were designed to be fired from the longer forward tube rather than *Drake's* shorter side tubes, as the drones had no engines of their own. With their active sensors turned off and no drives to give them away stealth drones were very hard to detect.

Their only drawback was that they were severely limited in the amount of information they could send. Designed to report back to their mothership in burst communications that mimicked background radiation noise, theoretically at least, their transmissions were impossible to detect. However, in mimicking the background radiation only small amounts of data could be transmitted at a time.

Before *Drake* began to move towards the fifth planet Fisher launched the first stealth drone down their original course, the combined speed of *Drake* and the acceleration of the rail gun sending the drone off at 0.2c. Once *Drake* was lined up on her new course she fired off the second, tracing out their line of progression into the system.

After watching both drones being dispatched into the system James sat back in his command chair and prepared himself for a long wait. *Drake* had a maximum speed of 0.31c. Her valstronium armor protected her crew from the cosmic particles and radiation she would encounter at that speed. Technically, *Drake* was also equipped with gaseous shields that allowed her to reach a top speed of 0.35c although this was only for emergencies.

Gaseous shields were a holdover from the days before valstronium had been discovered. When starships had been made entirely out of nano-carbon composites they needed extra protection in order to reach speeds anywhere near the speed of light. They worked by venting a charged gaseous mixture into space. Electromagnetic fields projected by the ship would then form the gases into a cone shape in front of the ship, giving additional protection from cosmic particles.

The techs of the RSN were constantly working on the armor configurations and shielding technology to try and the increase max speed. The most recent RSN ships were able to get 0.35c without their shields but that tech hadn't existed when *Drake* left the construction yard eight years ago.

Including the time it would take to reach 0.31c, *Drake* would pass the fifth planet in eleven hours. If he wanted to enter orbit around the third planet they would have to start decelerating for a further two hours. James however, just wanted to pass the planet, use *Drake's* survey scanners to have a look at it and then move on to the next system. Even so, it would take them almost seventeen hours to pass the planet and exit the system's mass shadow again. He therefore wriggled into his command chair and prepared for the long wait.

Three hours later Fisher's sensor station began to beep. "Sir, the first stealth drone is indicating it has picked up some ionized particles," Fisher reported. "Stand by, the next data package will come through in ten seconds."

Moments later she turned to the main holo-display. "It's confirmed sir, there seems to be a trail of ionized particles running roughly parallel to the path of the drone."

On the main holo-display the track of the drone appeared with a faint blue line roughly parallel to it two hundred thousand kilometers off its port bow. As the next data package came in Fisher updated the bridge. "The drone's passive scanners are picking up a faint gravimetric signature. It could be from the mass of a spaceship sir but it is faint."

"Will the drone be able to re-orientate its visual scanners in time?" James asked.

The stealth drones had maneuvering thrusters but using them would guarantee detection. To avoid this they had the ability to redistribute some of their internal mass, causing a slight spin. By shifting its internal mass again it could halt the spin and thus bring their most powerful visual scanners to bear on anything they detected.

"I'm not sure sir," Fisher replied. "The drone will pass whatever it has picked up in twenty seconds so we'll know soon enough."

Thirty seconds later the next data package came in the form of a visual of the object the stealth drone had detected. The drone managed to get twenty high powered shots of the object and so for the next ten minutes images were sent back to *Drake* by the drone. Sub Lieutenant Hanson had been pulling a double shift in order to man tactical and so it fell to him to try and identify the ship from the visuals. At four hundred thousand kilometers whatever it was,

was at the very edge of the drone's visual range and so the images were very poor. Yet estimating the length and breadth of the ship was a simple task for *Drake's* computers. The ion trail from the ship's engines gave an accurate position of the ship relative to the drone and it was simple mathematics to determine the size of the object in the visuals. Its speed was quickly calculated as the change in angle of the visuals combined with the known velocity of the drone indicated the direction and speed of the unknown ship.

After the last visual came through Hanson addressed the Commander. "Sir, the computer estimates that the unknown vessel is approximately two hundred and fifty to three hundred meters in length. It's travelling at roughly 0.05c on a course parallel to the done heading towards the third planet. Its engines mustn't be at more than 1% or else the drone would have picked up their energy signals rather than just their ion wake."

"And can the computer identify what the ship actually is?" James probed.

"No sir," Hanson responded, "the visuals are inconclusive."

"Ok, well let's assume that the ship is Chinese for the moment. We have had enough strange discoveries today without adding aliens to the list. Hanson, bring up known Chinese ships that fall into the profile of our unknown friend."

On the holo-display three ships appeared, slowly rotating to give a 360⁰ view of each one. As he always did when he saw Chinese warships James paused momentarily to stare. Of all the various star faring powers, the Chinese starship designers seemed to take the most pride in their work. British ships were designed and built almost purely on functionality. That in itself gave them a certain look of sturdiness that was beautiful in its own right. By comparison the Chinese ships looked like a single missile would crumple them. Of course being armored in valstronium this was a mistake and so James wondered, as he often did, why the Admiralty couldn't design ships to match the Chinese in beauty.

"Hanson, run us through what we're looking at here, without looking at your terminal please," James asked. He already knew each of the Chinese ship designs off by heart but he wanted to test Hanson and give the rest of the bridge a chance to digest the information.

"Yes sir," Hanson began nervously. After a slight pause he continued a bit more firmly, "the first ship on your left is the most recent Chinese survey ship. Larger than their previous designs she carries a sensor suite almost equal to ours and is armed with four missile tubes and a single plasma cannon."

"Thank you Hanson," James interrupted. "We can probably discount our friend being a survey ship. Intelligence suggests the Chinese have only completed six of them so far and I can't see them wasting one by leaving it sitting around a star system. You may move onto the other two if you would."

"Yes sir, well the other two ships are both Chinese destroyers. The one in the middle is the older Luda class. She is slightly smaller with a length of two hundred and sixty meters and a mass of twenty two thousand tones. She carries eight missile tubes and two plasma cannons. I believe intelligence indicates the Chinese have at least fifty in commission. The second destroyer is their newer class – the Luyang class. She is two hundred and eighty meters long with a mass of twenty five thousand tones. Offensively, she carries ten missile tubes and two plasma cannons. Her armor is estimated to be a whole twenty centimeters thicker than the Luda class."

"Very good Lieutenant Hanson and what would be your tactical conclusions?"

Without blinking Hanson immediately replied to his commander. "Well sir, with a broadside of four missiles even the smaller Luda class has enough firepower to blow us to pieces. If we come out of stealth we may force her to power up her drives and come after us. That way we'd be able to get a confirmed ID but we may not live long enough to report it back to anyone."

"My thoughts exactly Lieutenant," James said with a nod. "I think we'll stay as we are. There's no other reason why our friend should be where he is unless he plans to ambush anyone trying to survey the habitable planet."

Hanson turned back to his terminal trying to hide a delighted grin.

James continued, "If he is Chinese then the Chinese haven't reported their discovery of the Void to the UN yet. At least they hadn't when we were last in port six months ago. Navigation, plot his estimated course, how close will he be to the third planet when we are making our approach?"

James nodded at the answer. The Chinese ship would be nowhere near the planet when they approached it. That would allow them to redirect their heat vents away from the Chinese ship as they passed behind the planet. With luck, the Chinese Captain would never know they were here.

"Ok, keep us on this trajectory until we round the fifth planet. We'll make one pass on the third and then head back out of the mass shadow and one light hour beyond the shift limit. Then we'll jump out and head to V17 and see what else the Chinese are up to. I have a feeling the Admiralty is going to be very interested in our report!"

Several Sub Lieutenants nodded in agreement and Hanson tried but failed not to break out into a smile again.

Chapter 5 – Riches

Before the introduction of alien tech into the Human Sphere, the economy in the First Interstellar Expansion Era revolved around four things; valstronium for ship construction, He3 for fueling the fusion reactors on ships, starbases and planetary surfaces, a vast array of rare elements discovered outside the Sol system and, finally, consumer goods. With over thirty-five habitable worlds colonized by 2450 there was an ever-growing desire for all four resources.

-Excerpt from Empire Rising, 3002 AD

23rd November 2464. HMS *Drake*, the Void.

As *Drake* passed V2 all her passive sensors turned to focus on surveying the third planet. Once again Fisher was manning the sensor terminal after she had spent the last six hours off duty. James had given her permission to power up the active sensors for a limited scan of the planet. She was restricted to a brief scan of the equator for fear some radiation would seep around the planet and alert the Chinese destroyer.

As she looked up from her terminal, Second Lieutenant Gupta saw the same look she had seen in her eyes only hours ago when she had first reported the possibility of a dark matter bubble.

Glancing past Gupta she looked to the commander, "Sir, I'm not quite sure I can believe what I'm seeing."

"Well please don't leave us in suspense," James replied.

"It appears that there are significant deposits of valstronium around the area of the equator we surveyed. Given what our passive sensors have also picked up, the computer is estimating that the pockets we know are there for sure, continue sporadically across the entire planet."

Gupta looked back to the commander to take in his reaction. The British discovery of valstronium on their second colony was the main reason Britain had been able to keep up with the other major world powers in the space race, which had, in turn, led Gupta's family to immigrate to Britain. Before that discovery, almost two hundred years ago now, the only source of the metal had been from mining asteroids that orbited Sol and other stars. Typically only those with wide orbits contained the metal and even those were rare. Britain's discovery had meant that they could build as many spaceships as they needed and still export some of the almost priceless valstronium. This success and the overbearing weight of the Indian caste system had led Gupta's family to Britain in the hope of a brighter future for their offspring.

Gupta could hardly keep a grin from her face but as she watched the commander she controlled herself. As James read the details Fisher had sent to his display, his face didn't move an inch. Scolding herself for wishing to be like her stuck up commander, Gupta turned back to her own terminal. The findings were indeed impressive. Since the founding of Britannia, the other space powers had discovered their own limited sources of valstronium. However, the sheer quantity of valstronium the sensors suggested were present on V2 would mean that the British would once again have a near monopoly, if they could exploit it.

James eventually broke the silence that had encompassed the bridge. "Very good Fisher, I see the Admiralty is indeed going to be pleased with our discovery. What else have you found?"

Surprised at the commander's nonchalance over their discovery,

Fisher had to look back at her console to recheck the other details. "The planet is 15% smaller than Earth. It is also closer to its sun so although the sun in this system omits less solar energy than Sol's, the average temperature is 5⁰C higher. I'm not sure any settlers are going to want to live out in the open around the equator but the north and south hemispheres are perfectly habitable. The atmosphere is also similar to Earth's with a slightly elevated oxygen count. The land mass is largely made up of small islands although there is a sizeable continent in the south that would make a good initial base."

"Interesting," James replied, "I think we may want to suggest to the crew that they reinvest their prize money into this system. I can see V2 becoming the center of our expanding colonial empire for decades to come. Anything else of interest, how about plant and animal life?"

Gupta had to hide a snarl at the commander's comments as Fisher consulted her console again. It was well known that Commander Somerville came from an exceedingly rich family. Despite his current difficulties, it was hard to imagine the commander needing to think about how to invest a measly one million credits. When Gupta's family had come to Britain they had had no choice but to scrape a living from nothing. Her parents had worked two jobs each and spent their meager life's savings to send her to the RSN Lunar Academy. Now, as a Second Lieutenant, she was able to begin paying them back out of her wages and to help send her younger siblings to university as well. She still held out hope of a command someday. That would allow her parents a level of luxury they could only dream of. Yet, Somerville's promotion to commander had been a kick in the teeth and had left her father complaining to her over the datanet for weeks before *Drake* had left Earth's orbit.

Gupta's thoughts were broken as Fisher looked up from her console to answer her commander's question, "We only got data from the active scans so I can't tell you about the north and south hemispheres, just the equator. There seems to be abundant plant life although no sign of any sizeable animals, certainly no signs of intelligence."

"That's a relief," James said with a half-smile. "We don't need any more surprises; aliens would be just too much! Tactical, any sign of our Chinese friend?"

Now that *Drake* had passed the third planet, her heat vents were pointing away from the suspected position of the Chinese ship whilst all her passive sensors were aimed at where they estimated her to be.

Sub Lieutenant Becket who was now manning tactical took control of the main holo-display, replacing the rotating projection of V2 Fisher had up with the estimated plot of the Chinese ship. "If she hasn't altered her approach speed or angle, based on the recon drone's data we should expect her to be somewhere in this region, so far we haven't picked anything up yet."

Gupta sat forward in alarm. They had expected to pick up the Chinese ship on thermal scanners immediately after passing the planet. It made sense for the Chinese ship to be venting their waste heat towards the planet as that was the one place they could be reasonably sure no British ships were. Without waiting for Somerville's permission Gupta reacted. "Re-orientate the thermal scanners. Do an expanding sweep from where we last picked up the Chinese ship. It is out there somewhere and we need to find her."

Becket quickly turned back to the tactical console and her fingers began to fly over the controls. The main holo-display began to update itself, gradually expanding the view of the system out from the point they had expected to pick up the Chinese ship. Something caught Gupta's eye. "There, sector thirty seven point four. Re-orientate the thermal scanners and focus in on that sector."

Becket worked the tactical console again and this time the holo-displayed zoomed in and a number of data streams appeared beside the growing blip. As Gupta sat back in relief James took over, "Becket what are we looking at?"

"Sir, the heat signature is consistent with that from the recon drone. It doesn't appear as if the Chinese ship has boosted up their reactors. From the wave length distortion it seems the ship is heading away from V2. They must have turned around as we approached the planet and are heading back out of the system. They are not following the vector they came in towards the planet but they are on a roughly parallel course."

"Any chance they can detect our heat signature from their new position?" James queried.

"No Commander, our vents are still directed one hundred and seventy two degrees away from them. I'm realigning them to be the full one hundred and eighty now."

The bridge sat in silence for another twenty minutes as the passive sensors remained focused on the Chinese ship. Once he was satisfied the Chinese didn't intend any more course corrections James got up out of the command chair. "Lieutenant Gupta, you have the bridge, I'm going to retire to my quarters. Shannon, I want you to plot a series of micro jumps to V48 and V31. We're going to jump in at the edge of the system and launch a spread of recon drones. Then plot us a course to V17. That's the closest habitable plant to Chinese space; we need to see what's going on there so we're going to have a look for ourselves. We can then swing back and pick up the other recon drones. Call me when we are ready to begin our first jump.

Nodding Gupta stood and took the commander's chair. Inwardly she was already trying to control her anger. The commander was a glory hunter, of that she was sure! They had just made the greatest discovery in the history of the RSN. They should be high tailing it back to Earth to tell the Admiralty and let them sort out the political landmines. If there were more Chinese ships at V17 then *Drake* would be running a needless gauntlet. Clearly the Chinese intended to keep the Void a secret. This was a situation for the Admiralty. Yet Somerville wanted to go poking his nose into places he shouldn't. To shake her thoughts she began to review the data on the planet and the Chinese ship.

Yet, forty five minutes later she was still struggling to control her anger. The planet certainly looked like the best find the British had yet made. V2 had the potential to fill the British government's coffers for years to come. In time it would be developed into a major industrial center and then become the springboard for new waves of exploration and colonization out beyond the Void. Her other distraction, the Chinese destroyer, was clearly up to no good. Their small course corrections indicated that the destroyer was intent on patrolling the main line of approach from the Cambridge shift passage to V2. They wanted to catch any British ships that might happen upon the Void and head for V2. Still, despite these distractions, her thoughts had returned time and again to her Commander. With a groan she stood up from the command chair and headed out of the bridge. Her doubts would not leave her alone and, as much as she didn't want to confront her immediate superior, Somerville wasn't just toying with his own life.

*

Sub Lieutenant Becket approached the Captain's ready room. Adjacent to the Captain's quarters it provided him with a more private briefing room than the tactical briefing room. She had a report she felt needed to be passed up the chain of command and the ship's sensors said that both the Commander and the Second Lieutenant were here. As she raised her hand to activate the chime on the door to request permission to enter she heard raised voices.

"This is insane sir! Your lust for glory is going to get us all killed!" Lieutenant Gupta's voice could be clearly heard despite the sealed doors.

Instinctively, Becket turned to leave. It wasn't unknown for *Drake's* Commander and her Second Lieutenant to get into shouting matches. Under such circumstances it had become the Sub Lieutenants' custom to get on with their duties and simply record an audio message for either the Commander or Second Lieutenant to look over in their own time. Something about the strain and desperation in Gupta's voice made her hesitate though. Although she knew she should not, she lowered her hand and continued to listen.

"We've discovered the Void, we've identified that the Chinese are already here. The Admiralty needs to know what we know," Gupta continued, just as loudly as she had begun.

"Listen carefully because I'm only going to say this once!" James sharply retorted. "How many times in the six years before I took over command did *Drake* return to Earth for a refit or upgrade to the sensor package?"

"Six times sir, we had a yearly upgrade cycle which you know full well," Gupta spat.

"And how many times have we been to Earth since I took command? James followed up.

"None."

"And where have we undergone our upgrades? Not even in Britannia, but at Cambridge. Where the parts and the equipment had to be shipped in just for us at a much greater cost to the Admiralty. Haven't you figured it out yet? My promotion to command *Drake* wasn't because I used my family connections to get a foot up the ladder. And it wasn't about your lack of command ability. I was banished!"

James paused and eyed Gupta to let his last sentence sink in. "Sent out here, away from the high life of London and the nobility. I'm not doing this because I have a blood lust for fame and fortune. I'm doing this because it is all I have. If I don't command *Drake* to the best of my ability and somehow grind my way out of this situation, I will likely be here until I retire an old commander long forgotten on Earth.

"So get a grip of yourself. I read all of Captain Hank's reports on you. She recommended you to take over her position when she was promoted or at least to get a promotion to First Lieutenant and a chance to prove yourself on a combat ship. If you still want to be angry with me then fine. I can deal with that. But understand that you are stuck here passed over for promotion not because I tried to use my connections to steal what you had earned. This is a punishment for me, not something I sought out. I'm sorry you have been hit in the crossfire. But if you can possibly, just for one minute try and set your grievances aside and consider my proposals from a military perspective maybe you will understand my actions. Can you do that?"

Again James paused for effect but before Gutpa could begin to answer he went on. "If we go back now what do we have to tell the Admiralty? There is this Void, yes, but what else? A single Chinese warship? How are they going to make any decisions on such a scrap of information? And it will take them weeks or months to get any more up to date intelligence. We are the ship on station. We need to get home with the fullest report possible. Neither of us is paid enough to make the big decisions but our job is to help those who are. That Chinese ship was not laying out the welcome mat for us. Who knows what else the Chinese have in the Void, this could easily mean war.

"You are an officer in the Royal Space Navy, not a spoiled brat; it's time we got over this impasse. I will admit I have been taking out my frustrations on you. That has been my fault and I apologize. But now we are in a serious situation here. We need to focus on the task at hand. We are both naval officers."

Slowly and reluctantly Gupta relaxed, uncoiling her tense shoulders and clenched fists. She opened her mouth to speak but then paused. Instead she looked her commander in the eyes and gave a small slight nod. Then she turned sharply and began to walk out of the ready room shaking her head.

"Banished?" James heard her whisper faintly as she swiped the door control. Still shaking her head, Gupta didn't even notice Becket standing on the other side of the door with her mouth hanging wide open.

As Gutpa left James sighed. Opening up to Gupta had been something he should have done months ago but he had been too angry over the situation himself. He knew Gutpa hated him. That was as plain as day on her face when she had first walked into the briefing room. Yet he hoped their heated conversation had at least served to clear the air between them.

Looking up, he caught sight of Becket standing beside the door before it closed behind Gupta.   "Yes Sub Lieutenant, do come in," He called out.

Startled back to reality, Becket entered the commander's private briefing room. Without looking him in the eyes she explained her presence. "I was doing some analysis on the other planets in the system and I thought you would want to see what I found."

Without waiting for a reply she reached over and handed James a datapad. As he began to scan through her findings she summarized for him. "As you know there are two gas giants in the system. The larger of the two isn't anything we haven't seen before. The second one however, has the highest hydrogen mixture we have ever seen."

Nodding, James managed to finally catch her eye. "And why am I only being informed of this now?" He asked.

Clearing her throat Becket tried to keep her hands from fidgeting. "It's my fault sir, we were so focused on going over the data on the planet and rechecking the valstronium data that we didn't get round to the other planets until now."

Chuckling at her nervousness James sought to sooth her. "Well, given the circumstances I think your oversight can be excused. Give me a rundown of what you think this means for He3 production in the Human Sphere?"

Summoning back her courage Becket tried to project an air of confidence. "Well our analysis has only been brief so far. But if we can get a military gas mining station up and running within the year we should be able to meet sixty percent of the RSN's fuel requirements within a further six months. If we open it up to private investors V2 could begin to compete with the USA's Utah system. Certainly we could take over supply for civilian traffic in British, Chinese and French space."

"Agreed" James said as he set the datapad onto his desk. "Well, leave this with me and go and carryout a more in-depth economic analysis. In fact, inform all the Sub Lieutenants that I want separate tactical and financial reports on the implications of these discoveries by the time we get back to Cambridge. Dismissed."

"Thank you sir," Becket said as she turned to leave.

Focusing his attention back on his own data terminal James realized he had a dilemma on his hands. He had already begun to compose his briefing for the Admiralty before Gupta had interrupted him. Initially, he had intended to report the discovery of valstronium as the single most important discovery since Britannia. Yet now he wasn't so sure. The valstronium deposits would ensure the British had a monopoly on its production for decades to come. Yet in the short term the gas giant might have a bigger financial impact. It's small gravimetric pull and high hydrogen concentrations meant that the extraction costs would be far less than at any other gas mining stations except those in the Utah system. In turn, this meant that whoever got the rights to extract He3 from V2 would be able to undercut their competitors and grab a large share of the market.

Deciding he would leave his report for another time, James made his way to his quarters for a quick nap before *Drake* was due to make her jump out of the system. He hoped his 'heart to heart' with Gupta would have some effect. James didn't know if divulging some of his personal difficulties with Georgia would help their relationship but he'd finally decided it couldn't make it any worse. And if he was right and the Admiralty intended to keep him effectively locked up in *Drake* for the foreseeable future then he may as well attempt to make things a little smoother between himself and his Second Lieutenant.

Chapter 6 – The Lion's Den

Whilst the first battleships were not constructed until 2461 AD, they soon became the status symbol of all the naval powers. With the armor and defenses to withstand a fleet of smaller ships, they also carried the missile throw weight to reduce anything else to dust in one salvo.

-Excerpt from Empire Rising, 3002 AD

23rd November 2464. HMS *Drake*, the Void.

Drake exited shift space two light hours outside the V17 system after visiting V48 and V31. In both systems she had deployed a spread of recon drones on slow ballistic courses into each system. Their slow velocities were designed to give *Drake* a chance to survey V17 and the end of the Void before returning to recover the drones. That way all their data could be downloaded into the ships main computers for analysis without having to rely on their limited burst transmissions.

James and Gupta were both on the bridge when *Drake* re-entered normal space. James had taken Gupta's silence on their current mission as a sign that the Second Lieutenant had changed her mind. Although, it was just as likely that she had filed a report detailing her severe misgivings with the mission and intended to throw it in James' face if they made it back to Earth.

Immediately upon entering the system *Drake* shut down all of her non-essential systems and went into stealth mode. James had carefully considered what route to take through the system. They could head straight for the habitable planet and make a close pass as they had done in V2. Yet, of all the planets, this was the most likely to be occupied by the Chinese. If there were ships orbiting the planet, or even a ground or orbital base, then it would be impossible to avoid detection.

Going for the safest option possible, James had chosen to drop back into real space two light hours from the shift limit. That way *Drake* could slowly work up to her full speed before she entered the system proper. In addition, he didn't plan to get any closer to the planet than five light minutes. That would allow *Drake's* passive sensors to get a good look at the planet and anything in orbit and yet give *Drake* a lot of maneuvering room in case she had to make a quick escape.

"Ok navigation, take us in along the pre-set route. It's time to enter the lion's den again," James said to the bridge at large.

There was an air of trepidation among the bridge crew on duty. They were aware that picking up the first Chinese destroyer had been a turn of very good fortune. If there were similar ships lurking around in this system, the first notice they might get would be a missile or plasma bolt hurtling towards them.

The V17 system made matters worse. Its star out massed V2's by thirty percent, meaning that it had a much larger mass shadow. Added to the fact that *Drake* had jumped in two light hours from the edge of the mass shadow meant it would take a total of twenty-one hours for *Drake* to transit through the system. No one on board was looking forward to spending so long in stealth mode, not knowing whether the next few seconds would be his or her last. They hadn't even entered the system and already nerves were on edge.

As *Drake* approached the edge of the system's mass shadow, Sub Lieutenant O'Rourke transferred the feed from his terminal to the main holo-display. "Sir, I'm picking up a number of heat signatures from orbit around the planet. There are also two or three intermittent sources further out. The computer can't quite make them out yet but the ones around the planet are definitely ships."

"So I see Lieutenant, very good." As James spoke the plot updated showing that as *Drake* approached the planet the ships would just be coming up over the horizon. *Drake's* passive sensors would get a good look at them as they went past.

A further hour later *Drake* was traveling at her maximum velocity of .31c. O'Rourke had managed to firm up the other heat sources. He estimated that one was a cruiser and the other two were smaller, possibility destroyers or frigates. The ships wouldn't come into range of their optical scanners for a number of hours, so there was no way to get a clearer picture yet. A fourth signal had been picked up beyond the planet but it was still too fuzzy to be confirmed.

As the plot firmed up, revealing that the other two contacts were indeed destroyers, the crew became increasingly nervous. It was now obvious that one of the destroyers, clearly assigned to patrolling the approaches to the planet, would come very close to *Drake* as she coasted through the system. Unless she changed course in the next hour, the destroyer would come within two light minutes.

Over the next forty-five minutes the tension grew steadily. The only distraction was the constant updates from O'Rourke as the passive sensors updated the bridge on the other ships in the system. The fourth heat source beyond the habitable planet did indeed turn out to be another ship; a destroyer, clearly following a patrol pattern that mimicked the other ships.

Orbiting the planet, the cruiser had turned out to be playing escort to five freighters. The freighters had clearly carried in enough materials to construct a pre-fabricated orbital base of some description. Judging by the heat emissions, work was going full pace to put together whatever it was that they had brought with them.

"Sir, the destroyer is altering course," the sensor officer reported.

James peered at the holo-display as it charted the destroyer's new course. It had only altered its trajectory by a few degrees but it meant *Drake* would pass even closer to it. "Navigation, I want you to engage our aft maneuvering thrusters. Use micro second bursts to direct us away from that destroyer. We can't let them get within a light minute of us or they will pick us up."

Over an hour ago *Drake* had begun to pick up faint traces of the active radar waves the destroyer had been firing out into space as it monitored its assigned patrol route. *Drake*'s valstronium armor had been covered with a thin layer of the latest radar-absorbing tech. If she ever saw action, it would be the first thing to be burnt off the hull by a proximity hit but until that day she was able to absorb significant amounts of radar energy.

Yet the destroyer's change in direction meant that she would get close enough for her the radar emissions to reflect off *Drake*'s hull. The radar-absorbing coating could only handle so much before it became overloaded. James had to take the risk of engaging the maneuvering thrusters or else they would be picked up for certain.

For five minutes Sub Lieutenant Thirlwall sporadically engaged the maneuvering thrusters slowly turning *Drake* away from the destroyer. As they passed each other the crew on the bridge let out a sigh of relief.

Yet almost immediately everyone held their breath as O'Rourke broke the silence. "Commander," he shouted with alarm. "The destroyer is turning again, she's bringing her high-energy radar projectors around to look in our direction."

James let out a silent prayer. For every second the destroyer delayed powering up its main radar, the gap between them opened exponentially. Both ships were on almost perpendicular paths, giving *Drake* a glimmer of hope.

Eventually the destroyer managed to bring on its main radar projectors. Too powerful to run all the time, a ship's high-energy radar projectors were usually kept in reserve until battle was joined as they wore out quickly from over use.

This time James let out a prayer of thanks. The destroyer was searching a broad spectrum of space and so the radar's strength was being diluted over a vast area. Whatever the destroyer had picked up it hadn't got a clear fix on it. As the gap quickly opened James began to relax, the chances of a broad-spectrum sweep overcoming their radar absorbing outer skin were quickly diminishing.

Yet even as he began to think they had made it past the destroyer, the situation changed again. Even though they were all watching the tactical plot O'Rourke needlessly informed the rest of the bridge crew, "the destroyer is decelerating, she is angling to come back along our trajectory."

Almost simultaneously, the radar sweeps changed from a broad-spectrum search of *Drake's* area of space to more tightly aimed blasts of radar waves. Whoever was in charge aboard the destroyer had figured that if there really was something out there the only way it could be so close and avoid detection was to have radar absorbing tech. They were now trying to overload *Drake's* absorbing capabilities with more powerful electromagnetic energy.

Immediately James sprang into action. "O'Rourke figure out what sector of the destroyer's sensor gird must have detected us." James knew they couldn't have got a radar return or they would have immediately been able to lock in *Drake's* position. The destroyer must have picked up a stray radiation leak from *Drake.*

"Sir, if they didn't get a radar return they must have detected something with their port forward sensor nodes," the Lieutenant answered.

"Tactical," James snapped as he turned to face Becket. "I want you to prepare a recon drone, get ready to fire it off along vector, ah, thirty seven point five six." James said as he consulted his own console.

"I want the drone to fire off one of its maneuvering thrusters once it enters the sensor cone of the destroyer's port forward sensor nodes. Then ready a second drone."

Becket's fingers were already flying over her console as he spoke, "Aye sir, it will take another ninety seconds to load the recon drone into missile tube two."

James tried to wait patiently as the destroyer continued to send focused radar beams all around *Drake.* Someone on the bridge gasped as the outer edge of a beam passed within sixty kilometers of *Drake.* The seepage from the focused radar beam alone was almost enough to overload *Drake's* radar absorption tech.

Finally his console beeped to inform him that Becket had fired off the recon drone. "Navigation, estimate the course correction the destroyer will need to make in order to bring its radar to bear on the recon drone when it fires its maneuvering thrusters."

"Tactical, prepare to fire the second drone along a trajectory that will bring it into the destroyers forward aft sensor range as well. I want the drone to fire off its maneuvering thrusters when it reaches the same point as the first drone."

Before Becket could reply James swung back to watch the plot. The first drone would be in position in ten seconds; they just had to keep their luck a little longer.

Moments later O'Rourke shouted excitedly, "Sir, the destroyer is turning."

It took the computer a few more seconds to estimate the destroyer's new track as *Drake's* passive sensors fed it all the data they could pick up.

This time it was Becket's turn to curse, "Sir the destroyer has turned to allow it to keep its main radar on us while bringing one of its secondary systems to bear on the drone. I'm going to have to update the second drones firing solution."

James only nodded. Chinese and British warships had auxiliary high-energy radar projectors. Usually, they were only there for redundancy purposes. If a ship lost its main projector, it would severely reduce its defensive capabilities. In a missile duel, a ship's radar was used to coordinate the fire of the anti-missile missiles and point defense plasma cannons. If the radar went down a ship's defenses would be immediately reduced. *Drake* had two reserve high-energy radar projectors for just such a situation. Clearly the Chinese weren't as strict about protecting their reserve equipment from wear and tear.

With the destroyer still filling space around *Drake* with powerful radar beams, James knew they were really riding their luck. Even a random search pattern would happen across them eventually. Another beep from his console told him the second recon drone was away. Yet as the seconds passed doubt began to well up in James.

His trick was a long shot, if it didn't work they would be detected soon enough.

Becket's voice pierced through James doubts and the silence on the bridge, "Sir, the recon drone should have just fired its maneuvering jets. If the destroyer detected anything we should see a response any time now."

Just as she stopped speaking, the destroyer began to change its course again. Rolling, it brought its main high-energy radar projector to bear on the area of space the second recon drone was in and began a wide-angle sweep of space.

Everyone on the bridge let out a cheer of relief as the last radar beam swept past *Drake*. After only a brief scan of space the destroyer altered course again, reverting to its original vector.

Sub Lieutenant O'Rourke looked over to his commander with wonder in his eyes, "Sir I can't believe that worked. You made them think they had a sensor glitch rather than *Drake* on their scopes."

"Thank you Lieutenant, but that isn't a trick I'd recommend trying again. That's as close to being detected and destroyed as I think any of us are ever going to experience. Any closer and it would have been a reality." James replied in an attempt to take the wonder out of O'Rourke's eyes.

In fact he already felt guilty. Gupta had just come within a hair's breadth of being proved right. It might impress a Sub Lieutenant but James knew that none of his instructors at the academy would be using his tactic as a training exercise in the future. Certainly, the pool of sweat running down his back and legs and gathering in his boots was telling him he didn't want to go through anything like that again!

Over the next hour *Drake* continued on her ballistic trajectory in towards the habitable planet. As they approached the point where they would be closest to the planet James brought up the optical feed. At this distance James was looking into the past at the Chinese ships but he still wanted to be able to see what they were up to as O'Rourke gave a run down on what the passives told him.

"Sir, it's confirmed. There are five freighters and a medium cruiser. The medium cruiser appears to be one of the older Ning Hai class of ships. She is making sweeps with her low-intensity radar but we're well within the safe distance for our radar absorption. Three of the freighters appear to be fleet resupply vessels but the other two are different. I think they are civilian construction craft. I have fed the readings from the station they are putting together into the computer. It is currently trying to figure out what they are building based on known Chinese designs."

Ten minutes later as *Drake* rounded the planet and headed back into open space O'Rourke brought up the computer's results. It projected that the finished station would mass approximately one hundred thousand tones; roughly the size of a battlecruiser. James surmised the two construction ships had not been able to bring all the materials that would be needed, so the Chinese would be expecting reinforcements. As to its function, the computer believed that it would serve a dual purpose as both a resupply station and a limited repair yard. The last piece of information was the estimated time of completion. Provided the Chinese got all the materials they needed, the station would be completed in two months but it would be able to provide limited functionality in just three more weeks.

"Sir, the sensors picked up a couple of anomalies in close proximity to the station. I have had the computer enhancing the images we took of that area." As she spoke Sub Lieutenant Becket pointed to one of the secondary holo-displays.

What it projected was unmistakably a missile defense platform. Used by all the major space powers, they were nothing more than a cluster of single fire rail guns loaded with a standard anti-ship missile. The rail guns could accelerate the missiles to a set velocity before the missile's engines took over. They were used widely because they didn't require all the manpower and outlay of resources that came with building and maintaining a proper defense station. Yet they were limited because once used there would be no second salvo.

"Well," James addressed to the bridge at large, "clearly the Chinese think they are here to stay. I want a review of all the data we collected, let's make sure we didn't miss anything else. And double check the optical take of the space around the station, make sure there aren't any more missile defense platforms."

As the bridge crew went to work, James felt that he could finally relax. They were through the worst of it. The third destroyer would be nowhere near *Drake* as she passed through the area of space it was patrolling. If he wanted James could even fire up the main engines and alter course away from the destroyer and head straight out of the system. Of course he would prefer not to let the Chinese know he had even been here. Once *Drake* picked up the recon drones from V31 and V48 he fully intended to take Gupta's advice and head straight back to the Admiralty and let them deal with all this mess. This run into the system had been a close thing. Even if the next few hours would be a lot safer, James knew the tension in his shoulders wouldn't completely leave him. He had had enough of being a hero. He had much more important things to live for. It was time to head home and let those who were paid better make the big decisions. With a quiet sigh he settled himself and prepared to wait out the rest of the journey towards the safety of the system's mass shadow.

*

Still tense James almost jumped when alarms began to go off all over the bridge as *Drake* approached the edge of the system's mass shadow. He wasn't the only one, everyone on the bridge looked startled.

"Sir, we're picking up intense gravimetric anomalies ahead. There are a number of ships dropping out of shift space right on the shift limit. Correction. I now make at least thirty ships exiting shift space. They're about ten light minutes from where we planned to make our jump out."

"Understood," James called out. Sensors train everything we have on this fleet as we go by. Navigation, we're going to have to cruise out to at least one more light hour from the shift limit before we jump. Start to recalculate our jump if you please."

He didn't want to take the risk that their jump out would be detected by this fleet or another ship that might jump in after it. "Sensors, is there anything you can tell me about this fleet yet?" James queried.

He had no concern for their safety. *Drake* was well outside the range at which their radar absorption would be overloaded yet close enough for their passive sensors to get a good read on the Chinese ships as they radiated electromagnetic and heat energy into space.

"Well sir, they clearly have no desire to hide," O'Rourke began as he reviewed the current sensor feed. "The entire fleet has just begun a high acceleration burn. We are getting a clear read on forty-one ships. The computer has classed them as eleven cruisers, including a battlecruiser, twenty smaller combat ships along with eight more freighters. There are also two other ships producing signatures the computer doesn't recognize. They produced the largest gravimetrical anomaly I have ever seen coming out of shift space. I'm going to tentatively designate one as the new Chinese battleship we have been hearing all about, the other I'm not sure what it is."

That pricked James's interest. The Americans and the French had both begun to construct a new class of ship. Larger than a battlecruiser it was also significantly slower. Yet it traded speed for firepower and the Americans boasted one of their battleships could go up against any two battlecruisers and come away without a scratch. James had put that boast down to American bravado yet the stats were impressive all the same.

Their design and production had come after years of pushing by American and French top naval advisors for a larger class of ship capable of taking on a Russian Behemoth. In the last interstellar war, the Russian Space Federation had tried to invade New France and take it for themselves. A joint armada of British, American and German ships had pushed the Russian offensive back but not without loss. The Russians had never been able to source their own valstronium and no one else had wanted to sell them any. As a result they had been forced to build all their spaceships out of nano-carbon alloys. This gave their ships a slower maximum speed and less acceleration than their main rivals. In an effort to reduce these disadvantages the Russians had fully committed to their design philosophy.

To the amazement of all their rivals, they had secretly constructed a number of what became known as the Behemoth class spaceship in their colonial worlds. Mounting over thirty missiles on each broadside the Behemoths sought to overcome the disadvantage of their weaker armor, with very powerful offensive capabilities. The armada's ships were able to fly rings around a Behemoth but if they wanted to actually get in close to attack one they had faced a withering amount of fire.

In response to the defeat at New France, the Russian fleet in orbit around Earth had attacked their British and American counterparts. They had been quickly beaten but not before they had attacked many of the orbital installations of the other space faring powers. Two stray missiles had entered Earth's atmosphere. One had burnt up on re-entry but the second had impacted in the Philippine Sea. The resulting tidal wave had killed thousands of people in the Philippines and Indonesia. As a result, the UN Interplanetary Committee had banned the Russians from building or basing anything larger than a frigate in the Sol system and every other space faring power had quickly signed up to the Sol Demilitarization Act that banned armed conflict in the Sol system. The Committee had also demanded that the Russians pay reparations for the damage done to the Sol system.

Initially the Russian leaders had made it look like they fully intended to pay the repatriations. However, secretly they had been relocating most of the strategically important Russian population to their colony worlds. Then, once the second installment of their reparations had been due, they had announced they were abandoning Earth for their colonies. It had turned out that their entire government, along with five percent of their population, had been shipped out. Next the Russians offered a lucrative cash incentive for anyone who wanted to relocate to their colonies. This resulted in a mass exodus of the general Russian populace along with not a few volunteers from other countries.

Today there were a handful of shipping companies which owed their formation to independent freighter owners who had made so much profit shipping colonists into Russian space they had been able to start their own companies. Yet within a year, the Russians had closed their borders and there had been no communication with the rest of the Human Sphere for over twenty five years.

At first the other powers had hoped that the Russians would be content to live in peace in their own colonial empire. Yet recent stealth ships sent into the single Russian system that bordered the rest of human space rarely returned. If they came back at all the reports showed a steady buildup of Russian military vessels. The American and French response had been to begin the construction of battleships and China, not to be outdone, had embarked on her own construction program. The RSN however, had opted to continue its focus on battlecruisers. With so many systems to defend, the Admiralty felt that speed and flexibility was still the order of the day. That might just all change if the RSN ever had to go up against the battleship on the main holo-display James was looking at.

Not wishing to dwell on Chinese strengths James focused back on the matter at hand. "Navigation, have you updated our jump calculations?" James questioned.

"Yes sir, we'll be ready to jump to intercept our drones from V31 and V48 as soon as we finish our deceleration burn."

"Very good," James commented. "We'll watch this fleet for as long as our passive sensors can get good data on them. Once it's safe we'll begin deceleration for our jump to shift space. Then we're heading home people."

Chapter 7 - Home

The King or Queen of Britain was the second most powerful person in British politics after the sitting Prime Minister. Their personal wealth alone meant they had considerable clout. The popular support they could control in elections could sway the balance of power in the House of Commons. On top of this, the coalitions they were able to build up in the House of Lords gave the ruling Monarch of Britain significant political influence.

-Excerpt from Empire Rising, 3002 AD

10th January 2465. HMS *Drake*, the Sol system.

Thirty-eight days later Commander James Somerville, Duke of Beaufort, was once again sat in the command chair of HMS *Drake*. He silently rolled his tongue over his full title. When he had left Earth two years ago it had been in disgrace and ignominy. Then his promotion to commander had been a punishment and banishment all rolled into one. Now he was once again able to appreciate the beauty and wonder of the Sol system, a home he hadn't been sure he would have seen again for decades.

Sub Lieutenant Fisher had put up the tactical plot on the main holo-display. The Sol system was ablaze with ships. The heaviest traffic was flowing between the mining facilities in the Oort cloud on the edge of the system, the numerous gas-mining stations in orbit around Jupiter and humanity's Homeworld; Earth itself. There was also significant traffic between Earth and Mars. Highlighting just how important Mars still was to the human race despite the now abundance of more habitable planets amongst the stars. Even after

James had surveyed all this traffic, there were still more than a hundred other ships making their way to more out of the way destinations in the Sol system. There were well over three hundred government backed or independent colonies and space stations all within the Sol system. Some built by entrepreneurial miners, others by those who wished to escape the governments of Earth. Others were carrying out research experiments too volatile to be conducted anywhere near a habitable planet.

Earth was still the center of the growing Human Sphere, the name that had been given to the ever-expanding area of space inhabited by the different space powers. Cultural norms, fashion styles and social trends were all still formed on Earth and then quickly flowed out to the various colony worlds. As the son of a key nobleman, James had grown up with his finger on Earth's social heartbeat. Along with his friends, he had spent his late teen years frolicking in the joys of wealth, nobility and power.

Even as he looked at the projection of Earth on one of the secondary displays, he conceded that a little part of him was eagerly awaiting the chance to re-join his peers. Yet he had to admit that the last two years of command had changed him. In fact, if he was honest, a little bit of distance had made him realize that even from his time in the RSN Lunar academy things had begun to change. Parties, clothes, gossip and image had still been a big part of his life but a love and respect for the navy and its traditions had also begun to seep into his psyche. His years as a Lieutenant and now as a Commander had only served to strengthen his growing identity as a real naval officer. Not just the show he had been putting on to obey his father.

Keying the ship wide COM he addressed his crew. "Attention everyone. Before we enter orbit around Earth I wanted to pass on my congratulations to you all. It has been a pleasure to be your Commander over the last two years. Your excellence has never been in doubt but your actions and efficiency in the Void served to confirm what I already knew. What's more I'm glad to report that we have officially made the quickest journey from Cambridge to Earth, we'll be going into the Admiralty's record books!"

He paused to let the crew enjoy the moment before going on, "I'm afraid I have one more request of you. It's one you're not going to like. We can't let the Chinese know that we've found out about the Void – at least until the Admiralty decides to let them know. To that end, I'm going to have to postpone any leave until I get permission from higher up. For appearance's sake we'll be carrying out a complete systems check before any of you can take some shore leave."

James felt as if he could hear the crew's groans through the ship's nano-carbon bulkheads. Yet he knew they would take it in their stride. Everyone knew the Void would be a game changer. It was essential they not mess up at this stage. They had already succeeded in their first goal, a swift return to Earth.

After briefly stopping to pick up the recon drones from V31 and V48 James had red lined *Drake's* shift drive and impulse engines. He had received angry threats from the system commanders in Cambridge, Britannia and Cook but he had faked collision damage to his COMS array. As *Drake* passed through each system on full military power, she had been broadcasting a repeating message informing the system pickets and admirals that she had suffered a collision with an asteroid and was on her way home to Earth for repairs. James wasn't sure anyone had bought it but *Drake* had been going too fast for any of the system pickets to intercept as she skirted the edge of each system.

"Communications, open up a link to *Vulcan*," James requested. As well as the RSN's main shipyard *Vulcan* also served as its headquarters. "Contact them on a civilian channel, this isn't a military matter. Put me in contact with the First Space Lord."

Admiral of the Red Jonathan Hugh Somerville was James' uncle and the First Space Lord of the Admiralty. As such, he was in overall command of the operational functions of the RSN fleet. No doubt the family connection was another barb that constantly pricked Gupta's barely checked resentment over James' promotion.

As Sub Lieutenant Graham opened the channel James recorded the message he wished to send. "Uncle, it will be good to see you tomorrow at Jack's birthday party. I presume now that I have made it home in time I'll be getting an invite? Oh and could you let me know if His Highness is going to be attending. I am very much looking forward to rekindling our acquaintance."

After replaying the message to ensure he had convincingly portrayed his warmth for the King, James sent the message over the channel Graham had opened for him.

"Commander, should I send a situation report to *Vulcan* through a military channel?" Graham asked after his personal message had been sent.

"No need Lieutenant my message will suffice."

"Sir," Gupta began. "You may be the first Space Lord's nephew but I hardly think a personal message to him will suffice. Protocol calls for us to send a situation report before we approach Earth."

Looking at his Second Lieutenant James explained himself, "my cousin's birthday isn't tomorrow. It was yesterday. We were best of friends growing up. My uncle will know that I would never get his birthday wrong. And besides, do you remember our discussion in the Void of my little problem?" James asked.

As Gupta nodded her head he continued, "Well the King was the one who personally requested my assignment to a survey ship. Hell will freeze over before either of us will be warmly embracing. My uncle will get the message."

Gupta's face broke out into a confused stare but she quickly got it under control. The King was behind Somerville's banishment? She was beginning to realize that she had severely misjudged James' posting to *Drake*. Yet if the King wanted rid of James he must have done something awful. Gupta was aware of the disgrace James' father had brought onto his family and the nobility in general. But that certainly hadn't affected the First Space Lord's career so how could it be the reason behind James' banishment?

Still, she thought it would look strange if *Drake* didn't send any situation report upon their return to Earth. That might draw attention in and of itself.

"Hanson," Gupta called out. "Bring up the navigational data on the shift passage to the Void." As the view of the main holo-display shifted Gupta considered it for a moment. "I want you to create a new navigational file on the passage. Make it look like the passage is a dead end after the minor passage we labeled X37."

She turned around to look at her Commander who was staring at her searchingly. "Sir, if we don't send a situation report we'll look suspicious, especially to any Chinese spies. If we send all our survey data bar the Void no one will want to take a second look."

"I take your point Gupta," James began, "but we'll be sending a deliberately falsified report to the Admiralty, are you ok with that?"

When Gupta nodded James smiled. His uncle would most probably be mad at him anyway so what was one more log on the fire?

"Very well, Graham, make it so."

*

Even before *Drake* had docked with *Vulcan* James found himself summoned to the First Space Lord's office. Clearly his uncle had guessed he carried some sensitive information. His request to bring *Drake* into an isolated section of *Vulcan* had been permitted.

Now he was standing outside his uncle's office awaiting permission to enter. As the doors whooshed open, James walked in noting the various paintings his uncle had hung around his office. They all depicted some form of naval vessel in the midst of battle. There were ancient wooden ships from the days of Nelson, battleships from World War II and then three modern spaceships. James knew that each was one his uncle had commanded. The last was a medium cruiser, small by today's standards. In the painting it was swooping in on a Russian Behemoth, firing missiles and plasma bolts at the Behemoth's engines.

His uncle did not stand to greet him. Instead he waved James into a seat opposite him before giving his nephew a cold stare.

"I hope you have a very good reason for all the inconsistencies in the report you sent to *Vulcan*. Your personal message made me go over your report with a fine tooth comb as *Drake* decelerated into orbit. According to your survey logs you are missing three days from your collision through to your arrival at Earth. I also had my flag Lieutenant have a look over your ship as she was docking. There is no sign of any collision damage."

"You are quite right of course," James said as he handed over the datapad he had brought with him, trying to look calm and composed. "Here is our real survey report. I felt that given the circumstances secrecy was the best approach."

"You did?" Somerville asked with more than a hint of sarcasm. He had always thought there was a glimmer of potential in James but he feared he had too much of his father in him. After the incident with the royal family he had decided James' future in the RSN would go no further than command of a survey ship.

After eying the datapad Somerville instead looked back at his nephew, "you give me an overview of what I'm going to find in here."

After clearing his throat he proceeded with the report he had been practicing all the way from the Void. "Well sir. *Drake* was surveying a shift passage that led away from Cambridge when we discovered a pocket of space devoid of any dark matter. After a brief survey of the border of the pocket we concluded that it was indeed a dark matter bubble."

Inwardly James smiled, he could see his uncle had already slightly shifted forward in his seat. After clearing his throat again he went on. "The dark matter bubble is approximately twelve light years in diameter and contains fifty-six systems. Our astronomical data from Earth identified five of the systems as having planets in the goldilocks range so we proceeded to survey them before coming back to Earth with the news. Four turned out to be able to sustain human life. Two of them fall within our own borders, the other two are in open space. Out of all the systems only eight actually fall within Chinese space. More important is the system we designated V2. It is one of the systems with a habitable planet in our space. Our survey found significant amounts of valstronium ore on the planet and one of the system's gas giants has the highest concentration of He3 discovered outside of the Utah system. Our initial projections indicate that if we can develop this one planet alone it will be able to fund our expansion program for the next half century."

Before going on James again paused to take in his uncle's reaction. If anything he looked sterner than when James had begun. Clearly he was trying to control his feelings.

"But that is not all. When we entered the first system we did so under stealth. I thought that the wisest course of action as we didn't know anything about the Void or its planets. By chance one of our recon drones managed to pick up a Chinese destroyer lying in stealth in the system. It was patrolling a direct route from the Cambridge shift passage to the habitable planet. What's more, when we surveyed the habitable system closest to Chinese space, we encountered a light cruiser, three more destroyers and a number of freighters that were constructing a repair and resupply base. On our way out, we then detected another Chinese fleet jumping in. There were over thirty ships and my sensor officer is convinced that one of them was the new Chinese battleship. It is my assessment that the Chinese fully intend to keep the Void a secret and claim it all for themselves. If they do, they will get an advantage over us we may never be able to pull back."

James had found himself staring at the closet painting on the wall as he had finished his last couple of sentences. As he looked back to his uncle, his head was bowed deep in thought. The implications of their find were potentially colossal. Ever since the Russian attack on New France, the expansion race had increased three fold. The nuclear detonation on Earth had reminded everyone that it was foolish to have all their assets on one planet. Further, each space faring nation knew that if it was left behind the military and economic might of their rivals would curtail any further expansion. If any one space faring power could ring in another with colonies and military bases, there would be no more room for expansion. The UN Interplanetary Committee sought to limit this threat somewhat and give lesser nations an opportunity to found their own colonies. However, the threat still remained. Naval intelligence estimated that China had eighty percent of its survey ships operating around the British border trying to accomplish just that. And if China was willing to ignore the UN, all the success Britain had had over the last two centuries could come to a sharp end.

Without looking up, Somerville keyed his COMS unit and spoke to his secretary. "Janet, I want you to contact Admiral Russell and get him to meet me in my office immediately."

As he reached for the datapad, Somerville glanced at James. "You can go out and wait in the receiving room. I need to read this before Russell gets here. I will say this though, it appears you have done a very good job, excellent in fact, but this is over your head now."

Nodding, James got up to leave. Admiral Russell was head of the Royal Space Navy Intelligence and had served with Somerville during the New France campaign. James knew Russell was his uncle's closest friend and rumors around the fleet were always talking about them being as thick as thieves. Together they had successfully steered the RSN's and Britain's expansion over the last thirty years.

*

An hour after Russell had entered his uncle's office James was called back in. Russell then spent twenty minutes grilling James, ferreting out every scrap of information he hadn't included in his report. Finally, he sat back in his chair and relaxed, clearly satisfied that there was nothing more he could learn.

His uncle spoke for the first time since James had re-entered the office, "your move with the Chinese destroyer was brilliant – an extreme long shot to be sure but brilliant none the less. Clearly you've got more potential in the navy than your father ever intended you to have when he made you apply to the academy."

"Thank you sir, but you are as much to thank for that maneuver as me. I got the idea from one of your sea faring novels. A Captain in one of them played a similar trick back in the days of sail and cannons."

Russell did not even try to hide a chuckle, "you made the boy read those awful things, they have almost no bearing on historical reality."

Ignoring Russell's comment, Somerville smiled with satisfaction, "well, I guess those books came in handy after all then. My esteemed colleague and I feel that as you made the discovery you have the right to know what we're planning. Plus, we're going to be making extensive use of you in the coming weeks. I have already dispatched a corvette to Britannia warning Rear Admiral Jensen to prepare her fleet for departure.

We are going to have to form a larger task force from the defenses at Cook and New Edinburgh but that will take time. If our plan is approved, Jensen is going to have to move into the Void first and secure V2 with what she has got.

As you can guess we don't plan to just roll over and let the Chinese take what they want. Russell has an idea that might just win us some time. We're going to have to get you before the UN Committee on Interplanetary Affairs though. They have a session tomorrow so if I can pull a few strings expect to be summoned."

The COMS unit on Somerville's desk chirped for attention. Reaching over he spoke into it. "Yes Janet, what is it?"

"Sir, your guests have arrived, shall I show them in?"

"By all means don't keep them waiting." Somerville replied.

Looking up he caught James' eye with a piercing stare. At that exact moment Russell appeared to have grown a sudden interest in one of the wall paintings. "We are about to entertain some distinguished guests. I want you to be on your best behavior. Is that clear Commander?" His uncle asked him.

Being caught off guard by the sudden shift, James could only nod. As the doors opened realization dawned on him. In walked the Prime Minister of Great Britain, closely followed by the King, His Royal Highness King Edward XI

James had to fight to keep down the anger that welled up inside him. The King was the source of all his problems. If it would not have earned him a court marshal and a prison sentence his uncle would already be pulling him off the King. Grinding his teeth, James tried to calm down.

Noticing James' difficulty, his uncle stepped in front of him to greet the Prime Minister. "Prime Minister Fairfax," Somerville said as they shook hands, "it is a pleasure to host you in my private office. "My King, it is good to have you here as well. You all know Admiral Russell and this is my nephew, Commander James Somerville."

The Prime Minister offered his hand to James but King Edward didn't move. Before the tension got any higher Somerville showed his two guests to their seats. "As you know this is a highly unorthodox meeting but matters have arisen that I think need to be dealt with swiftly and in secrecy - at least for now. Commander, can you give us a summary of your discoveries out beyond Cambridge?"

James had been wondering why he was still here and so he had to shake himself as he turned to his audience. As he was recounting his discoveries one more time he made a point of only addressing the Prime Minister. Finally, after a couple of questions he was allowed to take his seat.

Somerville then stood and took over. "I think it goes without saying what the Chinese are planning and that we can't let them control the Void. Russell's office has managed to identify the large ship Commander Somerville picked up among the fleet he observed entering V17. It is their colony ship, *Henna*. Officially, it left Earth orbit two months ago to carry out some extended space trials. We thought nothing of it, as the Chinese had no colonies to establish. However, it now appears they were already putting in motion plans to claim the entire Void for themselves. To prevent this Russell and I have a plan. The Politburo has made a mistake in not going public with this and it gives us a chance. With your permission here's what I plan to do."

Twenty minutes later their conversation was interrupted by Somerville's COM beeping again. In frustration he answered, "What is it?"

"I'm sorry to disturb you sir but the frigate *Surprise* has just been sighted approaching Earth. She appears to have significant battle damage and has already sent us a full report. I've transferred it to your console."

Ignoring his guests Somerville turned to his console and after a few seconds handed Russell his datapad. Both men quickly scanned through the information.

Russell was the first to look up and break the suspense. "The Chinese have attacked convoy 3.2 as it was returning through Chinese space after visiting the Reading system. All nine of our freighters were lost along with a light cruiser, *Resolution,* and the flak frigate *Renown*."

"What happened," interjected the Prime Minister, "our ships have strict orders not to provoke the Chinese."

"No blame can lie on Captain Turner," Russell interjected, "it appears he handled himself well, giving his life trying to protect the convoy. A Chinese fleet jumped into the system just behind our convoy. They were clearly on transit to another destination, as they didn't try to enter the system's mass shadow. Yet two fast attack cruisers broke off from the fleet and pursued the convoy as soon as they saw it. *Resolution* and *Renown* managed to take out one cruiser before the other destroyed them and the freighters. It seems Commander James isn't the only one with a trick or two up his sleeve. Commander Lightfoot of the *Surprise* managed to trick the second cruiser into plasma range and destroy her.

"What's more," Somerville added as he finally looked up, "the fleet they encountered can only be the one James encountered approaching V17 in the Void. The convoy was attacked over five weeks ago. It has taken *Surprise* this long to creep through Chinese space with all her battle damage."

There was a pause in the conversation as everyone imagined the difficulties of commanding a damaged ship through hostile territory for over six weeks. It was a wonder *Surprise* had made it back at all.

King Edward broke the silence, "So what does all this mean for your plan then Admiral?"

"I'm not sure yet," Somerville replied, "but I think we can use this to our advantage. If you will excuse me gentlemen I have to deal with this quickly. We need to keep *Surprise* under wraps until tomorrow if we can."

The Prime Minister and King both got up to leave. As Edward XI walked out of the office he paused at the door, looking back at James he left a parting shot. "Don't think this changes anything boy."

Chapter 8 - Subterfuge

After the discovery of the shift drive and the Alpha system, international tensions on Earth threatened to spiral out of control. Before the discovery of Beta, Gamma and Delta it appeared that whoever controlled Alpha controlled humanity's gateway to the stars. The UN Interplanetary Act was passed to try and bring order to the scramble into space.

-Excerpt from Empire Rising, 3002 AD

11th January 2465. UN Interplanetary Offices, New York.

James sat in his assigned seat next to Commander Lightfoot. From his position he had a clear view of the UN Interplanetary Committee. Each of the thirteen representatives sat in a raised semicircle overlooking the audience chamber. Below them was seating for the various applicant parties. The clear divisions in the seating indicated that the designers had envisioned the committee handling complicated disputes with up to four parties involved. In front of him, occupying most of one of the seating areas sat his uncle, surrounded by a host of his aides and legal representatives. After the formal proceedings that announced the beginning of a session, James watched as his uncle stood and approached the council members.

"My esteemed fellows, I have two vitally important issues to bring before this committee today. To that end and in agreement with Mr. Blake, the British representative on this council, I wish to present a request for this session to be a Closed Session."

After receiving a nod from the Chairman, Somerville returned to his seat. His words had been enough to begin the protocol for holding a closed session. Now he had to wait and watch the cogs of the committee spin into action.

The UN Interplanetary Affairs Committee was made up of representatives from each of the space faring powers, along with four representatives from the long list of countries that had applied for colonies themselves. To hold a closed session of the committee, the proposal needed three representatives to approve the request.

The committee had been formed after the disputes over the Alpha system had almost erupted into nuclear war back on Earth. The Interplanetary Act had formalized the claiming rights of planets and how future interstellar borders would be drawn up. Over time the power of the committee had grown. They were now responsible for the administration of the Alpha, Beta, Gamma and Delta systems, as well as the colonies at Beta and Gamma. It also provided a mechanism for countries that did not have the ability to fund large exploration fleets to have access to their own habitable worlds. This last function had given rise to the UN Planetary Allocation Lottery. It allowed any sovereign state to apply, provided they could demonstrate they had the financial capability to start and maintain a colony beyond the Sol system. If they passed the checks, they went into the lottery system, the UNPAL.

The space faring powers had agreed that every third habitable planet they discovered would go to the PAL and be allocated to whoever the lottery system picked. With two exceptions, no class 1 planets would be given away and the space faring powers reserved the right to hold onto strategically important planets. Instead they could offer up another planet as a replacement.

Somerville had already contacted his direct opposites in the United States Space Fleet and the German Interstellar Marine. The Americans still had a good working relationship with the British, even to the point of sharing R&D projects. The Germans were even more concerned about Chinese military buildup than the British. They also shared a border with China and, having a fleet not even two-thirds the size of the British, the Chinese had been pressing them hard over the last two decades. In the end both representatives had proven easy to persuade. He hoped that both of his counterparts had found the time to ensure their representatives on the committee would cooperate. He hadn't informed them of his topics for discussion today and so they were operating completely on faith.

Smiling, Somerville relaxed as first the US representative seconded his proposal and the German representative followed suit. The Chairman of the committee, Japanese representative Akiyama, stood and addressed Admiral Somerville.

"It seems you have gotten you wish Admiral. I now declare this session closed. No communications with the outside world will be permitted and any information disclosed to the committee will remain confidential until a decision has been reached on whatever matters you are bringing before us."

"My thanks Akiyama-Tono," Somerville replied adding the proper honorific.

Again he approached the committee, this time bringing his datapad that allowed him to access the large holo-display in the center of the room.

"It is with great displeasure that I have to report an act of war by the Chinese Fleet. Exactly forty-six days ago, a Chinese fleet attacked a British convoy returning from a supply run to our colony in the Reading system. A mining colony awarded to us by this committee. The Chinese fleet destroyed a light cruiser, a frigate and eight freighters. A ninth had to be abandoned after the battle. In total one thousand two hundred and forty eight men and women were mercilessly killed."

As he had been speaking, Somerville had been watching the Chinese representative. His quickly hidden shock was a clear sign that the Politburo hadn't informed him about the incident. Somerville couldn't help looking back at Admiral Russell and winking. If the Politburo had kept their orders to fire on British shipping a secret then maybe they had also kept the Void itself from the Chinese representative.

"I have with me today Commander Patrick Lightfoot. He is the commanding officer of the frigate HMS *Surprise*. With a great deal of skill and not a little luck, he managed to escape from the Chinese attack, rescue the crew of the ninth freighter and get his damaged ship back to Earth. I'm now going to call on him to talk you through the battle."

As Lightfoot approached the holo-display Somerville keyed in the command to begin the recording of *Surprise's* sensor feeds from the Damang system. Calmly and methodically Lightfoot talked the committee through the entire engagement. Only when he spoke of *Resolution* and *Renown's* charge towards the Chinese medium cruisers did he show any passion.

The whole chamber watched in silence as Lightfoot finished recounting his ordeal. Somerville had found it impossible not to see himself in the same position with his old ship *Adventure*. Stuck over sixty light years behind hostile territory, nursing home a heavily damaged ship that had lost its radar absorbing coating. It truly was amazing that Lightfoot had managed to avoid detection all the way back to Earth.

Finally, after a few brief clarifying questions Lightfoot returned to his seat beside James. Exchanging glances with his peer James readied himself, as he knew he would soon have to repeat Lightfoot's briefing to the committee. First though, his uncle had to conclude this part of the hearing. As James watched he stood up taking Lightfoot's place.

"So there you have it ladies and gentlemen of the Committee," Admiral Somerville began, "all our evidence has been presented. I wish to request that this Committee demand a clarification from the Chinese government regarding their actions and that immediate reparations be paid to the Royal Space Navy and to the families of all the deceased."

"Just one moment Admiral," Akiyama interrupted. "I think it would be appropriate for us to get an independent review of the information you have presented before we come to any decisions. You and Committee member Feng Liao may each select one of the military attachés not involved in this dispute to present their view on this incident."

Somerville had expected this complication but it didn't concern him greatly. The evidence spoke for itself. The Chinese approached his convoy first. They fired the first missiles and they refused to acknowledge any of the hails *Resolution* had sent them throughout the engagement. He could call on almost any of the attachés and expect the same result.

Just to make that very point, he called for the Argentinian attaché after Feng Liao had requested the Indian. Argentina and Britain had never had the warmest of relationships and it hadn't defrosted any since both governments had extended their influence to the stars. India too did not enjoy good relations with Britain. They saw the British support for French expansion as a direct threat to their own. In reality, the British saw the French as the best stop gap against Russian aggression and so did all they could to help strengthen France's colonial empire.

Somerville tried not to look bored as both the Indian and the Argentinian attachés came to roughly the same conclusions. The Chinese were clearly the aggressors. Without a declaration of war, their actions were illegal under UN law. Reparations were a justifiable demand given the circumstances.

Satisfied that the first part of his plan was about to be accomplished, Somerville addressed the committee again. "Chairman Akiyama, unless Representative Feng Liao would like to add anything to this hearing I request that the committee move to vote on my request for reparations."

Akiyama looked over to Feng Liao and when he didn't move Akiyama turned back to Somerville. "Very well, we will take a vote on your request."

Somerville almost had sympathy for Feng Liao. A closed session meant that the matters presented had to be decided before the committee could retire. Feng Liao had been caught between a rock and a hard place. He couldn't contact his superiors to warn them about what was going on and, because his superiors had not informed him about the attack on the convoy, he could not present any counter evidence to delay the proceedings.

As expected, the vote was a foregone conclusion. China did not have any strong allies on the committee and the evidence had been overwhelming. The committee agreed to seek a response from the Chinese government regarding their intentions towards British shipping. They also demanded that reparations be paid for the ships destroyed outside a state of war.

Taking a deep breath Somerville prepared himself for the next stage. Everything so far had just been building up to this. He hoped the main blow to the Chinese was about to come.

"Ladies and gentlemen of the committee. I would now like to bring my second matter before you all. As you know, section two point three of the Interplanetary Act stipulates that all discoveries of new systems must be presented and approved by this committee. To that end I wish to inform you that yesterday HMS *Drake* returned from surveying space beyond the Cambridge system. She returned to report that she had discovered a dark matter bubble containing no less than fifty-six star systems, four of which are habitable."

There were audible gasps from some of the aides to the committee members and even from Somerville's own people. He had informed them about the first order of business but he had been keeping the Void under tight wraps.

Akiyama took a moment to compose himself and then gestured towards Somerville. "Do go on Admiral, I think we all want to hear about this."

Somerville nodded, "of course Chairman."

Tapping on his datapad brought up a map of the border between Chinese and British space. Cambridge was clearly visible. As Somerville manipulated the map a shift passage appeared linking Cambridge to a large sphere containing fifty-six blinking dots.

"As you can see this dark matter bubble, which we have been calling the Void, has a diameter of approximately twelve light years. Fifty-six star systems are contained in the bubble. There are no other known shift passages leading into the bubble although *Drake* didn't get a chance to fully survey all of it before Commander Somerville returned to inform us of his discovery. Speaking of whom, I have brought the Commander along to give you a rundown of his findings. You will find all the details in the standard discovery report I am sending to you all now but I thought you would like to get an overview first."

Without turning around Somerville motioned for James to come forward. James took this for his cue and so he got up and approached the speaking area in front of the committee.

As he did with Lightfoot's presentation, Somerville stood to the side and allowed his subordinate to carry out the presentation uninterrupted. As James went on, Somerville began to relax. Things could have become tricky if Feng Liao had known about the Void and the Chinese presence already there. His silence meant he truly did not know anything and couldn't question the data his nephew was presenting. Of course it was all true, it just left out a few critical details. The Chinese for one and the extent of the valstronium deposits for another!

Once James was finished recounting his journey through the Void and no more questions were forthcoming, Somerville nodded to James, giving him permission to return to his seat.

Then he got up again and stood in front of the committee. "As you can see Chairman Akiyama the significance of this discovery cannot be over stated. I'm sure you're well aware that my government and I would like to begin expanding our influence into the Void as soon as possible. To that end we would like to offer the planet we have designated as V17 to the Chinese as a sign of peace and goodwill. We do not desire a shooting war between our two nations and we certainly don't want a repeat of the Damang Incident. Further, we do not think we have the resources to make the best use of three separate habitable worlds. Even though our latest discovery has just gone to Canada via the lottery we would like to offer the habitable planet that falls outside our borders to the lottery fund as well."

"That is a very generous offer Admiral. Can I be assured that you speak for your entire government in this matter?" Akiyama asked.

"Yes sir, you can, I have with me a signed document by the Prime Minister and King Edward XI laying out our offer."

As he spoke an aide brought the letter to Akiyama.

"Indeed you do." Akiyama said after scanning over the letter, "and what then is it that you want in return for this generosity?"

"Nothing beyond what is expected in these circumstances Mr. Chairman," Somerville answered. "It is simply my wish that this committee ratify the division of planets and the new interstellar borders that would result."

Tapping his datapad Somerville brought up a new map of the Void and the surrounding Chinese and British territories. The Void was divided into three unequal sections. One, in red, represented what would fall under British ownership if the standard rules of the UN Interstellar Act were applied. Britain would assume control of V2 and V48 along with twenty six of the other star systems. A flashing white section centered on V34 represented what would be given to whomever won V34 in the lottery. A further fifteen systems fell within the white border. Finally, V17 had been added to Chinese space along with the remaining eleven uninhabitable systems within the Void.

"Chairman, I must object to this proposal," Feng Liao interjected before Somerville got a chance to continue.

"Yes, and why may I ask?" Akiyama said as he turned to face Feng Liao.

"The British have just claimed that we have carried out an act of war. Why would they then offer us a planet in the Void that the laws of this committee do not demand them to offer?"

Feng Liao was beginning to sweat very heavily. It was evident that he had figured out the obvious. In his final map of the Void, Somerville had included a wider shot showing the positions of Cambridge, Damang and Reading. It was clear to any half-witted observer that Damang was in close proximity to the Void. If there was a shift passage linking the Void to Chinese space then it would likely connect with Damang. Putting two and two together only came up with one reason for such a large Chinese fleet to be operating in and around Damang.

Somerville hoped the other representatives would be able to come to the same conclusions themselves. If he had of came to the committee with evidence that the Chinese had already discovered the Void they would have had little choice but to offer the two habitable planets that fell outside British space to China, as technically they would have discovered them. Yet, as things stood, China had not announced their discovery. The committee had to act on the basis that the British alone had discovered the Void. And if they could figure out the Chinese knew about it even better.

The committee usually came down very hard on any breach of the UN Interplanetary Act. If some of the representatives suspected China had covered up their discovery of the Void, they would not react favorably. Certainly Somerville hoped that the more astute representatives would realize that the British generosity was actually a ploy to wrestle away control of the Void from the Chinese without having to resort to war.

"Do go on committee member Feng Liao. I hope you have a better reason for objecting than the British are being too generous." Chairman Akiyama said sarcastically.

Feng Liao frantically looked around for help but none seemed to be forthcoming. "They are up to something, can't you all see that?" He shouted rising to his feet.

Chairman Akiyama stared at Feng Liao until he took his seat. "Thank you committee member Feng Liao, I hope that is going to be your first and last outburst or I will have to ask you to leave this meeting. Now, unless Feng Liao or anyone else has other information that they feel should delay our vote on this issue, I believe the time for a decision has come. The British offer is indeed very generous and I see no reason not to accept all their suggestions."

The voting itself took another forty-five minutes, all of which Somerville spent laying plans for the future. He didn't think the Chinese would take his little coup lying down. He had already made as much preparations as he could before this meeting but now that things would be out in the open he would have to act swiftly. His one advantage was time. On a zoomed out map of shift space the distance between Earth and the Void was roughly the same through Chinese or British space. Yet zoomed in things were different.

The shift passages that connected Wi, the nearest inhabited Chinese system, to Damang and Damang to Reading were particularly narrow and twisted. It typically took the convoys over a week to traverse the two shift passages. RSNI didn't know exactly where the Chinese shift passage to the Void matched up with known Chinese space yet even a conservative estimate gave the British a week advantage in sending messages to the Void. Somerville planned to use it ruthlessly. He would have a British fleet in orbit around V2 before the Politburo could even get a message to their fleet in the Void, let alone send in reinforcements.

By the time Somerville had surveyed all the RSN deployments, looking for some more ships he could reassign, the voting was coming to an end. As expected, the motion passed almost unanimously. The Brazilians and Argentinians had abstained, yet with only the Chinese and Indians opposing the proposal passed into law.

Somerville could not help but smile. Usually the bureaucracy of Earth and British politics was the bane of his existence. This time he had been able to manipulate the setup of the UN Committee in his favor. From the beginning, the Committee had been structured to allow decisive decisions to be made to stop any confrontations from coming to a head. Now it meant the Chinese had been unable to react to his plan before it was too late.

After Akiyama delivered the Committee's decision Somerville again approached the Committee members. "Sir, I have one more request before we adjourn."

"Yes Admiral, what else could you possibly have to bring before us?" Akiyama asked in annoyance. The meeting had already run well past lunch.

"Don't worry chairman; the Void was my last surprise. I would simply like to request that the recordings of this committee meeting be immediately released to the public."

At this Feng Liao jumped off his seat shouting, "that is out of the question you insolent...."

Before he could finish, Akiyama cut off the feed from Feng Liao's mike, although almost everyone still heard the expletive that followed.

Pretending he had heard nothing, Somerville pressed on, "my legal aides assure me that under section seven point eight of the Interplanetary Law a supplicant to this committee may request that the proceedings of a closed Committee meeting be made public. I know this section does not normally apply where armed conflict has taken place. However, subsection three does specify that the Committee Chairman may waive this restriction if the armed conflict was an unprovoked act of aggression and the victim agrees to waive their confidentiality."

"I must say," Akiyama began, "this is highly unusual given that you were the one who requested this meeting be a closed session in the first place. Yet, your actions are perfectly in accord with the Act governing this Committee so I'm going to grant it provided we can adjourn now?"

"By all means Mr. Chairman, I am as eager for lunch as you are."

"Very well, permission to publicize this closed meeting is granted," Akiyama said, as he brought down his ceremonial hammer closing the meeting.

Before turning to leave the chamber Somerville could have sworn that Akiyama had winked at him. The sly dog, he thought as he collected Russell, Lightfoot and his nephew, he knew what was happening all along.

"Well," he said to the three other men outside the chamber, "it seems we got everything we wanted. Let's just hope the rest of our plans go as smoothly."

Chapter 9 - Recruitment

Whilst the significance of the discovery of the Haven colony went largely unnoticed at the time, the brewing Void War having taken precedence, its discovery would prove to have a more long lasting impact on human expansion into space than even the discovery of the Void itself.

-Excerpt from Empire Rising, 3002 AD

11th January 2465. New York.

After the UN hearing, James invited Lightfoot for a drink in a local bar. The UN Interplanetary Committee was based in New York alongside the other UN administrative buildings. James had heard of this bar from other RSN officers. Lightfoot had politely declined; citing all the work he had to do in overseeing the repairs of *Surprise* as an excuse. James didn't blame him, if *Drake* was damaged he wouldn't want to leave her until he had seen his ship put back together. Still, he decided to go on his own. He needed some time alone to think.

On the news screens scattered around the bar a number of reporters where excitedly talking about some recent news. James immediately focused on the reports. It seemed that a French exploration ship had discovered a lost colony. Or at least they had made contact with a ship from the colony in another star system.

In the years before the shift drive had been discovered almost one hundred sub light speed colony ships had been sent out into space. A few had been rediscovered after the discovery of the shift drive. Almost all of them had managed to establish small colonies on habitable worlds however, they had all been struggling. Other colony ships had left no sign of themselves even after the planets they had set off for had been linked into the expanding Human Sphere. Still others were presumed lost forever, the dark matter near the systems having been mapped without any way to actually get to the planets being found. If the colonies had proved successful there was no way of finding out short of sending in a sub light speed ship. Such a trip could take decades and no one was interested in volunteering for such a mission.

It had been over one hundred years since the last lost colony was reconnected to human space. As the exploration ships of the space faring powers had headed deeper into outer space they had long since passed the point where the first sub light speed colony ship sent from Earth could have reached. Many stories and holo-drama's had sprung up around the possibility of encountering another human planet, one that had been separated from the Human Sphere for over three hundred years. No one quite knew what to expect. Would the rest of humanity be welcomed with open arms? Or would a whole new culture have developed hostile to the rest of mankind?

Well, it seems as if we're going to find out James thought. The French exploration ship had made contact with a human shift drive capable ship over seventy light years from Earth. That was well beyond even the new Canadian system of Quebec. The ship had claimed to be from Haven; however, the reporters were not reporting the location of the colony. That was strange, wherever it was, it must be closer to Earth than where the two ships had met. That meant there was an entire network of shift passages that would lead closer back towards Earth out there.

One news reporter had shifted her focus to a wealthy billionaire called Harold Maximilian. He had set out back in 2198 with thirty thousand volunteers in a colony ship he had largely funded himself.

His writings, she was reporting, spoke of a planet free from overbearing governments and nanny states. It seemed like the holo-drama writers might just be getting everything they wished for. If this colony had developed the shift drive independently of Earth it clearly had a good tech base. If they still carried the independent philosophies of its founders then it wouldn't be rushing into the arms of one of the space faring powers. James made a mental note to look up all the data he could through military channels once he got back to *Vulcan* and *Drake*. This was going to throw a whole new dimension into the interstellar politics of Earth. How would the UN Interplanetary Committee react to a colony that wanted its independence? Whatever the finer details, the discovery was likely to throw off all the RSN exploration deployments. There was going to be a rush to survey the space around this new colony.

Sitting back in his chair, James dwelt on the implications for a few minutes before he stretched and looked around the room. A short blonde woman in a dark, tight fitting uniform caught his attention. He had noticed her coming in and now she was staring straight at him. Judging by her facial features she couldn't be more than twenty-two or three, certainly not old enough to command a spaceship. That was strange he thought; junior officers were rarely called to the UN so what was she doing in New York? Sighing, James nodded to the woman, signaling to her that it was ok to intrude upon his solitary drink.

"Good afternoon Commander, my name is Lieutenant Ricks. I'm with the RSNI attached to their UN section here in New York."

Nodding, James realized that the uniform was almost identical to that worn by Admiral Russell only without the rank insignia. Clearly on Earth the RSNI wanted to keep the feeling of being in uniform without drawing too much attention to themselves.

"Admiral Russell sent me to keep an eye on you. He said I was to allow you to enjoy your drink but not to let you talk to anyone else."

"He did now did he? And what would happen if I decided I wanted to strike up a conversation with a beautiful French or Spanish Captain as I enjoyed my drink?" James asked.

Smiling Lieutenant Ricks reached up and undid the top two buttons of her uniform. "We are taught many skills during our training to enter RSNI, I'm sure I could manage to play the part of a jealous girlfriend without too much difficulty."

Chuckling, James lifted his lager and finished it in one gulp. "I guess there's no point staying around here too long then, you'll just spoil my fun. Do you want to accompany me to the shuttle docks?"

"My orders are to see you off Commander, so I go where you go," she replied.

"Very well then, there's nothing else keeping me here." James said as he stood.

Looking up at the news screens as he walked out James happily noted that every reporter had forgotten about Haven. They were all playing the footage Admiral Russell had released to the press of *Surprise* coming in to dock with *Vulcan*, her battle damage plain for all to see.

*

11th January 2465, 6:30am. Petworth, West Sussex.

Major Samuel Johnston RSNM, retired, was cooking breakfast for his wife who was still in bed. The sausage, eggs and bacon were done; he was just waiting on the toast to pop when he heard a loud knocking on his door.

He groaned inwardly. Even though he had been out of the Royal Space Navy Marines for fifteen years he knew that strong measured knock. Someone with armed forces training was at his door. He had seen the news reports last night about what was being called the 'Damang Incident.' His wife had been concerned but Samuel had reassured her. The facts just didn't add up. There was no reason for the Chinese to attack a British convoy coming from Reading! If there was going to be war, it would be announced with a much bigger battle. Yet why was someone at his door?

As he pressed the command to open the door his suspicions were confirmed. Despite their civilian dress, the man and woman standing before him were unmistakably armed forces. The man, in his mid-thirties had obviously tried to select baggy clothing to hide his physique but to Johnston's trained eye his lean muscled body couldn't be completely hidden. The woman looked much younger, barely past twenty Johnston guessed. Whilst she didn't have a muscled body that suggested she was a marine or an army soldier she did carry herself with a poise that indicated she had some martial combat training. Her body language also shouted the fact she was junior to her partner and was deferring to him.

After giving Samuel a brief look over the man stepped forward. "Major Johnston?"

"Retired," Samuel answered.

"Yes of course. We're here on behalf of RSNI, do you mind if we come in? My name is Mr. Jones and this is my associate Sub Lieutenant Becket.

"If you must, I suppose, my wife is still sleeping though."

As his two visitors sat at the kitchen table Samuel poured them both tea from the kettle he had been boiling for his wife. "So to what do I owe the pleasure of your visit? Anything to do with that battle we're hearing about on the news?"

"You could say that," Jones said, "We have need of your services."

"Just hold on there one minute. I hung up my boots fifteen years ago and I have no desire to come back. I gave the marines forty years and I intend to give my wife forty more in return for her faithfulness to me."

"Yes, of course we understand that," Jones began in a conciliatory tone. "If you will just hear us out. We are not requesting that you come back to the marines. The RSNI wants to offer you a three-month contract. We have need of your expertise and we would like to hire you on a short term basis."

"And what exactly does the RSNI want with me?" Johnston asked.

"I'm afraid we can't give you any real details unless you agree to sign the contract. What I can say is that you will be going off world, you'll be working with and training Marines and we don't think you'll be needed any longer than three months." Jones replied. "You'll be embarking on a RSN ship, which is why Sub Lieutenant Becket is here. If you agree to join us she'll prepare your things to be transported aboard her ship."

As Johnston studied Becket more closely she smiled at him. Turning back to Jones he asked, "And what is in this for me?"

"Well, for a start we're offering you a very attractive salary for the three months and a similar rate for any additional months you may wish to remain in our employ. Of course, any astute observer might see the connection between this offer and recent news events. You can be assured that if you accept you will be serving your country." Jones answered.

"And when do I have to give you my decision?"

"This is a time sensitive mission so we need to know within the hour. We can give you that time to think it over and talk it through with your wife, if you want. If you agree though we will have to leave in one hour from now."

"Ok, well you can leave the contract with me and I guess I will see you in an hour," Johnston said, already considering what his wife would say.

"Thank you for your time Major, I hope you make the right decision, we'll call back in an hour," Jones said as he got up to leave. Becket followed him out of the kitchen and then out of the house.

Flicking through the contract Johnston groaned, it seemed like the RSNI's offer was too good to be true. Certainly he could use the money and he was as much a patriot as the next man. Yet letting the RSNI get its hands on you was almost never a smart move.

He looked up as his wife walked into the kitchen in her nightgown. "Did I hear voices?"

"I'm afraid so dear, we have had visitors from RSNI."

"RSNI?" his wife asked with a hint of concern.

"Yes, they want me to go work for them for three months. I have the contract here. They won't tell me what I'll be doing but they are willing to pay handsomely."

His wife's concern visibly grew, "does this have something to do with the attack on that ship, what was she called, the *Surprise*?"

"I think that is a safe bet," he chuckled. "I guess I may have been wrong after all, what do you think of their offer?"

His wife paused for a moment to think. Walking round she sat on her husband's lap and looked him in the eyes.

"As much as I have enjoyed having you at my beck and call, we both know we need the money. But more importantly, I know you. If this is important you can't turn your back on it. If there is going to be trouble with China then the best way you can protect me is by going, we both know that."

Samuel looked at his wife with pride. Deep down he knew he was thrilled at the prospect of sinking his teeth into something again. He hadn't wanted to leave his wife. Yet, instead of having to talk her around, she was sending him out. Leaning in he kissed her deeply, giving expression to his pride.

As they broke their kiss, Johnston handed her the contract to look over. After a few minutes she put it down. "They really are offering to pay you well aren't they?" she said.

"Yes, this Damang incident must have been more important that I thought. I think we need to talk contingencies. Your sister has been inviting you out to visit her at Cook for months now. I think maybe you should contact her about taking a trip out there while I am gone. If things turn nasty between London and Beijing then Cook is a much safer place. Plus you won't get bored and lonely while I am gone. What do you think?"

Jackson watched as his wife considered it. "Well," she began, "I have wanted to see the new village they are setting up. And you know I have always loved to fish. Your pay will certainly cover the cost of getting a passenger freighter out to Cook. Plus, having something to do will help keep me from worrying about you too much. How long until you have to leave?"

"They only gave me one hour to decide," Johnston replied. "If I say yes then I'll have to go with them right away."

"In that case you better sign that thing quickly," his wife said. She was pulling him to his feet and towards the stairs to the bedroom before he had even set the pen down.

*

11th January 2465, 10am. Beijing China.

Once again Na Zhong, the Minister for Exploration, found himself looking around at his fellow Politburo members. Thankfully this time he didn't have any new information to share and so he was not the focus of attention. Instead, the second most powerful man sitting around the table, the Minister for Development, Wen Xiang, was speaking.

"This is totally unacceptable, worse, this is a blunder of the greatest magnitude. The UN may be a puffed up group of babbling fools but the other powers respect its rulings and the general public follow its decisions through the news outlets. How could we not have a more competent representative on the committee? And how could we not have informed him of our discovery of the Void? This is not going to end well for us now."

In frustration, Wen smashed his hands down on the table and sat down with a thump. The Defense Minister looked over to Chang and when Chang nodded he got up to speak.

"We were all here when we voted to keep this from our diplomatic services, that included our UN representative. I will admit that yesterday's events were a blind spot to us. No one here thought the British would claim the discovery of the Void for themselves. Everything we have on their exploration efforts indicated that it would take them anywhere from one to three years to find the Void. But even if they had, we were expecting a formal protest at the UN, not a declaration of discovery."

Chang smiled, he didn't think Quin's speech would dissuade those on the Politburo who shared Wen's anger. However, he wanted to move the meeting on, not spend time dwelling in the past. Politburo politics were complicated. If he were to cut off Wen and try to move on it would have cemented the resolve of those who wished to vent their anger. Instead, he could now cut off his own ally and no one would see it as a slight.

"That's all very good Minister Quin," he began. "The real question at hand however is what do we do now? We must all take some blame for yesterday's blunder. But today we must limit the damage as much as possible. Can you give us a rundown of the current military situation instead?"

"Well, as everyone knows, we sent elements of the third fleet into the Void. They should have arrived approximately seven weeks ago, though, as yet, we haven't heard anything from High Admiral Zheng He. Prior to this, we had a light cruiser and four destroyers stationed in the Void. With third fleet now stationed there the numbers have risen to one battleship, one battlecruiser, ten other cruisers and nineteen screening units. I fully expect the British to begin to move elements of their fleet into the Void to protect the planets the UN Committee have awarded them. We will enjoy military superiority for the immediate future, however, that is likely to change. The British enjoy almost a two-week communication advantage over us to the Void. They could already have orders out moving ships into the Void and we can't even warn Admiral Zheng before their ships will begin to arrive. I'm confident our High Admiral can deal with anything the British initially send into the Void. In the long term though he is going to need some help."

"And what were these ships doing when the British survey ship was in the Void anyway?" Wen asked.

Clearly he was not going to give up as easy as Chang hoped. "Have we even heard a report back from the Void informing us of any British activity?" he continued.

Every eye looked to Quin. "No, I'm afraid not." He began, "however, the time lag means that we wouldn't be expecting any communication from the Void for probably another three days if they have detected any British ships."

Chang felt it was time to take over. "Because of our disadvantage in communications, I would like to purpose that we immediately send reinforcements to High Admiral **Zheng**. As Quin said, he should be able to deal with anything the British initially send into the Void. Nevertheless, it is going to become a race to see who can funnel in the most ships first."

"Wait a minute," Na said as he stood.

Chang looked at him with clear disdain.

Trying to ignore Chang's look Na continued.   "You are talking as if war is inevitable. Surely we could be talking to the British and working something out. They have already shown us that they are willing to share the Void. If we go to the UN and reveal that we discovered the Void first we will get a slap on the wrist true. But they will also have to recognize our right to the Void. We can demand that we get two planets, give one to the UNPAL and one to the British. That way we will control the Void and sidestep a costly and pointless war. Space is a big place, there should be room for all of us."

This time it was Wen who interjected and when he spoke, Na knew his voice on the Politburo was about to lose even the meager weight he carried. "The time for politics had passed. We have made some colossal mistakes so far, but, as we agreed months ago, the Void must not be allowed to fall into British hands. Nothing has changed that. And besides, if I understand Quin right, High Admiral Zheng already has orders to engage any British shipping in the Void. For all we know war could be raging there as we speak. What I want to know is what the British are going to do. Minister for Foreign Affairs?"

Minister Fen was known for his bouts of anger but, unusually, he had kept himself under control so far. "I would think that would be obvious," he said. "We have carried out an unprovoked attack on one of their convoys and killed over a thousand of their people. The public opinion in Britain and its Sol holdings have truly galvanized against us. The images of that battered ship *Surprise* coupled with the joy over the discovery of the Void have firmly set the public's mood against letting us have anything. There have already been protests outside the British parliament against offering us one of the planets in the Void."

"And even if the public was against any form of retaliation, Admiral Somerville would still be plotting against us." Quin added, "He is a veteran of the New France Campaign and our intelligence reports on him suggest that he isn't likely to back down from a fight."

"So there you have it," Chang summarized as he stood. "We have no other option but to forge ahead with our plans. War with Britain has been looming over us for decades now, we cannot allow them to go on enjoying the expansion and economic success they have had. We have towed the line of the UN for too long. It no longer serves our best interests to obey them blindly. It's time to take a stand, to establish China as an independent power once again. No one will dare attack us here on Earth. If they did it would turn into a nuclear bloodbath that would envelope the whole UN. The Void has given us a chance to smash the British fleet away from Earth and the intervention of the other powers. If we can smash their fleet it will take them decades to recover and by then we will have left them far behind. Our course of action is set. I expect all of you to go back to your ministries and prepare to transition into a war footing. The UN regulations prevent any form of open hostility within the Sol system. We will abide by those laws, as they will serve us as much as they will the British. However, every other colonial world must be made ready for war. Is that understood?"

As every head of the senior Politburo ministers around the table nodded Chang sat down. With a wave he motioned Quin to his feet, "Minister Quin, can you share some of the military plans we have ready to put into action?"

*

11th January 2465, 11pm. HMS *Drake*, docked at *Vulcan* shipyard.

James sat at his desk in his private quarters aboard *Drake*. He had been reviewing the RSNI's report on the battle at Damang. They had completed their analysis of the Chinese weapons and tactics and produced a number of recommendations for RSN commanders as well as a new force analysis. The RSN fleet centered around ten battlecruisers and a further eighty heavy, medium and light cruisers. The Chinese had their battleship, eight battlecruisers and an estimated ninety-six other cruisers. On paper, the Chinese fleet out massed the British by almost twenty percent. Yet the Damang Incident had demonstrated that British technology could begin to undo this imbalance. James was sure the Chinese would be furiously working to negate the British advantages whilst RSNI would be trying just as hard to find new ways to ensure the British stayed ahead.

Closing down the RSNI report he switched to a memo from his accountant. Andrea Clements was an old friend from the academy. They had been unlikely friends. Andrea was from the slums on Mars whilst James was the son of a Duke. However, she had been a computing wiz kid and James had respected her skills, especially when it came to getting up to mischief. She, in turn, had seen James' friendship as an opportunity. Being from a poor background she had not had the contacts or support she needed. As well as being a computing wiz kid she also had a passion for numbers and wanted to start up her own investment company. The academy and her subsequent four years as an ensign and then Sub Lieutenant had simply been her way of overcoming her background. No one would respect a kid from the slums. But a graduate of the RSN Lunar Academy who had four years of military service was another matter. She now commanded enough respect and social standing to head up her own company and deal with the other major players in interstellar finance.

During their academy years James had watched her turn her family's meager earnings into a small fortune by their standards. Soon after he had begun to send some of his father's trust fund money her way. They had parted company when they had been assigned to different ships after the academy but he had continued to help fund her investment ventures. After the death of his father James had found himself inheriting the family property and business. James had been shocked to find out his father had gambled away most of the wealth his family had once been renowned for. Immediately, he had placed Andrea in charge in the hope she could salvage something. It had turned out to be a prudent move for within weeks he had been banished to exploration duty aboard *Drake*.

Within a week of his father's death the news had hit that he had left the Dukedom of Somerville in serious debt. Almost all the companies were insolvent and James had been forced to sell much of the family's stock portfolio in order to stave off disaster. Even so, in the end almost sixty thousand workers had lost their jobs. The news stories, protests and calls for an investigation had lasted for weeks.

Initially, James had not been too surprised when he had found out he was to inherit the family assets. His elder brother was an irredeemable drunk. James had never got on with his father but he had thought his father did not want the family fortune to be drunk away. However, when the news broke he finally understood. His father had not been able to live with the shame but he had no problem with his second son having to.

Over the last two years James had received sporadic updates from Andrea. She had used his remaining stock investments to balance the books on many of the larger established companies James had inherited. Then she had sold them off one by one, ploughing the money from their sale back into his smaller businesses and investment opportunities Andrea had identified. She had slowly allowed them to grow again, before they too were sold off. What was left was a core group of businesses and investments in enterprises Andrea deemed to have the best long-term futures. Judging by the most recent update, they were already beginning to turn a handsome profit and Andrea was already looking for further opportunities.

During his exile, James had also been happy to note that Andrea's business had been slowly growing. His Dukedom was still her largest client but she had been steadily building up a long list of medium size clients. This also benefited James as he had provided Andrea with a large part of her startup capital. He was a silent partner in her business.

Before closing the report, he wrote a quick message to her. He wanted to let her know that she was to reinvest his reward for the discovery of the Void back into the companies that would be awarded the development rights. That was as far as he could go without coming close to a charge of insider trading. Technically, he was not telling her to invest any of their personal wealth. The RSN reward scheme allowed recipients to reinvest a percentage of their reward back into the system they discovered at attractive rates.

Often this opportunity wasn't taken up but James knew valstronium had been discovered there. He had a feeling the Void was going to become very profitable. He hoped Andrea would be able to read between the lines and direct more of his wealth towards the Void as opportunities arose.

The COM unit on his desk began to flash, telling him that a low priority message was awaiting his attention from the bridge. Activating the COM unit he contacted the officer on watch, thankful for the distraction. "Lieutenant Fisher, there is a message for me?"

"Yes sir, an intelligence officer showed up at the docking hatch with *Vulcan*. He said he had a message for your eyes only. He passed on a datapad; it's waiting for you at your command chair. Apparently the datapad has to link into the chair for it to activate," Fisher explained.

"Thank you Lieutenant, I'll be up presently."

As curiosity got the better of him he abandoned the report he was reading and headed for the bridge.

Chapter 10 – Reunion

Despite the tensions between the spacefaring powers because of the colonial race, the First Interstellar Expansion Era was one of relative peace. Devoid of the interspecies commotion, dread and often panic that would over shadow the end of the First Interstellar Expansion Era, the public of the Human Sphere loved a scandal. In Britain the politicians and nobility were almost always at the center of this attention.

-Excerpt from Empire Rising, 3002 AD

13th January 2465. HMS *Drake*, docked at *Vulcan* shipyard.

James had debated putting on the dress uniform he had worn in New York, in the end he had settled for his standard Commander's tunic. The intelligence officers probably wouldn't want him drawing too much attention to himself. The datapad had summoned him to a secret meeting aboard the starbase *Gemini*. *Gemini* was a semi-independent starbase, used by shipping lines to load and unload shipments of cargo and passengers. As it was in geosynchronous orbit over Europe, it mainly served the European powers. Britain had a substantial stake in the starbase and operated some of its private levels. Even so, it was strange that he had to leave *Vulcan* to have a meeting with RSNI.

The message he had received last night said a shuttle would be waiting for him in shuttle bay seven on board *Vulcan*. It also stipulated that he was to leave *Drake* at exactly 0700 hours and head straight for the shuttle bay.

As James walked through the docking hatch, he thought it strange that the RSNI security detail was nowhere to be seen. Officially in place to protect *Drake* from infiltrators who may try to steal her information about the Void, they also ensured that no one from *Drake* could leak the same information. Shrugging, he walked the fifteen minutes to shuttle bay seven.

Inside the shuttle bay there was only one shuttle. A single pilot sat in the cockpit, wearing a tight fitting non-descript uniform. Her size and demeanor led James to think she was some kind of security officer. On their flight over to *Gemini* he couldn't get any information out of her confirming his suspicions.

As they docked, again in a deserted docking bay, and another similarly dressed officer escorted him into an adjacent meeting room. There he was told to wait and someone would be in to see him shortly. At this point James was beginning to get nervous. He had never heard of the RSNI acting this way. If Admiral Russell or one of his subordinates wanted to see him they could have just met in *Vulcan* or ordered him to the Ripley buildings; the ground offices of the Admiralty in London.

The whine of the door opening alerted James that someone had finally come to see him and he quickly turned to see who it was. All his apprehension fled. In less than a second he was on his feet and rushing towards the figure that had just entered the room. Reaching out his arms he caught her as she threw herself upon him.

"It has been too long," James heard her whisper as she buried her face in his shoulders.

After almost two minutes James gently prized her off his shoulder. Holding her face, he looked down into her eyes and smiled the widest smile of his life. Slowly he leaned in and gently kissed her lips. As he began to pull back she reached over his shoulder and placed her hand on the back of his head. Forcefully, she pulled his lips back towards hers. At the same time she moved her own lips up to kiss him with a vigor that startled him.

She placed her other hand on James' chest and began to guide him backwards, never breaking their kiss. Before James knew it, he had fallen back into a seat and she was above him straddling his legs. After another few moments of passionate kissing this time she broke the embrace. Looking down at James she mimicked his smile from before and then moved in to kiss him even more passionately.

Forty five minutes later James sat with Princess Christine Anne Elizabeth Windsor, second in line to the British throne, on his lap. He was slightly embarrassed that they had let their passions get the better of them. They were in a public meeting place after all. But even so he had no regrets, it had been two years since he had last held the love of his life.

"There were times when I lost all hope of seeing you again. Two years in a survey ship out beyond Cambridge felt like an eternity away. How did you manage to pull this off?"

Before answering Christine gave him another hug. "I had begun to despair too. I thought my father would keep you out there until your ship broke apart from rust."

Smiling devilishly she continued, "The head of my security thinks I am meeting a daughter of an American senator who wanted my advice. I told him she was in some personal trouble that was of a delicate nature. I managed to get him to order his subordinates to allow me to arrange a meeting without them knowing expressly who it was with. As long as you were unarmed they were to let you in."

At the last sentence her cheeks had reddened slightly. "I'm afraid they insisted on having a live video stream of the room to make sure I remained safe."

"What?" James asked with incredulity as he looked around the room. "You mean someone has been watching us the whole time?"

This time her cheeks really reddened. "I didn't think we would get so carried away but moment got the better of me!" She said as her devilish grin returned.

"But if someone was watching your father will eventually find out. There is no way you can stop all of your security detail from talking." James warned.

"Don't you see though? Everything has changed." Christine countered. "We don't need to fear my father anymore. Yes, everyone knows your name," she delicately said trying to avoid saying James' father's name. "Yet now they know it for a different reason. Your face is on all the news outlets as the one who discovered the Void. You are already making a new name for yourself. You could take your reward from making the discoveries, reinvigorate the businesses your father ran into the ground and re-establish the Dukedom of Somerville as a major economic force. My father would have to take you seriously then."

Stroking her hair, James ran his hand down to her neck. Hanging there she had a heart shaped locket. James opened it to reveal a small picture of a red rose.

"You still have it?" He asked her.

"Of course my love. No one will ever take it from me."

"Good," he replied with a smile as he leaned in to gently kiss her again. "I'm afraid I have already met your father since my return.

He and the Prime Minister came to my uncle's office to hear my report. It certainly didn't seem like he has changed his mind. In fact, he went out of his way to let me know nothing has changed."

Christine bowed her head to stare at the ground for a moment. As James watched, a small tear left her eye and ran down her cheek to touch her mouth. Wiping her cheek she gritted her teeth and looked back at James.

"My father is a stubborn man but that just means we have to be stubborn too. One way or another he is going to have to realize that what we have isn't going to pass in a month, a year, or even a decade. He can send you to the outer reaches of space again if he wants but I promise you, I'm not going to give up on us."

James couldn't stop himself from kissing her again. He didn't care who was watching, this might be his last chance to see her in person before her father tried to part them again.

When their lips parted, Christine tried a different approach. "Maybe you could retire from the navy. You could invest in the Void; become the champion of our colonial efforts there. That would get you world recognition and praise. If you made a success of one of the colonies you would get a lot of political power as well. That way our marriage would be advantageous to my father. I know what he is thinking. He wants me to marry for politics, not for love." As she spoke Christine clenched her fists, betraying the suppressed anger that had been building up over the years. There had been countless arguments between her father and her about her future, even before she had met James.

"Never worry my love." James soothed her. "We'll figure something out. If I can continue to progress up the chain of command, your father will have to take me seriously."

"I know," she said. "But we have already been waiting for years. How much longer are we going to have to wait? I want to start our life together now, not in ten years."

Silence descended on the room as they both held each other, thinking of the future. After more than ten minutes of just enjoying being so close, Christine spoke up. "Let's talk about something different. Tell me about the last two years. Are you enjoying commanding a spaceship?"

James didn't reply immediately as he reflected on the last two years. His feelings about the RSN were constantly changing, initially, when his father had sent him to the RSN academy, he had looked on the whole experience as a joke. He had grown up as the second son of one of the wealthiest nobles in all of Britain. He had always dreamed of having a bigger role to play in the world than serving as a Lieutenant out in the far reaches of space. Slowly over the four years of training he had come to see that there was a much stronger sense of family in the RSN than he had ever experienced at home. He was actually able to earn the respect of his tutors and, in time, develop real friendships with them and his classmates. Indeed, it was through his tutors that he also began to see the significance of the RSN and the pride that ran through it. In reality, the navy was the only thing standing between a continued British presence in space with all the wealth and freedom that came with it and another space power coming in and taking everything Britain had spent the last four hundred years building.

Then, as he had spent his first two years after graduating aboard HMS *Percy* as an ensign he had his first taste of real responsibility. Growing up, his entire life had been one big party where he was always at the center. In hindsight James knew he had been a spoilt brat. What the academy had not been able to drive out of him, the Captain of HMS *Percy* had finished; he had ruthlessly forced his new ensigns to grow up and live up to the responsibilities they had been entrusted with. For the first time in his life, James had found himself actually feeling like he was doing something worthwhile.

After attaining his promotion to Sub Lieutenant James' responsibilities had continued to grow. It was only then he had seriously begun to consider the possibility of continuing a long-term career in the navy. That had only been cemented when he met Christine. He had fallen in love overnight and James knew that if he were to have a serious chance of marrying her he would need to be seen as a respectable consort to a princess, even if she was only second in line to the throne. His party boy past would not have been acceptable and so throwing himself into the navy gave him his best chance of getting what he wanted.

When the news of his father's misdeeds had broken, the navy had also offered him a refuge. Aboard the battlecruiser HMS *Lion,* where he had reached the lofty rank of Third Lieutenant his family problems hadn't changed anything. His colleagues and subordinates already knew and respected him as an officer. His father's fraud and subsequent suicide had meant he had not been able to set foot anywhere on Earth without being surrounded by journalists. Only in the navy had he found peace and normality when the rest of Britain was calling for answers and even that justice be dished out to the rest of the Somerville family.

Then Christine's father had found out about their relationship. Even if the navy had still respected James, the nobility had done everything they could to distance themselves from his father. James and his older brother Richard had become toxic overnight. No one wanted to be seen with them, for it immediately brought up all the images of corruption and greed the nobility went to great lengths to disassociate from their public images. Christine's father had been no exception, for within days of finding out about their relationship he had pulled enough strings to get James promoted to Commander, given *Drake* and sent off on a two year cruise out far beyond civilization and the public eye. That had soured his view of the navy. Suddenly those who he had respected and admired had become the ones who had allowed themselves to be manipulated and used to punish an up and coming officer, simply because of who his father was. In those first dark months James had begun to think that everything he had believed about the navy had just been a façade. Behind the sense of duty and the camaraderie, it appeared that the Admiralty was just as corrupt and self-serving as the nobility. In those months, he had become disillusioned with everything; even the prospect of a future with Christine had seemed distant.

Even so, as time wore on and James had begun to step into the role of Captain, especially since the discovery of the Void, he had changed his mind again. Being a good Captain, leading his crew members well, fulfilling his duty to the navy and Britain had all been ambitions that had slowly grew on him.

As James began to speak, all this and more came spilling out. Christine listened carefully, glad that James could open up to her so easily despite having been separated for the last two years. She knew this was the man she wanted to marry. As he spoke, he only confirmed it. His concern for his duty, for the men and women under his command, impressed her. Command had matured him. She also respected his desire to repay all the families his father's lies and greed had hurt. As he told her about his plans to get Andrea Clements to begin offering compensation packages to all those who had lost their jobs two years ago when his father's businesses had begun to go under Christine resolved to quietly contact Andrea and offer to help her finance the packages.

"So you see," James concluded, "it is becoming a part of who I am. I don't think I can give it up. We'll find a way to convince your father but I think it needs to include earning his respect and if I can prove myself in the navy he and the rest of the nobility will have to respect me.

"I understand," Christine said once it was clear James had finished. "You've certainly matured in the last two years. It suits you. I guess we'll just have to see how we can speed up your promotion to Captain and then even to Commodore or Rear Admiral. My father will have to respect you then. And you'll no doubt look very handsome in a flag officer's uniform," she said breaking into another devilish smile and giving James a kiss.

"So tell me, what was it really like in the Void?" she asked as she sat back and enjoyed the moment as James excitedly told her all about his adventures.

*

Sub Lieutenant Becket had been summoned from the bridge to the boarding hatch with *Vulcan* by the RSNI security detail. It seemed that *Drake* had some visitors that needed escorting aboard. The Commander was on his way back to *Vulcan* from a meeting while the Second Lieutenant was busy overseeing the installation of the latest sensor tech onto *Drake's* hull. That left the meet and great to her. As she approached the boarding hatch, she realized why someone had been called down. There were twelve men waiting to board *Drake*. Each had a large pack over his shoulder. Behind the men were a number of techs organizing crates that were twice the height of Becket. As she walked through onto *Vulcan* two of the men approached her. It took her a couple of seconds to recognize them as they were both in uniform but when she got close they both smiled at her, obviously pleased to see her again.

"Good afternoon Lieutenant, my name is Mr. Jones I'm with the RSNI and this is Major Samuel Johnston RSNM, formerly retired," Jones said formally, acting as if they had not met before. "My men and I have been assigned to *Drake*, I have orders that I am to personally hand to your Commander."

Becket shook hands with Jones and then Johnston. "Very well Mr. Jones, welcome aboard *Drake*. She is not the biggest ship so you and your men may be a bit cramped but I'm sure we'll find some room."

Becket eyed the crates behind Jones. "We may have to get the pursuer here to ensure we get all your equipment aboard. The Captain is away from the ship at the moment although he has just signaled that he is on his way back."

"Odd," Jones said. "I thought he was not allowed to leave *Drake*. No matter, we'll get settled in and then I can meet him."

An hour later Gupta walked into the briefing room, she was the last to enter. It was as full as she had ever seen it. All the Sub Lieutenants were present, along with the Chief Engineer, Mr. Jones, Major Johnston and the Commander.

As Gupta sat, James stood and addressed the assembly. "By now all of you know we have some visitors with us aboard *Drake*. Well, we have also received our orders. We'll be heading back to the Void."

Murmurs ran through the Sub Lieutenants, there had been a betting pool running over whether *Drake* would get to go back to the Void.

"As I'm sure you can also guess Mr. Jones' presence here has something to do with this. What you're about to hear is rated top secret. As of the beginning of this meeting all outgoing COMS on *Drake* have been disabled. They will remain so until we leave Sol. Mr. Jones, if you would like to take over."

Standing, Jones addressed the crew of *Drake*. "For all intents and purposes my name is Mr. Jones. I have been with RSNI for over twelve years. I oversee special operations, typically insertions. With me is Major Johnston. He is here to help train my men."

Major Johnston stood so everyone in the room could see him. Despite having been retired for fifteen years Gupta thought he looked very comfortable amongst fellow officers again. And he certainly didn't look out of shape. Gupta listened closely as Jones continued.

"RSNI have seen an opportunity to retrieve valuable intel from the Void. Specifically from the Chinese destroyer *Drake* identified in the V2 system. Before he retired Major Johnston designed and tested a scenario involving an EVA boarding of an enemy ship. The Major was testing the idea in case the marines ever had to deal with a hostage situation on a ship. It is our intention to proceed to V2 and attempt to locate the Chinese destroyer. If she is still there we will board her and capture her. If we can take her intact there will be a wealth of information we can make use of."

Again murmurs ran through the Sub Lieutenants. Gupta tended to agree with the surprise. What Jones was proposing was an act of war.

Sensing the mood James stood to speak. "By now you have all had a chance to go over the details of the Damang Incident. There can be no doubt that the fleet that attacked *Resolution* and *Renown* was the one we saw in the Void. If their orders remain unchanged, they will likely attack any British ships they see. For all intents and purposes there is already a state of war between China and Britain. The politicians may well be explaining away the Damang Incident as a misunderstanding. We, however, know better. I have my orders from the Admiralty. We will be going back to the Void but we will not be alone this time. This mission is simply the first step towards securing our new planets and ensuring we have the breathing space to colonize and develop them."

Satisfied that his crew was on the same wavelength, James turned the meeting back to Jones with a nod as he sat down.

"We just have one more thing to discuss at the moment." Jones began. "Over the coming weeks, as we travel to the Void, we will be war gaming the scenario many times with you all. At this stage though we need a volunteer. My men and I will be making the EVA jump yet we have no training in flying a spaceship. We will be fitting in as many lessons as we can between here and the Void but that will not be enough. We need a volunteer to go over to the Chinese ship with us. Someone with command experience yet someone who isn't too important. That is you Sub Lieutenants. There is no need for me to explain how good this will look on your service records. Yet, I also need to add that this will be difficult and dangerous. Currently our simulations give us a sixty two percent chance of success. We hope to improve this as we refine the plan on our way to the Void, however, there will be no guarantees. I have sent you all more information on what will be expected from whoever volunteers. I want you all to read it over and make a decision within the hour. Think hard. You are dismissed."

As the Sub Lieutenants filed out Gupta walked over to James. "Sir, don't you think one of us should select who is to go on this mission. If it is as vital as Jones makes out we need to make sure there is no room for failure."

"I agree, but the risks involved are very high. We can't order anyone to take this mission. That said I'm fully expecting all of the subs to volunteer. Even if we are facing war, the opportunities for promotion will be slim. This is an opportunity no one can pass up. I have already reviewed their files. If Becket volunteers, I'm going to recommend to Jones that she take part in the mission. Her hand-to-hand combat and weapons training scores at the academy were very good. She has also studied Chinese engine design, of all the sub lieutenants she is probably the most familiar with their designs and controls."

A short time later Sub Lieutenant Becket skipped as she left the Commander's private office. She had just met with him and the mysterious Mr. Jones. They had picked her to go on the EVA mission. Already she had been assigned a mountain of reading. She had to familiarize herself with all of the known Chinese command and control terminals. On top of that she had to undergo hours of simulated EVA training, brushing up on her combat skills whilst helping to train Jones's men on how to pilot a spaceship. Thankfully, the Commander had given her half duty shifts until the mission commenced to give her time to prepare. She loved working with *Drake's* chief engineer and her shifts in engineering were the highlight of her week. Yet now she was positively drooling at the prospect of getting her hands on a Chinese designed and built ship.

*

Hours later, as *Drake* disengaged from *Vulcan* and headed out of Earth orbit James' personal COM unit on his command chair went off. He punched in his password and the feed turned into a video message from his uncle.

"You've done it this time boy. I have just had the king biting off my ear. He is furious. If *Drake* wasn't already on her way out of the system I think you would have been relieved of command. Look, I'm going to be honest with you. I see real command potential in you. But if you keep this up there is nothing I can do for you. My protection only goes so far. You're going to have to make a choice, continue pursuing this relationship or your career."

Before James could reply something caught his uncle's attention. He held his hand up and looked away from the screen. Before he turned around James heard a number of strong expletives.

"Someone has leaked the video of you two onto the datanet. I'm going to have to go. Do not, and I mean do not, make any other communications with Earth. Don't stop until you meet up with Rear Admiral Jensen.

As James sat in the command chair officially overseeing *Drake's* departure from the Sol system, his mind was elsewhere. Even as *Drake* accelerated away from Earth she was still updating her data banks with the latest holo news broadcasts. On his personal terminal James was able to watch the news break in London and then spread across the world and the solar system. The Royal Princess of Great Britain had been involved in an affair. Clips from their secret meeting were played and replayed. He was quickly identified as the son of the infamous late Duke of Somerville, then as the Commander who had discovered the Void. He was the princess's secret lover.

James' breath caught in his throat as the BBC interrupted their coverage of the story for some breaking news. The Princess herself had contacted the BBC to make a statement. The feed switched to a picture of the princess standing beside a BBC reporter. The audio soon followed.

"It is with great disgust that I wish to acknowledge that the leaked images of myself and Commander Somerville are real. I have no regrets over my actions. I am happy to confirm that James and I have been pursuing a relationship for the last three and a half years. You all know of James and his father. Well, when my father found out he banned our relationship; he didn't want to be touched with James' disgrace. Many of you will know that true love cannot simply be switched off, even if a King orders it. It is our hope that one day my father will give his blessing so that James and I no longer have to meet in secret. But, let me repeat my disgust. My love life is not a thing of entertainment and James is not some low life. He is a well-respected, successful Commander in the RSN. Our relationship should not be a thing of entertainment."

As *Drake* slowly slid away from Earth James longed to reverse course and return. He wanted to stand beside Christine and declare their love to the world. He wanted to stand up to her father as she had just publically done. Yet he knew he had a duty to his country, to his crew and to Christine. The next few months might determine the future of the Britain's colonial ambitions, his Princess' kingdom. And, if he was honest, he was not sure if Christine's course of action had been the wisest. Her father would never forget this. The leak of the video was bad enough; Christine's public appearance would mean that this news story would go on for weeks.

A gasp from the bridge brought him back to reality. Gupta's mouth was hanging open and she was staring at her Commander. Sighing James tried to put Earth and Christine out of his mind. It would take *Drake* three and a half weeks to reach Britannia and he needed to be one hundred percent focused for the sake of his crew. Yet he couldn't. Christine was his life, his future. Despite everything his uncle had said he opened up a data file and began to compose a statement. In it he spoke of his love for Christine and his commitment to their future even if they didn't win her father's approval. After rereading it several times James was finally happy. He hoped Christine would appreciate his words.

So as to avoid his uncle's wrath he waited until *Drake* was about to jump out of the Sol system, then he beamed the statement to one of the main British news outlets back in London. Now he could focus on the upcoming mission. He would deal with whatever consequences came his way for standing by Christine later.

Chapter 11 – Boarders Away

The Royal Space Marines had won little glory for themselves during humanity's expansion into the stars. With few wars of expansion there was no need for an army that could be landed on a hostile planet and begin offensive operations. However, as we all know, at the end of the First Interstellar Expansion Era this was to change.

-Excerpt from Empire Rising, 3002 AD

28th February 2465, HMS *Drake*, the Void

Becket felt *Drake* shudder as she excited shift space. Quickly, she charged her opponent, ducking under his guard in the hope the slight shift in the inertial compensators would throw him off. She had no such luck. For the hundredth time since *Drake* had left Earth one of Jones' men dodged her attack, kicked her legs out from under her and dumped her onto the floor. Groaning she rolled over and extended her hand to her opponent to get helped back up.

Her bruises had been multiplying since Britannia. Initially the marines had gone easy on her but as they approached the Void they had stepped it up. She felt reasonably confident about having to command the Chinese destroyer, if they captured the bridge intact. If there was some battle damage she thought she could probably make do. However, her training with the marines and Mr. Jones had shown her that her combat skills left a lot to be desired. Back at the lunar academy she had excelled in the hand-to-hand combat training. Yet she could barely land a punch against these men.

Their gun skills also far surpassed her. Her father had enjoyed hunting and had taken her and her brothers on hunting trips to Canada and so she had been no stranger to a gun. Yet the marines were a whole different kettle of fish. Their speed, accuracy and precision were almost inhuman. She knew that the Special Forces' marines were selected from the regular RSM for their excellence. She had heard that they underwent some kind of genetic and biomechanical alterations as well. The marines themselves were very tight lipped about it but seeing what they could do up close startled her. If it came to a gunfight, she would be staying behind them until the bad guys had gone down.

Her training had gone well though she thought. She had picked up some good tips from the marines and the hours and hours she had spent sparring with them were having an effect. Though she had to admit she was still quietly scared about what lay before her. Going EVA was almost every spacer's worst nightmare. Going EVA without a tether back to the ship had been unthinkable. At least until Mr. Jones and Major Johnston and had their say. No doubt if they made it to the Chinese destroyer a firefight would break out. A plasma rifle firefight in the small confines of a ship's corridors was not something to be entered into lightly. Yet Becket knew that if she made it that far, she would be relieved. The thought of going EVA from one ship to another had been giving her nightmares since they had left Earth.

*

Aboard the battlecruiser *Valkyrie,* Rear Admiral Jensen watched her fleet appear out of shift space around her flagship. She had spent the last year patrolling the approaches to Britannia; finally she was doing something proactive. *Valkyrie* was one of the newest RSN battlecruisers. Whereas the other powers had opted for battleships, the RSN had instead brought out an updated battlecruiser class. *Valkyrie* boasted a twenty missile salvo, three more than any Chinese battlecruiser. She was also equipped with two of the new flak guns, giving her a much greater defensive punch than anything but a battleship. With luck, Admiral Somerville would be able to get her two sister ships to the Void before they had to engage the Chinese battleship. If they could, Jensen was sure that the battle would show the wisdom of the British construction program.

She had jumped her fleet to within two light days of the Excalibur system, what had until recently been designated V2. Once she was satisfied the cruisers and destroyers had formed a tight defensive sphere and the frigates and corvettes were covering them in an outer cone she sent the signal to *Drake*.

Minutes later, after charging her jump drive capacitors, the small survey ship disappeared off the plot. Seven other ships quickly followed her. Apart from *Drake,* they were all off to try and find the Chinese shift passage into the Void. For now though, Rear Admiral Jensen and *Valkyrie,* along with the seven other cruisers, five destroyers and twelve frigates and corvettes under her command, had nothing to do but wait while others went into harm's way.

*

It only took *Drake* milliseconds to complete her jump further into the Excalibur system. The shifting of the internal compensators to accommodate the entrance and then immediate exit from shift space left everyone on board feeling slightly nauseous. The plan was for *Drake* to accelerate to 0.1c and then slowly coast into the system. Once the holo-display updated, showing no signs of enemy ships within the system, James gave the go ahead.

When *Drake* reached 0.1c her engines were shut down and a spread of twenty recon drones were shot into the system to search for the Chinese ship. That was double *Drake's* usual compliment but she had been loaded with spares for this mission.

As James watched them head off, he secretly thought they would not find anything. It had been over two months since *Drake* had first encountered the Chinese destroyer. He would be amazed if it was still in the system. On the other hand, if it was there it meant the crew must be getting very weary from their monotonous task. Traveling back and forth along the same track with all the main systems shut down for months could destroy a crew's moral and alertness. If they were there, they would be ripe for the taking.

Two hours passed before something happened. First the bridge erupted into a hive of activity and then the message was sent to the marines. Sub Lieutenant Becket jumped as the holo-display she had been staring at began to flash red. She, along with the other marines had been going over the mission one more time in the main debriefing room. The signal meant the Chinese destroyer had been located. A count down soon appeared on the holo-display. It would take *Drake* another three hours to get behind the Chinese ship and begin a slow deceleration burn. The plan called for *Drake* to close in from behind the Chinese destroyer, flying right down her engine exhaust plume. That would be where her sensors were the weakest. With luck, *Drake* would be able to get within a few light seconds of the destroyer. Then it was over to Mr. Jones and Becket.

The flashing light was the signal for Becket, along with the other marines to leave the debriefing room and head for the cargo bay that had been set up for them. Three hours was still a long time to wait but they all wanted to get into their EVA suits as soon as possible. Her heart was already racing. Up until now she hadn't really thought she would have to go through with what basically boiled down to being fired from a cannon from one ship to another. The mission had always seemed like a distant dream rather than something that could become reality. Now that it was at hand, she had to admit her fear was increasing. No one had tried going EVA from one ship to another untethered, let alone across a distance of two light seconds. If she missed the Chinese destroyer, she would likely float off into space forever. At least she only had oxygen for six hours, so forever wouldn't be too long.

After getting into their suits, there was nothing to do but sit and wait. Jones came around and gave everyone a pep talk but Becket was hardly listening. She was using her suit's miniature holo-display to review the Chinese destroyer's flight characteristics.

Half an hour before it was time to launch everyone was loaded into the five specially built air cannons. The twelve Special Forces marines were tethered into groups of three to be fired towards their target. Becket was to go with Mr. Jones in the fifth tube. As they were about to be tethered another figure in an EVA suit appeared. A small cheer erupted across the COM channel from the other marines followed by Major Johnston's voice.

"I thought you boys could use an extra pair of hands, no sense in spending all this time training you up and then seeing it all go to waste when you mess up."

After they had been tethered together Jones activated the private channel for their small group. "Are you sure you want to do this Major, I know you have a wife back on Earth?"

"It's for her I'm doing this," he replied after a moment's pause. "If the Chinese think they can start something against us I want to finish it quickly, before they take it to Earth or our other colonies."

Becket was embarrassed to be intruding on such a personal conversation between her superiors but she had little choice. She was also slightly ashamed; her thoughts had been all about her own survival and the potential promotion for taking part. She had forgotten that there was a wider world out there beyond herself and *Drake*. No doubt many of the men on the mission with her had families they wanted to get back to. This wasn't just an adventure for them. They were risking their lives for something they believed in, they wouldn't be here otherwise.

Thinking about the wider implications of the outbreak of hostilities distracted Becket as everyone waited for the mission to commence. She was startled out of her thoughts five minutes before launch as the cargo bay doors opened. This was the most dangerous part of the mission for *Drake*. With her cargo bay doors open her radar-absorbing tech would be useless. If the Chinese destroyer sent out even a low powered radar sweep *Drake* would light up like a Christmas tree.

As the countdown reached thirty seconds, Becket found herself crossing her fingers and closing her eyes. Mr. Jones would be controlling the small maneuvering thrusters that would direct their tethered trio once they got closer to the Chinese ship. All she had to do was remain tethered to Jones and Johnston until they got there.

A large hissing noise followed by a very slight sense of acceleration was the only sign that they had been shot from their air cannon. The Chief Engineer had complained for days when he had first been instructed to fit them into the cargo bay. He had been especially vocal about having to tear up most of the nano-carbon floor to fit them into place. Becket tried to replay the argument she had seen between the Chief and Mr. Jones. She was searching for anything to distract her from the weightless sensation of floating through space.

Eventually she worked up the courage to open her eyes. Immediately she was overwhelmed by a sense of vertigo. Everything around her was dark and she couldn't get any sense of which way was up or down. They had been fired feet first out of *Drake* and so she looked back to try and see if she could see the ship. Clearly, she had waited too long to open her eyes for they had moved well beyond where she could see *Drake*, even with the enhanced vision of the EVA suit. Slowly, Becket began to control herself as her training kicked in. It was not unknown for people to go into shock and panic when in an EVA situation. With deep breaths she calmed down and began to look around her more carefully. With no close point of reference, it seemed as if she was just floating stationary in space. She couldn't feel the velocity she knew she had been fired out of the ship with and she couldn't see anything around her zipping past to give the appearance of moving. Still, as Mr. Jones and Major Johnston appeared to be satisfied with how things were going she assumed they were heading towards their target. Looking around, Becket had to admit the stars in this part of space were beautiful. The Void was close to the Galileo Nebula and a faint red twinge could be seen in part of the starscape. As she continued to look around her Mr. Jones brought up a counter on everyone's EVA suit. It was tracking their progress from *Drake* in kilometers and giving an ETA for when they would reach the destroyer.

When the countdown hit zero and they were just one thousand meters away from the Chinese ship Jones fired their deceleration thrusters. They contained just enough force to reduce their approach velocity to a few meters per second. Becket braced herself as her EVA boots hit the deck of the frigate with a loud thud. She was sure that someone would have heard her landing but Jones had assured all of them that nothing, except setting off a large explosion, would alert anyone to their presence. As she realized they had made it relief washed over her. They had actually done it! It was a first in human history. All her fears suddenly turned into a giddy elation at having survived but as the rest of the marines began to move around the hull Becket tried to focus on their mission.

As she looked around the strange hull of the Chinese ship she made a mental note to herself. When she got back to *Drake* she would send a request to the Admiralty to look into placing sensors that could detect EVA suits along the hull of RSN ships. Having been out here herself she knew she would always be paranoid that an intruder would be walking around *Drake's* hull unnoticed.

Major Johnston was the first to spot the thicker armor section that identified where an access panel into the destroyer's hull was. Keying his COM unit he signaled to the rest of the Special Forces squad. Within a minute they had their equipment set up.

The marines had brought a plasma-cutting tool specially adapted to cut through valstronium armor. Normally the valstronium armor would flow around itself, filling any gaps created by the cutting process. This cutter inserted a titanium alloy strut into hole being cut that held back the valstronium. Once the cutting tool was set up it got to work automatically.

Samuel was already beginning to relax. In many ways the hardest part of the mission was over. EVA boarding missions had been dismissed as too chancy to attempt. Yet here they were. Now that they had made it onto the hull of the destroyer, things were starting to feel familiar again. Soon they would be past the hull and into the ship. Then Jones and his fellow marines could do what they did best; close quarters combat. Their intel suggested that the destroyer's crew numbered about two hundred. With luck most of them would be naval crew members and not the Chinese equivalent to the marines. If there were any soldiers aboard things would certainly be getting interesting.

The cutting tool sent a beep to signal that it had competed its task. Looking over Samuel saw a square hole in the valstronium armor. One of the marines, the demolition expert, had already stepped into it and was setting his shaped charges.

The schematics RSNI had provided for a Chinese Luda class

destroyer indicated that the ship's bridge should be exactly three decks below where he was standing. The plan was for the team to blow their way through the outer hull into the first deck. Then they would split up.

The marine setting the charges stood away from the hole and held up five fingers. Everyone braced for the coming explosion. A flash of light was the only sign anything had happened but, as soon as he saw it, Samuel swung into action. Three marines were already through the hole by the time he got there and jumped through.

The first things to greet him were two bodies, both with large holes blown in them from flying metal shrapnel. On his HUD display a red arrow appeared, directing him to the hatch that would lead deeper into the ship and towards the bridge. Before heading further in he turned to check on the other marines. Two groups of three marines were already heading off towards the rear of the ship.

One fire team was tasked with taking out the portside weapons control center; the other was going to secure the engineering section. Everyone else was preparing themselves behind him. When their eyes met Jones nodded, nodding back Samuel turned and headed off, following his HUD directions.

The first two corridors he came to were deserted but as they rounded the third, two Chinese crew members were struggling for breath, the air still rushing out the hole they had made in the ship's hull. Neither attempted to put up any resistance.

At the end of the third corridor, they came to an airlock that had automatically locked in place. Stepping aside Samuel allowed another marine to begin to work on the airlock. As he looked past the marine through the airlock's window he could see four Chinese setting up a blockade. Somehow they had managed to get a heavy laser turret in place to greet them. Samuel didn't even try not to swear. The Chinese response was a lot quicker than their intel suggested. Had they somehow found out about the British Special Opps procedures for boarding another ship? Samuel's first thought was to dismiss the possibility. Everyone knew the British counter intelligence services were very good. The Chinese couldn't have got their hands on the intel. But then he thought about it for a couple of seconds. He had established the protocol almost twenty years ago. What were the chances it was still a closely guarded secret? Probably everyone at the Marine headquarters back on Earth had long since dismissed the idea. It was only Mr. Jones who had resurrected it. Maybe the Chinese had got whiff of the British idea and implemented regulations to counter just such an attack. Whatever the reason for the quick response Johnston wasn't going to take any chances.

"Change of plan marine," he said over the COM channel, "blow the air lock, I want the next section sucking vacuum as well."

The initial plan had been to dump their EVA suits as soon as they came to an airlock. However, the marines had not been able to wear their combat armor under the suits. If they got into a heavy firefight they would be at a disadvantage. Speed was their best weapon.

Everyone shielded themselves as the airlock blew. Samuel rushed through the opening, plasma gun blazing. He was counting on the sudden depressurization to throw off the Chinese crewmen's aim. Luck was with him as the first two laser bolts blasted past him. Over the COM channel he heard a grunt as one of the marines caught a laser bolt full in the chest. It was too late however, by now three of his group were through and the combined fire from all their plasma rifles overwhelmed the blockade and the laser turret exploded as it took a plasma bolt to its energy cell. The Chinese crew had been stuck between trying to defend themselves and pull on their oxygen masks. In the cold hard expanse of space a human only had seconds before they would lose consciousness due to the drop in pressure. The naval uniforms every spacer wore were designed to give the crew of a ship a few extra vital seconds and limited protection from the cold. They weren't, however, designed to function in a combat situation.

Samuel rushed past the blockade and bundled into another group of Chinese in breathing masks. The cold of the vacuum would be making life difficult for them but their masks would allow them to resist for a minute or so. As they raised their guns to engage him, his finger was already depressing the trigger of his rifle. Plasma bolts vaporized all three.

Finally, he reached the access hatch that would allow him to descend to the next floor. His HUD was telling him that the hatch to the bridge was only five meters beyond the access hatch at his feet.

Without needing to wait for confirmation he opened the hatch and a marine threw in three stun grenades. As their suits registered the flash, Samuel and the marine jumped through the hatch onto the deck below them. Six Chinese crewmen were writhing on the floor. Samuel left the other marine to deal with them as he approached the hatch to the bridge. As expected it was sealed shut. Through the window he could see the bridge crew frantically preparing themselves. Checking his timer he saw that they had only been in the Chinese ship for three minutes. It was a pity they couldn't blast their way into the bridge; they could already be storming it. Instead they had to wait while Jones connected a RSNI datapad to the door controls. Jones had assured them that this piece of RSNI tech would be able to override the door's controls and open them in less than a minute. The RSNI had obtained the Chinese air lock and access hatch software and worked out a hack that would let them control it. Largely thanks to the Chinese never expecting to have to defend themselves from an internal hack, it would quickly have the door open.

As the datapad got to work Samuel took stock of their position. Above them the final marine was guarding the hatch they had used to gain access to this floor. The marines who had jumped through the hatch along with Sub Lieutenant Becket, were guarding the other end of the corridor while he and Jones waited for the door to open.

Patiently, Samuel forced himself to count his breaths as he waited. The seconds ticked by slowly. Finally, Jones held up his hand to signal that the hack was almost complete.

Reaching behind his back Samuel pulled out his electric stun gun. It fired a highly charged electrical bolt capable of immediately knocking out anyone it hit. It wasn't very accurate as the electric charge jumped through the air somewhat randomly, however, the bridge's command consoles would be protected against electrical surges, meaning that he didn't have to worry too much about accuracy. The gun would allow him to take out the bridge crew without harming the functionality of the ship. Samuel had designed the guns himself over twenty years ago and he was pleased that he would finally get to try one out for real.

"Becket get up here and switch to your stun gun." Samuel called out, looking back as he spoke. He was slightly embarrassed for the Lieutenant as she jumped when he spoke her name. So far their operation had been carried out in almost complete silence.

As the bridge door finally slid open, Samuel and Jones each threw two stun grenades in. They both rushed in after them, closely followed by Becket. All three spread their bolts of electricity around the bridge, scoring hits on almost all of the crew.

One man, dressed in what Samuel assumed to be a Captain's uniform jumped at Jones from out of nowhere. He was wielding a plasma knife and he drove it into Jones' leg. The RSNI officer grunted and fell to one knee. Before the Captain could pull it out and thrust it home again, Becket was at Jones' side and had driven her fist into the Chinese Captain's face. His body crumpled as her powerful punch, strengthened by the EVA suit's enhanced force, disintegrated his skull.

Before his body had even come to rest, Becket was already shoving him out of the way of the Captain's command console. With a practiced flick of her wrist she disconnected the gloves of her EVA suit. Somewhere behind them another airlock had closed so the bridge was still fully pressurized despite their advance. Immediately, her hands began to fly over the inputs as she attempted to assert control over the ship.

Jones had managed to get himself into a seat and was looking at the hole in his EVA suit that led to his leg. Grimacing at the pain he saw on Jones' face Samuel contacted the other fire squads. "This is Major Johnston, we have secured the bridge. Request status update over."

Sergeant Gera, who was commanding the fire team sent after the engine room answered first. "This is fire team three, the engine room is secure also. We are dealing with a heavy counter attack but the Chinese don't seem to have any combat armor on-board so we are holding them off."

Corporal Almaty's voice then came over the COM. Samuel grimaced again; Sergeant Harte was meant to be leading the second fire team. "We are still pushing towards the port weapons control section. Sergeant Harte is down. I'm not sure we will be able to take it intact, we're going to have to go with plan Zeta and set charges to blow the whole section."

Samuel thought about it for a second. Ideally they wanted to capture the Chinese ship intact but the ship had a separate control section for each of its main missile batteries. If one was destroyed the other would still be available for the tech guys to go over. On the other hand, the charges would send metal shrapnel shooting through the ship, possibly damaging nearby sections. Quickly he decided that losing two men on this mission was already enough.

"Permission granted, continue with plan Zeta if you can't secure the weapons control section, over."

Samuel looked up just in time to see Becket jump with excitement. "I did it, I'm into their command and control network, the ship is basically ours. I'm beginning to lock out local control of all the ship's main systems now."

Most of the ship's minor functions were only controlled from the bridge. Navigation and propulsion could also be controlled from engineering and each battery of missiles from their local command sections. With engineering captured, the remaining Chinese crewmen couldn't maneuver the ship. Once the port weapons control section was destroyed they also wouldn't be able to defend themselves from further boarders, for *Drake* was coming up along the destroyer's port side, ready to dock with her prey.

"Becket, I want you to close and lock all the access hatches. We need to keep the remaining crew from being able to meet up and organize a more serious counter attack. Then prepare to shut down all communications throughout the ship; we'll rely on our COMS units for now. Before you shut them down, I want you to open a ship wide channel."

It took Becket another thirty seconds to lock down all the access hatches. Once she had the channel open she nodded to Major Johnston and then began a full systems check of the ship.

On Becket's cue Samuel began speaking into the command chair's

COM. "Attention all Chinese crew members. My name is Major Johnston of the Royal Space Navy Marines. We have boarded your ship and taken control of your bridge and engineering."

Samuel paused and switched back to his personal COMS unit. "Corporal Almaty how long until your explosives go off."

"Thirty seconds sir," came the reply.

Switching back to the ship wide channel he continued. "In thirty seconds we will be blowing the port weapons control center. I suggest you evacuate it immediately." Johnston then paused and counted down the seconds. Right on time the entire ship rocked as Corporal Almaty's explosives went off. Satisfied that they now had the ship suitably under their control Samuel reached behind his back and switched on his locater beacon. It sent out strong radio pulses, which would alert *Drake* that the mission had been a success. With luck, *Drake* would be able to pull along the port side of the Chinese destroyer and extend a docking arm within thirty minutes. Then his men could be reinforced.

Again he switched to the ship wide COM channel. "Chinese crewmen, we have now secured your port weapons batteries. Our ship, HMS *Drake* will be closing to dock with this vessel and transfer the rest of our marines and a prize crew aboard. This is the first and only chance I will be giving you to surrender. Your ship was illegally within a system awarded to the Great Britain by the UN Interplanetary Committee. By lying in stealth, your intentions were clearly not friendly. Surrender now or face being treated as common pirates."

As he finished his call for surrender, Becket motioned for him to look at the holo-display. "Major, I have finished the systems check. As you can see the ship is almost fully functional. The upper two decks, ten and eleven, have almost entirely been vented into space.

However, no major damage has been caused. The explosion from the port battery control center has caused secondary damage to the sensor relays but the computer is working to bypass the damage now. I have full control of the ship from here. I'm going to begin a deceleration burn on the engines to allow *Drake* to come alongside quicker."

"Impressive Lieutenant, you have done well on this mission." Johnston commended. Now all his men had to do was hold tight for the next thirty minutes or so and hope the Chinese didn't try anything.

Chapter 12 – All Haste

The distances involved in interstellar war means that whoever is on the offensive almost always has the advantage. It simply takes too long for help to arrive after an attack has begun.

-Excerpt from Empire Rising, 3002 AD

28th February 2465, HMS *Drake*, the Excalibur system

Aboard *Drake*, James was beginning to get very worried. The mission timing was meant to be very precise. The marines and Sub Lieutenant Becket should have landed on the destroyer almost ten minutes ago. By now they ought to have signaled if they had managed to capture the ship.

Just then a small fireball erupted from within the hull of the destroyer. James had been watching the visual and so had seen it almost instantaneously. Fisher saw it on her console too.

"Sir, infra-red is picking up a small explosion from the destroyer. I estimate it to be coming from the port side weapons control center."

James had already surmised that from the visuals and so only nodded. Instead he addressed the bridge as a whole. "Blowing the control center was a fall back plan if they couldn't capture it. They must have the bridge or they would have blown the whole ship. Navigation, take us alongside them, keep us under their portside."

Seconds later Major Johnston's radio beacon sprang to life on the sensors but three more minutes passed before a communication finally reached *Drake* on the operations channel. "*Drake*, this is

Major Johnston, do you copy, over?"

"Major, this is Commander Somerville. What is your situation?"

"Ah, Commander, my long range COMS must have taken some damage, I am speaking to you through the ships communications array, we had to reactivate it. We have secured the bridge and engineering, the port missile batteries have been disabled. Sergeant Harte and Corporal Smith are both dead. Mr. Jones has sustained a nasty injury to his leg but he should be ok. We have begun a slow deceleration burn to allow *Drake* to come alongside sooner. Lieutenant Becket has the ship firmly under control."

Before replying James looked over to Thirlwall who was manning navigation. "How long until we come alongside them."

"Fifteen more minutes and we will have matched velocities sir." She replied.

"Ok Major, we'll be with you in fifteen minutes, you and your men just need to hold on until we get there," James said as he opened the communications channel again.

An hour later James was getting another situation update, this time from Lieutenant Gupta. "Commander, all the Chinese crew have surrendered. As far as we can tell there were a total of one hundred and ninety on board. Twenty-three were killed in the fighting so we have one hundred and sixty seven prisoners. Major Johnston is organizing the Marines from *Drake*. Some are guarding the prisoners in one of the cargo holds; the others are carrying out a sweep of the rest of the ship. I have my prize crew manning the Bridge and Engineering. We have locked everything else down for the moment. Oh, and by the way the ship's name is Tian'e."

"Very good Lieutenant, you and Becket have done a fine job. It's a pity neither of you can keep her as a prize, there is a RSNI crew with the Admiral that will be taking her home. I'm going to disengage the docking arm, we'll be back as soon as possible, try to stay out of trouble."

"Yes sir," Gupta replied. She watched on the Chinese destroyer's bridge holo display as *Drake* undocked from the destroyer and began to turn towards the mass shadow. It would take her three hours to reach the mass shadow of the system and then Rear Admiral Jensen's fleet another three hours to return to the destroyer. Six hours she had, six hours as the senior commander aboard a warship. It was what she had dreamed of ever since she had been a little girl. None of her family had been spacefarers. Her parent's trip from New Delhi to Britain had been their only space journey. Yet, ever since she had seen her first naval officer in uniform on the streets of London, she had wanted to join up. Sure she only had the command for the next few hours but it was hopefully a taste of things to come.

After giving herself a couple of minutes to savor the moment, she turned her mind back to her duties. There was a lot to get done. The ship had to be made ready for the RSNI types to come and take over. The damage done to the destroyer in the firefights had to be repaired and the prisoners had to be secured for the long voyage back to Earth. Every other ship that had come in Jensen's fleet was in the Void to stay. The destroyer would be the only ship leaving and so the prisoners would have to stay aboard her. That posed a risk. The crew would know their ship much better than Gupta and her crew. They would have to be secured properly to make sure they could not find a way to escape. Picking up her COM unit she contacted Major Johnston and arranged to meet him in an hour to go over his plan to detain the prisoners.

*

Rear Admiral Jensen had been in her ready room taking a nap. *Drake* had left her fleet hours ago and so she had taken the opportunity to go over her plans once more before catching some sleep. When her COM unit went off she was awake and alert instantly. An ability she was always thankful for being born with.

"What is it?" she asked.

"Admiral, *Drake* has returned, the mission was a success," Captain Chambers said over the channel.

"Ok, signal the fleet, break formation and prepare to jump into the system. Inform the RSNI tech team that they can ready themselves to take over control of the destroyer. Don't wait for me, take us in immediately."

Jensen had commanded the Britannia response fleet for over a year. In that time she and Captain Chambers had built up a very good working relationship. She had already recommended the Captain for a promotion to flag rank. However, with only a handful of fleets and task forces in the RSN there weren't enough commands to go around.

By the time she dressed and made it onto the bridge, the fleet had already formed into their jump formation. The communications officer had just finished informing Captain Chambers that the last ship had reported their shift drive fully charged. Before giving the command, Chambers looked over at Jensen. She simply nodded.

"Give the order to the fleet, we jump in thirty seconds," Chambers said.

Only milliseconds after making the jump to shift space, the fleet re-emerged on the edge of the Excalibur system. After sitting stationary for five minutes and closely watching the space around them, Jensen was satisfied that *Drake* hadn't missed anything.

"Signal Commodore Williams, tell him he can take his task force to Camelot and proceed with his mission. Tell him to keep the bulk of his force together, if they encounter anything I want them to be able to give a good account of themselves."

Jensen watched as a heavy cruiser, light cruiser, two destroyers and two frigates broke off from her main fleet and began to re-orientate themselves for the jump to Camelot. The system *Drake* had initially designated V48 also fell within British space and although it was less strategically important, the Admiralty wanted a British presence there as well. Jensen was concerned about splitting her forces, especially with a Chinese battleship out there. However, orders were orders.

"Ok, take us into the system. Inform *Norfolk* that she is to ready her passengers to disembark onto the Chinese destroyer. Once *Drake* has charged her drives and jumps back in, order her to make for the captured destroyer and begin to take her crew off. They won't be needed by then. Order the destroyers, scout frigates and remaining survey ships to begin operation Nimitz."

Nimitz called for the smaller ships that didn't specialize in point defense to begin a coordinated sweep of the system with their primary radar projectors. Jensen wanted to make sure there wasn't another Chinese ship lying in stealth somewhere.

"And inform *Respite* that she can begin her mission too."

Respite was the final survey ship in the fleet. She was tasked with jumping to the V17 system and delivering a message to the Chinese Admiral there. The message was simply the recording of the UN Interplanetary Committee meeting that had awarded the Excalibur and Camelot systems to the British. Alongside that there was a warning that if any Chinese ships entered British space it would be considered an act of war and they would be fired upon.

*

3rd March 2465, HMS *Drake*, the Excalibur system

Drake had spent the last three days scouring the Excalibur system along with the other light ships of Admiral Jensen's fleet, when her sensors finally picked something up.

Fisher alerted Lieutenant Gupta as soon as she detected it. "Lieutenant, a ship is dropping out of shift space approximately half a light hour away. It is right on the edge of the system's mass shadow."

"Alert the Commander and switch off the radar. Navigation, shut down our drives and put us into stealth mode. Once we are running silently, make a course correction towards their likely route into the system."

The ship that had just jumped into the system would almost immediately pick up the heat and radar radiation *Drake* had been pumping out into space. However, *Drake* hadn't been accelerating and so they wouldn't be able to track her using their gravimetric sensors. It would take the ship half an hour to realize that *Drake* had gone into stealth mode and by then *Drake* would be able to significantly close the range to whoever had arrived into the system.

Already the Chinese had sent two light ships into the Excalibur system. The first had broadcast a message claiming Excalibur for the People's Republic of China and threatening the destruction of the British ships if they did not leave. The second had sought to dive into the system and get a firm sensor reading on the British fleet.

Admiral Jensen had been keeping the main body of her fleet close to Excalibur and had been letting her ships go into stealth at random intervals. She was trying to keep her Chinese counterpart from getting a fix on her numbers.

A destroyer had chased the second ship off and had almost managed to score a hit. The Chinese ship had just succeeded in getting back to the shift space limit before the destroyers missiles caught up to it.

"Status report?" James asked as he walked onto the bridge and over to the command chair.

"A ship has just jumped out of shift space half a light hour away. We've entered stealth mode and are waiting to see what they do sir." Gupta replied.

With a glance James acknowledged Gupta's report and then turned his attention to the main holo display. After sitting stationary for a couple of minutes the ship that had just jumped in lit off its drives and headed into the system. The sensors weren't able to identify the ship based on its acceleration profile but given that it wasn't trying to hide, it was likely to be a friendly.

Twenty-five minutes later Sub Lieutenant Graham broke the anticipation that had been building. "Sir, I'm picking up a message from the incoming ship. She is the *York*, one of the survey ships Admiral Jensen sent out to survey the Void before we went after the Chinese destroyer. She is broadcasting her IFF signal and says she has an important message for the Admiral."

"Sensors, what do you make of her?" James asked.

"I can't say for sure sir, not at this range." O'Rourke began. "However, their acceleration rate is equivalent to *York's* maximum military acceleration and her heat seepage seems consistent with a Cook class survey ship."

"Ok, take us out of stealth, broadcast our IFF signal as well and return us to our survey route."

Three hours later *Drake* received a signal from *Valkyrie*. James had the message put up on the main holo-display for all the bridge to see.

"Commander," Admiral Jensen's image began. "I have some new orders for you. *York* identified a shift passage leading away from the Void towards Chinese space. I'm detaching the rest of my survey ships to explore it. I'm putting Commander Jackson of *York* in charge of the search. She will remain at the entrance to the shift passage and direct the search. I need regular updates so I don't want any ships running off on their own. You should be receiving the coordinates now, good luck Commander."

*

12th of March 2465 AD, HMS *Drake*, shift passage adjacent to the Void

James was beginning to remember why he despised the survey fleet so much. The last months had been full of all the excitement he had been dreaming about for the previous two years. Yet for the last week *Drake* had been transported back in time. Once again she was carrying out the monotonous task of micro jumping, surveying the dark matter, micro jumping again and surveying again. The main shift passage had reached a dead end after only three light years. However, so far *York* and her fellow survey ships had identified thirty minor passages leading away from the Void. Only five had been fully mapped out so far and any of the rest could lead to

Chinese space. *Drake* was currently sitting stationary, mapping out the surrounding space after a micro jump.

"Sir, I have finished the scan of the dark matter," Fisher reported. "There is a twist in the passage ahead, we're going to have to make a smaller than usual jump ahead to determine which direction it turns before we can head up it."

"Very well, send the navigation data to Hanson, we'll make the jump when you are both satisfied." James replied.

Suddenly the main holo-display automatically switched to show the gravimetric plot and a siren sounded twice to alert everyone on the bridge. At once everyone but Fisher shifted their focus to see what it was displaying. A large number of red dots were appearing just under a light hour away from *Drake's* current position.

"Gupta, put us into stealth mode immediately."

Thankfully, *Drake* wasn't accelerating anywhere so these newcomers couldn't detect them. *Drake* had only been at her current position for ten minutes so no infrared radiation should have reached this new fleet's position yet. With luck, they would just be rounding the twist in the minor shift passage and jumping as soon as their shift drives had charged. They would be gone before any sign of *Drake* reached them.

"Fisher, I want you to compare their jump signatures with those of the Chinese fleet that we saw jump into V17. See if you can estimate type and class for each ship and get me a final count on their numbers." James ordered.

Exactly thirty-four minutes after exiting shift space, the Chinese fleet jumped again. This time all of *Drake's* sensors were focused on them. After the last ship disappeared, Fisher put the computer's estimates on the main holo-display. "Based on the gravimetric anomalies created from their exit and entrance into shift space, the computer estimates that the fleet consists of one battleship, one heavy cruiser, four other cruisers and five other smaller ships." Fisher reported.

James stood up from his seat in shock. "Are you sure?" he demanded.

"Positive sir," Fisher replied. "We got a good look at that battleship at V17."

"Damn," James shouted. "They are only supposed to have one battleship." He reached over to bring up the intelligence on the Chinese construction program but Gupta was already ahead of him.

"The lasts intelligence report say the next Chinese battleship won't be completed for at least ten months." She commented sourly. "And that report is only two months old. There is no way they could have rushed her out of space dock that quickly."

"I agree," James said nodding. "They must have constructed a second one in secret. It's too similar to their first battleship. Intelligence says the new battleships they have under construction have had a few major alterations to their design. This one looks identical to the one at V17."

Everyone on the bridge seemed to be transfixed with the rundown of the Chinese fleet. At best, James knew that his uncle had been expecting it to take weeks for the Chinese to organize themselves before sending more ships. Yet for these ships to be here now meant the Politburo must have sent immediate orders for reinforcements to head towards the Void. The presence of the battleship showed just how badly they wanted to kick the British out.

"Ok everyone, we're just going to have to deal with the situation we've been dealt. Admiral Jensen needs to know just how badly outnumbered she is. Combined, the two Chinese fleets out mass Jensen's fleet at Excalibur by almost two to one. Navigation, plot us a least time course back to Excalibur, we have no time to waste. If I had to guess I'd say those ships are going to join up with their comrades and make straight for Excalibur. They'll be hoping to knock us out of the Void before we have had a real chance to establish ourselves here."

*

12th of March 2465 AD. HMS *Valkyrie*, the Excalibur system.

Admiral Jensen was sitting in *Valkyrie's* flag command chair. British warships typically had a main bridge and an auxiliary one. When a ship was used as a flagship the Captain was set up in the main bridge while the Admiral based on the ship took their station on the auxiliary bridge. That way the Admiral could direct the movements of the fleet without getting distracted by the running of their flagship.

Jensen still felt it was unnatural. Unless the ship was at battle stations, only a minimal crew manned the auxiliary bridge. She liked to pass her time sitting in her command chair but she felt naked without the bridge crew surrounding her as she had become accustomed to during the twelve years she had been a Captain. Even so, it was clear from those who were on the bridge with her that there was an air of excitement moving across the fleet. Everyone was eagerly looking forward to the next few hours. It had been over two days since the last Chinese scout ship had tried to enter the system and spy on her fleet. After the last attempt Jensen had decided to mix things up a little. Her light ships had now completed their full scan of the inner system. Up until that point she had been keeping her ships within the shift limit. The Chinese had, therefore, been jumping in only half a light hour from the limit before powering their drives and boosting into the system.

Since the last Chinese ship, Jensen had pushed all her light ships but the point defense ships beyond the shift limit. She had also worked out a signaling system that used the gravimetric acceleration profiles of her ships. That way, when one ship picked up an incoming Chinese ship it could go to full burn on its engines, immediately alerting the rest of her fleet about the newcomer.

For her benefit, the sensor officer on watch addressed *Valkyrie's* First Lieutenant louder than necessary. "Lieutenant, *Arrow* has just gone to full burn. Her course and speed indicate that she has picked up a vessel exiting shift space."

The main holo-display switched to show *Arrow's* position at the edge of the system closest to the Chinese end of the Void. A line extended from Arrow towards the shift limit, giving an estimate of where the ship she had picked up was. Moments later another blip appeared where the line intersected the shift limit.

"Sir, we have the new contact, they are going to full burn too."

Jensen sat up in excitement. No ships were expected back from spying on the Chinese fleet for another day and *York's* next progress report on the survey of the shift passage wasn't due for another three days. Whether a friendly or another Chinese spy something was finally happening.

Aboard *Drake,* James already had his ship accelerating at maximum toward Excalibur. As soon as *Drake* had come out of shift space and he had confirmed that the Chinese fleet wasn't in the system yet, he had sent a general message to all the ships in the system. The Chinese were coming.

Chapter 13 – First Blood

The first tactic taught at any naval academy when it comes to fleet engagements has always been this: ambush your enemy and destroy him before he has a chance to fire back. Yet, in reality, this almost never happens in space warfare. The distances are simply too great and ships are simply too hard to hide. Every now and again though it has been known to happen and these instances are always closely studied at every naval academy in an effort to try and repeat them.

-Excerpt from Empire Rising, 3002 AD

12th March 2465 AD, 8pm. HMS *Arrow*, the Excalibur system.

Twenty minutes after *Drake* had dropped out of shift space, her IFF signal reached *Arrow*. Along with her IFF, *Arrow* also received the data stream James had broadcast to the entire system. It gave a breakdown of the new Chinese fleet and James' belief that it was on its way to Excalibur. Commander Farquhar tended to agree with Somerville and so he ordered his navigation officer to alter *Arrow's* acceleration.

Aboard *Valkyrie, Arrow's* course change was immediately spotted, "Captain," her sensor officer called to Chambers who had just taken over the watch from *Valkyrie's* First Lieutenant. "*Arrow* has cut her acceleration. Wait, she is going to ninety percent now. That's the signal she has identified the newcomer as a friendly."

Just as everyone began to relax the officer called out, "She has cut her acceleration again." A few moments slowly passed as the officer hunched over her control terminal watching the sensor feed. "Sir," she shouted with concern this time. "Her new acceleration pattern is the signal for enemy fleet approaching."

"Acknowledged Lieutenant," Chambers said much more calmly than he felt, "forward your readings to the auxiliary bridge. Inform the Admiral we have a Chinese fleet on its way here. Then warn the crew they'll be called to battle stations soon."

On the auxiliary bridge Jensen had received the same message from her own sensor officer, even before the alert from the main bridge came to her command chair. She waited with apprehension. Her smaller ships were spread out around the system, trying to ambush a single Chinese scout. If the Chinese had decided to push their entire fleet into the system she would be caught without a good proportion of her screening elements.

After another thirty seconds she asked the question she already hoped would have been answered, "Has *Arrow* changed her acceleration pattern to give us a direction for this fleet?"

It was the Third Lieutenant who answered, he was with the navigation officer on the auxiliary bridge, looking over her shoulder at her console, "No Admiral, they are just sending us the same message, enemy fleet approaching."

"So be it. Order all our light ships to return to Excalibur. Get me *Broadsword* on a COM channel."

Moments later Captain Wolfe appeared in front of Jensen. "Captain, I think we have an enemy fleet approaching Excalibur; one that hasn't arrived yet. The friendly ship *Arrow* identified can only have come from the shift passage to Chinese space or V17. If there is a fleet coming, wherever they are coming from they won't be far behind our friendly. Here's what I have in mind."

Five minutes after Jensen went over her plan with Captain Wolfe and then Captain Chambers, *Valkyrie* and the other ships that had been lying in stealth around Excalibur boosted out of orbit under minimal thrust. Meanwhile every other ship in the outer system, bar one, went to stealth and turned to head for Excalibur and *Broadsword*. *Pelican* jumped out to warn Commodore Williams at Camelot. On Excalibur's surface, the men who had landed there began the tasks they had been assigned.

It took seven hours for *Drake's* message to reach *Valkyrie* but when it did Jensen breathed a silent sigh of relief. She had taken a big gamble by splitting her forces. Even more of a one given how many more Chinese ships were bearing down on Excalibur than she had thought. Everyone on the bridge was shocked by the news that they could be facing two battleships. No one expected *Valkyrie* to stand up to one, never mind two.

However, her smart thinking had given them chance to get in the first decisive punch, hopefully it would be enough. She had already altered course on the assumption that the delay meant that the Chinese would be coming from V17. Now all she had to do was wait and hope the Chinese Admiral hadn't adjusted to fighting in the Void yet. If the Chinese approached from a completely unpredictable direction, she would be caught badly out of position.

Aboard *Drake*, James, along with everyone else was very nervous. They were the only ones who had seen firsthand both Chinese fleets. The thought that they had combined their strength and were on their way was frightening indeed. As more time passed, this possibility was becoming more and more of a certainty. James had half expected the Chinese fleet to beat them to Camelot. That they had not meant they must have gone to join up with the first Chinese fleet at V17. The next most logical course of action would be to head straight for Excalibur and strike before the British even knew they had overwhelming numerical superiority.

"Commander, where do you think Admiral Jensen is?" asked Lieutenant Becket, who was manning the tactical station.

James took a few moments to consider his response. "I'm not sure, but if I was a betting man I would put money on her laying an ambush somewhere. Either she had some ships in the outer edges of the system already in stealth or she took whatever was in stealth around Excalibur out of orbit when she got our message. One way or another she's going to try and hammer the Chinese if they push into the system."

"Then why are the rest of the outer pickets coming back in towards Excalibur under stealth," Becket followed up.

"Simple, if the Chinese jumped in and saw that every ship in the outer system was already firing off their drives at full burn they would know they had been made. The outer picket ships are coming under stealth so that by the time the Chinese do arrive they'll still be close enough to meet up with Captain Wolfe and *Broadsword* and yet not give away Jensen's plan. I understand your concern though. If Jensen is caught out of position, the ships still in orbit are going to be left well and truly isolated."

For his part, James had ignored Jensen's order to head for Excalibur. Having come out right on the edge of the system's mass shadow it would take him hours to reach Excalibur under stealth. If a battle were going to be fought he would only end up out of position and no help to anyone. Instead *Drake* was angling to get ahead of any fleet that would jump in from the direction of V17. Due to *Drake's* angle of entrance into the system, heading straight for Excalibur would have put him right in the firing line of the Chinese if they came straight from V17. *Drake* would either have had to remain in stealth and watch the battle or open fire and go down fighting.

As it was, James had put *Drake* in a position to choose her time of attack. Hopefully, the Chinese fleet would not get close enough to detect them and force their hand.

*

13th March 2465 AD, 4am, *Hai Hu*, approaching Excalibur system

An air of invincibility emanated from High Admiral Zheng as he sat in his command chair on the flag bridge of the People's Spaceship *Hai Hu*. His rage had been growing and growing over the last two weeks. The appearance of the British forces had caught him by complete surprise. The disappearance of the destroyer *Tian'e* had turned his surprise to anger and the constant British scout ships showing up at V17 had sent him over the edge. It had only been his own scout ships inability to get a good look at the British fleet that had prevented him attacking the system the British were now calling Excalibur. Then his reinforcements had arrived along with the latest intelligence reports. Minister Chang and his intelligence service estimated that the British couldn't have more than a handful of cruisers in the Void by now. Zheng had leapt at the opportunity. His reinforcements significantly tipped the balance of force in his favor and now he was on his way to crush the British at Excalibur and Camelot. He would send the British back to Cambridge with their tails firmly between their legs.

One of his flag officers broke into his thoughts. "Admiral, we will be exiting shift space in five minutes."

Zheng grinned; it was time to see what his battleships could do. As

Hai Hu came out of shift space he watched the sensors update the various displays. Faint traces could be detected of ships in orbit around the habitable planet but nothing else. Satisfied his own fleet was alert and in formation he ordered them to move forward.

As his fleet's acceleration gave their presence away, he watched the British react. First, the ships around Excalibur began to break out of orbit and form a cohesive unit. Then it seemed like every picket ship they had in the system came alive as they too went active and made to rendezvous with the larger ships.

Zheng waited for the moment the British would turn tail and run. His sensors had managed to identify no more than five cruisers in orbit around the planet. They were outnumbered more than three to one. This wasn't the *Damang* system, here they had nothing to protect. Yet as he watched, the cruisers finished forming up, turned towards his fleet and made their intentions clear. They were going to fight. It didn't make sense, Zheng thought, unless there was a reason he hadn't anticipated.

"I want a full sensor sweep of that planet. I want to know if there is anything there." Zheng called out. He had to wait impatiently for almost a minute as the sensors were redirected from the approaching fleet.

"Admiral, there appears to be at least a couple of energy sources on the planet. We can't make out anything more than that at the minute but their strength indicates that the British have at least a couple of colonies or military bases up and running."

Impossible, Zheng dismissed with a thought. They hadn't had the time. Yet how did they manage to get ships to the Void so quickly? Suppose they had known about it for longer than they had let on to the UN. Then they would have had ample time to get together the men and materials needed to begin to fortify Excalibur. Only they mustn't have had the time they needed to complete their orbital bombardment shelters. There was no other reason; the fleet approaching him must be seeking to protect a planetary base. Standard Chinese and British protocol was to build their colonies with bombardment shelters that would protect their military and colonists from everything short of a series of thermonuclear missiles.

The British fleet obviously hoped to delay him enough for the bases to be evacuated. Zheng knew he had a great opportunity before him. The British population was weak. If he could present them with a stunning defeat, one where their own colonists had been bombarded from space, they would lose their heart for war. They may even lose the heart for sending their children off to new colonies with dreams of wealth and success. The Void would fall to the Chinese by default! Sure, it meant he would have to fire on civilians, but wasn't that why he had been chosen for this mission?

"Signal all my Captains, inform them that I think the British are going to fight. Tell them to be prepared and to double-check their missiles. I want our first salvo to be devastating." Zheng ordered.

*

As the Chinese fleet charged into the system, Jensen watched them until they were only light seconds away. During that time she had been constantly weighing up the decision before her. She had almost pulled off the perfect ambush, almost. The Chinese were charging right for the planet as she had expected. However, their trajectory into the system was slightly off her prediction. Slowly, she had been working her fleet towards them but the differing speeds made things difficult. The Chinese were still accelerating and had almost reached their top speed. *Valkyrie* and her consorts had been limited to five percent of their maximum thrust to ensure they weren't detected. Getting her slow moving fleet to cross paths with the stampeding Chinese without being detected had been difficult.

As things stood, she had lined up her ships to get close enough for one passing shot at the Chinese with their plasma cannons, maybe two. She could alter course again. However, now that both fleets were so close, they might detect her ships maneuvering thrusters, getting closer would also give the Chinese the chance to react and fire back with their own plasma cannons. Jensen wasn't sure her fleet would survive such a volley.

Reviewing her options one more time she made up her mind and sat perfectly still, refraining from ordering anymore course corrections. Two volleys would have to do. It would leave Wolfe and *Broadsword* in a tight position but hopefully she could do enough damage to help them out.

Admiral Zheng was already composing his report for the Politburo. His fleet was about to put out the greatest missile salvo since the final battle of the New France Campaign. With almost two hundred missiles at his disposal he had aimed them all at the five cruisers approaching him, ignoring the smaller ships. With over thirty missiles targeted at each one he was sure none would escape damage, with luck they would even all be destroyed in the first salvo.

There was still an hour to wait but he had already ordered most of his light ships to form a protective screen ahead of his main fleet. The British had a slight range advantage and he wanted to make sure neither of his battleships took any damage. With only limited repair capabilities within the Void he didn't want to have to send either of them home unnecessarily.

A sudden explosion drew his attention back to the main body of his ships. One of the frigates he had left guarding the rear of the fleet had disappeared off the tactical plot, indicating that she had stopped communicating with the flagship.

"Admiral," his sensors officer called out in a panic. "I have multiple heat sources and drives coming on line, bearing zero seven seven point three. They are almost dead astern!"

Zheng had been replaying the visual feed from the frigates last known position. All he could see was an expanding ball of debris. With his sensor officer's report he quickly put two and two together. That's why the other ships didn't run away, he thought, they are not alone.

Jensen smiled as the only frigate that could have warned the Chinese crumpled under her plasma cannons. This was the signal for the rest of the ships to drop out of stealth and open fire. As one, every ship fired and a hail of plasma arched out to strike the Chinese ships. She had ordered the first volley to target the smaller ships, as she wanted to whittle away their point defense. *Valkyrie* was the only exception. Her larger guns were aimed at the lone Chinese battlecruiser. She wasn't sure *Valkyrie's* guns could punch through the larger battleship's armor at this range but she knew they would make quick work of the Chinese battlecruiser.

Mere seconds later the battlecruiser visibly shuddered on the visual display. Jensen saw at least one of the four heavy plasma bolts punch right out of the other side of the battlecruiser. She wasn't going to last long. Simultaneously, a light cruiser, four destroyers and the remaining rear guard frigate exploded.

The rest of the Chinese ships continued on as if nothing had happened. Their crews too stunned to react. Thirty seconds later *Valkyrie* and the heavy cruiser *Achilles* fired their plasma cannons again; they were the only ones with large enough caliber guns to do any damage at the ever increasing range.

Each ship had targeted one of the battleships and explosions rippled across their armor. Neither dropped off the plot though and no secondary explosions were detected. Instead Jensen's attention was drawn back to her ships, one of the Chinese heavy cruisers had managed to turn and return fire before the range became too great and the destroyer *Sandstorm* erupted into a ball of fire.

"Signal all ships." Jensen shouted over the noise of the bridge, "Everyone is to go to rapid fire on their missiles now!"

The Chinese were clearly getting their act together, even as Jensen's fleet fired their first salvo of fifty-five missiles the Chinese turned as one and returned fire with over one hundred and eighty. As Jensen's missiles approached the enemy it looked like the first salvo would do significant damage. Yet suddenly the Chinese forward screening ships appeared, decelerating between their larger brethren to add their counter fire to the battle.

"Target their new screening elements in the next salvo," Jensen snapped.

The Damang incident had taught the British a number of hard lessons. One had been that ships that specialized in point defense were much more effective at protecting other ships. Missiles that were accelerating straight for them were harder to intercept.

She watched as the Chinese began to engage her missiles. Silently she willed them through the point defense barrage and onto the two battleships. Every missile had been targeted at them in the hope that being caught with their screening units out of place would have allowed some to get through the battleship's defenses.

The forward screening ships had reacted faster than Jensen had anticipated and their additional fire was reducing her missiles quickly. In the end only four missiles got through, three scored proximity hits on one of the battleships, stripping off some of its armor, external weapons and sensor nodes in thermonuclear blasts. Yet it continued on.

As the Chinese missiles approached the British ships Jensen ordered another salvo fired and then the British ships switched their focus to point defense. The flak cannons reached out and began to engage the incoming Chinese missiles. Jensen had one flak frigate and three flak corvettes with her, combined with *Valkyrie's* two flak guns that gave her fleet seven. Each had been assigned a cone of space around her fleet and soon the incoming missiles had to go through a hail of fire, the likes of which had never been seen before in human interstellar war. One hundred and eighty were quickly reduced to one hundred, then sixty and then thirty nine. Next it was the turn of the point defense plasma cannons to open up, closely followed by the AM missiles. More slowly, they too began to whittle down the explosive force arrayed against Jensen's fleet. As the last ten accelerated up to attack velocity, the British ships went into evasive maneuvers and launched decoy drones. All but two of the missiles missed their targets. Yet, as the fleet reformed its formation, a light cruiser and a flak corvette were missing.

Jensen grimaced at the losses. Yet their initial ambush meant they were still giving better than they got. She checked the range. Her ships would only have time for one more missile salvo. As she was watching the Chinese ships they eventually managed to fire off their second salvo. It was actually larger than the first as their screening ships were able to add their firepower. In response the British fired their third salvo and then prepared themselves for the coming onslaught.

Silence descended on the flag bridge as the superior numbers of the enemy quickly reduced the British second salvo. In the end the missiles only managed to get hits on two frigates and a light cruiser. Both frigates exploded but the light cruiser continued, albeit falling behind her consorts.

As the second and last Chinese missile salvo rained in on her ships Jensen had to grit her teeth to remain still. Their first salvo had almost overwhelmed her defenses and now she was down two flak guns.

One hundred and ninety missiles became sixty from flak cannon fire. Then the plasma guns and AM missiles began to knock them off in fives and tens. Yet it wasn't enough. Fifteen reached attack range and went to their maximum acceleration. The heavy cruiser *Achilles* and the flak frigate *Bat* both exploded from direct hits. *Valkyrie* rocked as two missiles scored proximity hits.

"Damage report?" Jensen called out.

"This is the Fourth Lieutenant here at damage control, the Second Lieutenant has been killed. Reports are still coming in but it looks like we have lost the number two flak gun along with three of our starboard missile tubes."

Jensen felt a cold drop of sweat run down her back, they had stared death in the face and survived. Most of her fleet had not. She was down to *Valkyrie*, the light cruiser *Justice* and her two remaining flak corvettes. If the Chinese Admiral wanted too, he could decelerate and finish them off, Jensen only hoped they had caused enough damage to make him think twice. With Wolfe and the rest of her task force still out there the Chinese might not want to run the risk of being engaged on two fronts. It was a long shot though.

Aboard *Drake*, James watched as Admiral Jensen's third missile salvo closed with the Chinese. As soon as she had opened fire with her plasma cannons she had went to full military power after the Chinese fleet. However, the velocity the Chinese had been carrying into the system meant that both fleets had already fallen out of range of each other. Only the British rapid firing ability and range advantage had allowed her to get off one more salvo than the Chinese ships.

Of that third salvo only two missiles managed to get through the Chinese defenses but both scored a direct hit on one of the heavy cruisers. Seconds later, as its reactors overloaded, it detonated in a colossal fireball

As James continued to watch, both fleets reformed the ships they had left into the best protective formations they could. Then space seemed to go quiet once more. The Chinese still had their two battleships, eight cruisers and six screening ships left. James couldn't tell if the battleships had taken any serious damage. Even though a number of missiles had scored proximity hits to add to the plasma bolts from Jensen's second volley they were still heading into the system, towards the second British fleet. Admiral Jensen had managed to punch well above her weight. Yet Wolfe and the rest of the fleet were still outnumbered almost two to one.

Then the Chinese fleet moved most of their screening ships forward again. They were preparing to engage the second British fleet. Wolfe and *Broadsword* were now angling away; they had completed their mission of luring the Chinese into the system. Yet their opponents were altering course to try and close the range. By James' estimate, Wolfe was going to take a hammering before she could escape.

"Gupta, alter course." James requested. "Get us in front of the Chinese fleet's new angle of attack if you can. We need to try and pull some of their screening units away from *Broadsword*.

"Tactical, once we have our new position locked in I want you to start calculating missile timings and trajectories. We're going to flush as many missiles out of our single tube as possible and leave them on a ballistic trajectory. Once the Chinese fleet passes us we'll signal them to go active. Hopefully the different angles of attack will confuse the Chinese and let us get away. More importantly though, it might make them paranoid, they won't know who else is out here. We have to give Captain Wolfe a chance."

Ten minutes later everything was ready. The Chinese fleet was twenty-five minutes away from engaging *Broadsword* and her colleagues. As the Chinese passed in front of *Drake* she began to flush missiles. Without having to feed them targeting data she was able to get off three in quick succession. James waited another minute and then gave the order.

"Send the signal, tell the missiles to go active."

There was only a few milliseconds' delay between the signal reaching each missile and their response. Almost at once, all three went active and began to accelerate along the ballistic course they were already traveling. At the same time their active radar seekers came online and began to look for a target. All three locked onto the solitary frigate that was at the rear of the Chinese formation and began to turn towards it.

High Admiral Zheng was fighting to keep control of his anger. Somehow the British had known he was coming. They had laid an ambush for him. Both his precious battleships were damaged. Not badly enough that they were out of the fight but enough that he knew he was going to be called before the Politburo. And those blasted flak guns. They had allowed the first British fleet to survive his two salvos. Well, he wasn't going to let the second fleet get away so lucky. Once he had smashed them and their bases on the planet he would turn around and get his revenge.

"Admiral, *Xing Lun* is under attack. Three missiles have just appeared and are angling towards her," one of the bridge officers called.

"What! Where did they come from? Have they more ships behind us?" Zheng demanded.

"I'm not sure sir, the missiles seem to have been fired from a ship or two in stealth. We are searching the area now with our high intensity radar."

Zheng could only watch as the three missiles closed in on *Xing Lun*. She tried to weave and duck but alone beyond the protective point defense fire of the fleet she could only destroy two of them. The third struck a glancing blow but it was enough to set off its warhead and *Xing Lun* disappeared in the explosion.

A moment of panic flashed through Zheng, how many more ships were out there lying in stealth? The second British fleet was angling away from his. They clearly didn't want to enter plasma range but they weren't running away with abandon. They might just be trying to keep the range open for a missile duel to lure him into another trap of some kind.

"Sensors, are we close enough for a visual inspection of the second fleet yet?" Zheng asked.

"Yes sir, I'm reviewing the take now."

"How many of their flak ships does this second fleet have?"

"Hold on sir, I can make out at least two of their flak corvettes and one, possibly two flak frigates."

Everyone on the flag bridge looked away as the Admiral let out a string of curses in mandarin. He had to grip his hands into fists to stop them shaking. His anger was turning into fear. Even if the British didn't have any more ships out there in stealth, this second fleet would be able to soak up a lot of his missiles. It would take a while to hammer them into dust in a long-range missile duel. And their ECM missiles would ensure they continued to get hits on his ships.

He made up his mind. "Tactical, plot us a route out of the system. We can't risk the battleships. We can repair and come back again to finish this."

"Aye sir, I'll transmit the orders to the fleet."

"Good, once that is done I want you to work up a firing solution on those colonies. We'll fire a salvo of ground attack missiles as we pass."

Ground attack missiles were missiles tipped with pure titanium instead of nuclear warheads. Accelerated to high speeds they would penetrate deep into the planet's crust, causing colossal local damage. At least he would have the last say in this engagement Zheng consoled himself.

Captain Wolfe had been watching the entire battle longing for the chance to get her ships into range. She had felt the death of each of the British ships. She was proud of what they had achieved but now she wanted to get her revenge. Her fleet could fire a much larger salvo compared to Jansen's and she wanted to make it count.

"Captain, the Chinese are changing direction," her sensor officer reported. "It looks like they are trying to avoid action."

"What?" she questioned.

It didn't make any sense. The Chinese still out massed her by more than two to one. Her flak guns and ECM penetrator missiles would even the odds some but the Chinese would still have the advantage.

"Navigation, try and keep them in range. I want to get off as many salvos as we can before they blow past us. And be prepared to reverse course, it may be a trick to try and get us to come into plasma range."

Despite her and her navigation officer's best efforts Wolfe couldn't prevent the Chinese from escaping. The fleets passed close enough for them to fire one missile salvo each. The British ships put out eighty-two missiles. Knowing that it would be her only salvo, Wolfe had ordered that her cruisers load two ECM penetrator missiles each.

The remaining Chinese could only manage a salvo of one hundred and eighty but it was still significant. When it became clear that almost all the missiles were targeted at the flak frigates and corvettes, they pulled away from the rest of the fleet. The British had learnt from the Damang Incident. Each ship ignored the missiles angling towards it and instead focused on protecting her sister ships. The move worked well, knocking out most of the Chinese missiles but, in the end, both flak frigates took proximity hits and exploded. Almost all of the other missiles aimed at the rest of the fleet were knocked out with one exception. A lucky hit took out the light cruiser *Demise*.

On board the battleship *Hai Hu* concern tinged the sensor

Lieutenant's voice as he shouted, "Admiral, they have more ECM missiles in this salvo than normal. They are going to hit us hard."

Zheng could do nothing but watch the coming destruction. All he could hope for now was that the fleet he had sent to Camelot had achieved more success. Once he combined his forces and licked his wounds he knew he would be back.

One by one the British missiles disappeared off the plot. Ten made it into attack range and a medium cruiser and a destroyer both took direct hits and exploded. *Hai Hu* shook as she took another proximity hit that knocked out more sensor nodes and another missile tube. After ensuring no more serious damage had been caused, Zheng gave the order to fire a final volley of missiles at the planet's surface. Everything that remotely looked like a British piece of equipment was targeted.

Unopposed, Zheng smiled as he watched the missiles rain down destruction on the planet as he led his ships out of the system. Even though he was leaving the system in defeat he could at least hold onto one success. The British efforts to settle the planet had been thwarted for now, and he knew he would be back.

Onboard *Valkyrie* Jensen also smiled. Unknown to Zheng his last act of vengeance proved to be impotent. One of her first acts when she came to Excalibur had been to organize her engineers to set up fake colonies. She had hoped it would give her another tactical option in any battle. In the end they had served their purpose perfectly, luring the Chinese Admiral deeper into the system, setting up her ambush. Finally she allowed herself to relax, the battle was over. It had cost them dearly but they had achieved the impossible, they had managed to drive off two Chinese battleships.

Chapter 14 - Aftermath

First Battle of Excalibur: battle report

On the 13th of March 2465 AD a Chinese fleet under High Admiral Zheng attacked the British forces guarding the Excalibur system. The British forces commanded by Rear Admiral Jensen were outnumbered by a factor of almost three to one. However Jensen managed to get a portion of her fleet into plasma range and rake the Chinese warships. Soon after the Chinese were forced to retire from the system.

Chinese loses: One battlecruiser, a heavy, medium and light cruiser along with five destroyers and four frigates.

British losses: One heavy and two light cruisers along with one destroyer, three frigates and one corvette.

Outcome: British victory.

-Excerpt from Empire Rising, 3002 AD.

13th March 2465 AD. HMS *Pelican*, the Camelot system

HMS *Pelican* excited shift space on the edge of Camelot's mass shadow. Her Captain was about to order Admiral Jensen's warning to be transmitted when his sensor officer stopped him.

"Sir, I'm picking up lots of radiation bouncing around out there. I think we are too late. The readings are consistent with a high number of nuclear detonations."

"Shit," Jennings said, "are there any signs of friendly ships?"

"Negative sir, I'm not picking up any vessels in the system."

"Ok, continue scanning while our jump drive charges. Navigation, I want to jump us a further six light hours out of the system, let's see if we can pick up anything from the battle."

Jennings had always thought it strange that a ship could jump further from a system and in effect look back in time. If he could get a telescope powerful enough he could jump to a position where he could watch his great, great grandfather back on Earth. Yet now it was going to prove useful. He could jump further out of the system and look back at the battle that had already occurred.

Half an hour later the entire bridge watched silently as the sensors picked up a large group of Chinese ships heading into the system. The British had already reacted and Commodore Williams was leading his forces to engage the intruders. At this range it was impossible to do anything more than identify the number of heat sources. Estimating type and class was out of the question. They could however, detect the heat and radiation of nuclear explosions.

The Commodore's ships survived the first two waves of missiles and managed to take out one of their opponents with their return fire. However, as the third set of explosions blossomed around his ships two of Commodore Williams' eight blips disappeared. Then two more disappeared in the next salvo. Finally, the fifth salvo from the Chinese ships destroyed the last British ship. In all, four Chinese ships had also disappeared from the plot yet no one on board had cheered their loss. The RSN had never lost an entire task force before. No amount of Chinese losses would make up for the men and women that had just disappeared in front of *Pelican's* eyes.

*

15th March 2465 AD, HMS *Drake*, the Excalibur system

Two days had passed since the first battle of Excalibur. Most of Rear Admiral Jensen's ships were in orbit around Excalibur effecting repairs. The initial joy over the defeat of the Chinese had given way to dismay at the news from Camelot. Almost all of the ships in the Void had served as one unit back at Britannia and so everyone had lost friends in one or both systems.

James was eager to get out of Excalibur and return to V17 to see what the Chinese were up too. Yet every functioning ship was needed to patrol the approaches to Excalibur in case a Chinese ship tried to sneak into missile range. Admiral Jensen had contacted him personally to commend him on his actions in the battle. She suspected the Chinese would have driven on and destroyed Wolfe's task force if *Drake* hadn't spooked them off. As a reward, she had promised she would release *Drake* to go and watch the Chinese fleet, but not until enough ships had been repaired to set up a proper picket system.

"Commander," Sub Lieutenant Fisher said from her position manning the sensors console. "Two ships have just lit off their drives and are coming out of orbit from Excalibur."

"Acknowledged Lieutenant," James replied. "Navigation, plot us a course out of the system that will line us up for a jump to V17."

It took just over two hours for the message James had been expecting to reach *Drake* from *Valkyrie*. Admiral Jensen had sent a video message and so James put it on the main holo-display.

"Commander, we now have enough ships back in fighting trim to allow me to spare you. We need to know what the Chinese are up to. I want you to jump into V17 but don't enter the mass shadow. Watch for as long as you need but once you have a good idea of their strength and intentions, head straight back. And again pass on my thanks to your crew."

When James had first spoken to the Rear Admiral after the battle she had looked tired and haggard. Now she seemed back to her calm and controlled self. That was reassuring.

"Navigation," James ordered, "Bring us onto our new vector, it's time to return to the lion's den."

*

Hours later, Rear Admiral Jensen watched *Drake* disappear from the system. She had been desperate to send someone to poke their nose into V17 but she hadn't had enough ships to properly protect her fleet. Already she had sent one badly damaged destroyer back to Cambridge with news of the battle and a request for immediate aid. The Chinese light cruiser that had been damaged and then surrendered was almost ready to be sent home as well.

Currently, she only had *Valkyrie* and six other cruisers under her command. She had lost almost a third of her force when the two Chinese battleships had tried to force their way into the system. If Commodore Williams' task force was added to the equation the proportion lost approached half of the ships she had entered the Void with. Those losses had been taking their toll on her. They were all men and women who she had spent the last year commanding. Now they were simply gone. Thankfully, she had more than enough responsibilities to keep her busy and stop her mind dwelling on the losses for too long.

The last two days had been nerve wracking, to say the least. She had feared the Chinese would either come back in strength to finish the task or send their smaller ships to coast into Excalibur. The Chinese still had more than enough firepower to destroy her fleet if they came against her with everything they had. On the other hand, a small ship could enter the system under stealth and possibly get close enough to launch a spread of missiles. With so many damaged ships she hadn't been able to properly cover all the approaches.

Her only source of hope had been the damage she had managed to deal to the two battleships. *Valkyrie* had scored some direct hits with her plasma cannons and a review of the battle had shown that some missiles had scored proximity hits as well. Both battleships were a long way from being inoperable. They had show that with their last salvo at Wolfe's task force. However, Jensen hoped she had done enough damage that the Chinese Admiral wouldn't want to risk them again until they were fully repaired.

A week before the battle she had received an update from the Admiralty. Vice Admiral Cunningham was only weeks away from being ready to leave Cook and make for the Void. It had taken the message three weeks to reach her. Cunningham should be on his way by now. All she had to do was hold on.

*

17th March 2465 AD, HMS *Drake*, edge of the Excalibur system

"Communications, send the report to *Valkyrie*," James ordered once the sensors had updated to show that everything was as expected around Excalibur.

Drake had just jumped into the system after spending four days patrolling V17. They had not managed to locate all the Chinese ships they were expecting to be there after the battle. James guessed some were lying in stealth within the system. However, they had identified the two battleships. They were both in low orbit around the habitable planet in the system. James had sent in a number of recon drones to try and get a look at what they were up to. Three of the four had been spotted and destroyed by the picket ships. The fourth had managed to beam back some visuals before it too had been destroyed. It seemed that both battleships were docked with the repair station the Chinese had under construction. The drone hadn't been able to get a good look at the damage they had sustained but the fact they were both docked at the station spoke for itself. It gave the British a good bit of breathing space. As long as both ships were receiving repairs they couldn't be mounting any offensives.

As his report was beamed into the system, James kept *Drake* just beyond the mass shadow. He expected to be ordered right back to V17 and so didn't want to waste any time heading into the system. That said, it would still take over fourteen hours for his report to reach *Valkyrie* and a response to be sent out to the edge of the system.

Once the report was sent, James headed back to his quarters to change out of his uniform. He had ordered the cook to prepare a meal for all his senior officers. Everyone had been on edge for the last few weeks. The stress of constant patrol duty had only been heightened since the battle of Excalibur. Everyone on board had now seen real action. No one was particularly keen to have to go through it again.

He had planned this meal to help everyone unwind and relax. Only Sub Lieutenant Hanson wouldn't be there as he was on watch. The officer's mess had been the only room large enough for everyone to fit in and so he was getting a rare opportunity to come into the world of his subordinates. Andrea, his friend and accountant, had sent on board a case of expensive French wine from the Bordeaux region when they had their short stay on Earth. It had been a celebration for his estate finally turning a profit.

Ordinarily, the crew of a RSN spaceship was not allowed to

consume alcohol. The regulations did however, stipulate that in special circumstances the Commander or Captain had the authority to waive the rule. James had decided that now was a good time. With *Drake* sitting on the edge of the system powered down, and in stealth, they would be all but undetectable unless a ship came out of shift space right on top of them. Realistically, this was the only chance they were going to get to enjoy a period of relative safety. James wanted to make the best if it.

Satisfied that he was dressed suitably, he made his way to officer country. Along with Second Lieutenant Gupta and his Sub Lieutenants, the ship's pursuer, who oversaw the stores of *Drake*, the chief engineer and the RSN marine Lieutenant all shared the officer's section. Tradition meant that every British ship still carried a small compliment of marines. *Drake* had only ten, yet they had come in handy in their mission to capture the Chinese destroyer.

As he entered the dining area he saw that everyone was already there. Walking over, he took his seat at the head of the table. "Welcome everyone, or should I say thank you for welcoming me into your home," James began with a smile. "This is probably going to be the only chance we get to relax and unwind over the next few weeks so I want you all to enjoy yourselves. Don't think of us as commander and subordinates, we're all equals at the table tonight, so relax. Of course," he continued as he winked at Sub Lieutenant Becket. "Those who are on duty in a few hours should remember to take some detoxing stimulants after they have enjoyed tonight's lovely wine."

As James sat, a number of crew who had been drafted in by the cook to help serve the food, appeared and began to distribute the first course. It was a blend of a traditional British vegetable soup with a popular recipe from Britannia, which mainly used native plants.

For the first few minutes everyone ate in silence. Just as James was about to give up on seeing his officers open up, Gupta broke the silence and came to his rescue. "Fisher, I hear you and Becket had a bit of fun earlier today, care to retell the story for the rest of us?"

Fisher had to set her spoonful of soup down as she tried to hold back a giggle. In contrast Becket looked up from her soup aghast.

Before either got a chance to reply, James mouthed a thank you to Gupta. Becket then began to tell the story but Fisher quickly shushed her. "I think the story should come from me – I got the best view after all." Before Becket could protest Fisher launched into her account of the story. "Chief Harkin had sent us both down to check on the power relays around number two reactor. Becket had been boasting that she had read of an engineer who could check a power relay simply by touch. She had claimed he was able to judge the power levels going through it, just from the static it gave off.

"When we got there, she insisted I put my plasma spanner away and allow her to check the relays by hand. What she hadn't realized was that they had been fluctuating quite badly. As soon as she touched the second one, her hair shot up and she began to jerk and jolt like crazy. Even when she managed to take her hand away from the relay, the current still jumped out and kept the connection. She had to take four or five steps away from the relay to break the connection. And all the time she was still jerking and shaking! The engineering crew had a right laugh. Every time they see her now they break into a jerking robot dance! In fact, I got a message from one of them, they managed to get the security holo-recording."

Fisher reached over to an input terminal on the table and after a few clicks had turned on the holo display in the room. Becket tried to grab her hands away but O'Rourke grabbed Becket in a bear hug, holding her off. Moments later a recording of the entire ordeal began to play out in front of the officers. Becket hung her head in embarrassment all the way through the recording.

As the laughs died down, James showed his approval. "Well I think we know who the prize for *Drake's* best dancer goes to! Though the award for most promising engineer may have to go elsewhere."

Everyone knew that next to the Chief Engineer Becket was the most knowledgeable when it came to *Drake's* impulse or shift space engines. James hoped this incident would keep her from getting too big headed.

He sat back as the conversations began to flow. Fisher was continuing to mock Becket and she even got up to give everyone a rendition of the jerking dance. Thirlwall was telling the pursuer all about her childhood on Thames, one of Britain's newest colonies. The conversation eventually turned to the war and both O'Rourke and Graham were prodding Gupta about her views.

"Come on sir, do you really think the Chinese will keep coming at us? We gave them a real licking. The terms of the UN agreement are very generous for them. They get to keep the planet they have now and no more blood has to be spilled."

"That's all perfectly true of course," she replied. "But if you know your history you will know that the human race rarely gives away anything it thinks is theirs. The Chinese did discover the Void first. They obviously think they own all of it. Their actions at Damang and here at Excalibur show that they are more than willing to shed blood to keep what is theirs. We have hurt them, but they still outnumber us, and they have many more ships they can send into the Void.

On a slightly more fearful note Becket asked, "Do you think they will be back soon then sir?

"You have all seen the take we got from V17. Their battleships are under repair so I don't think they'll be here in the next few hours. But yes, they'll be back."

"What about you Commander, when do you think they will be back?" Fisher asked. James was pleased that she was obviously overcoming some of her shyness around him. As he paused before answering, every other conversation ceased. All eyes turned to him.

"Gupta is right, she has clearly thought things through. We all know the Chinese have been lagging behind us when it comes to the expansion race. Their population just hasn't had the same drive to get out into space. That has hurt the speed at which their government can ramp up their economic and industrial growth on new colonies. Added to that is the fact none of their colonies have been class I or II habitable planets. Cook is a paradise compared to Wi Liang or Parcal and Britannia makes everything they have pale into insignificance. Two of the planets in the Void, Camelot and V34 are both Class II and Excalibur isn't too far behind. Yet they have been awarded neither by the UN. Think about things from the Politburo's point of view. They see us as their enemies. We've been slowly pulling ahead of them. If we get Excalibur and Camelot, we will only get stronger. Their only advantage over us is the size of their military and we are working hard to come to parity with them in that department. As Gupta said, they have already shown their ability to shed blood. I see no reason for the Politburo to stop now. If they give up, they are basically accepting that they are second best. I don't think that's even a possibility in the Chinese mindset.

"I have grown up all my life around people who thought they were at the pinnacle of power. I used to think that too before I was assigned to *Drake*. I know what it's like to fall from grace. The Politburo won't back down. Not when the alternative is a slow fading into insignificance. My father faced the same choice when his first business venture failed. Rather than admit defeat he covered it up and tried to fix the problem by firing good money after bad. I have seen how that worked out but I'm not sure the Politburo can see the folly of a long protracted war."

"Is that why you were sent to *Drake*, because of your father? I thought it was because of the Princess?" O'Rourke asked.

This time every eye turned to O'Rourke. He was the youngest person around the table and he seemed to shrink back from all the attention. Gupta began to change the subject but James waved her to stop.

Sighing he said, "I suppose you have all seen the news reports from when we left Earth. Well, as you can imagine things are complicated. As you know the nobility protects its image with a vengeance, the King more than anyone. Christine and I hope to have a future together, the King thinks otherwise. That's really all I'm going to say on the matter."

As James went back to his meal everyone followed suit. Slowly the whispered conversations grew back into a noisy ruckus as the wine continued to have its effect. As desert came out and everyone's attention was elsewhere Gupta leaned over to her Commander. "I think your idea has worked well sir. Everyone seems to be enjoying themselves. I'm sure you and Christine will be able to work things out in the future."

"Thank you Lieutenant," James whispered back. "Christine shares your enthusiasm, I just hope you are both right."

As the conversations continued to flow, James sat back in his chair and relaxed each of his muscles in turn. He was happy not to be drawn into any more conversations. Instead he enjoyed watching each of his subordinates unwind and show a side of themselves that they usually kept hidden from their Commander.

Fourteen hours after the message from *Drake* had been sent into the Excalibur system, James was back on the bridge awaiting the reply from *Valkyrie*. Sure enough, a message came back from Rear Admiral Jensen almost exactly when he was expecting it. *Drake* was to head back to V17 and watch the Chinese fleet. She was to stay there until she had something important to report or she was relieved.

After reading through the order twice, James looked over to Sub Lieutenant Hanson, who was manning the navigation console. "Are the coordinates locked into the jump drive?"

"Yes sir, everything is ready."

"Ok engage the engines, take us to V17.

Chapter 15 – Superiors

The command structure of the Empire's navy was taken from the British Royal Space Navy, which in turn was taken from the Royal Navy before it. The Royal Navy had the longest and most prestigious history of any of the navies that combined to form the Empire and so assuming its command structure was the obvious choice.

-Excerpt from Empire's Rising, 3002 AD

25th March 2465 AD, HMS *Drake*, edge of the Excalibur system

Once *Drake* dropped out of shift space James watched the holo displays update themselves. They had spent the last week doing what *Drake* had been designed for. After arriving at V17 they had spent a day slowly coasting up to the shift limit. There, *Drake* had silently watched the Chinese fleet as it began to reassemble itself. One of the battleships had finished its repair work and, with a number of the cruisers, was drilling battle formations. After collecting lots of data on their drills, James had jumped *Drake* to the other side of the system and repeated the process.

Finally, once he had been satisfied that they had managed to identify most of the Chinese ships patrolling the system, he had taken *Drake* on two passes into the system. Neither entered the inner system as it was too heavily patrolled, however, he still managed to get a reasonably good look at the Chinese fleet. All in all he felt he had a very accurate picture of the Chinese ships present at V17.

Things had gotten a little hairy when another British scout ship had jumped into the system. One of the Chinese picket ships had picked it up and given chase. A number of other Chinese ships also joined the chase and the ensuing commotion had almost led to *Drake* being discovered as well. Thankfully, some quick thinking had kept them out of detection range.

After the second pass through the system he had decided to return to Excalibur. The second battleship was still undergoing repairs but the rest of the Chinese fleet looked like it was battle ready. The ships the Chinese Admiral had under his command were more than capable of blowing Rear Admiral's Jensen's fleet into space dust, even without the second battleship. As they looked about ready to make a move, James had decided he better get back to Excalibur. He didn't know how much information the other scout had managed to get.

The new ships that had jumped into the system as he had been leaving had hastened him. More reinforcements, in the form of a battlecruiser, a heavy cruiser, six other cruisers and twelve smaller ships had jumped into the system and lit off their drives. James hadn't been able to get any more firm information but he knew their arrival meant the Chinese Admiral would be able to resume offensive operations. It was time for *Drake* to get back to Excalibur.

As the initial readings of the Excalibur system came up fear pierced his heart. For a moment he thought that somehow the Chinese fleet had found a way to beat him to Excalibur. There was a large number of ships moving into the system. Their impulse drives were lighting up the gravimetric sensors. James relaxed as logic took over. There was no way the Chinese fleet could have gotten so far into the system ahead of him. The ships must be reinforcements! Vice Admiral Cunningham had arrived.

Over the next couple of minutes the plot gained more detail, as Sub

Lieutenant Fisher, who was manning sensors, was able to identify a number of the ships. There were two new battlecruisers in Cunningham's fleet along with five heavy cruisers and another twenty smaller cruisers. Fisher wasn't able to get a positive ID on the smaller classes of ships at this range but there were over thirty other support ships.

Further back from the main body of the fleet there was another squadron. None of the drives matched known British vessels. Fisher had designated them as unknown friendlies and had identified one light cruiser and three smaller ships, probably destroyers. They seemed to be escorting three other ships; one of them was rather large.

James put the mystery to the back of his mind. No doubt he would find out soon enough. "Send our report to *Valkyrie* and take us in towards Excalibur, I'm sure we're going to be getting new orders."

Looking around the bridge he smiled. "If the Chinese try to jump us anytime soon they're going to get nasty surprise."

*

Several hours later James found himself aboard HMS *Churchill*, Vice Admiral Cunningham's flagship. Sat around him were over forty other Commanders, Captains and Flag lieutenants. They were all crammed into the battlecruisers tactical briefing room. As he finally managed to squeeze into his own seat, a side door opened and Vice Admiral Cunningham walked to the front of the room accompanied by Rear Admiral Jensen and Commodore West.

James studied the man closely. He had taken some of the Admiral's lectures at the lunar academy. Cunningham looked just as sharp and distinguished as ever. He had been over one hundred and twenty when James had sat under his teaching almost eight years ago and yet he still walked with the ease of someone who had undergone expensive anti-aging treatments. Apart from a few tinges of grey hair around his ears, there was no sign that the Admiral was of his great grandfather's generation.

The main medical discoveries with regard to anti-aging treatments had only happened fifty years ago and, initially, they had only been available to the super rich. Today they were readily available, if still somewhat expensive. It was standard practice to offer them freely to all RSN graduates from the lunar academy. James had been assured that he could expect to live to at least two hundred before he would begin to feel the effects of old age. For Cunningham to still be on his feet, he must have received one of the first anti-aging treatments. They weren't as effective as the modern ones but clearly they hadn't done Cunningham any harm.

Whatever the Admiral's age, James knew his mental abilities were impeccable. As part of their training, the cadets were made to run simulations against their instructors and, whether in a fleet engagement or single ship combat, Cunningham had wiped the floor with James a number of times. As a close friend of his uncle's the Admiral had been approachable and ready to offer help. James looked forward to remaking the Admiral's acquaintance.

"Ok, everyone please be seated," Rear Admiral Jensen shouted over the hum of conversations going on in the briefing room.

When everyone had finally quieted down Admiral Cunningham spoke. "Well everyone, welcome to Excalibur. For those of you were already here I want to offer my congratulations on holding the system. I have read over Admiral Jensen's battle report and I am suitably impressed with everyone's performance.

"I have called this meeting because I want you all to know our plan for prosecuting this war to its finish. The Government and the

Admiralty have no desire to get embroiled in a long term war of attrition with the Chinese. We don't want their systems, we don't even want total control over the Void. Space is big enough for all of us. That said, the Chinese have clearly shown us that they don't share these sentiments. With that in mind we're going to make sure they can't cause any more harm.

"My plan is simple. Rear Admiral Jensen and I will take our forces to V17 and set up a blockade around the system. No Chinese ships will be allowed to leave. It is the Admiralty's hope that once the Politburo and Chinese Admiral see that every ship they send to V17 becomes stuck there, they will be willing to come to terms. However, if the Chinese at V17 do want to fight then we will show them what the RSN is made of. We now have nearly twenty percent of the total RSN tonnage operating within the Void. We have a powerful force under our command ladies and gentlemen. We will be getting more reinforcements but they will be trickling in, for now it's up to us. We will be expected to do our duty with what we currently have; it's our job to do everyone back home proud. Are there any questions at this stage?"

Captain Adams of the destroyer *Sparrow* stood and asked, "sir, as you know I was here when the Chinese attacked us three weeks ago. I have seen their resolve first hand. How likely do you think it is they will want to fight again?"

"A good question Captain," The Admiral began. "We have brought with us new intel from RSNI. We believe the Admiral in charge of the Chinese is Admiral Zheng. He was able to handpick his Captains, at least those of his original fleet. We believe he will put up a fight. He has nothing to go back to, if he goes back empty handed he will be exiled for his failure. For that reason, we need to be working from the assumption that he will try to force a confrontation. If our blockade of the V17 system is successful, we may be able to starve him of fuel before he can force a large-scale engagement. That is our hope at least. If it comes to it though we need to be ready to fight. Admiral Jensen has already shown us how it's done."

Wolfe was the next to raise her hand. "Admiral, what about the Swedish ships, can we expect any help from them if it comes to a fight?"

James finally got an answer to his question. The second squadron keeping its distance from the combined British fleet must be Swedish. They must have come to lay claim to V34. As he continued to watch, the Vice Admiral switched the image on the holo display to show the small squadron James had been curious about.

"I'm afraid not Captain. As you can see our Swedish neighbors have brought a few combat ships, two supply freighters and their colony ship. Their plan is to found a colony on New Stockholm as soon as possible. Officially, they are neutral in this combat. Unofficially, they are afraid the Chinese won't respect their neutrality and end up dragging them into the war.

"They therefore have no intention of doing anything that looks like supporting us. In fact, I think they wish we would all just disappear or better yet that they could get a colony somewhere else. However, they can't and we won't. As this is the only opportunity they're likely to get for decades to found their own colony, they're stubbornly pushing ahead with it.

"The governor in charge of founding the colony is keeping his plans close to his chest. My guess, however, would be that once we establish our blockade around V17 he will take his ships to New Stockholm and start constructing their colony. It certainly wouldn't hurt our cause if they joined the war but that is not going to happen anytime soon.

"Now, if that is all the questions, you should be receiving your orders on your personal datapads. Please check them now and report to your commanding officer for further briefings."

James pulled out his data pad and immediately checked his new orders. He had been assigned to Commodore West's squadron. She had been given the task of overseeing the continued fortification of the Excalibur system. Apart from her flagship there was nothing larger than a destroyer under her command.

In frustration James switched off his datapad. He had been at the center of everything that happened so far. *Why was he being sidelined now?* Looking through the crowd of departing faces James spotted the Vice Admiral. Making his way over he held out his hand as he approached.

"Admiral, it is good to see you again. I am pleased that you have been given this command. I know firsthand how good your tactical skills really are."

The Vice Admiral merely eyed James. "Somerville, I remember you of course, from the academy. What can I do for you?"

Pausing, James waited for the Admiral to take his hand. When Cunningham merely continued to stare at him James was taken aback by the standoffish greeting. Determined he pressed ahead anyway, "sir, as you know *Drake* and I have been at the center of things here in the Void. I was hoping my crew would get the opportunity to see things through to the finish. We have spent over two weeks within the V17 system and *Drake* has proven her ability to sneak around the Chinese fleet.

The Vice Admiral's face darkened. He grabbed James' elbow and directed him towards an unoccupied corner of the debriefing room.

"Listen here Commander Somerville. I will not deny that you have proven yourself very useful in this campaign so far. Before I left Cook I received a full download of all the news stories from Earth, as well as a personal communication from the King. I suggest that if you want your career to progress, you try to be more careful in the future. If it were up to me you would be leading the fleet into V17. But it's not; we all have to respect our betters. You can begin now by obeying my orders."

As the Admiral spun and walked off, James had to work quickly to hide the look of shock on his face. He had looked on the Vice Admiral as a close confidant back at the academy. Now the Admiral was acting as if they had never met before. *"The King!"* James whispered through gritted teeth. It seemed as if he was never going to get away from the King's attempts to punish him for his feelings.

In a daze, James headed to his assigned briefing room aboard *Churchill*. When he arrived he was the last to enter. Everyone else had been waiting for him. Without acknowledging James' tardiness Commodore West began to outline her plans.

"As you have all read by now we have been given the job of securing Excalibur and the surrounding systems while the others get to go off and play. You may be disappointed but let me remind you of the causalities we suffered at the battles of Excalibur and Camelot. Going to V17 isn't going to be a holiday. Further, there's no guarantee that the Chinese won't be able to break out of Vice Admiral Cunningham's planned blockade. If they do, they'll be heading straight for us. We are going to be prepared for that eventuality. Here are my purposed deployments...."

As the Commodore droned on about her plans for fixed defenses and picket patrols, James lost focus. He was still seething. He had proven himself. He had won some honor back for his family name and he was working to undo all the financial harm his father had caused. The King had no right to interfere with his career like this! I'm going to get my own back, James thought to himself. If I survive this I'm going to make sure the King regrets his pettiness!

"Commander Somerville, are you listening?" The Commodore's voice brought him back to reality. Looking up he only nodded.

"Very good, well then you will know that I'm assigning you to the V34 system. I want you to survey it for any Chinese ships lying in stealth. Then you are to monitor the system. It is the Vice Admiral's belief that the Swedes will head to the system after the blockade is set up. If they do, you will be there to observe what they get up to. You are not to contact them or reveal your presence at any time. If anything happens you can jump out quietly and come and inform me. Is that understood?"

"Yes sir," James responded without any enthusiasm.

Patrol duty. Patrol duty in a system not likely to even see any action. If the Chinese did manage to break through the blockade and head to Excalibur, the first *Drake* would hear of it would be when news of a victory or defeat got to V34, probably days later.

Shaking his head, James got up to leave as soon as the briefing was over. He didn't wait around to chat to his fellow Captains. Instead he made his way to one of *Churchill's* flight decks. When he got there, he ordered the first available shuttle to take him back to *Drake*. He didn't have to wait long as he was the first to request transit back to his ship. Sitting in the shuttle James had time to think over his situation. Once he calmed down, he began to see the pros and cons.

If there were a battle, and Vice Admiral Cunningham seemed to think it likely, then it would be a costly one. The British may have the tech advantage but the Chinese had already shown just how much damage they could deal out. Being assigned to an out of the way system meant his chances of getting back to Earth and Christine had just gone up considerably. Yet, he would be returning with no glory and quite likely no prospect of promotion. If the British fleet won a victory, there would be no end to the stream of successful officers returning home with combat experience. James would be pushed down the list.

Realization dawned on him. King Edward must have had quite the dilemma. If he had used his influence to get James posted to V17 there was a good chance he would get rid of him. Yet there was also a chance that James could win more fame for himself and rise further in the public's eyes. Instead King Edward had gone for the safer option. By keeping James out of the way he was ensuring the media would forget about him and he wouldn't have a chance to force his way further up the command chain.

As his anger began to fade, James steeled himself for the future. His earlier vow would not be forgotten. If he got back to Earth, he was going to repay the King in kind, even if it took fifty years. For the present though, he would make do. If he were going to be assigned to a secondary system then he would make sure he carried out his duty to the best of his ability. When the opportunity for promotion came he would be ready. He wasn't going to remain a lowly commander with a tattered name and little financial power or political clout forever.

As the shuttle approached *Drake,* James leant over to look out the viewing port. He couldn't help but feel proud. *Drake* was beautiful in her own bulky way. Her single starboard missile tube was open as a tech team carried out repairs. The electromagnetic rings that formed the missile tube glowed blue as they were tested. They made the open tube look like a giant glowing eye. On her top side the single heavy plasma cannon gave *Drake* a menacing image.

Intermittent sparks of electricity could be seen coming from amidst the various sensor nodes on *Drake's* belly.

Just before he had left the ship James had approved the installation of a towed array. It was a hastily designed external mount that housed a single recon drone. Like the stealth drones, it was engineless the extra space taken up by all the latest passive sensors. The external mount also housed over five hundred kilometers of thin nano carbon cabling.

A freighter had brought enough of the towed arrays to outfit all the survey ships operating within the Void. The thinking was that the towed arrays would give a ship in stealth two points of contact with an enemy vessel. It would allow *Drake* or any of the other survey ships to triangulate any contacts they detected to get a better sensor reading and, if necessary, compute a better firing solution.

James thought it rather ironic that *Drake* was one of the first ships to be outfitted with one and yet she would not be going to V17. No matter though, he was already thinking of a number of ways that he could use the towed array.

One the shuttle docked with *Drake* James made his way to the bridge. He wanted to see how the repairs and new installations were coming along. When he got there Gupta was sitting in the command chair, she nodded to him as he entered.

"Don't get up, I'm not here to relieve you, I just want an update on how things are going?" James asked.

Gupta cleared her throat and then began to give a rundown of everything that had happened in the five hours James had been away. As she finished she asked, "how did it go with the Vice Admiral, what is our next assignment?"

James grimaced, but they would find out soon enough so he spoke up for the rest of the bridge to hear. "Vice Admiral Cunningham will be taking the bulk of the fleet to V17 to set up a blockade of the system. We have been assigned to Commodore West's squadron and given the task of patrolling V34."

"What!" Sub Lieutenant Fisher almost shouted before she realized where she was. "I mean, I'm sorry sir, but why aren't we going to V17? *Drake* has proved herself, surly we have earned the right to go with the fleet?"

"Those were my thoughts exactly Lieutenant," James replied. "I voiced them to the Admiral but you won't be surprised to know that it's not our job to deal out assignments. We'll go where we're told and do our duty."

As he turned to leave Gupta got up from the command chair and followed him to the exit of the bridge. "Commander, surely there must be a mistake. I know we have to follow orders but look at what we have done already. Can't the Admiral see that we, that you, will be useful in the battle to come?"

James took a moment to reply, he was a little taken aback at Gupta's concern. "I can't speak for the Admiral's views but I will tell you this, he received a letter from the King. We have the only assignment we going to get."

A look of disgust came over Gupta's face. James didn't know if it was directed at him for getting them into this situation or at the King for his abuse of power. Either way he wanted to defuse the situation. Gupta was meant to be the officer on watch. Reaching out he rested a reassuring hand on her shoulder.

"I apologize for this. My actions have cost you a promotion and now they have gotten us assigned to a backwater system. I promise you, I'll do my best to see that when *Drake* next returns to Earth you will be ear marked for a promotion to Commander yourself."

James realized his words had done the trick when Gupta's anger seemed to turn to embarrassment. With reddened cheeks she replied, "I'm not angry with you, sir. You have proven yourself over the last few months; I am beginning to enjoy serving under you. My family was held down and walked all over on New India for generations because of their social status. Those in power did everything they could to keep them down. I may not know first had what it is like to be bullied by someone in power but I have heard all about it. My anger isn't for my own promotion opportunities. The RSN needs officers like you, our King shouldn't be jeopardizing that."

Stunned, James had to take a step back. He had noticed that their working relationship had been slowly improving since their showdown. Yet he hadn't realized she had warmed to him so much. Replacing his hand on her shoulder, he smiled at her and said, "Well I'm encouraged you feel that way. I'm glad we can understand each other better. I have to admit, I misjudged you. My anger when I took over command of *Drake* soured our relationship. I hope we will be able to get over that."

Before Gupta could reply James went on, "You will be getting that promotion but for now we have a ship to see too."

Blushing again, Gupta hurriedly turned around and headed back to the command chair without a word. After a moment James also turned and went back to his quarters for a much needed shower. His time on *Churchill* hadn't left him feeling particularly clean and relaxed.

*

Three days later James and Gupta were both on the bridge again. *Drake* had spent the last eight hours making her way out to the edge of Excalibur's mass shadow. The whole crew by now knew that they were being sent away from where all the action was to be. Reactions had ranged from anger to disappointment and even to relief. James had been keeping an eye on the crew. He was worried about morale. His crew had put their lives on the line time and time again over the last few months. They were taking the snub hard. It hadn't helped that *Drake* had been put to the back of the refueling queue. They had been made to wait for two days while every other ship in the fleet had gone ahead of them to refill their stores of He3 from the supply freighters that had come in with Cunningham's fleet.

As *Drake* had been nearing the end of her fuel supply, they had had to power down some of the non-essential equipment just to make sure they had enough left to maneuver to the tankers. James had protested and demanded *Drake* be moved up the list, yet with no avail. *Drake* had been deemed a low priority.

Trying to put that behind him, James stared out at the stars. They were about to make the jump to V34. He consoled himself with the thought that at least he would be able to enjoy the freedom of independent command again.

Chapter 16 - Best Laid Plans

It has been the same story time and time again down through human history. We do not know when to give up. When we invest in something we cling to it even when it begins to fail and let us down. War is no exception.

-Excerpt from Empire's Rising, 3002 AD

7th April 2465 AD, Beijing, Earth

This time Minister Quin hadn't been able to keep his anger in check. With a loud thud he smashed his fist against the conference table. "This is unacceptable, I promise you High Admiral Zheng will be severely punished. He outnumbered the British, there is no excuse, it was his own incompetence that has caused this defeat. He must be punished."

Na was barely listening; a British courier had just brought news of the battle of Excalibur. The British were keeping most of the details of the battle to themselves but what had leaked to the media had been telling. A small British force had managed to drive a larger Chinese fleet away from the system they were calling Excalibur. The defeat was all the more telling because everyone around the table knew the force makeup of the Chinese fleet that was operating in the Void. No one had expected their two battleships to be defeated. It had seemed impossible that the British would have been able to stand against them. Yet they had found a way. Even worse, there was no information on Chinese losses. For all they knew both battleships had been destroyed. Na realized that the battle would reflect badly on the Chinese construction policy. Quin, the Minister for Defense, was simply trying to cover his posterior. His anger was probably being fueled by fear as much as actual animosity. High Admiral Zheng had been Quin's personal choice to command the fleet sent into the Void. Quin was in trouble.

It seemed that no one else was paying much attention to Quin's rant either for as soon as there was a lull in his shouting Minister Xiang broke in, "We can find a scapegoat later. Now we need to address the situation at hand. Chang, surely your intelligence networks have managed to get more information from the RSN than the media outlets?"

Na sighed inwardly. The Politburo had always been more about power plays than actually cooperating to accomplish a goal. Xiang, the Minister for Development and Chang, the Minister for Intelligence, were the two most powerful men at the table and they were direct competitors. Currently Chang held sway over the politburo and the president was his puppet. Yet things could change. Xiang was clearly angling to lay much of the blame for this catastrophe on Chang and his associates.

Glaring at his opponent, Chang reluctantly stood and brought up a number of files on the holo display. "As it happens we have managed to get some further information. You are looking at a personnel file listing the deceased RSN officers from ships operating in the Void. After cross checking this with personal assignment information, we already have an estimate the British losses. Our best guess is that they lost a heavy cruiser, two light cruisers, a destroyer and some smaller ships.

"Apart from some new super weapon there is simply no way the British could have heavily defeated our forces and not taken greater losses. My analysts have concluded that whatever victory the British have had, they can't have caused us too much damage."

Chang made a conciliatory glance at Quin before continuing, "Granted, High Admiral Zheng will still have to give an account of his actions. However, we don't think that he has managed to lose all the forces under his command yet."

As Na looked over to Quin, he saw him visibly relax. Chang's glance had been enough to reassure him that the blame for the defeat would rest squarely on the High Admiral's shoulders and not his immediate superiors. As Minister for Defense, Quin wielded oversight of the Chinese naval and ground forces. That included the building program that had decided to push ahead with the new battleships at great expense. If it turned out those ships had been easily defeated, it would be hard for him to avoid the ramifications.

Seemingly without noticing the effect his glance had, Chang continued, "The reason I called you here was not to cry over the defeat at Excalibur. Rather, we need to press on. As I said, my analysts indicate that High Admiral Zheng should still have most of his force intact, if somewhat damaged. By now he has already received another set of reinforcements and there is a further squadron on the way to the Void. It is my understanding that this last set of reinforcements are just a week away from reaching the Void."

Again Chang looked over to Quin, this time waiting long enough to get an affirmative nod before continuing. "Minister Quin has already informed me that we cannot spare any more ships to send to the Void. Not without leaving our systems uncovered and tempting the British to attack us elsewhere. As that is the case we have to discuss other options. It just so happens that there are already a few plans ready to implement."

Sitting down, Chang waved to one of the fleet officers sitting behind his chair. Na wanted to get up and shout that this was all insanity. Blood had already been shed over the Void. Clearly the British weren't going to roll over and accept Chinese demands. That fact alone should have changed the Politburo's approach. Never mind the bloodshed. Instead they were pushing on full steam with a plan that would only lead to more senseless loss.

The only thing that kept him in his seat was the fact that he was already working to bring the war to a close, that and the knowledge that speaking up would do no good. He had already lost the respect of his peers. He had been voicing his concerns about the war but they had been falling on increasingly deaf ears. Chang and Xiang had both made it clear that peace was not an option. Na did not want to betray his country but this war was going to do more harm than any peace. Yet, because the two most powerful men in the room were set on continuing the conflict, there was no hope of stopping it from this room. All his continued protests would accomplish would be to lose him further support. There were other means he could explore though.

Oblivious to Na's hidden thoughts the meeting continued uninterrupted. The naval officer took control of the holo display and brought up a 3D image of a small space ship. "Ministers, I have been asked to brief you on the X32. This is a top secret project we have been working on at naval intelligence. As you can see the X32 is a small craft, much smaller than even the corvettes the British use for point defense purposes.

"Previously, military planners in our navy and others have dismissed the use of small, fast attack craft. The amount of valstronium needed to protect them from cosmic radiation is prohibitive. Plus, the fact that they could only carry a small payload and were not significantly faster than other larger ships limited their development among the other powers. However, given the recent advances in inertial compensators and stealth tech, we believe we have found a use for such a craft.

"The X32 is what we are calling a missileboat. They are outfitted with two anti-ship missiles. Their planned role is for surprise attacks. A squadron of X32's will be inserted into an enemy system by a mothership, essentially a carrier in space. The X32's will then accelerate to their top speed of 0.32c and coast further into the system. Their anti-ship missiles pack quite a punch but at the cost of only having a limited range, thus they will have to get close. Yet once in range of their targets, preferably stationary ones, or targets that have a predictable orbit, they can launch their missiles with devastating effect. Their stealth tech should make it almost impossible to detect them prior to launch and after launch their maneuverability and high speed should ensure that they exit the combat zone unharmed.

"The X32's are therefore a first strike craft. Designed to be used to attack enemy hard points, industrial nodes or ships in orbit, they will soften up a target before the fleet moves in."

Hanshon, the Minister for Energy raised his and asked a question, "and how are the ships recovered. Surly a ship that small won't be able to carry the fuel to reverse course and return to its mothership?"

"Correct," the fleet officer said. "The ships were designed to be expendable if it comes to it. They will have enough fuel to decelerate and come to rest at the other side of the target system. If they can be recovered after a battle they will be. Obviously their recovery will not be a high priority in the middle of a battle but once hostilities are finished they can be picked up. If, for some reason, they cannot be recovered the damage they should be able to inflict will still be worth their loss. With that in mind the X32's have been highly automated and only require a crew of three. For the most part the X32's will be manned by volunteers."

Standing Chang nodded to the officer, "Thank you Commander,

that will be all." Briefly he scanned the faces of his colleagues around the table before continuing. "As you can see we still have a few tricks up our sleeves. Given recent developments I believe it is time to bring the X32's to the table."

Na couldn't help himself. "But Minister Chang, these weapons are first strike weapons. Fighting is already well underway in the Void. Do you mean to expand the fighting to other systems? If we launch a surprise attack against another British world it could spell disaster for us, they will respond in kind!"

"Sit down!" Chang shouted. "If I want the opinion of a junior minister around this table I will ask. And let me make this clear Minister Na, I do not want to hear one from you!"

Chang stared Na down until he relented and returned to his seat. A new wave of frustration and helplessness washed over Na. His seniors had almost brought the People's Republic of China to its financial knees with their mismanagement and military spending. Now they were going to threaten their own nation's priceless infrastructure by giving the British a thirst for revenge. There would only be one response from the British if one of their home systems were attacked.

Satisfied that he had intimidated Na into silence Chang continued, "As I was saying, we need to show the British that we do not intend to back down. Both we and the British have committed a significant percentage of our fleet to the Void. What we have left is needed for defending our systems. I can only assume the British are in a similar situation. The X32's will allow us to strike a decisive blow against their infrastructure and force them to pull ships out of the Void. That should give High Admiral Zheng and the rest of our reinforcements enough time to hit back with their own counter attack as well.

"It is my wish that we take a vote on this issue immediately. I therefore propose that we vote to approve a series of strikes by X32's on the Cook and Britannia systems."

As Xiang stood, Na desperately held onto a flicker of hope that he was going to try and stop the attack.

"There are inherent risks with this approach. If we open up another front in the war the British will follow suit. What guarantees do you have that they won't hit us back just as hard?" he asked instead.

"It's simple," Chang replied, "we will hit them hard and fast. The X32's will cause devastating damage. Once we have demonstrated their power and our willingness to use them, we will offer the British terms. They will have to vacate the Void but apart from that we will offer to go back to the status quo. We won't try to take any other systems or reparations from them."

Nodding, Xiang was clearly thinking about Chang's answer. "And what if something changes in the meantime. It could take weeks or months to mount such an attack. If the British can drive High Admiral Zheng out of the Void they will think victory is in their grasp. Even if we hit them hard they may not want to surrender."

"That won't be a problem," Chang countered. "Two squadrons of X32's are already in place outside the Cook system. On our orders they will immediately begin their attack and then move onto Britannia."

"Wait a minute," Minister Hanshon interjected. "What if the British already know of these ships? They could be preparing to mount an attack of their own. We all know how good their intelligence service is."

"Not this time," Chang assured the assembly. "Each squadron has been berthed within a *Mustang* class transport freighter. They are of American design and almost exclusively owned by independent American traders. Already both freighters have passed through the shift passages to the Alpha and Cook systems without being stopped by British checks. As we speak, they are sitting on the edge of the Cook system awaiting orders. All we have to do is approve their orders and the attack will commence. We have another freighter, this time of Japanese construction, ready to be sent to rendezvous with them and give the go order. All we have to do now is vote. Are there any other questions?"

When no one stood or raised a hand Chang sat and pressed a button on the conference table. A group of aides entered and began to distribute the ballot papers. A hold over from generations ago the paper voting was meant to keep it anonymous. The reality was that each member voted with his faction, there was never any suspense.

Na watched the vote in despair. As a junior member he didn't have a vote on tactical decisions. Instead he had to watch his 'betters' unanimously agree to plunge his beloved country further towards the brink of destruction. Na had earned his position thanks to his grandfather's and great grandfather's foresight. Both men had invested heavily in the first Chinese colonies. Na and his father had followed their lead and, as a result, Na was one of the wealthiest men in Chinese space. For the last twenty years he had been using that wealth to promote further colonial expansion and exploration. Eventually it had landed him his role on the politburo as Minister for Exploration. Yet, because of his wealth and his off world investments, he knew just how precarious the situation was in the colonies. All of the political power in the communist party still resided on Earth. His fellow politburo members only looked to the colonies as a source of wealth and raw materials to be used to build up China. As a result, the economies of the colonies were delicately balanced, constantly trying to stave off disaster as the men in power funneled much of their wealth and profits back to Earth.

The war had changed all that. With trade being limited and industrial output being focused on military matters, the colonies were being neglected. Na had been using his personal wealth to try and alleviate some of the worst problems yet it was just a drop in the ocean. Already he had noticed significant opposition to the war developing among the populace. Many of the older couples in Chinese society had children who had moved to the colonies. In turn, many of the students that attended the best Chinese universities were children of off world settlers. Through both lines of communication, news of the effects of the war was spreading back to Earth. People were unhappy. The rest of the politburo members had not realized the window of opportunity that this was opening but Na had.

When the voting was completed, Chang sent his naval aid out to convey the Politburo's orders to the awaiting freighter that would then travel to Cook with the orders to attack. Satisfied that he had gotten his way he yielded the floor to Minister of the Interior.

"I wish to bring you all up to date with domestic affairs here on Earth. As you know we have refrained from mobilizing our ground forces as they are not likely to be needed and we didn't want to cause too much strain on the economy. There have been some problems with switching other areas of our economy to a war footing. Supplies both at home and in our colonies have been running low, though we are largely on top of the problems. As a result, our people have not had to feel much strain, overall their optimism is high.

"We are getting some indications of organized student opposition to the war. At the moment it doesn't look like it is going to cause us a great concern. It does indicate a more widespread problem however. My general read on the populace is that they are confused. They know the importance of the Void and they are not too worried about the strain the war is putting on our economy. However, most believed the information coming from the UN. We have tried to put our spin on it but so far we had little success. As it stands, it looks like we fired first, both in the Damang Incident and in the Void. It also appears that we have rejected a fair British offer to share the Void. In another country I would say we should begin to worry. I believe our people will remain loyal however. They may not understand our actions but they all trust the faithfulness of the Communist Party, we can rely on them to back us, no matter what."

Na was not surprised at this attitude. The Communist Party had ruled in China for over five hundred years. It had gone through some changes in philosophy and structure true, but China was still a one party state and the people were loyal to their party. The expansion into space hadn't been easy for some of the more democratic countries. The liberal American government had fallen to a conservative coup that had wanted American to regain the lead in the space race. France and Britain had just survived an Islamic revolution after the Meccan incident and whilst Britain had quickly gotten back on her feet, it had taken France decades. Other countries had gone through their own troubles too yet China had remained strong. Her people had remained loyal.

"What about the recent news of defeat, how do you see that affecting the populace's mood?" Chang asked.

"It is too early to tell at the moment." The Minister of the Interior answered. "If we can control the spin on the battle, we may be able to undo much of the damage. I feel we need a win and quickly though. If the people see us losing and can't understand why we are fighting in the first place, the situation may change quickly. My fear is that the spin coming out of the UN and from allies of the British may also begin to persuade some of our people. In the long run I am confident they will remain loyal but we may experience the occasional short term problem."

"That's all very well," Xiang said. "I think everyone would agree that we don't want to take any chances though. What measures are you taking to ensure we don't have to divert any resources to handling the populace?"

"To date," the Interior Minister began, "we have severely clamped down on any independent media sources that have tried to operate within our sphere of influence. We have also greatly increased our cyber warfare division. The British are trying to flood our datanet with propaganda about the war but we now have enough specialists to take down their uploads as soon as they appear. My PR division is putting the finishing touches on a release concerning the battle as we speak. The general line will be that the so called battle at Excalibur was simply a skirmish by a light Chinese squadron testing the British defenses."

"There is one problem with that approach," Xiang announced. "If you portray it as a small skirmish then the public will be expecting a decisive victory to follow. In fact, given everything that has happened so far, I think that is exactly what they need to hear about. I would like to purpose that we send orders to Admiral Zheng to bring the British fleet to battle. Only by forcing a decisive victory will we be able to show our public that this war is in our best interest."

"For once I agree with you Minister," Chang said. "It's time we brought this war to a close. The attacks on British systems will be a first step. Defeating their fleet in the Void will finish them off and appease our populace at the same time. Now, if the junior members of this meeting would excuse us, I wish to discuss the finer details with my colleagues."

With that Na got up and left. He knew now that Chang and Xiang would never end this war. They were taking China to the brink of disaster. Thankfully, he already had contingency plans in place. It was time to activate some of them.

*

7th April 2465 AD, HMS *Vulcan*, Earth

As Admiral Somerville was sitting at his desk a chime from his office door alerted him someone wanted to enter. With a command he opened the door and Admiral Russell walked in.

"Good afternoon sir," Russell began and, without letting Somerville welcome him he continued. "I have just received some sensitive intelligence information. One of my operatives in China was contacted by an intermediary claiming to bring a message from Minister Na."

"Minister Na?" Somerville asked.

"He's a junior member of the Politburo responsible for overseeing the Chinese exploration efforts."

"Ah, I thought his name was familiar, what has he got to say to us?"

"That's just it. I'm not sure if we can take it seriously or not. He is claiming that he represents a faction within the Chinese government that wants peace, a faction that didn't want to go to war in the first place. But that is not the most time pressing issue. As evidence of his sincerity he has passed us information on the next Chinese plan of attack. He is claiming that they have secretly constructed a number of missileboats, essentially small fighter type ships. They are supposed to already be in the Cook system awaiting orders to attack our orbital installations. According to Na the Politburo gave those orders an hour ago."

"Right," Somerville said as he jumped up and sprang into action. "If there is even a chance this is true we need to act immediately." On his control terminal he punched in the commands to open a COM channel with the courier ship *Swift*.

"Commander, I have no time to talk. I need you to immediately boost towards the Alpha shift passage. You'll be taking orders to Cook. I'll transmit them to you once I have them ready. You have my permission to break all the safety procedures. Get to Cook as fast as you can."

After the Commander nervously acknowledged his orders Somerville ended the COM link. "Right," he said turning back to Russell. "We have four hours until we need to transmit our orders to *Swift* before she jumps out. We need to decide what orders to send to Cook and how we're going to respond to this escalation. Then we need to decide what to do with Na. We have been looking for an opportunity to unite the popular unrest in China against the Politburo. This might just be our chance."

Chapter 17 – Incursion

The greatest fear in warfare is the unknown. This hasn't changed since the dawn of time. What is the enemy planning? Where are his troops? Ever since humans stepped foot into space, this fear has been magnified. With the constant ongoing revolution of technology, commanders must deal with the unending question; what is the latest trick the enemy is going to use and can it be countered?

-Excerpt from Empire Rising, 3002 AD

11th April 2465 AD, HMS *Ghost*, destroyer class, outer edge of the Cook system.

Third Lieutenant Rosin Johnston was sitting in the command chair on the bridge of HMS *Ghost* when the sensor officer motioned for her to come to his station. *Ghost* had just left Cook's main shipyard a month ago and was in the last phase of her work up before she could be deployed.

"The sensors have been picking up some intermittent thermal signals, Lieutenant. At first I thought they were just a bug we hadn't worked out of the system yet but they are too regular."

Leaning over the sensor officer's shoulder Lieutenant Johnston remained silent as she looked at the information the consoles was displaying. "What vector are these readings coming from?" she asked.

The sensor officer manipulated his console to display a 3D image of the Cook system. *Ghost* was at the very edge of the mass shadow caused by Cook's star. She was out here calibrating her deep space sensors and preparing for a stealth run into the system as the last check of her systems before she could be declared battle worthy. The whole crew was looking forward to seeing how far *Ghost* could sneak into the Cook system before the local defenders spotted her. The 3D image marked out a line proceeding from *Ghost*, heading further out of the system giving an estimated position of the sensor readings.

"As you can see Lieutenant the computer can't get a good estimate of the range of the thermal signals, only their angle."

"That's strange," Johnston thought out loud. "Whatever it is it's even further out of the system than us. There is no good reason for a ship to be so far from Cook." Speaking up for everyone on the bridge to hear her she continued, "navigation, plot us a course towards these signals, though don't take us directly towards them. Approach at an angle so we can get a better fix on the range. Sensors you have the bridge; I'm going to go and inform the Captain. Oh, and don't take us out of stealth." The Lieutenant ordered as she left and walked down the corridor towards the Captain's quarters.

An hour later Captain Lightfoot was the one sitting in the command chair contemplating what was going on. After surviving the Damang Incident and safely returning to Earth he had found himself a bit of a celebrity. He had been forced to endure a lengthy debrief and then had been assigned to the RSN Tactical Think Tank. Basically a group of RSN officers and other specialists brought in from outside the RSN, the Think Tank's job was to assess new battle tactics and incorporate new technologies into the RSN's existing tactical doctrine. He had enjoyed the mental stimulation but with the Think Tank based in London he had been plagued by the media. Eventually, the Admiralty had given him a newly minted destroyer, HMS *Ghost*, as a reward and he was glad to be aboard a spaceship again.

As his ship continued deeper into open space he reviewed the sensor readings once more. The strange thermal blips had continued for another ten minutes before disappearing. The sensor officer had backtracked his readings and identified another five blips the computer estimated were a part of the same pattern. All in all that made thirty estimated blips. What would make such a small thermal blip and yet hope to go anywhere? They were hours away from Cook itself. If the heat emissions were from a ship they hadn't been large enough to do anything more than effect a course change. Yet the blips had all originated from the same location. Whatever was causing them wasn't moving. If they were from a fission reactor restarting or experiencing difficulties it had to have been the smallest fission reactor in space. What purpose could it serve? The rhythm his fingers were strumming on his command chair suddenly stopped as it hit him!

"Navigation, make a direct course for the blips, take us there at full stealth acceleration."

"Yes sir," came the reply.

"Tactical, I want you to run a number of simulations based on our data of the Cook defense network. Assume those blips are either thermal leakage from a long-range stealth missile's drive kicking in or from a small fission reactor starting off. See what the chances are of Cook detecting such a missile before it could get into attack range of the industrial complex in orbit."

Fusion reactors powered all British anti-ship missiles. They were smaller and easier to produce in large numbers. A missile with a fission reactor would have a much greater range. However, they would be slower and any target they could attack would have lots of time to get out of the way; unless, of course, the location of the missile's targets could be predicted: like the geosynchronous orbit of an orbital shipyard or factory.

"Communications, I want you to prepare a brief information packet to send back to Cook. Detail our findings and my belief that the thermal readings could be from some new form of Chinese missile designed to approach the inner system under stealth. Let them know what to look out for."

Lightfoot paused and looked back to his navigation officer. "How long until we can get into visual range of the area?" he asked.

"Another hour at this rate of acceleration sir."

*

Aboard the battlestation *Chester* in orbit around Cook, Commander Harte was on watch. Five hours ago a courier from Earth hand jumped into the system. It had been accelerating at full speed towards Cook ever since. Only five minutes ago the first message from the courier had reached the battlestation. It was broadcasting a warning that RSNI believed there was an imminent Chinese plan to attack Cook and its orbitals. Harte had already sent the information to Admiral McGreevy, who was in charge of Cook's defenses. The Admiral was on his way up. When the second message from HMS *Ghost* arrived Harte sat up in his chair. He had hoped to leave any big decisions to the Admiral. Yet the Admiral wouldn't thank him for delaying if there was a serious threat to his system. Speaking loudly he addressed the various officers who were manning the sensor and tactical stations that made up the battlestation's command and control center. "I want us to bring the system's defenses to alert status one. We have a credible threat. All ships and battlestations are to go to powered active scanning. I want our pickets to establish an outer ring thirty light minutes from the planet. Nothing is to get close to Cook without us knowing about it. Pay special attention to this vector," he said as he brought up the data from *Ghost*. "Our Chinese friends may be sending us a few unwelcome presents."

*

As the first visual images were picked up by *Ghost*, Lightfoot had to admit he was surprised by what he was looking at. He had been expecting some kind of Chinese warship. Instead there were two American built freighters. Could the American's be carrying out some sort of espionage on the Cook system? It hardly made sense. American freighters passed through the Cook system all the time. They had no need to go around sneaking about in the outer system. The Chinese must have bought them he concluded. "Tactical, what does the computer make of the images? Is there any sign that the freighters have been modified to fire missiles?" he asked.

"No sir," the tactical officer replied. "As far we can tell the freighters are the same as when they left their American shipyards. If there are any changes they must be on their underbelly, it's the only side of the ships we can't get a visual of."

"What systems do they have fixed to their underside?" Lightfoot snapped.

"Nothing much sir, most of the underside is taken up with the loading bay. This class of freighter is designed to allow atmospheric craft to fly up from the surface of a planet, enter the loading bay and then return directly to the surface with their cargo."

"What is the likelihood they are unloading missiles through the docking bay and using some kind of small craft to reorientate them before firing them into the system?" Lightfoot followed up.

"It's possible sir, but I don't think it is very likely"

"Why not?"

"Well," the tactical officer began. "You would want to be very careful unloading any missiles, especially from a ship not specifically designed to handle them. Even if they had two tugs to take the missiles out of the freighter and line the missiles up, it would take quite a while to unload thirty missiles. All our sensors blips occurred in pairs. That would suggest two tugs, yet we haven't spotted any yet. And even if they are there the time between blips was very short. It seems more likely that whatever was coming out of the docking bay was maneuvering itself."

At that the bridge went silent. Everyone was thinking the same thing but it was the First Lieutenant who was the first to voice it. "Some kind of small fighter like craft?"

Lightfoot had his doubts but before he could voice them the tactical officer chimed in, "it's possible sir, given enough spare valstronium a small ship could be made reasonably safe for high velocities. If it could be kept relatively stealthy they would make good surprise attack craft. They'd be damned hard to spot at anything more than close range."

Slowly, a new picture dawned on Lightfoot as he seriously considered the possibility. The Chinese must have bought the two freighters and converted them to house these small attack craft. The freighters would have had no problem passing the checks in the Sol and Alpha systems unless someone actually boarded them and obviously no one had. Whatever armaments the small attack craft were carrying were going to be bad for the defenders of Cook. "Communications send a signal back into the system. Inform the Admiral that we believe these two freighters have just deployed a group of fighters. Let them know that the fighters may be coming in on a different attack vector than the one we sent them. If they are in any way maneuverable, they will alter course before lining up for their attack run. A straight line into the system would only lead our defenses back to the two freighters."

"Message away sir."

"Good, navigation how long until we get within weapons range of the two freighters?" Lightfoot asked.

Instead of replying the navigation officer frantically danced his fingers across his command terminal. "One moment sir, the two freighters have just powered up their drives and are altering course."

There were two beeps in quick succession from one of the secondary display screens. Each beep indicated the gravimetric sensors had detected a ship jumping into shift space.

"I'm afraid we have lost them sir. Both freighters just jumped into shift space. The computer is trying to calculate their precise route now. It may take up to thirty minutes though. The only thing I can say for sure is that they didn't jump towards a shift passage. It looks like they jumped somewhere further round the edge of the system."

"Damn," Lightfoot swore as he punched his fists down on his command chair. Before saying anything else that might give away his disappointment he began to think. Whatever size those fighters are they can't have their own jump drives. That means they have to meet up with those freighters again if they want to get out of here after their attack. "Tactical, bring up the rough estimate of the direction the freighters jumped."

When the image appeared on the holo display Lightfoot studied it. "It looks like they jumped at an angle to make their way around the mass shadow and towards the Britannia jump passage, what do you think tactical?"

As the tactical officer began to run the numbers, Lightfoot pictured the Cook system in his mind. Every solar system created a mass shadow within which the shift drive wouldn't work because of the system's gravimetric field. That same gravimetric field also created a bubble in the dark matter that was strewn about the galaxy. Often the gap between the mass shadow and the outer edge of the dark matter bubble was negligible. Yet, in certain systems like Cook, it was large enough to allow ships to make a series of shift drive jumps around the edge of the system. Doing so, allowed ships to move from one shift passage to another without having to enter the inner system. Since Cook was colonized the British government had had problems collecting transport fees from shipping companies who ordered their freighters to skirt around the edge of the Cook system to avoid any fees.

"It's possible sir," the tactical officer began after reviewing the data, "the Cook system has one of the largest bubbles of dark matter. If they jumped far enough out, they could turn around and jump back along the mass shadow towards the shift passage. That or they could disembark another flight of fighters to make a second attack run on the system from another angle."

Lightfoot almost didn't hear his Lieutenant's last sentence. If they sortie another attack there was nothing he could do, but if they were planning to regroup with their fighters and then go to Britannia and launch another strike… that he could deal with.

"Navigation, plot the likely least time jump pattern those freighters would use to reach the Britannia passage. Then plot us a series of jumps to follow, only keep us 1.1 light hours back from them. They probably don't have military grade gravimetric sensors but I don't want to take the chance they get a sniff of us.

*

237

"Flight Leader, this is *Red Dragon Two*. The power readings on our impulse drive are fluctuating beyond the safety parameters. We're going to have to drop back out of formation."

Flight Leader Le cursed after he keyed an acknowledgement. That was the second missileboat that had been forced to drop back. After an initial burst of their impulse engines to clear the freighters, his ships had cruised into the Cook system for an hour before lighting off their engines again. If they were spotted they didn't want to draw any attention to the freighters that were their only ride home. He now had his flight of twenty-eight remaining missileboats making a slow burn up above the star's ecliptic. Once far enough away from the freighters, they would turn back down and charge into the system to deal out as much destruction as possible.

As his ships continued their cruise, Le began to zone out his surroundings and enter into the meditation technique he had been teaching himself. Ever since the first day of training for operating the new missileboats he had had to endure long simulator runs. Almost every attack plan his superiors had been able to come up with involved long engine burns into a system toward their targets. It could play havoc on anyone's nerves, being so closely confined for up to ten hours at a time. The only way Le had stayed sane during his training had been using a mediation technique he had downloaded off the datanet and had been teaching himself. When the time came for his missileboats to alter course and begin their dive into the system he gave the order, barely noticing it. Even when another missileboat reported engine trouble and had to drop back he was able to stay calm.

Eventually they got to within one light hour of their target. Slowly Le brought himself out of his meditative state. Almost as soon as he did his ships began to report active radars ahead. At this range Le knew they could only be from a ship's main search radar. Someone knew they were coming. Instead of being able to carry out a simple sweep in towards Cook, he now had to contemplate dancing his way past a number of patrols before he could get close enough to launch his missiles.

Before leaving Chinese space he had drilled for just such a situation with his fellow pilots. Everyone knew what to do. Their one advantage was that their ships were too small for the system pickets to hit with their anti-ship missiles. They would have to close to plasma cannon and anti-missile range. If Le could manage it, he should be able to dart through the picket line before they realized that they would have to close with him.

For the next ten minutes he allowed his missileboat's computer to analyze all the radar energy his flight was picking up. Soon he had a rough plot of where all the picket ships were. Carefully, he planned out a route past them all and sent it to the rest of his ships via laser links. Any radio transmissions would give them away.

When the final missileboat acknowledged Le sent out the order. As one, the missileboats turned onto the new vector. He was reasonably confident that the pickets wouldn't pick up the thermal readings from their small maneuvering thrusters. However, they would have to make their next course adjustment only twenty light minutes from one of the picket ships. That was going to be close.

All of a sudden the radar sweeps from the pickets began to change. The sweeps switched from a regular pattern to random high-powered beams. It also seemed as if the pickets themselves had given up their pre-set flight path and were now deviating their trajectory randomly. *They know we're not missiles*, Le thought to himself. Or at least standard missiles, they think we can maneuver past their pickets. Le smiled. With luck they wouldn't realize just how good their stealth tech was. It had been one of the Chinese intelligence services' better successes. His missileboat and the other twenty-six of his remaining flight were covered in an outer layer of the latest British radar-absorbing tech. Even the picket's random search patterns shouldn't be able to detect them all.

Le looked down as the computer beeped. The new trajectories of the picket ships meant they would have to make their next course change soon. If they delayed any longer the thermal bloom from their engines would be detected. Yet their new course would also now bring them closer to several British ships.

After sending the updated course to his flight Le keyed the audio link. "This is Dragon Leader. We're going to pass close to three British ships. If they detect you I want you to go to full power and make a run at the ship. See if you can take it out. Hopefully that will get everyone's attention and allow the rest of us to get through to our target. We all volunteered for this and we knew what we're signing up for. Good luck. Dragon Leader out."

*

Aboard the frigate *Ajax*, Commander Montgomery wasn't sure what the Admiral was thinking. Currently Montgomery had his ship powering through space making random course changes, often severe ones. That and having to run his primary search radar for so long was going to mean *Ajax* would be making a trip to the repair yard at Cook sometime soon for a replacement. He understood there was a creditable threat to the system's industry, but fighters? And ones that would be able to sneak past the outer picket the Admiral had set up – it seemed far-fetched! Orders were orders though and if *Ajax* had to spend some down time at the repair dock his crew would enjoy the shore leave.

Just then alarms went off around the bridge. "Commander," shouted one of the bridge officers, "we have picked up two small anomalies twenty light seconds off the starboard beam. They are very small but they are in the range of what we have been told to look for."

Montgomery tried to shake himself out of his doubtful thoughts but it was difficult. "So you think these are the fighters we are expecting?"

"They appear to match the data *Ghost* sent to the fleet sir," the officer replied.

"Very well, can you get a missile lock on them?"

"Not a clear one, they must have some radar absorbing tech. Even at this close range we're struggling to get a read on them," the tactical officer said.

"Ok here's the plan. We'll launch two missiles at each of those craft and then we'll come about and head for them at full power. Hopefully, when we get closer our radar will be able to burn through their protection and give the missiles something to lock onto. In the meantime we will try and get into plasma cannon range, we won't need a firm lock to begin to pick them off with plasma."

Before he had finished speaking the tactical officer had already updated the missile's firing solutions. "We're ready to fire when you give the word Commander," he reported.

"Navigation, are you ready to bring us about after we fire?"

"Yes sir."

"Ok Tactical, fire!"

Almost as soon as the four missiles left the acceleration tubes the two anomalies plus a third craft began to maneuver. Their engine plumes immediately gave them away, allowing the missiles to get a firm lock on them. It only took *Ajax's* tactical officer moments to fire another two missiles at the third craft. Yet as the missiles approached their targets, it was clear they weren't going to get things all their own way.

Two counter missiles shot off from each of the small craft, taking out two of the incoming missiles. Then the small craft went to full power and began drastic evasive maneuvers whilst powering up their ECM jammers. Three of the remaining four missiles missed their targets but one managed to get a proximity detonation. The small craft simply vanished in the expanding nuclear fireball.

As soon as the other two ships were clear of the missiles pursuing them they swung around and headed straight for *Ajax*. Commander Montgomery looked at the status of the missiles tubes. *Ajax* had expended all her missiles and it would take another two minutes to reload. By then the small craft would be within range of *Ajax's* counter missiles, never mind her plasma cannons.

"Tactical, target the main plasma cannons, then use point defenses to take them out if you have to."

Montgomery watched as the main plasma cannons had little effect. *Ajax's* cannons were designed to punch through the valstronium armor of another ship, not swat these smaller flies. The random jerks and twitches the two small craft were making made it impossible for the plasma cannons to track them.

Before Montgomery could think of a new plan the tactical officer broke his thoughts.

"Sir, I'm detecting two more launches from each of the fighters. They're not firing counter missiles, these things are bigger, anti-ship missiles I think."

As he stared at the plot the two incoming ships ceased their jerking to line up their shots. One blew up as a plasma bolt finally managed to make a direct hit yet the fighter had already got away its two missiles.

Quickly Montgomery worked out the closing speeds in his head. *Ajax* was heading straight for the fighters at 0.2c. The fighters were closing at 0.35c. If they had acceleration tubes their missiles could be coming in at over 0.4c, never mind the acceleration they would put on once their own engines kicked in. They would be closing at almost the speed of light!

Even as he shouted orders to put the ship into reverse and bring the point defense network to full, he knew it was too late. The sharp thud of counter missiles being fired off in rapid succession by the ship's automated defenses told him the missiles were already very close. Before he could finish his next thought he was thrown out of his command seat and right across the bridge as the concussive force of a missile hitting his ship threw everyone to the floor. As the missile detonated, *Ajax* exploded, leaving nothing behind but atoms in space. Alone the kinetic energy from the missile that had hit the ship vaporized the front nose section. The nuclear explosion finished the rest of the ship off.

Chapter 18 - Devastation

In contrast to the later wars humanity would get itself embroiled in, only rarely did the wars between the different human space faring powers overspill into attacks upon orbital and planetary targets. Yet when they did, the destruction always proved devastating.

-Excerpt from Empire's Rising, 3002 AD

11th April 2465 AD, inner Cook system.

Flight Leader Le didn't know whether to be overjoyed or depressed. He had managed to steer his flight of missileboats through the outer picket of Cook's defenders. After hours of cruising into the system they were now only ten minutes out from their target. Yet of the thirty missileboats he had begun the mission with, three had dropped back because of engine problems. The pickets had destroyed a further five, although his ships had taken out a frigate and a light cruiser. Now he only had twenty-two missileboats left. That gave him forty-four missiles, not enough to get the job done. Dismissing his pessimism, Le instead turned his mind to the task of re-evaluating his targets.

Three destroyers were frantically making their way towards Cook's orbital shipyard while a frigate was settling into position to cover the planet's main defensive battlestation that was in orbit over the largest city. A second frigate was boosting around the planet to join the defense of the battlestation.

Bringing up the visuals of the nearest frigate, Le knew his fears were justified. The frigate was one of the new flak frigates and that meant the second frigate likely was too. Since the intel from the Damang Incident, his officers had run simulations going up against the new British flak frigates with missileboats. They never ended well. While their small size and stealth technology made them hard to hit with conventional missiles and even heavy plasma cannons, the flak rounds were another matter. Only the front thirty percent of his missileboats were armored with valstronium to protect against cosmic particles. The rest of the missileboats only had titanium armor and a flak round traveling at even 0.1c would shred his boat apart. Never mind the fact that the frigates would be able to knock down more of his missiles as well.

Quickly, he readjusted his attack plans and then transmitted them to the other missileboats. As each ship acknowledged he watched as his force split into three groups. He had ordered first flight to attack the shipyard while the ten missileboats of his third flight headed for the main battlestation. One of the missileboats of second flight carried a special weapons package so the rest of that flight would escort it to its target.

As the shipyard was the closest target, Le had a few seconds to watch first flight's attack commence. Racing in at 0.35c, the missileboats released their missiles as soon as they came into range. The three destroyers had already fired their own anti-ship missiles and were filling space with plasma rounds as well.

Ignoring the threat to their own lives the missileboat commanders kept their ships directly on line with their target until all their missiles had been deployed. Only then did they begin evasive maneuvers as they turned away from the shipyard and tried to put some distance between themselves and the defending destroyers. Too late for some, for two anti-ship missiles managed to get proximity detonations, taking out three missileboats. The rest managed to escape as both the destroyers' and the shipyard's defenses switched over to trying to take out the incoming missiles.

Compared to the attacks on the system pickets the closing speed of the incoming missiles was a lot less, giving the defenders a few vital seconds to target the oncoming threats. Of the sixteen missiles launched at the shipyard, five fell to the point defense plasma cannons of the defenders. AM missiles took out another eight but three managed to penetrate the defensive fire and strike the shipyard, sending shockwaves along the large structure as they exploded.

Le didn't have time to watch as he began to led his own flight on its attack run. If he had, he would have seen the shipyard quickly break into a number of large pieces, all of which were dragged down towards Cook by the planet's gravity. A number of them quickly burned up in the atmosphere but three large sections of the shipyard continued on to plummet towards the planet's surface, forgotten by both the attackers and defenders in space as the battle raged on.

Le's ten missileboats soon became nine as the battlestation opened up with all its heavy plasma cannons. Not designed for point defense, the larger plasma cannons were all but useless against missiles. Yet the sheer weight of fire the battlestation could put out meant his missileboats had to go into evasive maneuvers. The flak frigate also began to rapidly fire rounds off at the incoming missileboats as they approached but, at its outer range, the fire was spread too thin to be a real threat and only one more missileboat was hit.

As the missileboats finally entered the range of their own missiles, time seemed to slow down. As one the remaining eight ships ceased their evasive maneuverers and turned towards the battlestation. Immediately, one missileboat exploded as a flak round detonated in close proximity to it. Within two seconds the remaining seven missileboats fired off their fourteen missiles. The gunners aboard the battlestation *Chester* and the flak frigate *Crossbow* took full advantage of those two seconds as plasma cannon fire destroyed two missileboats and a flak round took out another.

As with the attack on the shipyard, the remaining missileboats managed their escape when the defenders switched their fire to the incoming missiles. Confident that he was safe, Le watched the missiles make their final attack runs. Pumping his fists he urged the missiles on. Fourteen became eight as the flak frigate filled space with a withering hale of explosions. Then the point defense plasma cannons added their fire. Eight became seven and then six. Finally the AM missiles were launched from the battlestation and frigate and six became two. Both struck the superstructure of the massive battlestation and Le saw it buckle as two explosions erupted from deep within. Yet, no secondary explosions followed and in dismay Le watched as the battlestation used its maneuvering thrusters to reorientate itself and open fire once again on his remaining missile boats with its large plasma cannons. Automatically setting his craft into a series of evasive maneuvers Le tried to pick out second flight from all the information on his holo display.

Second flight's target had been on the other side of the planet and so they had headed up over the northern hemisphere of Cook. Decelerating as they approached their target, their missiles would have the smallest closing speed though their target was also the smallest. Sitting in geosynchronous orbit, the battlestation *Oak* was a much smaller version of *Chester*. Her job was to protect the small valstronium mining operation on the planet's surface.

As all but one of second flight's missileboats launched their missiles at *Oak* she tried her best to swat them out of the sky. Two fell to plasma fire and another two to AM missiles but that wasn't enough. Multiple missiles struck *Oak* and she simply disappeared. Coming in sixty seconds behind her sister ships, the last missileboat of second flight fired off her two special missiles. They immediately dived into the atmosphere of Cook and used their ground penetrating radar to lock onto the underground mining facilities. Upon striking the surface, their valstronium cores allowed them to penetrate down almost a kilometer before exploding. Their momentum alone caused an explosion of several kilotons and the thermonuclear detonations of the two missiles ensured that nothing of the mining operation survived.

Once he had led his flight out of range of the remaining battlestation, Le waited for what was left of his other two flights to join him. Their numbers were severely depleted; of the initial thirty missileboats he had lost half. Yet they had accomplished their primary target, the shipyard was destroyed. The British would also no doubt have felt the loss of the valstronium mine and would have to divert important resources to repair their large battlestation. The mission had been a success. As the missileboats joined up and aligned into a single formation Le began to plan out the attack on Britannia. If Cook was anything to go by not many of his missileboats would make it out of Britannia alive. Still, that was what they had signed up for; they would do their country proud.

*

For the last several hours, Captain Lightfoot's fists had been clenching into smaller and smaller balls as he had watched the updates come in from Cook. The initial destruction of two of the picket ships had been a shock; no one had expected the Chinese fighters to be able to take on a warship. What had happened next almost threatened to rewrite the rulebook on space warfare. Less than thirty enemy fighters had destroyed a shipyard and a precious valstronium mining facility. The officers on *Ghost's* bridge had been trying to quietly discuss the significance of the attacks without Lightfoot hearing. Initially he had agreed with their shocked conclusions that the attack had left the RSN's fleet obsolete. After having time to review the data as *Ghost* continued her journey around the edge of the Cook system, he had changed his mind. The flak frigate assisting the battlestation *Chester* had handed out a lot of damage to the attacking fighters and had also almost stopped all their missiles. If the second flak frigate had made it to *Chester* in time the battlestation probably wouldn't have taken any damage. Likewise, if the shipyard had been fitted with three or four flak cannons, it too probably would have survived. The Chinese' main advantage had been surprise and, if he had anything to say about it, they wouldn't be getting that advantage again.

Ghost had dropped out of shift space 1.5 light hours from the shift passage to Britannia and in stealth he had begun to creep towards the area he expected the freighters to be in. For the past several hours the missileboats had been on a steady course towards the freighters, the gravimetric signals from their engines, now working at full power, giving them away. Only twenty minutes ago they began to decelerate and from this new data his navigation officer had been able to work out exactly where the freighters were waiting. No doubt they were powered down to avoid detection and Lightfoot planned to use this to his advantage.

"Sensors, let me know when you get a visual," Lightfoot requested.

Before waiting for a reply, he switched his holo display to bring up the face of Lieutenant Beckford, the commanding officer of *Ghost's* marines. Usually a destroyer warranted a full Major to command her marine contingent but as *Ghost* hadn't officially passed her space trials one hadn't been assigned yet. "Is everything ready at your end Lieutenant?" Lightfoot asked.

"Yes sir, my boys are suited up and ready to go. We're about to load into the two shuttles now. I'll be leading first platoon, while Sergeant Jamison leads second. I've selected a number of navy personnel to accompany us on the shuttle in case we need them on board the freighter," Beckford replied.

"Very good Lieutenant, I want you to run a final test of your jamming equipment five minutes before go time. It's vital they don't get a signal out." Glancing away for a moment at another screen, Lightfoot then turned back to the marine. "We're twenty minutes out now, good hunting."

As the marine saluted before switching off his screen, Lightfoot walked over to the tactical station. Looking down at Lieutenant Johnston's console he watched the Lieutenant for a few seconds. "Are you confident you can do what I'm asking?" He said.

"Yes sir," she replied. "I've reviewed the technical designs of the American freighters. From the visuals, the computer is certain they're both Liberty class freighters. All of their communications relays are mounted on the aft mid-section of the hull. Our point defense plasma cannons should be able to take the relays out without causing any other damage; we just need to get into range. I've also reviewed the most recent American freighter designs, in case these freighters have been updated with any new tech. If they have any secondary communication relays we'll identify them and take them out before they can be powered up."

Satisfied that Johnston had things under control, Lightfoot patted her on the shoulder and returned to his command chair. After reviewing the details of the plan once more he spoke to the bridge at large to reassure them. "Ok everyone we're ten minutes out from point defense plasma cannon range. You all know what to do. If you see even a hint that they are going to resist or are going to get a signal out you are to bring up our jammers. Otherwise let's sit tight and let the marines have some fun for a change."

Slowly the timer on Lightfoot's holo display counted down, as it reached zero he began to bark out orders. "Johnston, now! Sensors begin transmitting. Lieutenant Greaves, open the shuttle bay doors, give Lieutenant Beckford the go ahead. Navigation, begin our deceleration burn."

At once Lightfoot's plan sprang into action. Six low powered plasma bolts shot out from *Ghost* and hit targets along the aft sections of the freighters' hulls. Just as the Chinese officers on watch began to receive damage updates, their passive sensors began to beep furiously alerting the crew that a ship, impossibly close, had just opened its shuttle bay doors. Johnston's shots had only taken out their outgoing communications relays and so into the mix the COMS stations aboard the freighters began to demand attention, for *Ghost* was bombarding their remaining laser COM receivers with a message to surrender.

"Chinese freighters, this is HMS *Ghost*. We have disabled your communications relays and are sending over a boarding party. Surrender immediately or be destroyed. You have carried out an act of war against Great Britain and we demand your surrender. Chinese freighters, this is..."

Lightfoot watched as the Chinese freighters remained inactive. Either their bridge crews were frozen in fear or they were simply overwhelmed by their situation. Either way it didn't matter. The couple of minutes of inactivity had given the two shuttles enough time to latch onto each freighter and the boarding parties were already cutting their way into each hull. It was just as well that *Ghost* had been unable to slow down her approach for fear that the fighters would pick up her engine emissions and be spooked off. Even though the navigation officer had already begun to decelerate, *Ghost* was already passing out of point defense plasma range and couldn't offer any support to the marines without giving her presence away to the approaching fighters.

Yet, now that the marines were on board, Lightfoot knew nothing short of a miracle would save the freighters. Even if the Chinese had a marine equivalent of their own, the short warning wouldn't have given them time to prepare. His marines were going in fully equipped in powered combat armor. Checking his holo display, he could see a small energy reading coming from each shuttle, indicating they had deployed their jammers, stopping any personal communicators from sending a warning to the approaching missileboats. Confident that the first phase of his plan had gone well, he turned his attention to phase two.

*

By the time *Ghost* had worked her way back to the two freighters the Chinese missileboats were only fifteen minutes away. Once back in range of laser COMS, Lightfoot had contacted Lieutenant Beckford and was getting a report on the boarding action.

"So that sums it up sir. Both freighters are space worthy. Six Chinese crew were killed, we lost one marine to an armed Chinese officer and another injured."

"Acknowledged Lieutenant," Lightfoot began, "Have the engineers you took over with you had a chance to look at the fighter bays to give us a better idea of what we are facing?"

"Better than that sir," Beckford answered. "There are ten more of the craft in each of the freighters. I'm sending you all the technical data the engineers were able to find or deduce themselves."

"Thank you Lieutenant, I'll be back in touch after I have reviewed the data," Lightfoot said as he closed the COM channel and put the new data up on the bridge's main holo display.

Without hesitation, the First Lieutenant began to walk the bridge through the engineer's findings. Gomez had been with Lightfoot on *Surprise* as a Second Lieutenant and already, since *Ghost's* commissioning a month ago it was obvious he wouldn't be staying a First Lieutenant for long.

"It appears the Chinese call these fighters missileboats. They are equipped with two high acceleration low yield anti-ship missiles and a single plasma cannon. Their top speed is 0.35c and their acceleration is fifteen percent higher than ours. The engineers indicate that only the forward thirty percent of each craft is armored with valstronium so they are very vulnerable to proximity kills, either from a missile detonation or a flak round. The data we have from the battle around Cook indicates that each of the remaining missileboats fired of all their missiles so we just have to worry about their plasma cannons."

"Ok," Lightfoot interjected. "We'll go with plan alpha then. Navigation begin to move us away from the freighters."

The dilemma Lightfoot faced was simple. He knew where the enemy was going but he simply didn't have the firepower to stop all of them. With over a dozen missileboats heading right for him, he couldn't hope to take them all out with his plasma cannons before they were able to return fire and potentially cripple *Ghost*. If he tried to fire his missiles at them he would only warn them of his presence and give them a chance to escape. That left him with only one option; he was going to bluff.

Once far enough away from the two freighters, *Ghost* began to jettison missiles from her tubes. Without their engines engaged they simply floated in space. *Ghost* continued doing this for as long as time allowed before she turned around and headed back to the freighters. Just as the missileboats came to a stop 3000km, from the freighters *Ghost* turned to bring her main plasma cannons to bear on them.

"Captain, Lieutenant Beckford has informed us that the missileboats are contacting the freighters by laser COM. They are requesting the freighters turn on their running lights and open their cargo bay doors," the COMS officer announced.

"Tell him to ignore them," Lightfoot ordered. "Tactical, how many missileboats do you have targeted?"

"I have three lined up with our main plasma cannons and six more with the point defense cannons. Two more are within range of some of the missiles we released," Johnston informed her Captain.

"COMS, when Johnston opens fire, I want you to immediately begin broadcasting," Lightfoot ordered. "Johnston switch your targets as soon as you have a confirmed kill. On my mark. Fire!"

Bolts of plasma immediately shot out all over *Ghost's* hull as every weapon that could bear on the fighters opened fire. At once, three fighters evaporated as heavy bolts cut right through them. Within a couple of seconds six more disappeared as smaller bolts peppered them and quickly punched through their weaker rear armor. Almost simultaneously with the explosions that marked the deaths of the first three fighters, two thermonuclear explosions erupted in the midst of the missileboats formation taking three more with them.

A number of the missileboat commanders immediately began to accelerate away from the area of destruction. Others, seeing a message being broadcast from *Ghost* hesitated just long enough to think through what it said.

"Coms, status update, has our bluff worked?" Lightfoot queried after the first shots were fired.

"I think so sir," the COMS officer replied. I'm receiving surrender messages from all but three of the missileboats."

Without looking over to Johnston, Lightfoot knew she was firming up firing solutions on the three remaining missileboats. As he watched, two heavy plasma bolts reached out and plucked one from the tactical display. Instinctively he knew that the other two were likely to get far enough away to allow their evasive maneuvers to work well enough to escape. Quickly Lightfoot accessed the tactical feed himself and took control of the missiles *Ghost* had dropped. None were in range of the fleeing missileboats but four were close. Selecting them he sent their detonation signals and then flicked open a communication channel.

"Fleeing missileboats, you are in a mine field. Repeat you are in a minefield. The next detonations will not be a warning."

Almost in unison both ships cut their drives and began to power down, announcing their surrender. Lightfoot let out a sigh of relief. He wanted to get all the missileboats. With their speed and agility it could have taken days to capture them, all the while they could have been harassing freighter shipping in the system.

Without the firepower to stop them, Lightfoot had decided to try and trick the Chinese commanders into thinking they had been trapped in a minefield. It wasn't that unbelievable given the fact the Chinese commanders must have realized the RSN had found their freighters. Lightfoot was just glad more hadn't tried to flee or worse, had opened fire on the freighters.

*

Half a day later *Ghost,* joined by the light cruiser *Righteous,* who had chased the missileboats out of the system, were escorting the two freighters back towards Cook. Already two courier ships were well on their way to Earth and Britannia, one to warn of a possible attack and the other to report back to the Admiralty. In his private office Lightfoot was reviewing the intelligence data the boarding parties had sent back when the officer on watch interrupted him.

"Captain, we have received a communication from Admiral McGreevy on the battlestation *Chester*. It's for your eyes only so I've sent it to your office terminal."

Intrigued, Lightfoot keyed an acknowledgement before turning to put the message on the holo display. When the Admiral's face appeared he looked somewhat haggard and his uniform was crumpled but the smile on his face was genuine.

"Captain Lightfoot, it appears congratulations are in order again. Not only did you give us plenty of warning about the incoming attack, you have likely prevented an even more devastating attack on Britannia. You seem to be blessed by lady luck herself. I'm sure the Admiralty will be rewarding you for what you have done here. However, your work isn't over yet. It seems the Admiralty got wind of this Chinese attack through some RSNI agents and they have already decided to retaliate in kind. The courier that arrived in system just ahead of the attack also contained orders for you. You are to take *Ghost* into the Void and deliver the orders I'm sending to the commanding officer at Excalibur. If I had to guess you'll be taking *Ghost* on into Chinese space to repay the damage they've done to us here. I also have orders to dispatch two frigates back to Earth. It looks like a second force is going to go up the shift passage from Earth to Beta and then into Chinese space so you'll not be alone. Give them hell for me Captain. McGreevy out."

The message had taken a number of hours to reach *Ghost* and so there was no point sending back a reply. Instead, Lightfoot ordered the COMS officer to send an acknowledgement that they had received their orders. Then he set about recalling his boarding parties and handing over control of the two freighters to the light cruiser *Righteous*. There was an in system shuttle bringing the rest of his assigned crew from Cook. Once it arrived they would be ready to head on to the Void, the official ceremony declaring *Ghost* space worthy had obviously been shelved for the time being. It looked like *Ghost* would be seeing action again very soon.

Chapter 19 - Uncommon Valor

As in the Earth navies before the dawn of the space age, courage and bravery have been the hallmarks of what the Empire seeks to instill into its recruits. Whilst these attributes were exemplified in the wet navies of Earth the legacy handed down to the Empire's navy was forged in the colonial wars of the first Interstellar Expansion Era.

-Excerpt from Empire's Rising, 3002 AD

16th April 2465 AD, HMS *Drake*, New Stockholm system, previously designated V34

Aboard *Drake*, James was sitting in his office rereading the first old style novel his uncle had given him. He had finished the last novel months ago on *Drake's* return journey to Earth after discovering the Void. Since then he had been too busy to even think of them again. That had all changed once *Drake* had been posted to New Stockholm. For nearly two months *Drake* had been circling the system, watching the Swedes begin to set up their colony on the habitable planet. Initially, James had tried to resist the urge to go back and reread the books in case they distracted him from his command. A week ago he had given in. With nothing happening and not even any news coming through from the rest of the Void, he needed a distraction.

As he turned another page, the buzzer on his door went off. With a flick of his wrist he hit the button to allow the door to open and Gupta walked in. James was surprised to find that he was happy to see her. Since their heart to heart and everything that had happened to them after, their relationship had been changing. It was the duty of a ship's second ranking officer to run the day to day needs of a ship on behalf of its Captain, only bringing problems up the chain of command that warranted attention. Initially, when James had taken over command of *Drake*, Gupta had used this tradition to freeze him out. She had never come to him with a problem or involved him in the running of the ship. At the time James had been happy with the arrangement as he drowned in his own self-pity. In return he had shut her out of the command decisions that fell on his shoulders.

Since they had come to New Stockholm things had changed. Gupta had begun to consult him when it came to the running of the ship and the crew, he, in turn, had begun to share his thinking and plans with her. Their relationship still wasn't functioning like the well-oiled machine he had been taught to expect at the academy but it was getting there. James had also been enjoying the closer relationship he had been able to forge with the rest of his crew now that Gupta had opened that world up to him. He believed he had earned their respect with everything they had been through so far but now he hoped that in the last couple of months had also begun to earn their friendship.

Shaking himself out of his thoughts, he motioned for Gupta to take a seat opposite him. "So what can I do for you Lieutenant?"

"Sir," Gupta started but before she did James interrupted as he raised his hands. "James, you can call me James in private."

"Yes sir, James I mean. And it would be my pleasure if you call me Georgia. As I was saying, we both know the crew are beginning to get restless. Not only are we stuck here while the war rages on around us. We haven't heard any news for nearly two months. Worse, being permanently stuck in stealth mode has meant we've had to limit our use of non-essential equipment. There is a long waiting list for most of our leisure and entertainment platforms and it's growing all the time. The virtual reality suit and sports simulators are usually the only things that keep a crew sane during a long commission. I'm not sure I can vouch for their happiness or even willing cooperation if this situation continues much longer."

As she paused, James took up the conversation. "I'm well aware Georgia but you know we've been doing everything we can to distract them. There's nothing more I can think of. We have tripled the number of combat simulations. We've made competitions out of everything we can find and we've even allowed those interested to spend some time in other posts to develop new skills. I'm not sure what else we can do."

"You're right sir," Gupta agreed. "I haven't come with any new ideas but I might have a new approach. I've been reviewing our inventories. Our fuel tanks are just above sixty percent but other things are starting to get pretty low. We only have a few weeks of power cells left and we've had to change out a number of secondary processor units from the ship's main computer. We can make do if we run out of either but ideally we need to be resupplied. I know it's a pretty weak excuse but it might be enough for us to make a quick trip to Excalibur and see if we can locate the supplies we need. I think the break from New Stockholm and some news would do the crew a world of good."

James was distracted from Gutpa's ideas by a flashing on his office console. "Hold that thought Georgia." James intentionally used her first name even though Gupta had slipped back into calling him sir. He was determined to break down the last walls that stood between them. "We might have to make your plan work but for now it looks like we have something to break the monotony. Sensors have just picked up a ship accelerating into the system."

Both James' and Gupta's eyes went to the gravimetric data being displayed on the main holo display as they entered the bridge. It would take hours for any electromagnetic radiation the ship was giving off to reach *Drake* but the gravimetric disturbances caused by its rapid acceleration give them an instant fix on its location. As they watched the ship disappeared off the display. It reappeared a few seconds later on a new vector ninety degrees to its original course. Then it vanished again only to reappear heading straight out of the system.

Immediately James sprang into action. "That's the prearranged signal indicating Chinese ships have broken out of the blockade. Sensors, what are the Swedes doing?"

Without a means to transmit messages faster than light, the RSN had developed a simple set of signals a ship could use to communicate with ships deeper in a system. By following a set acceleration pattern other ships could pick up the acceleration via their gravimetric sensors and interpret the signal. The meaning of some of the acceleration patterns had been shared with the Swedish forces. A Chinese break out had been one of them.

Sub Lieutenant O'Rourke, who was manning sensors, only took a few seconds to reply, as the Swedish reaction was swift. "Sir, the Swedish warships are maneuvering. It looks like the two destroyers on picket patrol are heading to meet up with the light cruiser and destroyer that are protecting the colony ship."

Smart, James thought. Outside the Void, attacks on a system usually came along a set vector, as ships were limited on where they could go because of the dark matter strewn between solar systems. In the Void, the Chinese could attack from any direction and so it didn't make sense for the Swedish to split their forces.

"Ok," James spoke to the bridge at large. "Let's assume that Admiral Cunningham managed to get off this warning before the

Chinese ships succeeded in jumping away from V17. That gives us a little bit of time before they get here. Their most likely target is going to be Excalibur but we need to be prepared. Navigation, plot us a course closer to the Swedish squadron. I want to be able to lend our support if we are needed. Take us there at six percent thrust.

*

Two hours later everyone in the New Stockholm system got the answer to the question they were asking. The Chinese had decided to hit New Stockholm. Back during his days at the academy James had loved to gamble. If it hadn't been inappropriate for a Captain to make bets with his crew, he would have wagered a considerable amount on the Chinese bypassing New Stockholm. Yes, the Chinese had laid claim to the whole Void but they couldn't expect the UN to let them keep it all. They were already at war with the British; it made no sense to attack another power.

Yet here they were and James had to make the best of it. Almost in silence the bridge watched four ships begin to accelerate into the system. They could only be Chinese as they weren't altering course to make any of the prearranged signals. When it was clear they were hostiles, the Swedish warships accelerated out of orbit around New Stockholm to meet them. James understood what the Swedish Admiral was thinking. The Chinese goal was to force the Swedish to abandon the system. If they lost their warships, the colony ship and accompanying supply ships would have to return to Earth. The Admiral was offering the Chinese his ships in the hope they would then leave the colonists alone. Brave, but foolish. The Swedish were at least thirty years behind the Chinese in military tech. If the four Chinese ships were anything bigger than frigates they would blow their way past the Swedish warships and the colony ship would be at their mercy. RSNI estimated that the Swedish colony ship could hold up to forty thousand colonists.

As the Swedish warships rose to meet the Chinese, Gupta turned to

James. "Shall we follow them sir and give them what assistance we can?"

"No," James answered. "We don't have the firepower to alter the course of the coming battle. We would just lose this ship for nothing. The Swedish Admiral should have tried to run for it. If they had tried to keep the Chinese at maximum range, they may have managed to take out enough missiles to survive long enough to jump away. If they had tried, we could have added our defensive fire to theirs. But we can't change the outcome of a missile duel to the death. The colony ship may yet need us so we'll stay here."

As Gupta nodded in recognition, James gladly gave the order he knew he should. "Navigation keep us heading towards the colony ship. If they change their orbit or try to break orbit, match their course but don't exceed ten percent of our maximum thrust." Helping the Swedish warships was suicide; everything he said to Gupta was true. But it also allowed him to hide his other motives. He wanted to get back to Christine. He loved serving in the navy but he didn't want to throw his life away for nothing. He had other things that were more important.

*

A deathly silence had descended on the bridge during the three hours it had taken the two groups of ships to enter missile range of each other. In that time *Drake* had entered orbit around New Stockholm and was slowly creeping up on the colony ship. Not being equipped with military grade sensors it was unlikely the Swedes would detect them.

Suddenly the gravimetric plot erupted as the four Chinese ships opened fire using their superior missile range to hammer the Swedes. Sub Lieutenant Fisher, who had been manning sensors since the Chinese had arrived in system had managed to identify the four ships as *Luda* class destroyers. Just before entering missile range they had turned perpendicular to the approaching Swedish ships and presented their broadside missile tubes to them. Twenty new contacts had then appeared on the gravimetric plot as the Chinese opened fire with every missile tube they could bring to bear.

With both groups of ships closing on each other so fast, the Swedish had just been able to get one missile salvo away before the first from the Chinese hit them. As the battle was taking place nearly a light hour from *Drake*, they could only watch the gravimetric sensors to get a real time indication of what was going on. As the first Chinese salvo crashed into the Swedish their three destroyers disappeared off the plot. The remaining light cruiser fired off another salvo of their own before the second wave of Chinese missiles, already homing in on it, caused it to disappear from *Drake's* screens as well. The twenty five missiles the Swedish had managed to get off all closed in on the Chinese destroyers but as they disappeared they didn't manage to take any ships with them.

Clearly satisfied that Swedish forces had been destroyed three of the destroyers began to decelerate and turn back towards the mass shadow of the system. One however, kept coming.

James couldn't help but curse aloud. "Those bastards, they're going for the colony ship!"

Moments later a transmission was broadcast out into the system by the Swedish colony ship. It wasn't encrypted so Sub Lieutenant Graham put it on the main holo display.

The visual showed an aged man who was visibly trying not to shake with what looked like a mixture of rage and fear. "Chinese vessel. My name is Governor Olsson. I am in charge of this colony ship and the colony being set up on New Stockholm. You have destroyed our warships. I offer you our complete surrender. On my word we will vacate this system and return to Earth. There doesn't need to be any more bloodshed. Again I repeat. I offer you our complete surrender."

It would take almost an hour for the message to reach the approaching destroyer so James sat back into his command chair to see how things were going to play out.

Twenty minutes after the destroyer should have received the message it was still accelerating towards the colony ship. Knowing his ship could never stand up against the destroyer James still felt trapped. Everyone on board expected him to help the colony ship. Hell, they probably expected him to find a way to save the day! Yet he knew better, how could *Drake* come out of this in one piece? They would all die. His dreams for the future would evaporate. As he hesitated he could feel everyone on the bridge watching him. Could he live with the shame of running away? He would have to face a court martial when he got back to Earth. They might find in his favor. Revealing his presence would certainly end in the destruction of his ship. If he fled any inquiry would have to admit that he took the most prudent decision. Yet, the court martial would be a public affair. All of Britain would know he ran away. How could he ever hope to marry Christine then? What choice did he have then? He was damned if he did and damned if he didn't.

All of a sudden his thoughts turned to the Damang Incident. Captain Turner had not hesitated in charging straight for the Chinese cruisers in order to protect his freighters and he had had no hope of surviving. That was what was expected of a British naval officer. James had gone through the academy knowing that but he had always thought the rule applied to others. He was the heir to a Dukedom. His life was too important to be thrown away so easily. Yet, now he knew it wasn't so simple. If he ran he would lose everything, Christine and the navy. Neither would look at him the same. He could already feel the questions of the bridge officers. Every one of them had been trained to throw themselves into harm's way; they would already be questioning his delay. But no matter what way he looked at it he really had no choice.

James struggled with the decision for another two minutes. As every second passed by he could feel the pressure from the bridge crew building. They were waiting for orders. Finally he made the only choice that seemed to offer him any hope of still having a future with Christine, slim as it was.

"COMS, get us a laser link with the colony ship. Tell them not to do anything that might alert the Chinese to our presence and get me Governor Olsson on the line."

Seconds later the governor's face appeared on James personal holo display. "Governor, it appears you could use some assistance," James said putting on a brave face. If he was going to do this no one else needed to know how close he had come to backing down.

Smiling, the governor replied, "I've been fighting tooth and nail to keep your RSN ships out of our new system but boy I am glad to see you Commander. How did you get so close to the planet without my warships spotting you? And more importantly can you handle this Chinese destroyer?

"For the first, you know our stealth is good Governor," James answered. "And for the second I'm afraid not. I command HMS *Drake*, a survey frigate. We only have a couple of missile tubes so the Chinese Captain can handle anything we throw at him. The best I can offer is that we can add our point defenses to yours. It's not much but if I guess right the Chinese Captain will not want to waste any more missiles on you than he has to. I suggest you evacuate the two supply ships and put their defenses on automatic. You need to take the colony ship out of orbit and make it look like you are making a run for it. We should be able to match your speed while remaining in stealth. With luck the Chinese ship will only fire one salvo and turn to re-join its buddies. If some of the missiles are targeted at the two supply vessels, we might have a chance of taking out the rest between us. That's the best I can offer you."

Nodding, the governor accepted James' plan, "Very well Commander, I don't think I have much choice. Don't think I don't know you could stay in stealth and avoid any danger. On behalf of my people I want to thank you, whether this works or not."

*

Forty five minutes later as James and Gupta were reviewing their final plans, Fisher suddenly shouted out excitedly to the rest of the bridge. "Six ships have just begun to accelerate rapidly into the system. It looks like they are coming in under full military power. I recognize the drive harmonics of one of them. It's the medium cruiser *Voyager*. Wait. The three Chinese destroyers have just gone to full acceleration, they're trying to get away."

Switching to look at the gravimetric display, James saw that fortune was on the Chinese' side. The British ships had jumped into the system several light hours from the point the Chinese ships were heading towards to jump out. At full acceleration the British ships would get the chance to fire off one missile salvo but it would be touch and go as to whether the missiles would actually reach their targets before the Chinese managed to jump away.

A shift drive wouldn't engage within the mass shadow created by a system's star. Yet the actual size of the mass shadow was determined by the sensitivity of a ship's shift drive. As technology advanced, the shift drive continued to be fine-tuned, allowing it to engage further and further into a system, slowly decreasing the mass shadow of any given system. Over the last one hundred years the gains had been negligible yet it did mean that the RSN wasn't exactly sure how far out from a system's sun the Chinese could engage their shift drive, if they took all the safeties off. If RSNI data was to be believed the missile salvo from the British warships could catch them in time but it would be close.

The fourth destroyer on the other hand, was in a lot more trouble. Every second it delayed making a break towards the mass shadow it decreased its likelihood of escape. In theory it could continue to charge into the system past the colony ship and head towards the far side of the mass shadow. Outside the Void that would be the logical course of action and it would ensure *Drake's* destruction, as the Chinese destroyer would have ample time to fire salvo after salvo at her and the colony ship. Yet, being in the Void meant the perusing British ships could simply make a couple of shift jumps to the other side of the system and lie in wait for the Chinese ship. The Chinese Commander's best chance of escape would be to fire one salvo at the colony ship and then turn tail and run for the mass shadow at full speed.

James contacted the governor and passed on the latest developments, informing him that their plan was still the best chance they had. Now all they had to do was wait.

The crew were able to occupy themselves during the initial stages of the destroyer's approach by watching the unfolding chase between the British forces lead by *Voyager* and the fleeing Chinese ships. A collective groan escaped from the bridge crew as the Chinese ships all disappeared twenty seconds before the British missiles reached them. They had been able to jump away just in time. With that drama over, everyone's attention was focused on the lone Chinese destroyer.

A further fifty minutes later and James' prayers were answered. The

Chinese destroyer had started to decelerate to come to rest at her maximum missile range. Without wasting any time, she fired five missiles after the fleeing colony ship and boosted away, making for the shortest route to the edge of the mass shadow. The Chinese's Captain's actions had assured that if he wanted to come back for another salvo he would be guaranteeing the British warships caught him. Hopefully, that would mean James only had to deal with the one salvo heading for them.

Fired from maximum range and towards a target fleeing the opposite direction it would take the missiles over thirty minutes to catch them. A long time for the bridge crew on board *Drake* to watch nervously as almost certain death approached. Ten minutes out James keyed his console to open a ship wide channel.

"All hands, this is the Captain. By now you all know what we face. We have five missiles coming for us seeking to reign down death and destruction. Beside us are almost forty thousand civilians. We didn't ask to be their protectors but that is where we find ourselves. I'm not going to lie, none of us may be walking away from this but if we die we will die knowing we have done the duty of a British warship." Pausing to regain control of his emotions James continued to put on a brave face, dismissing thoughts of Christine. "If any of you have yet to transmit your personal messages to *Voyager* do so now, the Chinese missiles are less than ten minutes away. It has been a pleasure commanding all of you. Commander Somerville out."

As he finished he saluted, knowing that many of the crew were watching his last words to them on holo displays throughout the ship. As he looked up James saw that the entire bridge crew was standing to attention saluting him back, Gupta included. Momentarily at a loss for words, James simply motioned them all back to their seats. "Thank you everyone, I know you will all do your duty." Inwardly, James felt ashamed. He thought his crew had deserved the words he had given them but he knew how close he had come to running away and he knew his real motive for staying. He didn't deserve their respect and it shamed him. Still, he thought to himself, we are in it now. There is nothing to do but put on a brave face and live up to everyone's expectations.

At five minutes out, it became clear two missiles were targeted at the two supply ships. That left three for *Drake* and the colony ship to handle.

At three minutes out, the missiles all went into evasive attack patterns and switched on their ECM to confuse the defensive fire that was about to try and swat them out of space.

Two minutes and thirty seconds out, the colony ship and the two supply ships opened fire with their point defense plasma cannons. The unmanned supply ships ignored the missiles targeted at them and sought to protect the colony ship. Of the five missiles aimed at the colony ship one was hit and exploded.

The next thirty seconds were the longest in James life. *Drake* could drop out of stealth and open fire with her point defense plasma cannons but the plan called for her to wait.

At two minutes out, *Drake* went to full power. She immediately began to launch AM missiles and open up with all her plasma cannons. At the same time her ECM went to full power.

The remaining two missiles targeted at the colony ship seemed to pause for a moment as their targeting sensors tried to burn through the ECM and identify the new target. In those vital seconds one was knocked out by *Drake's* defensive fire. Yet the last one came on.

Thirty seconds from impact James knew they weren't going to get the last one. He almost couldn't believe the next words that came out of his mouth. "Navigation, move us directly in front of the colony ship. Put us between them and the last missile," he ordered.

As time slowed down, James thought it strange that even so close to death he was still able to appreciate how Sub Lieutenant Thirlwall immediately obeyed his final orders, even though it sealed her own doom. He then looked over to Gupta to see that she was still fully focused on overseeing the point defenses. The look of determination in her eyes showed she had no thought for what was about to happen, she was focused on the here and now. All across the bridge James watched as his crew were calmly doing everything they could to aid in the defense of the colony ship. Still, it's not enough, James thought as time suddenly seemed to speed up again and the missile came crashing in.

Just as the missile was about to impact Sub Lieutenant Thirlwall managed to interpose *Drake* between the missile and the helpless colony ship. The sudden merging of the two targets and the ECM from *Drake* confused the missile enough to cause it to over shoot the colony ship before exploding. The shockwave, however, still washed over *Drake*. On a larger warship such a hit could be brushed off but on a small exploration frigate it was devastating. On the bridge James was flung into the back of his command chair and everything went dark as the thermonuclear explosion burnt off *Drake's* valstronium armor and tore into her inner hull. Crumpled and without power she tumbled away from the colony ship.

Chapter 20 – Second Chance

Every naval officer aspires to command their own warship. This is without exception. Yet only the very best will ever rise above their colleagues and attain the rank of Captain.

-Excerpt from Empire's Rising, 3002 AD

17th April 2465 AD, HMS *Drake*, New Stockholm system

Slowly James became aware of a drum beating somewhere in the distance. It began to come closer and closer until eventually it felt like it was being held right up to his head. With an effort he tried to open his eyes. At first nothing happened but then, suddenly, they opened and piercing light flooded his vision. The pain was unbearable and instinctively he moved his hand to cover his eyes. In his groggy state, he misjudged the distance and ended up whacking himself in the face, sending the drum beat in his head firing off at an increased pace.

Noticing the movement, Doctor Wilson came over to stand by his patient's bed. "I see you are awake Captain. You'll have to take things slowly for the next few hours; you have received a nasty concussion. I had to put you into a temporary coma in order to stop your brain from swelling too much."

Concern coursed through James. How long had he been out? *Drake* needed him. Try as he might he couldn't get his mouth to form the words. All Doctor Wilson heard was "Hl on."

Having already anticipated the Captain's first question Wilson was able to decipher the mumble. "You've been out for just under twenty hours, Captain. You don't need to worry, Lieutenant Gupta has everything under control."

James tried to mull that over but the thumping in his head was still growing in intensity. "M hd, pan." He managed to croak.

This time the doctor had to pause for a second before understanding. "Yes, you're going to be in some pain for the next day or so but now that you are awake I can start to give you something for it, hold on."

A few moments later the doctor returned and pressed one of his instruments to James' neck. Almost immediately the drumming in his head receded considerably and he felt the rest of his body begin to relax too. After working his jaw back and forth a number of times, he finally felt confident enough to try his next question. "H.. how bad?"

Wilson considered whether to answer this question right away or to wait until James was at least back on his feet. After a lengthy pause that only served to deepen James' fears he decided the Commander deserved to know. "Personnel wise we were very lucky, only six dead. *Drake* on the other hand wasn't. The missile that detonated off our bow crumpled the forward twenty percent of the ship. We lost the forward missile tube along with our store of recon drones. Gupta says our point defense has been reduced by sixty percent and the damage to our forward section means we won't be able to hide from anyone. There was also damage to the forward plasma cannon and one of our fission reactors has had to be shut down. In short, it looks like *Drake* will be spending a lengthy time in a repair dock sir."

Relieved at the light causalities, James still felt a pang of pain for *Drake*. He had come to love her as his own and now his own had been almost turned into a wreck. "The colony ship?" He asked next.

This time Wilson broke into a smile. "The colony ship survived sir. There were a lot of shaken up colonists but the final missile exploded far enough away that it only damaged the ship's engines."

"And the Chinese destroyer?"

"Gone sir, after what she tried to do to us and the Swedes, *Voyager* and her consorts tore her to shreds, they didn't give them any quarter."

Lying back in relief, James cracked a small smile himself. He had done it, and against the odds, he had even survived himself. It was almost unbelievable. At the end he had been resigned to his fate.

After the moment passed, he tried to sit up again. *Drake* needed him, she may be heavily damaged but she was still his ship. They needed to get back to Excalibur and then to Britannia for repairs. That was his duty.

This time he opened his eyes slowly and allowed them to get used to the light of sickbay. Looking around he noticed he was alone with the doctor. "Where is everyone else?" he asked. If there were that many dead there should have been plenty of injuries too.

"Because of the damage *Drake* took, all our injured have been moved to the destroyer *Janice* or to the Swedish colony ship. Lieutenant Gupta insisted that you would want to remain on board," replied the doctor.

Relieved that the others were being well taken care of, James tried to swing his legs around in the bed to stand up. As he did he lost his balance and almost fell off the bed. If wasn't for Wilson's strong arms he would have.

"I do have experience treating stubborn patients Captain. Lieutenant Gupta is doing a fine job. She'll manage without you for another few hours. This will put you to sleep, when you wake up you should be ready to resume your duties." Before James could complain, Wilson had thumbed a new command into his medical device and pressed it to James' neck again. Within seconds James was asleep.

*

Two days later and James was back where he knew he belonged, sitting on *Drake's* command chair. The repairs had been going well. With the destroyer *Janice's* help, both *Drake* and the Swedish Colony ship had been made shift space worthy and were about to make the jump to Excalibur. After reviewing the repairs Gupta had been doing while he was in sickbay, James had had to admit to himself she had probably organized things better than he could. Once back on his feet, he had joined her and together they had thrown themselves into the repairs. Finally, he felt like they were a real team.

His first inspection of the ship had been surreal. Not only had he been unable to venture forward past the port missile tube due to the damage, there had also been a lot of missing faces. James had been dismayed to learn that Sub Lieutenant Shannon had been among the six dead. She had manned navigation and so he had worked closely with her over the last two years as they plotted out *Drake's* survey routes. As well as the fatalities, twenty crew members had been injured seriously enough to warrant being moved. Eight had been taken to the destroyer *Janice* while the others were aboard the colony ship. That left James with only forty personnel under his command. The gaps were obvious.

James suspected the injured on board the colony ship would be having an exhausting trip back to Earth. Already the crew still aboard *Drake* had been inundated with messages of thanks from the thousands of colonists aboard the colony ship. At least they could ignore the messages. Those members of *Drake's* crew who had to travel all the way back to Earth among the colonists wouldn't be getting a moment of privacy.

Tapping on his console, he made a note to send a message to them. It wouldn't do for them to try and take advantage of the situation. They would need to be on their best behavior. Sub Lieutenant Fisher was also among the injured aboard the colony ship. He would miss her the most but once she got back to Earth she would have the chance to take her Lieutenant's exam and finally get her promotion. Typing a personal message for her reminding her to keep *Drake's* crew members under control, James then opened her personnel report. He spent the next few minutes updating it and gave his recommendation that she be immediately assigned to a combat role after she passed her exam.

As he completed the recommendation, James' thoughts were interrupted by Sub Lieutenant Graham who was manning the COMS station. "Captain, both the colony ship and *Janice* report that they are ready to jump. *Janice* says that we have the privilege of giving the order to jump."

"Very well," James acknowledged. As the senior Captain *Janice's* commanding officer should be the one to order the ships to jump but he was giving *Drake* the honor out of respect. "Navigation, are we ready to jump?" James asked.

"Yes sir, our jump capacitors are fully charged," came the reply.

"Ok, COMS, order our ships to jump in three, two, one, jump."

As always, the slight flicker in the inertial dampeners indicated that *Drake* had jumped into shift space. Happy the jump had been successful James began to review the repair plans for the next few days. It would only take three hours for them to reach Excalibur and then another nine to enter orbit. When he had last been at Excalibur, almost two months ago, a number of construction ships from Admiral's Cunningham's fleet had begun to build a small repair and resupply facility. It would not be able to handle all of *Drake's* requirements but it could provide what *Drake* needed to get back to Britannia. James intended to have a full list of their needs ready as soon as they reached Excalibur so they could pick up what they needed and be on their way in good time. He wanted to see *Drake* back in working order as soon as he could make it happen.

After finishing his list of requirements, James began to work on his battle report. He had not had time to work on it since he had left sickbay. All his efforts had been given over to getting *Drake* and the colony ship ready to depart as soon as possible but Commodore West would be expecting a full report.

When the navigation officer announced they were coming up to Excalibur James was surprised by how quickly the time had passed. He had been lost in his thoughts reliving the battle. Writing the report had given him a chance to reflect on the life he had nearly lost. Between Christine, his growing love for the navy and his quest to rebuild his family name he had a lot to live for. He had nearly lost it all. Even though he knew they had saved almost forty thousand colonists he wasn't sure he would make the same decision again. He had acted in the heat of the moment, not considering the implications of his actions when he had given the final order to close with the colony ship. As he thought about it he wasn't sure that he was prepared to risk his future with Christine so easily. Still, now he had a second chance to make sure he got the things he wanted out of life.

As *Drake* excited shift space on the edge of the Excalibur system the bridge crew were on full alert. Within seconds the ships passive sensors were flooded with lots of data. "Tactical, what have you got?" James asked.

"Our gravimetric sensors are picking up a number of ships maneuvering around the system sir. They all appear to be following typical routes for system pickets. Around the planet itself, our passives have picked up a number electromagnetic radiation sources. The computer has identified Commodore West's heavy cruiser *Avenger* and Rear Admiral Jensen's *Valkyrie*. There are also at least another fifteen warships in orbit."

"Thank you Sub Lieutenant Becket," James responded. There were more ships in orbit around Excalibur than he had expected but if there had been a fight at V17 then it was likely some of the damaged ships were here affecting repairs. Satisfied there were no hostile threats in the system James stood to retire to his office. "Becket, you have the bridge," he said as he turned and walked out.

*

James waited patiently as he sat in the adjacent room to Rear Admiral Jensen's office aboard HMS *Valkyrie*. As *Drake* had made her way to settle into orbit around Excalibur, he had been surprised to get a summons to appear on board *Valkyrie*. Strictly speaking he was still under Commodore West's command even though he would have to take *Drake* back to Britannia. Yet here he was. After only ten minutes, the Admiral's aide appeared at the door and ushered him in before leaving James alone with the Rear Admiral.

As he entered Jensen stood and stepped towards James taking his hand. "Congratulations Commander, you pulled off quite a victory, I'm suitably impressed."

Slightly embarrassed, James knew not to contradict a superior officer but he couldn't help himself. "I'm sorry sir, but have you seen the damage reports on *Drake*? I allowed my command to be turned into a wreck."

"Nonsense," Jensen insisted waving her hand as if the damage was nothing. "You did better than anyone could have expected and from the way Governor Olsson tells it you'll be receiving the Swedish Medal of the Sword. It's the highest military medal they can award to a foreign national. You should be proud."

"I am sir," James quickly responded. "Proud of *Drake* and her crew but I didn't expect to receive any praise for my actions. I was just doing my duty, that's why we were at New Stockholm in the first place."

At that last sentence Jensen lowered her eyebrows and gave James a piercing stare. "I must say, I was surprised to see Vice Admiral Cunningham send you to New Stockholm. After your contributions so far I thought you would have come in useful at V17. Have you and the Vice Admiral a history?"

Wincing, James tried to control his emotions before replying, her change of tact had caught him off guard. "We knew each other from the academy. He took advanced tactics and I was in his tutorial group for the simulator side of the class. Before we met here two months ago, I counted him as a mentor of sorts." Looking down James reluctantly let out his next sentence, "I believe the Vice Admiral received a message from the King before he departed for the Void."

"I see," Jensen said carefully, a look of concern on her face. "Well, as I'm sure you can guess everyone is familiar with the news reports about Princess Christine. I guess it's not too hard to read between the lines."

Sitting down again Jensen motioned for James to join her at the other side of the desk. "In that case I have some good news for you. I'm not as close to the King as Vice Admiral Cunningham and I know a good officer when I see one. I have an offer for you. You may have noticed we have a few more ships here in Excalibur than strictly necessary, my own flagship included." As James nodded she continued. "Well, we'll be departing as soon as we finish up our repairs. We're needed back at V17 as soon as we are ready."

James nodded again; he assumed something had happened at V17 to let the four destroyers escape to attack New Stockholm.

As he didn't say anything Jensen continued. "In order to break the blockade we have set up around V17, Chinese Admiral Zheng feinted a large attack with his battleships. As we gathered our fleet into one unit a number of fast destroyers broke from the Chinese fleet and managed to get to the hyper limit. We tried to stop them but the Chinese Admiral brought his fleet into range and we exchanged a number of missile salvos. We only received minimal damage, as did they, but it was enough of a distraction to allow the destroyers to escape."

Though he didn't want to delay the good news, James also couldn't help asking, "What about the three destroyers that escaped from New Stockholm?"

"Sadly for them they decided to make a run at Excalibur," Jensen said grinning. "They came out of shift space almost right on top of my squadron as we were returning here for repairs. Once *Voyager* and the other pursuing ships got here, they were all but trapped. Two of them were destroyed and the third took some damage before it reached the mass shadow and jumped out. Vice Admiral Cunningham sent word back to say that it managed to slip through the blockade and return to V17."

"Good," was all James said though on the inside he was more than happy. Any Captain that was prepared to be involved in a mission whose's goal was to fire on civilian ships deserved getting caught under Jensen's guns.

As Jensen continued James' interest perked. "You can read the report of course. Why I'm telling you this is because one of the destroyers under my command took a proximity hit that momentarily knocked out her inertial dampeners. A quarter of her crew were killed and another two dozen severely injured. Her Captain was among the dead. I want you to take command."

As she paused to await James' response, he tried to speak. Feeling like he was back in sickbay aboard *Drake* he worked his jaw to try and say something as his mouth had gone completely dry. As the shock wore off he managed to get out a response.

"I'm honored sir, really I am. But I don't have command experience on a warship. Surly there is a frigate commander with the experience to make a more appropriate Captain?"

Smiling Jensen answered, "under other circumstances you may be right but we are at war. You may only be the commander of an exploration ship but you have proven yourself in combat. I've requested that you be seconded to my command from Commodore West's. She has already said yes."

Pushing over a datapad to James, she continued, "I have given you a field promotion to Captain. I'm sure if you prove yourself the Admiralty will be happy to make it official at a later date. Right now I want you to go over to *Raptor* and officially take command. Once you have a feel for the situation there, you're going to need to begin to fill in the missing personnel. You'll find some men and women from among the other ships here in Excalibur that are ready for a promotion and so can fill in some of the gaps aboard *Raptor*. For the rest I suggest you take as many as can be spared from

Drake."

Nodding, James asked, "What is to happen to her?"

"I plan to put Second Lieutenant Gupta in charge. She'll have to make do without the crew members you'll take but once she has completed enough repairs she will be taking *Drake* back to Britannia and then maybe to Earth. I suspect the Admiralty will want to give her command of *Drake* once the repairs are complete. Your report on her abilities certainly speaks well for her."

"Thank you sir," James said with relief. He was half afraid Jensen was going to appoint someone else to take command of *Drake* and take her home for repairs. "*Drake* will be in good hands with her."

"Very good Captain, now you have a lot to do. I suggest you make your way to *Raptor* and get to work. After you officially take command and get settled in, I want you to report to HMS *Ghost* at sixteen hundred hours. Captain Lightfoot is expecting you. The rest of the squadron and I will be returning to V17 but the Admiralty has something else planned for you two.

Recognizing the dismissal James rose. Before turning to leave he shook Rear Admiral Jensen's hand again. "I want to thank you again sir, I won't forget this opportunity."

*

As James approached HMS *Raptor*, he couldn't help but stare out the shuttle's viewport with an open mouth. He had always thought Chinese ships were beautiful but *Raptor* had a beauty all of her own. At twenty eight thousand tones *Raptor* was the largest destroyer the RSN had yet built. She was three hundred and four meters long and at her widest point she had a beam of sixty meters and a height of fifty. Armed with four heavy plasma cannons, each of which made

Drake's look like peashooters, she could handle herself in a close fight. For longer-range engagements, she had two forward and rear missile tubes and a broadside of six missiles tubes on both her starboard and port sides. Her streamlined construction reminded James of a cross between a battleship and a submarine from the old 20th Century wet navies. Her sleek hull mimicked that of a submarine while the large plasma cannons poking out above her superstructure gave her the menacing look of those ancient battleships.

With a crew of two hundred she was designed to easily defeat anything smaller than herself and the strategists back at the Admiralty believed that with the RSN advantage in missile ECM she should be able to take on a Chinese light cruiser and put up a good fight. That was yet to be proven, for only six of the *Crusader* class destroyers had been finished when the war broke out. To his knowledge none had seen real close quarters combat yet.

As the shuttle rose up over the bow of *Raptor* to approach the shuttle bay James caught a glimpse of another identical ship orbiting Excalibur. With the shuttle's view screen he zoomed in on the ship to see her name. HMS *Ghost*. So it seemed the Admiralty had a plan for their two *Crusader* class destroyers in the Void. As the shuttle docked, James took a moment before stepping off the shuttle and prepared himself to officially take command of his first warship.

Chapter 21 – A New Beginning

Destroyers are the workhorses of any fleet. In peace they are typically used as system pickets, convoy escorts and pirate hunters. In war, their fast acceleration and impressive stealth capabilities make them ideal for operating behind enemy lines. Yet, when larger fleet battles break out, they are always in the thick of the action helping to protect their bigger sisters.

-Excerpt from Empire Rising, 3002 AD

21st April 2465 AD, HMS *Raptor*, Excalibur.

Stepping off the shuttle, James was greeted by a loud shrill noise bombarding his ears. After a few seconds, it began to break apart into the recognizable sounds of a pipe and drum band welcoming their new Captain aboard. As both feet came to rest on *Raptor's* deck he offered a crisp salute to the assembled officers and crew. Not all the crew could fit into the shuttle hanger but a great many had tried.

A young looking man in an officer's uniform stepped out of the crowd and offered his hand. He had to shout over the din of the welcoming band, "Welcome aboard Captain, my name is Lieutenant Romanov."

James had to push down the tension that suddenly gripped his body. For the last half-century the Russians had been the bogeymen of children's bedtime stories. Yet, after the Russian government had fled Earth with a significant part of their population, hundreds of millions had been left behind. At present, the old geographical area that had been Russia was a war torn patchwork of rival warlords. Some of the surrounding nations had begun to claim territory for themselves but with the possibilities in space no one wanted the expense of having to pacify a militant population. The costs simply outweighed the benefits. Over the years though, many Russians had escaped old Russia and sought to make new lives throughout Earth, and indeed, all the human colonies. No doubt Lieutenant Romanov's parents or grandparents had been such people. Still, as much as he didn't want to admit it, he was sure Romanov had struggled in the RSN because of his background. If James' initial reaction had been one of caution, others would react with outright hostility.

With that thought James resolved to give Romanov all the respect he deserved as a RSN officer. Pushing away the last tension that had coiled around his body, he refocused on what the lieutenant was saying. "I was the third Lieutenant aboard *Raptor* but when our inertial dampeners failed Herrick, our First Lieutenant was severely injured and sadly Second Lieutenant Sanders died with the Captain on the bridge. I've been acting as the senior commanding officer for the last two days."

Nodding, James made a mental note to review everything Romanov had done in the last two days. It couldn't have been easy to be thrust from Third Lieutenant to senior commanding officer in the blink of an eye. James knew from personal experience; although he had been given a small survey ship not a damaged warship! A mistake or two would be understandable. As the last vestiges of the bos'n's pipes and drums died down, James replied, "Thank you Lieutenant Romanov, you have put together a fitting welcoming reception." Speaking louder for everyone to hear James continued, "I have to say that as the shuttle approached *Raptor* I got a good look at her. In my humble opinion she's the finest looking warship in the British navy. I'm looking forward to taking command and I'm sure you all will live up to the reputation the late Captain Hooker has already established for *Raptor*, thank you all for your welcome."

As he eyed the assembled crew he knew he had chosen the right words. On the shuttle ride over he had been able to briefly review *Raptor's* files and he had seen enough to guess Captain Hooker had been well respected and would be missed. No doubt the crew were apprehensive about getting a new Captain and he wanted to win their trust as soon as possible. With whatever Jensen and the Admiralty had planned for them, they would likely need to be working as a team fast.

Lowering his voice again James turned back to face Lieutenant Romanov, "Do you have the necessary ship wide COM set up?"

"Yes sir," Romanov replied, "this way." As Romanov led him through a gap in the assembled crowd, James fished in his jacket pocket to pull out his orders. They were printed on an old fashioned piece of paper. It was a tradition going back almost a thousand years in the Royal Navy and it had been carried over into the Royal Space Navy. When they came to the podium, Romanov stepped out of the way and allowed James to stand behind it. When Romanov had taken his place back among the assembled crew he shouted, "Crew, about turn."

With a single motion the crew turned through one hundred degrees and stood to attention with the sharp clang of their leading feet stamping on the shuttle deck. Looking down, James could see the podium was keyed into the ship wide COM so every crew member could hear him.

"Crew members of HMS *Raptor*," he began in a slow measured pace. "I am Captain James Somerville. I have with me orders issued by Rear Admiral Orla Jensen on behalf of the Admiralty, they read; 'Captain James Somerville upon receipt of these orders you are to report aboard HMS *Raptor* and assume the full responsibilities of the commanding officer. You are to carry out your duty in service to your country and your King. Upon reading these orders aboard

Raptor to her crew you will be designated her Captain."

Folding the piece of paper, James carefully put it back in his jacket pocket. He knew he would be getting it preserved as a keepsake. Then he looked back at the assembled crew. This was the point when Captains were often expected to make elaborate speeches to introduce themselves and impress the crew. James had already dismissed that idea; there was work to be done. "Crew members of *Raptor*, it's a pleasure to have the privilege of being your Captain but I'm going to end the formalities here. I believe we will be getting new orders to leave Excalibur within the next twenty-four hours. That means we all have work to do if we're going to be ready in time. I'll be making a full inspection of each department once I have reviewed the ship's logs. Until then I trust you to carry out your duty. You are all dismissed."

As the gathered crew began to disperse, Romanov approached James and asked, "can I give you a brief tour of the ship sir?"

"Not just yet," James replied, "take me to my office if you don't mind. I'm scheduled to meet with Captain Lightfoot aboard *Ghost* at sixteen hundred hours. I'm going to be reviewing *Raptor's* logs until then so I don't want to be disturbed."

"No problem sir," Romanov assured James, "I'll have a shuttle prepped and awaiting you in shuttle bay two."

"Very good," James answered, "now tell me, what state is *Raptor* in?"

"As you probably saw on your shuttle ride over here sir, outwardly she is almost as good as new. The proximity hit caused minimal damage; the valstronium armor absorbed most of the explosive force. It was a freak accident that our inertial dampeners took part of the shock of the explosion and overloaded. The repair crews at

Excalibur have been very helpful. We've replaced the sections of armor that were damaged and reapplied the stealth coating to them. We're practically as good as new."

Lowering his head to speak quieter his expression changed as he continued, "inwardly it's a different matter. Everyone has lost someone they were close to. It's strange sir. We look around and everything looks the same. There's no battle damage or sign of what happened, only the missing faces. We all respected Captain Hooker and I think many of the crew still turn around expecting to see him checking in on them or coming down to oversee some repairs being carried out. He was a very involved Captain."

It had not occurred to James before but as Romanov explained it, he realized *Raptor* was in an unusual position. Normally if a ship suffered causalities it was as a result of severe battle damage. The ship itself would have to go back to a repair yard and the surviving crew would get some down time to mourn and work through the trauma of combat.

A ship's inertial dampeners effectively created an artificial gravity field on board the ship. They also compensated for the g-forces a ship felt when it was accelerating or maneuvering. Without them, ships would be severely limited in what they could do as they couldn't accelerate or maneuver more than their crew members could tolerate without blacking out. When *Raptor's* inertial dampeners had failed it hadn't caused any secondary damage. Instead it had simply thrown the crew around with the force of the maneuvers *Raptor* had been undergoing to avoid the incoming Chinese missiles. Thankfully, the failure lasted less than a second before the backup systems came online. Yet their failure had been enough to cause injuries to most of the crew. Those unlucky enough to be thrown at the wrong angle or to be close to something solid had been severely injured and many had died, including Captain Hooker.

So *Raptor's* crew had lost many close friends without seeing the typical physical trauma to the ship. They would also not have the time to properly mourn their losses, as instead of returning to Earth or Britannia they would be going straight back into combat. James hadn't thought of this or the problems that might arise from it but it was clear Romanov was already encountering them.

"What steps have you taken to help the crew through this?" James asked.

"I have kept everyone as busy as I can over the last two days sir. That hasn't been hard as we're so down on personnel. The bodies of the dead have already been removed for transport back to Earth but I have a memorial service planned in the main shuttle bay at sixteen hundred hours. I've given all the crew two hours off duty before the service to prepare themselves and ready any tributes they want to make."

James was impressed with Romanov's initiative. Normally a junior officer wouldn't make such a bold arrangement with a new Captain on his way to assume command. "Very good Lieutenant, I'm sure that will go a long way towards helping everyone process what happened. I'd like to attend the service. Can you contact *Ghost* for me and inform them of the service and leave a message for Captain Lightfoot that I will report on board *Ghost* as soon as the service is finished."

"Aye sir," Romanov said eagerly, "the crew will be happy that you're joining us." Pointing to a large door in front of them he continued, "this is your office sir. Your quarters are adjoining on the starboard side."

"Thank you Lieutenant, you may contact me when it's time for the memorial service. Until then I don't want to be disturbed," James said as he stepped through the opening doors into his new office.

He was impressed by the size. *Raptor* was about a third larger than *Drake* but a significant amount of *Drake's* internal space had been given over to fuel tanks. Despite being a warship, *Raptor* had been designed with some level of comfort for the crew who would have to spend years serving aboard her. His office was over twice the size of the one he had aboard *Drake* and he guessed his living quarters would be the same.

Settling down at his desk, James promised he would give himself time to enjoy his new surroundings later. For now he had to get on top of what state *Raptor* was in before he met with Captain Lightfoot. After entering his RSN passwords into the main computer and being recognized as the new Captain he first opened the Captain's logs, went back six months and began to read.

Five minutes later he was disturbed with a beep from the door admittance system. Frustration caused him to lose his train of thought. He had asked not to be disturbed. Before he could give permission for whoever had requested entry into his office to come in he heard the whooshing sound of doors opening. Swinging round in his chair towards the main doors out into the corridor, James shouted in anger, "who gave you permission to..." His outburst was cut short when he realized the main doors were still shut and there was no one in sight.

Instead from over his left shoulder came a slightly shaky voice. "Excuse me Captain, I'm sorry to interrupt. I thought I should introduce myself and see if you need anything. I am the Captain's Steward, Arthur Fox."

Turning to face the man standing in the entrance to his personal quarters, James realized he had completely forgot that a Captain of a warship was meant to have his own attendant to cook for him and look after his needs. Typically stewards had free range of a Captain's quarters and office so it wasn't rude for him to just come into his office without permission. Standing, James strode over to take Fox's hand. "I'm sorry Arthur, I had forgotten that I would have a steward, I didn't mean to scare you."

"That's ok sir, I quite understand," Fox said as he looked at the ground, not meeting James' eyes. "I would understand if you already have your own steward from your previous command. I already have Captain Hooker's things packed and stowed, ready to be taken off the ship. I can arrange passage for myself with them, if you wish."

"Nonsense," James said worrying he had gotten off on the wrong foot with his steward. "I didn't have a steward on my last command. It was only a survey frigate. I'm sure I'll be delighted with your services. In fact I think I'll take a strong black coffee to help get me through the data files I'm reviewing. After that you can arrange to transfer my things from *Drake*. To be honest I hadn't thought about them yet. If you like, you can take a shuttle across and oversee the transfer yourself."

A look of relief passed across Fox's face. With a simple nod he scurried back into James' quarters and towards a door that James guessed led to his own personal galley. Clearly he was happy to have something to do and so James left him to his own devices. Turning back to his data files he began to read again, he had six hours to the memorial service.

*

Sitting in the shuttle for the short flight over to *Ghost*, James had a few minutes to reflect on the memorial service and his reading. He hadn't said anything at the service but had been content to sit at the side and observe. He hoped the crew had welcomed his presence and appreciated that he had given them space to reflect on their lost crew members. From his reading he had quickly realized that Captain Hooker had run a tight ship. Before the battle the crew's fitness reports were exceptional and in simulations *Raptor* had always performed well. Despite losing some good personnel with the failure of the inertial dampeners, the crew had come together and worked hard over the last two days. The fact so many holes in the command structure could be filled so efficiently, spoke of how well Hooker had trained his crew.

Before he left James had approved a number of promotions Lieutenant Romanov had made and then submitted the list of the replacements *Raptor* needed to Rear Admiral's Jensen's aide. Most of the losses among the lower ranks would be filled with crew members from *Drake* but the NCO's, Sub Lieutenants and Lieutenants would have to come from all the ships in Excalibur. Those in line for a promotion that couldn't be given aboard their current ship, would get a chance to join *Raptor*, a step higher up the ladder.

Within minutes of landing on *Ghost*, James was shown into Captain Lightfoot's office. Lightfoot looked just as James remembered him from the testimony he had given before the UN Interplanetary Committee. Short black hair, a black moustache and a thick neck that ran down to two square shoulders, all reminded James of a wrestler he had followed growing up. Lacking some of the fear factor, Lightfoot's six foot five frame still inspired an air of respect.

Despite his formidable appearance, Lightfoot's smile was genuine as he welcomed James into his office. "Welcome aboard *Ghost* Captain. It is good to see you again. I must apologize for the last time we met. RSNI had already scheduled further debriefs with me and so I had to rush off."

"That's quite alright sir," James began with a hint of relief. He had feared Lightfoot would be upset about him being over an hour late for their scheduled meeting. "RSNI ushered me back to my ship within minutes of ordering a drink so I didn't get to see much of New York myself. I apologize for my lateness. I hope my Third Lieutenant passed on that we were having a memorial service for the crew members *Raptor* lost. The service was already scheduled before I took over command and I thought it demanded my presence."

"I understand. May I call you James by the way, when it's just the two of us of course?" Lightfoot asked.

"Certainly sir." James said, "I get the impression we're going to be working closely together."

"Indeed we are and you can call me Patrick," Lightfoot responded with a knowing smile. "I take it you have read the most recent reports about the Chinese attack at Cook?"

As James nodded, Lightfoot continued, "Well I can tell you a bit more than the reports can. The damage to the shipyard at Cook means it is a total loss. It will take at least three years to rebuild the station and then another two to get production back to full speed. When I left Cook, the Admiralty hadn't yet heard about the outcome of the attack but I expect they will be furious. Though they won't be surprised."

Pausing for a second, Lightfoot let James ponder that before continuing. "You see RSNI got a tip off from a high ranking Chinese official that the Chinese Politburo had decided to step the war up a notch. They knew an attack of some kind was imminent and so a warning was able to get to Cook just before the Chinese carried out their attack. Even with this warning things were bad. In retaliation the Admiralty has decided to carry out raiding attacks in Chinese space. As the two Captains of *Crusader* class destroyers we'll be spearheading the raiding attack through the Void. The four other *Crusader* class destroyers will be moving up into Chinese space via Earth and the Beta colony. Their area of operations will cover the older, more established colonial worlds. We'll be hitting more backwater locations. Our targets won't be as fancy but there will also be fewer defenders so we have more chance of coming through this mission with the paintwork intact.

"Interestingly, along with the tip off about the Chinese attack we got information on the Politburo members who are championing this war. I'm reading between the lines here but I think the Admiralty is gunning for regime change among the Politburo. All our targets are either military or are owned by one of the leading Politburo members in favor of the war. So while it seems we are going be raiders for the next few months, we are to be raiders with a conscience. Tell me; is *Raptor* up to an extended long-range mission?" Lightfoot finished by asking.

James delayed his answer as he took a few seconds to take everything in. The British government and the Admiralty would only want a regime change if it were likely to bring peace. They must be hoping to target the more bloodthirsty Politburo members. If the plan worked, the targeted Politburo members would then either have to end the war to protect their personal wealth and power or else watch themselves topple as they lost prestige and influence. It was a long shot but it might just work.

"Yes sir, we are still waiting on replacement personnel but if they arrive in the next twenty-four hours we should be ready to leave. It will take a while to get everyone working together smoothly but we will have to make do," James answered.

"Granted, but you will have to do everything you can to speed up the process. We're likely to see action sooner rather than later so *Raptor* needs to be ready. Having said that, I have been given some leeway on how we approach our targets. The Admiralty has ordered us to hit the Wi system, the New Shanghai system and to liberate our mining station at Reading. After my tussle with Admiral Zheng at Damang, the Chinese sent a small force in to take over the station in case we used it as a resupply base. There'll be nothing there that is useful to us now but the Admiralty wants our people back. RSNI believes they are still being held captive on the base.

"Given your ship's situation, I've decided we'll hit Reading first. It'll take us a week to work through the shift passage from the Void to Damang and another three days to reach Reading. That should give you enough time to cement your new crew members in and be ready for whatever faces us there.

"Now," Lightfoot said as he stood and handed a datapad across the desk to James, "here is the latest RSNI info on our target systems. I would like your thoughts on how we should approach each objective."

*

Four hours later James finally set the datapad down. He was exhausted. He felt he had covered every possibility he could think of, given the data in front of him. James was pleased that Lightfoot and he had worked so well together. They had modified Lightfoot's original plans in a number of places. James now felt confident that their plans were as good as they could make them, without actually jumping into each system and laying eyes on what was really happening in each one.

After thanking James for his assistance as an afterthought Lightfoot added, "oh, I'm sending over the commanding officer of my marines to liaise with your men. He will get your boys up to date and then return to *Ghost* before we leave Excalibur. I think you have already met him, Major Johnston."

James was momentarily surprised; he had thought the Major had intended to return to his wife as soon as the mission to capture the Chinese destroyer at Excalibur had been completed. What could have changed his mind?

Chapter 22 - Friendship

Serving in the navy often forged friendships that would last a lifetime. Being assigned to the same ship for years would lead to many crew members thinking of themselves as family. Even so, it was rare that officers got to develop such connections. They had to remain aloof from their subordinates and as they moved from ship to ship more often than other crew members they rarely built deep lasting friendships.

-Excerpt from Empire Rising, 3002 AD

21st April 2465 AD, HMS *Raptor*, Excalibur

Stepping off the shuttle back onto *Raptor*, James paused to say farewell to Major Johnston. Back when Johnston had taken passage on board *Drake* to attack the Chinese destroyer, he had thought he had gotten on well with the Major. In the brief flight over to *Raptor*, James could already tell things had changed. Johnston hadn't been the most talkative marine he had ever met but he had barely said a couple of words during the flight. It seemed all he was interested in was the Reading mission. When James had asked about his wife a look of pain had crossed his face before he had regained control and fixed a steely expression in its place. James had waited for an answer but when none had been forth coming he had given up.

As he turned to say farewell to the Major a familiar voice distracted him. "Major Johnston, it's good to see you again sir," came the feminine voice of Georgia Gupta across the shuttle bay.

The Major grunted a reply before walking off in the direction of the marine barracks aboard *Raptor*. James on the other hand swung round. "What are you doing here Georgia? You're meant to be commanding *Drake*."

Instead of answering him she held out her hand, "Welcome back Captain and congratulations on your promotion. I'm sorry I didn't get time to call over the COM and congratulate you before now."

Taking a step back she smiled at James, "Do you like my new uniform?"

Only then did James notice the extra Silver Star on her shoulder, the mark of a First Lieutenant. "When the list of open spaces was sent around the fleet I applied for the open First Lieutenant spot, Rear Admiral Jensen assigned me here immediately based on you evaluation of me."

James was momentarily speechless, "But, you're meant to be commanding *Drake*. If you take her back to Earth and oversee the repairs, the Admiralty is bound to give you a promotion to Commander. That's why I wrote the evaluation for you."

"I know that James," Gupta said, smiling again as she used his first name and enjoyed the confusion that was all across his face. "But if I did that I would be sitting out the rest of this war on the side-lines. Britain is my home too and I intend to fight to protect her. Besides," she began as she turned and started to walk away, forcing James to follow her, "you seem to lead an interesting life as far as this war goes. I'm betting that if I stick close to you, I'll see plenty of action and get lots of chances to prove my worth to the Admiralty. Come to the bridge and I'll show you what Lieutenant Romanov and I have been doing in your absence."

James began to follow. By the tone of Gupta's voice it was obvious she already had a growing respect for the newly promoted Second Lieutenant. Given that their family backgrounds were so similar, they were likely to have a lot in common. Both were certainly good officers. "What about *Drake*, who has Jensen put in charge of her now?" James asked as they walked.

"Before I made my request I checked in with Sub Lieutenant Fisher," Gupta explained. "She has made a better than expected recovery from her injuries aboard the Swedish colony ship. She had already put in a request to be reassigned back aboard *Drake*. I simply approved her request and then included a recommendation that she take over responsibility for getting *Drake* home if my transfer was accepted."

Seeing wisdom in Gupta's decision, James simply nodded. Some independent command experience would do Fisher the world of good. She still lacked a bit of self-confidence. And it would also do her chances of making Lieutenant no harm at all. There wasn't many Sub Lieutenants who got the chance to put command experience on their file. She would never be able to keep command once she reached Britannia but even a couple of weeks of experience would look good.

As he strode onto the bridge James realized he was humming to himself. The weight of getting *Raptor* ready in time and finding enough personnel to replace those injured or killed had been weighting heavier on him than he had appreciated. Suddenly the weight had lightened a great deal.

Sitting down in the command chair, he listened to Gupta and Romanov detail how they planned to fit all the new crew members into the existing watches. Once they were finished he approved their plans and, with a few moments of peace, he turned his attention to something that had been bothering him. On his console he opened up Major Johnston's personnel file. After briefly reviewing it nothing seemed out of the ordinary. After completing the mission to board and take the Chinese destroyer he had returned to Earth for a lengthy debrief. Rather than dismiss him, the

Marines had decided to retain Johnston until the end of the war. He had then been posted to Cook. Why Cook though? Then James remembered. Johnston had once said that he had sent his wife to visit relatives in Cook in case the tensions between Britain and China spilled over into war.

With trepidation James accessed the details of the Chinese attack on Cook. He searched the list of deaths from the attack on the orbital shipyard and battlestations but Johnston's wife wasn't there. Then he spotted a secondary file marked 'collateral causalities.' As he read, he realized that as the shipyard in orbit around Cook had been destroyed it hadn't simply exploded. Too large to be completely destroyed by the smaller missiles used by the attacking missileboats, it had broken up. Several large chunks had broken through the planet's atmosphere and struck the surface. None had been large enough to do any serious damage but one had impacted the ocean. The collision had been near a series of villages that were being set up as fishing villages to provide food for the growing population of a nearby city. As he searched through the dead he found the name he was looking for. Noelle Johnston. Selecting her name brought up some additional details including her maiden name. Looking back at the list of collateral causalities, James saw other people with the same last names. Noelle's family in Cook must have been involved in setting up the new fishing villages. Many of them had been killed as a tsunami, caused by the section of the shipyard that had impacted the sea only a few miles from their village, had swamped the area.

Searching through some more files, James tried to find out where the Major had been when this happened. He was horrified to find out that he had been in the Cook system. He had just arrived hours earlier and had been in orbit aboard a passenger freighter when the attack had taken place. A few more seconds found that the freighter had attempted to contact the villages to warn them of the approaching danger. While everyone else's attention had been focused on the battle unfolding in orbit around Cook, one man's attention had been on the planet. The major cities all had their own missile defense systems to protect against invasion and any debris falling from orbit. The villages did not. Johnston's warnings had allowed the other villages to be evacuated just in time but the one his wife had been in was just too close to the impact.

Suddenly, James felt a new weight on his shoulders. He couldn't imagine what Major Johnston had gone through. To watch his wife die before his very eyes, the very wife he had told to go to somewhere he had thought was safe. Forgetting the other duties that were pressing upon him, James tried to think of how he could help the Major but when Gupta returned twenty minutes later needing his approval for another personnel change nothing had come to him.

*

Twelve days later *Raptor* and *Ghost* dropped out of shift space on the edge of the Reading system. They had stopped off in the Damang system to carry out some exercises and observe any Chinese shipping that was passing through on its way to V17. Admiral Cunningham's blockade of V17 was meant to keep the Chinese fleet locked up so it couldn't carry out any further attacks. Normally, when blockading a system it was easy to stop any ships getting in by simply patrolling the shift passages. In the Void this was impossible as a ship could approach from any angle. That meant the Chinese were able to run as much supplies and reinforcements into the system as they wanted. The only caveat was that once in the system it was difficult to leave. Any ships trying to make their way to the edge of the mass shadow were easily spotted, allowing Admiral Cunningham to get a blocking force in place.

Before they left, the latest intel from the Admiral had been that the Chinese were running supply convoys into V17 at a rate of about one every two weeks, although the gap had been slowly expanding. RSNI operatives imbedded with the Admiral's fleet suspected the Chinese were having problems finding enough freighters to keep sending into V17 when so few were returning.

By the time *Raptor* and *Ghost* had left Excalibur another convoy was expected and so they had waited in stealth to watch the convoy pass through. A light cruiser and a destroyer had been escorting it. As they had been too far away to sneak into close range under stealth, Lightfoot had decided to leave it alone. A long range shooting match with a light cruiser and destroyer would likely leave one if not both British destroyers damaged and unable to continue.

Now in the Reading system, both ships came to a stop on the edge of the mass shadow. Every passive scanner was focused on the inner system. "The gravimetric sensors are not picking up any ships at high acceleration sir," Sub Lieutenant Becket called out from her place at the sensors console. She was another of the crew from *Drake* who had been assigned to *Raptor*. James was pleased to have her.

Over the next ten minutes Becket and the other bridge officers worked to analyze all the data that was coming in. James purposely didn't watch the live feeds. He wanted his bridge crew to learn to work without his oversight.

After spending some time with Becket, Romanov switched on the main holo display. He also configured it so that the holo display on the auxiliary bridge would show the same image. All RSN military ships were fitted with auxiliary bridges that could take over the control of the ship in the event that the main bridge was damaged. When at battle stations, the First Lieutenant was assigned to the auxiliary bridge and was to be prepared to take over in a moment's notice. James was still getting used to the idea of having Gupta aboard and yet not on the bridge where he could pick her brains.

With a COM channel opened between the two bridges, Romanov gave James and Gupta a breakdown of his findings so far. "Captain, the mining station is definitely still operational, it's radiating heat into the third planet's atmosphere like crazy. The levels are actually higher than our safety or environmental regulations allow. I suspect the Chinese have expanded the mining operation or are running our equipment at full capacity. We've also been getting intermittent electromagnetic radiation from orbit around the planet. It wasn't enough to ID a ship but there's something in orbit. If it's not a ship it must be some kind of automated station."

Before James could respond the Sub Lieutenant manning Communications announced that *Ghost* had established a laser link and Lightfoot was on the line.

"Captain," James said to acknowledge that he was now receiving the visual of Captain Lightfoot. "My officers believe there to be a ship in orbit around the third planet. Probably keeping station above the mining facilities."

"As do mine, Captain Somerville," Lightfoot replied. "I've decided to go with plan gamma. You may begin transferring your marines over to *Ghost* immediately. We'll depart as soon as they are on board. Happy hunting Captain."

"You too sir," James replied as the visual of Lightfoot disappeared. Plan gamma called for *Ghost* to move into the system and assault the mining station while *Raptor* waited near the mass shadow to pick off any ships that tried to leave.

Typing in a series of commands, James sent orders for the marines to prepare to embark onto *Ghost*. Then he ordered the crew manning the auxiliary bridge to stand down. It would take hours for *Ghost* to creep into the system under stealth and he didn't want his crew to get worn out before the real fun began.

Major Samuel Johnston could feel his anger growing as *Ghost* got closer and closer to the mining facilities and the Chinese inside. During the time it had taken *Ghost* to get close to the third planet of the Reading system he had been briefing the marines from *Raptor*. Initially, he had planned to fully brief them when he had visited *Raptor* back at Excalibur but in the end he had only stayed long enough to give them the barest details. He hadn't expected to see Captain Somerville there let alone Lieutenant Gupta and Sub Lieutenant Becket. Seeing so many familiar faces had brought back memories of the mission to Excalibur and his fateful decision to leave Earth. Only Captain Lightfoot knew of his loss and he hadn't wanted to speak to any of the old crew members of *Drake*.

Every morning he woke up, he regretted his decision to agree to Becket's request that he be temporally reactivated in the marines. For days his anger had been directed at her and the RSNI spook Mr. Jones. Yet seeing her again had softened it somewhat. She had done well on the Excalibur mission and he respected her. He knew she had only been following orders when she had turned up at his house. In fact, he knew that ten times out of ten he would have accepted the Marines call to be reactivated and carry out his duty. But hindsight was sometimes a cruel mistress. Now, all he wanted was to go back and change his decision. And yet he couldn't. He couldn't change his decision and he couldn't change his current circumstances. So now he focused all his anger and rage on killing any Chinese he could get his hands on. They had killed his wife and now he was going to kill them.

All the marines were crammed onto the five shuttles in both of *Ghost's* shuttle bays. The shuttles themselves were packed closely together as two were from *Raptor*. As the commanding officer Johnston sat in the cockpit of the lead shuttle with the two pilots. He had a direct line to the bridge and was able to watch the holo image of *Ghost* and the third planet as they made their approach.

When they were close enough, visuals confirmed the presence of a Chinese ship in orbit. It had turned out to be a Chinese frigate. Some of the marines were placing bets on whether or not it would stay and try to fight or would turn tail and run when they spotted *Ghost*. Johnston hoped its Commander would be foolish enough to stay and fight. He was looking forward to seeing the frigate gunned down. The logical part of him not driven by his anger realized that it was very unlikely. The frigate could never hope to match itself against *Ghost*.

At the prearranged time a power fluctuation erupted from *Ghost's* number three fission reactor. It was so strong, it set off minor warnings on the control board of the shuttle Johnston was in. The Chinese couldn't miss it. Indeed, as Johnston watched, it only took the Chinese frigate seconds before it began to send out powerful beams of energy using its main search radar. Almost immediately *Ghost* went to full power, charging straight for the frigate. With luck it would look to the Chinese like *Ghost* had been trying to sneak up to the frigate and had been given away by a faulty reactor.

Now the Chinese Commander would know what he was up against. Would he stay or run? Johnston only had to wait thirty seconds to find out. After a brief flurry of electromagnetic radiation suggesting a signal was sent down to the mining facilities the frigate began to boost out of orbit, away from the approaching British destroyer. Someone on the bridge plotted the frigate's likely rout of escape given its current vector. At present speeds *Ghost* would be able to get off a few shots from her two bow tubes but then the smaller frigate's better acceleration would allow it to escape. Of course, *Ghost* had more acceleration up her sleeve but the Chinese weren't to know that.

As the frigate began to break orbit and head away from the third planet *Ghost's* vector took her gradually away from a direct approach to the mining facility and her speed continued to increase. Without knowing the route of escape the frigate would choose, it had been impossible to plan the next part of the mission precisely, but now that the frigate had begun to move someone on *Ghost's* bridge updated the shuttle with their flight plans. On her new vector *Ghost* would pass closest to the mining facilities in another five minutes sixty seconds. Three minutes before this point the shuttles would launch and immediately begin to decelerate in order to drop down into the planet's atmosphere and, hopefully, surprise the Chinese defenders. Unless the Chinese had shipped in expensive sensor packages for the mining facility, they wouldn't be able to detect the small shuttles. All they would see would be *Ghost* passing by the planet in pursuit of the escaping frigate. At the same time *Ghost* would turn on her jamming equipment to prevent the frigate from warning the planet. Johnston didn't know if Somerville or Lightfoot had come up with the plan but he was suitably impressed. He would be even more so if it worked.

When the timer hit zero, the shuttles began to launch from the two shuttle bays. One part of being in the marines Johnston hated was that he spent most of his life being a passenger. Now that the mission was a go he still had to wait and watch as the pilots guided his shuttle to its destination. Each shuttle had its own target and as they began to descend through the atmosphere the shuttles separated as the mining facilities covered an area of more than thirty square miles. Johnston and his first platoon would be leading the assault to recover the prisoners in conjunction with second platoon on board the shuttle keeping station with them. The other three platoons would secure the main control facilities, the landing zone and the equipment store. Details on the facility said there was enough explosive in the equipment store to blow up the entire facility. Johnston didn't want some suicidal Chinese taking out his entire assault party.

306

With their targets already identified, the other three shuttles began their final swoop down to land. A hail of fire sprang up from the ground at the shuttle making its way to the landing zone but it was cut short as the shuttle fired a hyper velocity missile at the defenders. Johnston ground his teeth as he waited for the co-pilot to work the shuttle's thermal scanners. "There," he shouted. "The greatest concentration of bodies is in the secondary housing unit, that must be them."

Johnston only had to glance at the holo display to confirm the findings. "Take us in," he ordered.

As the shuttle zoomed in towards its target, an alert had obviously gone out from one of the other objectives for men in combat armor began pouring out of one of the side buildings. The marine gunners aboard the two shuttles began to fire at them but the shuttles weaving through the mining equipment that towered into the sky put most of their shots off. All the same, three or four Chinese fell to the ground with gaping holes where plasma cannon fire had punched through them, armor and all.

While all this was going on, Johnston was reviewing the tactical scans of the area. Tapping his command console he spoke into his COM unit, "put us down over there, we'll take it from here."

Switching between channels, he continued, "ok Marines, our objective is coming up. Once we disembark the Chinese positions will be at our three o'clock. First and second squads, you are to lay down covering fire. Third squad you're with me, we're going to flank round to the right."

After a series of affirmatives from the squad leaders Johnston switched the COM channel again, "Lieutenant Albion, my men are going to lay down covering fire and flank to the right. Our flanking maneuver will only be a feint. I want you to give us thirty seconds and then take your men down the left flank, punch through the defenders and get into that building. Leave any stragglers to me."

In the Royal Marines each squad consisted of six men and three squads made a platoon. Destroyers carried a total of three platoons and, with one left on *Raptor* that gave Johnston a total fighting force of ninety men. He was confident that if he could get a full platoon of marines in combat armor into their target building, any defenses inside would crumble. They just had to get past what was waiting for them outside.

Before the shuttle hit the ground, Johnston was jumping out, trusting his power armor to cushion the fall. He had ordered the shuttle to put down behind some mining equipment so his men had a screen protecting them from enemy fire while they disembarked. As soon as they were out the first and second squads spread out through the mining equipment and began to fire at the makeshift barriers the defenders had set up in front of the building holding the hostages. Once third squad had formed up around him, Johnston sprinted off at an angle away from the barricade. He was constantly scanning his surroundings but was confident the defenders would be focused on the attack coming from their front. After sixty seconds, he slowed the pace of his sprint and turned back towards the enemy with third squad behind him. When he got to the point he could see the green flashes of the plasma cannons he crouched down and signaled the rest of the squad to fan out. Slowly they maneuvered around the various mining equipment until they all had good firing points.

When he saw that everyone was in position he gave the command. "Fire!" Suddenly, the defenders found themselves taking fire from two directions. The first three plasma bolts from his men all found their targets. After that the defenders ducked behind cover that would protect them from the new angle of attack, popping up occasionally to return fire. When Johnston heard a click over the radio to signal that Lieutenant Albion's platoon was in place he sent an acknowledgment back.

Peeking out from his cover, Johnston saw eighteen marines in heavy combat armor break out of cover from almost directly behind the new positions the defenders had taken. Assisted by the combat armor a marine could sprint at sixty miles per hour over short distances. Each marine had his plasma rifle aimed at a defender but they were holding their fire. It wasn't until the first defender had spotted them and began to turn to open fire that Lieutenant Albion gave the order to open up. At almost point blank range a hail of plasma bolts rained down on the defenders, killing more than fifteen of them. The rest abandoned their now useless cover and dove away from the secondary living quarters to find safety. A few fell to shots from his platoon while about ten escaped.

The gap in the defenses was all the encouragement Albion needed, he immediately ordered his men to alter their angle of attack and make straight for the now undefended entrance to the living quarters. Quickly, explosive charges were fastened to the large doors and the marines stepped back as they detonated. Before the smoke began to clear Albion and his squad were rushing through the door. Plasma bolts rained out the door past the entering marines. One struck Albion and blew him backwards to land in the dirt in front of his objective. Another marine fled clutching his leg but the sheer weight of return fire from the marines silenced the defenders and the rest of the marines were in the building in seconds.

Satisfied that second platoon would soon have the objective under control, Johnston switched his focus back to the defenders who were left outside. Over the COM he ordered first and second squads to move up while he took third squad round to flank them again. This time he made sure they were able to work their way right behind the enemy. Slowly, he crept closer and closer to the Chinese positions and then he jumped from cover and charged, ordering his men to follow as he ran. He had picked out two Chinese defenders who were in a smaller recon version of the Chinese army's combat suits. With his plasma riffle he sent five bolts into one of his targets, almost turning him to dust despite the armor plating of his suit. With his left hand he whipped out his long marine combat knife. As the second Chinese soldier began to turn to face the new threat he plunged the knife into his chest. The monomolecular blade easily cut through the armored suit and slammed right into the soldier's heart. As blood spurted out the gaping wound in the armor, Johnston savored the moment and the look of shock on the dying man's face. Shutting down any sympathy he felt, he summoned the image of the approaching tsunami crashing over the beach and the buildings where his wife had been staying. With a grunt he twisted the knife extinguishing the life force of the man whose people had taken the only thing he cared about.

After wiping his knife, almost ceremonially he returned it to its sheath and then began to refocus on the battle. Three of the remaining defenders outside their objective had surrendered, the rest were dead. As he was giving orders to restrain the prisoners, a voice came on the COM channel. "Major, this is Sergeant Anderson."

"Go ahead Sergeant," Johnston responded.

"We have the prisoners sir. Of the thirty that were here when the Chinese attacked, we have recovered twenty-seven. The survivors say the Chinese army commander killed their leader as an example. Two others with technical expertise were taken away before the troop ship that attacked the planet left orbit. They think they were taken off world to be interrogated."

"Good work Sergeant," Johnston commended. "And what of your

causalities?"

"We have two dead including Lieutenant Albion and another three wounded sir, none serious."

"Ok, get your wounded and the survivors to the shuttles and back to *Ghost*, she should be coming back for us in about thirty minutes. Unless our other teams find anything interesting, there's no point us sticking around any longer than we have to."

*

Aboard *Raptor* James was eagerly awaiting his first combat as the Captain of a warship. As things went, he couldn't have planned a better first engagement either for himself or to meld his crew into a single fighting unit. The Chinese frigate was almost heading straight for them. She had to leave the system through the same shift passage they had come in through after all. To get close to the frigate he had ordered a slight course correction but that had been two hours ago. Now *Raptor* was cruising along with all her systems powered down and her engines shut off. Being only two years old, her stealth tech was even better than *Drake's*. Thus, even though it was much harder to hide a destroyer James was confident the frigate wouldn't detect them until it was too late.

As far as he could tell, the bridge crew were as eager as he was for action, though he knew everyone was frustrated by not knowing what had happened at the mining facility. *Ghost* had turned back from pursuing the frigate over three hours ago and *Raptor's* passive scanners had picked up shuttles returning to the destroyer from the surface. Other than that *Raptor* was in the dark as to the outcome of their primary objective.

Nonetheless the crew were focused on the task at hand. James watched as Lieutenant Romanov personally took command of the targeting computers for the main plasma cannons. Engineering had reduced their power for the first shots and Romanov carefully aimed each cannon at the frigates own plasma cannon and its two missile tubes that were facing *Raptor*. Already the RSN had captured a Chinese destroyer thanks to James and *Drake,* along with a light cruiser that had been damaged in the battle at Excalibur. James hoped to add another ship for the intelligence officers to pick over. When all the cannons had locked onto their targets, Romanov looked up at James. He simply nodded and Romanov pressed the button to fire. Four heavy plasma cannon bolts struck the frigate and although they were fired with minimal yield, the frigate still visibly shook.

Immediately Sub Lieutenant Ferguson was on the COM channel demanding the frigate's surrender. "This is HMS *Raptor*, you have been crippled, surrender now or be destroyed. If you try to turn your other missile tubes to bear on us we will fire. I repeat we will fire. Surrender now. You have thirty seconds."

As Ferguson continued to count down the remaining time, James waited patiently. The frigate was heading out of the system at 0.3c. He had maneuvered *Raptor* to be on a roughly parallel course to what he had expected to be the frigate's route of escape. Yet, because he had had to stay in stealth, he hadn't been able to get anywhere near *Raptor's* top speed. As a result the frigate would be out of firing range less than forty seconds after the first shots had been fired. If they didn't surrender, James would have to blow them up.

Ten seconds before their time was up, the Chinese frigate cut its engines. A cheer erupted on the bridge that James had to hush down as the Chinese Commander contacted James to officially surrender. *Raptor* powered up her drives and took off towards the frigate while the frigate began to slow its vector out of the system. As soon as the distances had reduced enough, the last of *Raptor's* shuttles took, off bringing over a boarding party of marines and navy personnel. The intelligence types would be getting another ship to look at after all.

.

Chapter 23 – Raiders

The greatest casualty in war is always the civilian population. This was true in the Solar Expansion Era, the First Interstellar Expansion Era and the interspecies wars that gave birth to the Empire.

-Excerpt from Empire Rising, 3002 AD

10th May 2465 AD, HMS *Raptor*, Wi system

After the successful capture of the Chinese frigate, the morale of the crews of both *Raptor* and *Ghost* was high. The Chinese prisoners from the assault on the mining facility had been transferred to the frigate and a prize crew had been put on board to take her back to the Void and then to Earth. With renewed enthusiasm, both ships had begun the voyage back to Damang and then on to the Wi system. James was currently sitting on the bridge of *Raptor* watching the passive scans of the system. Discovered over fifty years ago, it contained two barely habitable planets. Humans couldn't walk on the surface of either unaided. Both were just on the edge of the goldilocks range, one closer to the system's star while the other was further out towards the edge of the system. With a bit of investment, the Chinese had managed to get colonies going on both planets but their size was limited. No one willingly came to either to Wi Li or Wi Liang as the two planets were called. Both environments were too hostile. Instead the Chinese used the planets as centers of research and mining. Together they boasted a population of half a million. That in itself demonstrated how much money had been invested into whatever the Chinese had going on here. Hopefully, thought James, they were about to ensure the Chinese got a very poor return on their investment.

The difficulty was in selecting what targets to hit. There were mining facilities scattered around the system's outer asteroid field and a gas mining station at the system's only gas giant. Obviously the two planets themselves presented juicy targets but it would be difficult to destroy anything vital to the Chinese war effort without spending a considerable amount of time in orbit carefully picking out their targets.

On top of that they had two more problems. The first was the system pickets. There were three frigates, two destroyers and a light cruiser patrolling the inner system. On their own, the two British destroyers could take any one of them out but together the Chinese ships would be too powerful to risk a confrontation.

The second problem was their orders from the Admiralty. They were only to attack targets owned by the Chinese military or directly owned by certain Politburo members. They also had to do everything in their power to prevent civilian causalities. Britain was already winning the public relations war and once news of the Chinese attack on the Swedish colony ship hit Earth, it would likely send a wave of sympathy through the populations of the other nations.

So, somehow, they had to identify the right targets and make sure they didn't kill any civilians, all the while avoiding a squadron of Chinese picket ships. James was glad he wasn't the senior commander of this mission. Lightfoot would have to make the final decision on how they proceeded.

Thankfully, RSNI had managed to give them a rough break down of who owned what in the system so they weren't going in completely blind. As he was reviewing the list of targets again, James' thoughts were interrupted by a COM message from *Ghost*. Captain Lightfoot was grinning as his face appeared on James' personal holo display.

"Not as easy as we thought it was going to be is it?" he asked.

"No sir," James replied, "After months in the Void and years out surveying the dark matter beyond Cambridge I'd forgotten how busy even a recently colonized system could be."

"I can well imagine. The shipping's not our priority though. If we can hit any freighters we can identify as legitimate targets all the better but it's the system's infrastructure we're after. Here's what I'm thinking at the moment. The system picket is the key. If we can destroy them or get the heavier ships to move away from the planets, we can make a quick run past them and take out any targets we can identify.

"I propose we go for the second option and try and force the Chinese ships to move away from the planets. We can revert back to trying to take them out if there is no other option. Ideally, I want to spend the next few months out here raiding Chinese space so the longer we can avoid a real fight the better. To that end I'm going to take *Ghost* into the system under stealth. I want you to prepare to make a micro jump along the edge of the system - as far as the dark matter will allow. Once you get as far as you can I want you to make a high speed run at these asteroid mining facilities."

On James' personal holo display a set of coordinates about forty degrees around the system's outer edge from *Raptor's* current location began to flash.

Lightfoot continued, "Those asteroids seem to be the biggest mining operation the Chinese have going on, apart from those on the two habitable planets. At the moment there is one frigate close to the asteroids protecting them and the freighter traffic loading ore there. Once they detect you coming I doubt they'll stick around to put up a fight. Hopefully, the system commander will then feel he has to detach some of the inner system pickets to come to the frigate's aid.

I want you to try and take out as much of the asteroid mining facilities as you can as well as any freighters that come under your guns. But your main objective is to force some ships out of the inner system to come and face you. So just make as much of a nuisance of yourself as you can.

"I'll take *Ghost* as far into the system as I can without being detected. If any holes in their defenses open as they move to confront you, I'll be ready to take advantage. I don't plan on taking any risks though. If things get hairy, I'm going to pull out and I want you to do the same. We have time on our side. Even if they send to New Shanghai for reinforcements, it'll take days for them to arrive. If this plan fails, we can regroup and try again. I'm sending you three new sets of coordinates. They will be our rendezvous points in case we lose contact."

"Aye sir," James responded, already eager to get going now that Lightfoot had a plan. "I guess this time it's my turn to say happy hunting."

"Indeed, I'll see you on the other side of the system. If this goes well, we'll make our way to New Shanghai and see what trouble we can cause there," Lightfoot replied as he nodded and switched off the COM channel.

When Lightfoot disappeared, James relayed the coordinates from his personal holo display to Sub Lieutenant Jackson who was the navigation officer on duty. "Plot us a series of micro jumps around the mass shadow to get us as close as possible to these coordinates. Then calculate a least time intercept course for the asteroid mining facilities. Aim for the largest one. I want an overall ETA until we enter firing range of the asteroids if we make our first jump in two hours. Send it to my personal computer in my office."

James didn't wait to hear the acknowledgement from the navigation officer but instead rose and walked out of the bridge. As he had been speaking, he had also keyed in a command for Lieutenants Romanov and Gupta to meet him in his office so he made his way there. After getting seated and manipulating the main holo display to show the latest sensor scans of the system, he waited for his Lieutenants to arrive.

Romanov was the first to enter the office, closely followed by Gupta. As they sat James began, "Lightfoot has decided our next course of action. He's going to try and sneak into the system while we stir up a hornet's nest further out and draw the Chinese forces to us."

As he was speaking, his computer beeped to let him know the navigation officer had sent him the navigational data. Putting it up on the holo display James continued. "We're going to wait two hours to let *Ghost* make her way in system then we'll jump to here," he said as he pointed to the last jump destination in Jackson's planned route. "Then we'll make for the asteroid belt at full speed. Every gravimetric sensor in the system will spot us so we'll get everyone's attention."

James manipulated the holo display where the computer estimated the system pickets would be when *Raptor* came out of stealth. "Based on our observations of the picket ship's patrol patterns this is how the enemy's disposition should look. If the system commander reacts quickly, he can send this destroyer currently orbiting Yi Liang. It will not make it to the asteroids in time to stop us destroying most of them but it will prevent us from chasing down the freighters in the area unless we want to stick around for a fight. Dispatching the destroyer certainly seems like the best option for the Chinese Commander. With luck *Ghost* will be able to take advantage of Wi Liang being uncovered and make an attack on the planet before Captain Lightfoot can be driven off. Do either of you have any suggestions for the plan?" James asked as he looked from

Romanov to Gupta.

Neither was quick to speak as they took everything in. Whether Romanov waited for his senior to speak or Gupta was just the quickest to come up with something, she broke the silence first. "What about if we were to make a run for the frigate instead? If we could close them down and destroy them, then we would buy ourselves more time to be able to pick off the freighters and swing round and destroy the mining facilities on the asteroids. It might even force the system commander to send in more ships to try and drive us off, giving *Ghost* more of a chance to hit a vulnerable target."

It was Romanov who said what James was thinking. "I'm not sure that will work. If we jumped out of shift space and went to full acceleration towards the frigate they would see us coming a mile off. We could eventually overhaul and destroy them but the chase would bring us dangerously close to the inner system pickets. If we tried to slow down to come back for the asteroids we could get caught by the inner system pickets as they accelerated out to meet us. Destroying the frigate would be ideal but I can't see how we do it without running the risk of biting off more than we can chew."

Gupta was nodding in agreement as Romanov finished his last sentence. She had obviously already moved on from her initial suggestion and had another. "What about if we only make it look like we're going for the frigate? That might still have the same effect, forcing the system commander to send more than the destroyer out after us but still enable us to keep out of danger and hit the mining facilities on the asteroids."

Intrigued James leaned forward in his seat, "Explain," he ordered.

*

Four hours later *Raptor* was cruising towards the asteroid mining facilities under stealth at ten percent of her maximum acceleration. She had slowly been building her speed up to 0.2c. As she reached the pre-planned speed, her main fission reactors were powered up to ninety percent and then her engines boosted up to ninety five percent of maximum thrust. With her reactors and engine working near their maximum *Raptor* had given up all attempts of being stealthy.

As she began to accelerate much more quickly, it only took a slight course correction to point her right at the Chinese frigate patrolling in the region of the asteroid mining facilities. James sat back in his command chair watching the main holo display. This part of their plan would take another forty five minutes and then things would get really interesting. At present all he could do was watch the feed from gravimetric sensors being displayed on the main holo display. The frigate was the first to react. Picking up *Raptor* from her acceleration on their own gravimetric sensors, the frigate immediately began to move away from the mining asteroids. Her starting speed had been rather slow as she had been keeping station with one of the asteroids and so *Raptor's* closing speed gave her an advantage. Still, the navigation officer estimated that *Raptor* would not reach the asteroids for another two hours; the frigate had plenty of time to run.

Nothing else happened for almost five minutes but then the next ships to react proved to be the light cruiser and destroyer in orbit around Wi Li. Together they began to boost out of orbit and accelerate towards *Raptor*. Strange, James thought as he considered the situation, he could understand the Chinese Commander, likely on board the light cruiser, wanting to meet the threat in person. But why leave the planet completely unprotected? Soon the answer became clear. The remaining two frigates in the system turned and began to make for Wi Li. It must have been a prearranged plan for there had been no time for a light speed communication to be sent to the frigates. James was both pleased and slightly concerned about the developments. The movement of the two frigates opened up the door for *Ghost* to attack the system's only gas mining facility around the gas giant, or Lightfoot could move in towards Wi Li. His destroyer should be able to easily cripple or destroy the two frigates. The planet would then be at his mercy, at least until the other ships returned. But with a frigate already in the vicinity of James' target and a light cruiser and destroyer on the way, his side of the mission had just got a little tougher. He was going to be hard pressed to pull off a successful attack and make it away in one piece. Still, for the moment, Gupta's plan gave them the most options so he remained quiet and watched the plot of the system.

Raptor reached her maximum speed of 0.35c after forty five minutes of acceleration. Gupta's plan called for her to continue on their current course for one more hour until she got to the edge of the inner system. When the allotted time was up, James nodded to Gupta. She immediately began to give orders. "Navigation, bring the engines down to six percent acceleration then prepare to rig the gaseous shields. Then bring us onto a new vector towards the largest asteroid." Moments later she had opened a COM channel to the engine room and was talking to *Raptor's* Chief Engineer Hugo O'Neil. "Alright Chief you can power the reactors down, just leave us enough juice to run the engines up to six percent and maintain our gaseous shields. Be ready to bring the power levels back up in a hurry though in case we get into an unexpected fire fight."

James had been impressed with Gupta's plan, especially the final point of using the gaseous shields. The shields were simply a mixture of ionized gases pumped out of the ship and held in place by electromagnetic fields. Originally they were used to help shield a ship's crew from harmful cosmic particles when the ship was traveling at high speeds. They had been made obsolete with the discovery of valstronium, for it provided a far better protection and gave ships much greater top speeds. The RSN hadn't done away with the shields though. Officially they been kept so that a ship that had its valstronium armor damaged could still travel through space. Unofficially, they could also be used to increase a ship's top speed. Combining the gaseous shields and her valstronium armor meant *Raptor* could reach speeds of 0.38c. With the engines powered down to six percent, it would take another fifteen minutes to reach her new maximum speed. Crucially though, the Chinese ships would be expecting *Raptor* to be approaching at .35c. The difference wasn't much but it would let them have a small element of surprise. Also, with her engines producing so little acceleration and her stealth systems engaged, now that her reactors were also powered down the Chinese wouldn't be aware of *Raptor's* change in vector. They would no doubt guess she had entered stealth to make a course change but they wouldn't know where to.

Gupta's plan called for *Raptor* to remain in stealth until they reached the mining facilities. The idea had been to force the Chinese ships to make a decision between two options, either of which would be advantageous to *Raptor* and *Ghost*. Either the Chinese Commander would order the frigate back to the asteroid field, leaving it vulnerable to *Raptor* or it would flee back to meet up with the coming reinforcements, leaving *Raptor's* target undefended. At the same time, the very fact that *Raptor* was now undetectable meant the approaching light cruiser and destroyer had to take precautions themselves. If *Raptor* managed to get close to them in stealth, they would suddenly find themselves being hunted rather than doing the hunting.

Ten minutes passed before anything happened but when it did James cursed. Of all the possibilities, he hadn't expected the Chinese Commander to get so spooked. Yet that was the only explanation. The light cruiser had begun to decelerate hard. Meanwhile, having a higher top speed, the destroyer had begun accelerating again, intending to meet up with the frigate and then rendezvous with the asteroid field. Suddenly James was faced with the worst of both worlds. The plot updated to show the new intercept times. *Raptor* would reach the asteroid mining facilities ten minutes before the destroyer and frigate. They would be able to destroy the asteroid mining facilities but at a price. They would be well within the missile range of the Chinese warships and would have to fight their way out of a missile duel. Meanwhile, the light cruiser would get back to Wi Li in time to stop *Ghost* causing too much damage.

Suddenly another thought occurred to him. "Navigation project the likely position of *Ghost* given the last data we had on her flight plan."

The main holo display updated, showing an estimated plot of *Ghost*. It was expected she was still another two hours out from the gas mining facility around the system's only gas giant. That had been their original target. A second dot appeared as the navigation officer called out. "This would be her expected position, if she had altered course towards Wi Li when the light cruiser and destroyer had boosted out of orbit towards us."

James studied the plot for a number of seconds. It looks possible he thought to himself. "Assume Lightfoot altered course again to try and intercept the light cruiser as it returns to Wi Li, where would he reach her?"

This time a red dotted line appeared in front of the second estimated dot of *Ghost's* position curving round to intercept the plot of the decelerating light cruiser. The cruiser had been heading for the asteroid field for almost two hours so it would take it that long to return to Wi Li. *Ghost* would intercept her an hour before she got there, long before the two frigates that had returned to Wi Li would be able to come to her aid. The question was, would Lightfoot risk it? If they could destroy the light cruiser, the threat of the Chinese defenders would be severely reduced. Alone, one of the Chinese destroyers couldn't take on *Ghost* and *Raptor*. The remaining forces in the system would have to regroup and come at the two destroyers together. That would take time. Time the two British warships could use to cause a lot of destruction. But *Ghost* couldn't hope to destroy the light cruiser alone, not without taking considerable damage. The new *Crusader* class destroyer's stealth tech was good, even better than that built into survey and scout ships like *Drake*. However, *Raptor* was built to be a warship and even its more advanced stealth tech couldn't hide all of its power hungry systems perfectly. The light cruiser would detect *Ghost* before she could sneak into plasma cannon range. It would be a missile duel to the end. If *Ghost* was severely damaged, she would have to return to British space for repairs and the mission would be over before it had hardly started.

Then it occurred to him. If he was thinking Lightfoot might be tempted by the opportunity to hit the light cruiser, maybe Lightfoot was thinking the same about him. "Navigation, plot us a new course. If we turn to pursue the light cruiser can we catch it in time to aid *Ghost*?"

"It's possible sir," the navigation officer replied. "It would be a close shave getting by the destroyer and frigate heading our way without being detected. Once we did, we'd have to ramp up our engines in order to arrest our current momentum enough to make the turn towards Wi Li. We could catch them but the light cruiser would know we're coming."

"Thank you Sub Lieutenant," James said instinctively, his mind already working out all the possibilities. If the Chinese cruiser knew they were coming what would he do? He could turn to face *Raptor* while the destroyer and frigate behind likewise turned and trapped his ship between two forces. But it would take time for the destroyer and frigate to decelerate. The light cruiser would be alone and would take a lot of damage. The other option was that the

Chinese Commander could continue on to Wi Li and meet up with the two frigates there and then turn to face *Raptor*. It was a risk though. Letting *Raptor* so close to the planet would give James the opportunity to bombard whatever he wanted. Whoever was commanding the Chinese forces didn't know the British warship's strict orders concerning civilian causalities.

James considered his options carefully. Going for the light cruiser was a gamble, but maybe one worth taking. If the Chinese Commander on board the light cruiser did fancy taking on *Raptor* alone then James would have to hold out for at least forty minutes before *Ghost* caught up with them. On the other hand, if he didn't try it *Ghost* might end up taking on the light cruiser on her own.

Banking on the fact Lightfoot and he thought alike, James made his decision. "Navigation engage your new course." Looking over to Gupta, James added for her sake, "it looks like we might have bigger fish to fry, we'll have to come back for the asteroid mining facilities later."

Chapter 24 – Lady Luck

Luck, it may seem strange to find a discussion of luck in a history book but if we are to examine the rise of the Empire then Luck cannot be ignored. We all know the pivotal characters who contributed to the founding of the Empire yet, any cursory examination of their lives shows us just how fragile their contribution was. The wrong decision here, an unlucky system malfunction there and things could have been very different.

-Excerpt from Empire Rising, 3002 AD

10th May 2465 AD, HMS *Raptor*, Wi system

It was time to see just how good *Raptor's* stealth tech really was, James thought. For an hour they had been slowly turning to head deeper into the inner system, towards the rendezvous point with the Chinese light cruiser that was heading back to Wi Li. They could not give away their position to the other ships in the system just yet, so *Raptor* had to change her vector by only using ten percent of her maximum thrust. Any more and the Chinese ships' gravimetric sensors would pick her up. Now the problem was that she was getting close enough to the Chinese destroyer and frigate still heading to the asteroid mining facilities that they were likely to pick them up through other means. All ships vented electromagnetic radiation into space in the form of heat and other stray emissions from equipment on board. *Raptor* was designed with systems that allowed her to vent her heat radiation away from a certain direction so she couldn't be detected. She also had a coating of radar absorbing material that would protect her from active scans, up to a point. Both systems worked well but they couldn't make a ship disappear.

In order to reach the light cruiser they were targeting *Raptor* had to pass very close to the Chinese destroyer and frigate. So close that if their vented heat didn't give them away, the radar waves being sent out by the two ships as they overloaded the radar absorbing material around *Raptor's* hull would.

As James silently watched, the distance between his ship and the two Chinese ships got smaller and smaller. Just before they got to the point where he expected them to pick *Raptor* up he shouted. "Fire!"

Second Lieutenant Romanov was waiting for the order and immediately six missiles erupted from *Raptor's* starboard missile tubes. Starting so close to their target, the missiles only had a flight time of eight minutes. Initially, there was no reaction from the Chinese ships. Then, after almost thirty seconds, both ships brought up their main search radar and began frantically trying to lock onto the missiles. It took another minute for them to begin to turn to face the new threat but when they had completed the maneuver they both fired their own salvo towards *Raptor*. Their response had been slow though, too slow. By the time they had fired, *Raptor* had already passed them and the distance was rapidly opening up as both sets of ships rushed away from each other at their maximum speeds. While *Raptor's* missiles were heading at a right angle towards the Chinese ships, the Chinese missiles left their tubes heading away from *Raptor*. They had to use their engines to overcome the momentum of their parent ship before they actually began to gain on *Raptor*.

As a result, *Raptor's* missiles crashed into the two Chinese ships long before their missiles caught up with *Raptor*. Crucially, they also struck before the Chinese ships could fire another salvo. James had decided it was unlikely they could take out the destroyer with one attack so he had targeted most of his missiles at the smaller frigate. Four homed in on the frigate while two targeted the destroyer in order to force it to focus on its own protection rather than helping its smaller consort.

Raptor carried two of the new penetrator ECM missiles that had proved so effective since the outbreak of war but James had kept them for the showdown with the light cruiser. That meant the destroyer had no problem swatting the two missiles aimed at it out of existence. It took too long though for when her point defense switched to tackle the four aimed at the frigate they only took out one. The frigate had already managed to destroy two more but that still left one missile to enter terminal attack range. Despite the frigate's ECM it managed to get a firm lock on its target. The missile hit the frigate's midsection and penetrated through the thin valstronium armor before exploding. It must have hit one of the frigate's fission reactions for two explosions spewed from the interior of the frigate and when they cleared there was no sign of the ship.

As if in anger, the destroyer barked out with another salvo of missiles at *Raptor*. Then it began to turn again, pointing its nose at *Raptor* so it could bring its main engines back to full power and begin to decelerate along its original vector, reversing course to follow *Raptor* as she dove into the system after the light cruiser.

As James expected, the light cruiser showed no sign of changing course yet. The Chinese Commander was wisely waiting to see if the two missile salvos heading towards *Raptor* would do any damage before he decided whether or not to take *Raptor* on alone. That meant James could focus fully on the two missile salvos coming his way.

The first salvo contained five missiles from the Chinese destroyer and two from the frigate, the second only five more from the destroyer. James nodded at Romanov, giving him permission to reveal *Raptor's* final surprise. With a flick of a switch at his tactical

328

console, a forward section of *Raptor's* hull began to part and a weapon emplacement began to rise up. Along with the penetrator ECM missiles the British fleet's biggest surprise for the Chinese had been their flak frigates. Construction on them had begun five years ago but they had been kept away from Earth and the prying eyes of Chinese spies. The older classes of British destroyers all had three twin plasma cannon turrets. The *Crusader* class had only been fitted with two. Officially, the story was that the destroyers needed the extra energy for their stealth systems. In reality, a flak cannon had replaced the third turret. Kept in a concealed compartment, James was confident that the Chinese intelligence services hadn't figured out the secret even though they now knew about the flak cannons themselves.

As soon as the first salvo came into range the turret reoriented itself and began to throw out a screen of explosive rounds into the path of the approaching missiles. The quadruple electromagnetic cannons each fired ten explosive cartridges a second. Each cartridge in turn exploded at a set range, releasing a thousand small explosive ball bearings. The ball bearings themselves spread out in a uniform sphere before they too exploded, creating a sphere with a diameter of roughly a kilometer, full of shrapnel traveling at high velocities. The valstronium tips of the incoming missiles brushed the shrapnel aside but the weaker titanium alloys used to armor the rest of the missiles couldn't cope with the combined relativistic forces of the shrapnel fragments and the momentum of the missiles themselves. Any time a piece of shrapnel hit a missile where its armor was weaker it easily ripped through and sent the missile spiraling off harmlessly into space.

Of the first salvo, four missiles disappeared in the field of shrapnel created by the flak cannon. The point defense plasma cannons took out another two, leaving one still homing in on *Raptor*. Her last line of defense was her short-range AM missiles. Ten of them shot out and two managed to get hits, exploding the last missile before it got close enough for even a proximity detonation. After the last missile disappeared, James released a deep breath he hadn't realized he had been holding. The first salvo had been the most dangerous. With two less in the second *Raptor* should be able to handle it.

Sure enough the flak cannon again proved its worth as the second salvo failed to hit *Raptor*. No doubt the destroyer's Captain was furious. He now knew his destroyer was simply outclassed. Alone it couldn't hope to penetrate *Raptor's* defenses, while *Raptor's* own broadside of six missiles would likely reduce his ship to atoms given enough time. Looking back to the plot, James could see that the Commander of the Chinese light cruiser obviously thought the same for he hadn't deviated from his original course. The two frigates that had entered orbit around Wi Li an hour ago had now began to boost out of orbit again to meet up with the light cruiser. Once they had joined forces James had no doubt they would turn and try to take him out. Combined they could throw out salvos of twelve missiles.

*

Two hours later and James was beginning to sweat. In moments *Raptor* would enter extreme missile range of the light cruiser. She would be able to get off one salvo before the cruiser could fire back. After that, it was likely the light cruiser would begin to pummel *Raptor* badly. A Chinese light cruiser had almost thirty centimeters more valstronium armor that *Raptor*. It wouldn't give a great deal of protection from the large British anti-ship missiles fired by battlecruisers and heavy cruisers but against *Raptor's* smaller missiles it might even be able to brush off a direct hit or two.

James had expected *Ghost* to make an appearance by now and have already begun to engage the cruiser. That she had not had James worried. Maybe he had misjudged how Lightfoot would react? The dice had already been cast though and James could do nothing but push his fears to the back of his mind. If he tried to maneuver *Raptor* out of the approaching engagement with the cruiser, it would only give the destroyer he had already engaged time to join the cruiser. Together they would make quick work of *Raptor*. If *Ghost* was somewhere else his only hope was to fight his way past the cruiser and make for the system's mass shadow.

When they got into range *Raptor* fired off her first salvo of six missiles. This time he had included one of the penetrator missiles. It would take twenty minutes for the missiles to cover the distance so, before the cruiser had even begun to fire off its point defense weapons, *Raptor* had fired one more salvo while the cruiser had fired off one of its own.

When the penetrator missile sensed the cruiser's point defense weapons powering up it went active. Immediately, the Chinese sensors shifted from detecting six missiles to seeing eleven. The sensors tried to burn through the fake missiles but the ECM on each real missile added to the confusion. In the end the point defense cannons and AM missiles took out five real missiles, including the penetrator, and four of the fake missiles. The remaining fake missiles disappeared with the penetrator but not before the final missile scored a proximity hit.

When the visual images reached *Raptor* for several seconds James watched the detonation. It looked like the explosion had been close enough to cause some damage to one of the cruiser's missile tubes. His suspicion was confirmed when the next salvo poured out of the cruiser only contained seven missiles.

When James's second salvo was ten minutes out from the light cruiser the gravimetric sensors began to beep wildly. The sensors officer called out excitedly. "New contacts, new contacts, I'm picking up six new missiles, they're heading towards the cruiser from sector four zero five point two four. It must be *Ghost*!"

James had already come to the same conclusion; no one else would be shooting at the Chinese warship. Lightfoot must have stayed in stealth, waiting for the opportune time to fire. Lady Luck was with them, now the cruiser had twelve missiles heading for it from two converging directions. It would have to spit its point defense. No doubt Lightfoot has used one of his penetrator missiles in that salvo too! A smile finally broke through the look of concern that had been growing on his face over the last half an hour. James had used his second penetrator in his second salvo so the Chinese point defense network was going struggle to cope. But, before he could watch the results of the missile salvos homing on the Chinese ship, he had one heading for his own ship to concentrate on.

Again the flak gun opened up at maximum range and began to whittle down the incoming missiles. Eight became six and then five. The flak cannon then went silent as the more accurate closer range point defense systems came online. Plasma cannon fire took out two more missiles and AM missiles another one. At the last second, Romanov dialed up *Raptor's* ECM to full and dove the ship into a tight evasive maneuver. One of the two remaining missiles was fooled but the second closed in and detonated off the ship's starboard bow. The shockwave threw the bridge crew about at their consoles.

Looking around James could see that no one was seriously hurt, just a little shaken up. "Damage Report," he demanded.

"The valstronium armor held," Romanov reported. We lost twenty percent of our point defense plasma cannons in that firing arc though. I'm also getting reports of minor damage and injuries in forward sections one through seven. All starboard missile tubes still report full functionality. Our next salvo will be ready to fire in two minutes."

"Very well, fire when ready," James responded, "see if you can re-train any of our other plasma cannons to cover that area before the next salvo gets here." Opening up a COM channel to Gupta on the auxiliary bridge James ordered, "Take over the damage control from Romanov, let him focus on getting ready to handle the next salvo."

With *Gupta* on top of the damage control, James shifted his focus back to the Chinese cruiser. He could only watch the gravimetric sensors to see what was happening in real time. The twelve missiles began to quickly disappear off the plot as they were destroyed. Whoever was controlling the light cruiser's defenses was good. Yet not good enough, for three missiles detonated close to the ship. As the visuals came through James saw that significant damage had been done to its stern. Still, the cruiser wasn't giving up for as James watched it fired another salvo, this time at *Ghost*. The cruiser must have managed to fix the damage to its eighth missile tube for it had fired a full broadside.

Moments later a message came through from *Ghost*. "*Raptor*, this is Lightfoot, clear the engagement zone. I repeat, clear the engagement zone. Our last salvo has significantly damaged their main engines. That cruiser isn't going anywhere fast, we'll have plenty of time to accomplish what we came here for before they can effect repairs. It looks like they still have all their offensive weapons working so we're not going to risk trying to destroy them. Please acknowledge. *Ghost* out."

James thought Lightfoot had tried to add an extra level of sternness into his command. Not that he really needed to with his strong voice and intimidating build. Lightfoot must have been worried that James wouldn't let an opportunity to destroy a Chinese ship pass. Certainly, there would be some British commanders who would pretend they hadn't heard the last message and move in for the kill. While James was tempted - it would look good on his record to have a cruiser down as a confirmed kill, there was a mission to complete.

Speaking to the communication officer he ordered, "acknowledge *Ghost's* orders." He followed this up by ordering the navigation officer to pull *Raptor* back to the coordinates Lightfoot had sent over with his orders.

As *Raptor* began to change direction, the second salvo of Chinese missiles altered course to follow. The flak cannon again began to fill space with shrapnel.

Ten seconds before it was programmed to cease firing to allow the other point defense weapons to open, the energy supply to one of the electromagnetic rings in the fourth barrel over loaded. The resultant surge in the magnetic force along one side of the barrel pulled the next three flak rounds off center before the safeties shut the flak cannon down. Two of the rounds excited the barrel, heading off in the wrong direction, but the third collided with the end of the barrel and exploded. As a thousand explosive ball bearings erupted from the explosion and detonated themselves the flak cannon was shredded along with a number of point defense plasma cannons.

Unaware of the confusion engulfing the bridge of *Raptor*, the remaining five Chinese missiles continued towards the ship. What was left of the point defense plasma cannons opened fire, taking out one missile. Another two fell as *Raptor* fired off as many anti-missile missiles as she could. Two still survived and they both homed in on the nose of the ship. As one they exploded only eight hundred meters from the ship when their seeker heads realized they wouldn't get a direct hit. The explosive force of the thermonuclear detentions quickly dissipated in the void of space but not before a significant amount of the force crashed into *Raptor*.

This time the bridge crew were thrown about much more forcibly and two officers lost consciousness as their harnesses failed to stop the excessive g-forces from impacting them. Disorientated from the shockwave and the flickering of the damaged lights on the bridge, James shook himself to try and refocus. Romanov was hunched over at his console. His head lolled about from side to side and a thick stream of blood was making its way from his hairline down the back of his neck. After getting full command of his senses James keyed his command console. "Medical assistance to the bridge immediately," he ordered on the medical COM channel. Then he switched command of the tactical console to his command chair. The first damage reports coming in showed almost all of the valstronium armor had been blasted off *Raptor's* starboard nose section. The life like metal was already flowing from other parts of the ship to even out the armor's thickness. It would strengthen the nose sections but would leave the rest of the ship generally weaker. Starboard missile tube six was reporting as inoperable but the remaining five were ready to fire. Checking that *Raptor's* gravimetric sensors were still working, James updated the missiles with the latest data on the cruiser's position and then pressed the command to fire.

He watched his own missiles streak off for a few seconds and then opened a channel to Gupta. "How bad is it Lieutenant?"

The auxiliary bridge was further forward than the bridge and Gupta looked well shaken up. Sweat was pouring down her face and her hair had shaken itself loose from her ponytail and was splayed everywhere. The look in her eyes was all James needed to see to be reassured that she was still in full control. "We've lost nearly sixty percent of our forward starboard point defensive network. Starboard missile six is damaged but I think it can be repaired. We've also lost our flak cannon. A review of the last few seconds of the attack indicates that the flak cannon malfunctioned and damaged itself along with some of our point defense cannons. So far

I have reports of two fatalities and five serious injuries. They are all being taken to sickbay now. Everyone else is working flat out on the repairs."

"Good work Lieutenant," James said, "let me know if there are any more fatalities or injuries." Before commanding *Drake*, James had not been on board a ship that had had a fatality. He had felt the deaths of his crew on *Drake* deeply and he knew it would be the same today. Maybe even some of the fatalities would be crew members who had followed him from *Drake*. Yet right now he had to get everyone else to safety and so he forced his feelings out of his mind and looked back to the holo display.

Ghost was making her way out of the cruiser's missile range at full speed. She had obviously weathered the cruiser's first missile salvo but the second one was about to enter engagement range for the point defense weapons. Her own flak cannon dealt with four of the incoming eight missiles. Only one survived the closer range weapons. For a moment James thought it had scored a direct hit as the explosion played havoc with *Raptor's* sensor feed. A few seconds later *Ghost* reappeared on the same vector, still accelerating at her top speed, indicating that any damage had been minimal.

From the cruiser another eight missiles shot out of their tubes towards *Ghost*. Someone had made a mistake though, probably out of rage. With *Ghost* and the crippled cruiser now pulling away from each other, the missiles didn't have the range to catch *Ghost*. In vain they accelerated after the British warship but eventually their small fusion reactors ran out fuel and they faded off the gravimetric plot as their engines died.

The final missiles from *Ghost* and *Raptor* on the other hand, crashed into the cruiser's point defenses five minutes apart. Only one managed to get a proximity hit and James hoped it had caused some internal damage to add to the time it would take for the cruiser to repair itself. From the visuals it was clear the light cruiser would still be able to put up a fight, if it could get into range of the British destroyers once its engines were back online, though James knew Lightfoot had no intention of sticking around to see how long that might take.

Chapter 25 - Hunted

By the later stages of the First Interstellar Expansion Era the British Space Navy had become obsessed with stealth technology. This would go on to prove very useful for the whole human race.

-Excerpt from Empire Rising, 3002 AD

12th May 2465 AD, HMS *Raptor*, Wi

A full two days after the battle with the light cruiser that had left the door to Wi Li open, James, Gupta and Romanov stood on the bridge of *Raptor*. They were watching the now fully regrouped ships of the system picket, including the somewhat repaired light cruiser, charging straight for *Ghost* and *Raptor*.

"They're certainly putting on a good show," Romanov said to the bridge at large.

"Indeed," James agreed, "too little too late I'm afraid." No doubt the Chinese Commander was trying to cover his back. At least it would look like he tried to engage the British destroyers once he had repaired his ship. It was just a pity his targets were about to jump out of the system, their mission complete.

After *Raptor* and *Ghost* met at the coordinates Lightfoot had sent to James, they had waited for over an hour before setting off together towards Wi Li. The wait had allowed the damaged cruiser and the two frigates that had eventually joined it to overshoot Wi Li. With the cruiser's engines damaged, it hadn't been able to slow down and enter orbit. Instead, it had been forced to continue further into the inner system and actually ended up well past the system's star and on its way out towards the far side of the system before its engines were repaired enough to arrest its momentum.

The damage to the light cruiser left only two destroyers to oppose the British ships, the one that had been guarding Wi Liang and the one *Raptor* had exchanged fire with. They had both retreated to Wi Liang and had sat in orbit, obviously concluding that a missile duel with two destroyers equipped with flak cannons would be futile. Thankfully, they hadn't realized that *Raptor's* had been damaged.

With Wi Li at their mercy, the two British ships had moved into orbit. The planet, being recently colonized, didn't yet have any orbital defenses. RSNI had identified two planetary weapons facilities, which *Ghost* had bombarded with ground assault missiles. They were simply anti-ship missiles with their nuclear devices replaced with a shaft of valstronium. Accelerated to very high relativistic speeds, when the missiles hit the surface of a planet the impact released megatons of explosive force without the radiation from a nuclear detonation. There had been a moment of alarm aboard *Raptor* when a third planetary defense installation had been identified. The first sign of it had been when it began to spew missiles that accelerated out of the planet's atmosphere and towards the ship. Thankfully, the installation had only been partially completed and so only had six missiles ready to launch.

Throughout the human sphere, orbital defense platforms were the preferred defensive fortification as missiles fired from a planet's surface spent a lot of their fuel boosting out of the planet's gravity. The only drawback was that a system needed a well-established orbital industry to begin constructing something as large as a battlestation. Thankfully for *Raptor*, Romanov was quick on his toes. His quick thinking led him to take *Raptor* down deeper into the gravity well as the missiles accelerated up to reach them. This meant when the missiles got in range of the point defenses they were still travelling at very low speeds as they tried to overcome the planet's gravity. The point defense network was designed to be able to intercept missiles coming at *Raptor* at speeds of up to 0.6c. The much slower missiles that were just breaking orbit didn't prove much of a challenge even with the damage *Raptor* had already taken to her defenses.

Once safely in orbit, both ships had then begun picking off targets the RSNI had identified as either facilities used in the Chinese military industrial complex or belonging to Politburo members. Everything in orbit had been destroyed but the ground targets had been selected more carefully. With a limited supply of ground assault missiles, they had been reserved for heavily protected facilities. In each case, the British ships had given the occupants at least an hour's warning before the facilities had been destroyed. For the rest of their targets, including ones that were in heavily populated areas, the marines had been sent in to plant demolition explosives. At a number of targets, firefights had broken out between the marines and the Chinese army contingents based on the planet. Yet there wasn't a centralized garrison to coordinate the defense. Whoever had sent the army units to the planet as guards had simply assigned platoons or companies wherever they were needed and left them in charge of their own area. Thus, there had been no way to mount a coordinated defense. That left the Chinese army units sitting ducks for the Marines. Wherever the defenses had been too strong the marines' shuttles had simply pulled back and poured heavy plasma cannon fire into the buildings, destroying them with their defenders inside.

After the first several hours a woman, claiming to be a RSNI agent, had contacted *Ghost*. She had been working on the planet for the last two years. Major Johnston had taken a squad of marines and picked her up. She had passed all the checks Lightfoot had been given before embarking on the raiding mission. She gave her name as Julia Bell and had provided the two destroyers with a number of secondary targets she had identified over the last two years. Two of which she insisted the marines assault in order to see what intel they could gather. To everyone's surprise Julia had also insisted she accompany the marines and from Major Johnston's report, she had clearly undertaken some special opps training in the past. After personally dispatching at least five Chinese soldiers, she had instructed the marines to carry out a number of Chinese computers and other hardware. The two shuttles carrying her and Major Johnston's men had been so full after their two raids that they had struggled to get back up to orbit. At the time James had wondered just how many RSNI desk jockeys it would take to go through all the data Julia was bringing them.

Along with the damage to the planet's infrastructure, the destroyers had also captured and destroyed six freighters carrying war material. In each case they had ordered the crew to abandon the freighters before they blew them up. The first Chinese Captain had refused and tried to escape out of orbit from Wi Li and head to the protection offered by the two destroyers at Wi Liang. Lightfoot had simply fired a missile with its acceleration reduced to minimum at the fleeing freighter. Without ECM or point defenses the freighter couldn't escape and *Raptor's* sensors had shown most of the freighter's crew had abandoned ship just before the missile had caught up with them. James had hoped that if anyone had been left on board, the foolish Captain had been one of them.

When the ships had exhausted the list of targets supplied to them by RSNI and Julia they had broken orbit. Behind them they had left a traumatized planet. Every major population center had numerous smoldering ruins where buildings had been. Just outside the three main cities there were huge gouges in the countryside where bombardment missiles had been used to take out the three planetary defense installations. Despite appearances, James had been confident that the people themselves would still recover. They hadn't destroyed anything vital to their economy nor to their food production or distribution. Despite the Marines best efforts, it had been estimated that around two hundred civilians had been killed. Both Lightfoot and James regretted every single one of them but short of risking the lives of the marines by sending them to visually check every square inch of each target, preventing them had been impossible.

On their way towards the mass shadow and the shift passage to New Shanghai, *Ghost* and *Raptor* had swung by the gas mining station. After calling for the workers to evacuate, they had poured plasma cannon bolts into the station until it had broken up and began to fall into the gravity well of the gas giant it orbited. Only then had the regrouped Chinese warships begun to charge after them, seeking revenge for the destruction done to Wi Li.

The plot on *Raptor's* bridge showed the Chinese ships would catch up to her in two more hours. Yet in only another ten minutes she would reach the edge of mass shadow of the system and would be able to jump to shift space. The next target on Lightfoot's mission brief was New Shanghai.

To pass the time as they waited to jump, James asked the bridge at large, "so how many billions of credits of damage does anyone think we have caused over the last forty eight hours?"

Romanov began to scratch his chin as he thought about an answer. Sub Lieutenant Becket was the first to speak. "It must be in the tens of billions Captain, I'd guess maybe eighty billion?"

Sub Lieutenant Graham, another transfer from *Drake* answered next, "It has to be way more than that. The gas mining station alone probably cost more than ten billion to construct. I'm going to go for two hundred billion."

"I would guess even higher," Romanov answered, "three hundred and fifty billion."

Secretly James thought all three of their answers were a little naive. Even though his father had lost most of the family's wealth, James still knew what it cost to operate and run even a moderate industrial enterprise. He suspected the damage done would run into the trillions. Before saying so he waited to see if anyone else would speak up. He didn't think anyone else would but he wanted to give them an opportunity. None of the rest of the bridge crew knew him like Becket and Graham did. Hopefully though, seeing the ease at which they spoke up would help to break down the barriers that always went up between a crew and a new commanding officer.

As he was about to speak, Gupta beat him to it. "Well, if I had to guess I think I would have to put it somewhere round one trillion four hundred and fifty billion," she said with a mischievous grin.

"Really?" James asked sarcastically, "and why exactly would you feel confident in being so precise may I ask?"

"It's quite simple actually," she answered again, smiling as she passed James a data pad. "In the last few hours Julia has been completing a preliminary report on the raid. That is her figure on the damage we have caused, including the loss in taxes the Chinese government will suffer from the reduced industrial output of the system."

Romanov whistled in surprise at the figure and the look on all the Sub Lieutenants' faces was priceless. None of them came from wealthy backgrounds and so James was sure they couldn't even imagine how much a trillion credits was really worth.

"It looks like we'll all have some interesting reading to do on our journey to New Shanghai," James said, as he waved the datapad in the air. Almost everyone nodded. A silence then fell on the bridge as minds were turned towards thinking about the damage they had just caused. Everyone was wondering what impact it would have on the Chinese government and the Politburo members who had just seen some of their wealth evaporate. James knew it was not much more than a drop in the ocean for some of the leading Chinese government officials but he also knew *Ghost* and *Raptor* weren't the only ships raiding Chinese space.

The silence that had descended on the bridge was broken by the COM officer, "*Ghost* has signaled that she is ready to jump."

James looked at the status board on his command chair. "Confirm we are ready too. Jump on their command."

With a brief flash both destroyers vanished from the Wi system, leaving an angry Chinese Commander behind. Three hours later another series of small flashes in the same area indicated a group of ships had just arrived, a squadron of reinforcements from New Shanghai. It took them a few hours to confirm what had happened at Wi but once they had, they turned around and jumped back towards New Shanghai in pursuit of the raiders.

*

After the stress of the assault on Wi Li James had felt drained and exhausted. The shift passage between Wi and New Shanghai was especially tight and twisty and so it had taken just over three days to reach their next target. During that time, James had made every effort to rest and prepare himself for what was coming next. New Shanghai had been colonized sixty-five years before the Wi system had even been discovered. It only had one habitable planet but the planet had an atmosphere that was breathable and, thus, as soon as it was discovered the Chinese government had begun to ship colonists out to it. Now it boasted a population of over a billion. On the two main continents, the original flora and fauna was all but a distant memory as animals and plants from Earth had been imported and seeded into the environment. In orbit there was a growing shipyard, numerous smaller facilities utilized by the mining and trade industries and three large battlestations bristling with offensive weapons.

Lightfoot's plan was very simple. He had decided to take a leaf out of Gupta's playbook. After lying in stealth for a number of hours to observe the ships in the system *Ghost* and *Raptor* would boost into the system under full acceleration. Intentionally alerting the Chinese to their presence, the ships would then switch into stealth mode when they reached their top speed. Being still so far out from the inner system and in stealth would mean they could pick any target and slowly make their way towards it. New Shanghai was what the RSN academy instructors called a target rich environment. The Chinese system Commander would know they were coming but he wouldn't know where they were going. Lightfoot and James would thus be able to see how he reacted and chose their targets accordingly.

As *Raptor* excited shift space, James watched as his bridge crew frantically analyzed all the sensor data coming through. Following standard doctrine, *Ghost* and *Raptor* had excited shift space one and a half light hours from the edge of the system's mass shadow. A ship exiting shift space produced small gravimetric disturbance detectable up to one light hour away. RSN stealth doctrine therefore called for ships to enter a system at least a one and a half light hours out so any ships patrolling the system's mass shadow wouldn't detect them.

Romanov was again manning tactical. He was the first to shout a warning, "A ship has just gone to full acceleration. Its half a light hour off our port bow, heading directly for us."

Before James could register the implications of the ship's presence the sensors officer called another warning, "Another ship has just gone to full acceleration right towards our position. This one is point two of a light hour to starboard."

As James was trying to decide what to do Lightfoot appeared on a COM channel. "It's a signaling system. A warning must have got out of Wi, they were expecting us. They must have ships strewn out along the end of the shift passage waiting to detect us. The last thing they will expect us to do is take on one of those ships. Follow the vector my navigational officer will send you." Without waiting for a reply, Lightfoot had already gone.

When the channel closed James cursed, he should have seen it sooner. The British were doing the very same thing in the Void. Their approach was a little bit more sophisticated with different course changes and acceleration burns signaling different things. Yet the Chinese system, crude as it was, would be just as effective. With two ships accelerating towards the same point, the Chinese system Commander would be able to know exactly where *Ghost* and *Raptor* had come out of shift space.

"Navigation, follow the course *Ghost* is sending over to us," James ordered. "Sensors, have you been able to identify either of the two ships coming towards us yet?"

"Yes sir," the officer replied. "The first one is a frigate, the second one a destroyer. I can't determine the class of either though."

"That's ok," James said. "That's all we need to know for now. Romanov ready a full spread of missiles. Contact the tactical officer aboard *Ghost* to work out the best defensive formation given the damage both ships have taken. We're going to be taking on that destroyer."

Even as he spoke, James felt *Raptor* come alive as she turned and began to make for the approaching Chinese destroyer. It had only been point two of a light hour away when they had emerged from shift space and already the range was closing fast as it accelerated towards the point they had emerged. Both *Ghost* and *Raptor* had emerged from shift space with the same velocity they had entered it. Traveling at 0.1c they were beginning to move away from where they had come into the system. It wouldn't be enough to avoid the destroyer though. They would have to fight.

For a moment James had to wonder at the speed of Lightfoot's reactions. While he had still been struggling to react to their situation, Lightfoot had already figured out what the Chinese were doing and had realized they couldn't avoid a confrontation. As James thought about it he was sure all the Chinese Captains who were patrolling the shift passage had orders to engage whatever came out of the shift passage. Only by pressing the British forces into a fight could the system commander know what he was facing. It was a cold logical approach. The System Commander was willing to sacrifice a frigate, or even a destroyer, in order to get intel on his enemy. Still, just like the signaling system, it would work.

Once Romanov had conferred with his counterpart on *Ghost*, he brought up their plan on the main holo display. "Here's our suggestion sir, *Ghost* will take up position above our forward starboard side. I'm still not happy with the repairs we have managed to do to the point defense plasma cannons in that section. This way we shouldn't have to use them. We have also planned a number of evasive maneuvers we can take together that will allow our best point defense weapons to keep engaging any incoming missiles. We'll have to come out of stealth and increase our speed before we engage the destroyer for them to work effectively. *Ghost's* tactical officer is running it by Captain Lightfoot now."

"And what about our flak cannon?" James asked. Romanov had been able to repair two of the cannon's barrels during their raid on

Wi Li, from spare parts on board *Raptor*. Without time in a repair yard that was the best he could do. With only two barrels the cannon's rate of fire was halved, along with the area of space it could fill with shrapnel.

"Diagnostics indicate the repairs are fully functional. I have slaved control of it to *Ghost's* tactical officer though. It will be more effective if he can use our reduced firepower to enhance his own flak cannons rather than use them as two separate weapons."

"Agreed," James said. "We'll be entering missile range in ten minutes, sooner if Lightfoot approves the acceleration," he spoke to the bridge at large, "inform the crew to prepare for battle."

*

Aboard *Ghost*, Lightfoot was reassessing his options. While everyone else was preparing for the duel with the approaching destroyer he had been reviewing New Shanghai's defenses. Agent Bell had been able to fill some gaps in the RSNI intel and even before jumping into the system, he had been coming to realize their mission might be impossible. The system was simply too well defended. Now, with all the data that was coming in from the sensors on the inner system he was more convinced. Included in his orders to attack New Shanghai and Wi was a secondary objective. It was secondary because it was more of a long shot but it looked like it would have to be bumped up the list. Still, if they could take out the approaching destroyer quickly, they could yet cause a bit of havoc in this system.

Switching his thoughts back to the coming battle, he reviewed his tactical officer's plans. "Approved," he called out knowing his officer would know what he meant. "Take us to full acceleration, fire as soon as we come into range." Even with *Raptor's* damaged flak cannon, the coming battle was all but a forgone conclusion, yet he didn't want to take any chances. His tactical officer's request for more maneuvering flexibility was a sensible one, even if it gave away their position a little sooner than he would have wished.

As the previous battles with Chinese warships had gone, his ships got to fire off the first missile salvo. Twelve missiles sped off towards the approaching destroyer. *Raptor* had used her two penetrator missiles against the light cruiser at Wi but *Ghost* had one left. Lightfoot had chosen to keep it in reserve; a couple of volleys and the enemy ship should be destroyed. The fact that the three ships were almost heading straight for each other meant the missiles closed quickly with their target. Nevertheless, the Chinese ship still managed to get off two missile salvo's before the first British missiles came tearing in on their target. The point defenses took out nine of them but three got into engagement range. Not one of them managed to get a direct hit but three proximity explosions rocked the destroyer. Immediately, it lost acceleration and began to roll violently. Lightfoot studied the visual feed carefully to observe the damage. The destroyer looked like it was out of the fight already but he didn't want the same trick he had played at the Damang to be played on him.

Satisfied that the ship did indeed look like it had taken serious damage, Lightfoot waited until *Ghost's* and *Raptor's* point defenses had taken out the first Chinese salvo of five missiles. Then he spoke to the COM officer, "hail the Chinese ship, inform them that we're going to close to plasma cannon range and destroy their ship. They are to evacuate now. If they don't evacuate we'll assume they intend to fight on and we'll send another volley of missiles their way."

"Yes sir," the COM officer replied, "sending the message now."

As the second Chinese missile salvo approached, it became impossible to see what the Chinese destroyer was doing as space around the two British ships was filled with flak explosions, plasma bolts, AM missiles and exploding Chinese missiles. When the sensor feeds cleared both *Ghost* and *Raptor* continued on, having shrugged off the Chinese missiles. Lightfoot could also see on the visual display that small escape pods were launching from the damaged destroyer.

"Tactical," Lightfoot ordered, "keep your missiles locked onto that ship but hold fire. If there is any sign of it turning to bring any weapons to bear on us fire immediately. As soon as we get into plasma range take it out. Then put us back into stealth. We are now the hunted."

Chapter 26 – Behind Enemy Lines

The Void War saw the first real use of warships as raiders operating behind enemy lines for long periods of time. This had been a tactic perfected by the wet navies of Earth centuries before but many of the skills had to be relearnt.

-Excerpt from Empire Rising, 3002 AD

16th May 2465 AD, HMS *Raptor*, New Shanghai

James felt more exhausted than he ever had before in his life. The closest he had come to how he currently felt had been when he had taken *Drake* through the V17 system. There he had to dodge a number of Chinese picket ships while trying to get a good scan of the planet. New Shanghai was turning out to be an entirely different kettle of fish. For the last five hours *Ghost* and *Raptor* had been slowly making their way deeper and deeper into the system. Only an hour ago they had actually managed to pass the line marking the system's mass shadow.

The Chinese System Commander had filled the exit of the shift passage from the Wi system with small patrol craft. After finishing off the destroyer, Lightfoot had taken them back into stealth and they had slowly made their way into the system. Every time they had detected a Chinese warship they had been forced to try and sneak around them. In *Drake* it would have been much easier but, even though the *Churchill* class of destroyer had impressive stealth systems, it was much harder to hide a fully equipped warship.

As if things couldn't have gotten any worse, three hours after they had defeated the Chinese destroyer another force had jumped into the system behind them. They must have been reinforcements sent to Wi that had returned once they learnt that *Ghost* and *Raptor* had already left. As soon as they had jumped into the system, they had spread out and were now slowly making their way into the system. All their active scanners were operating at full capacity as they sought to locate the two British ships.

The Chinese Commander was definitely a canny one. Even though he must have known *Ghost* and *Raptor* were trying to sneak further into the system, he hadn't ordered his outer system pickets to go to active scanning. Instead they had remained quiet and undetectable unless the British ships got close to them. That meant that James and Lightfoot had to be prepared to come under fire at any second.

Further into the system things were a little different. Around the planet the System Commander had two light cruisers in orbit to lend weight to the battlestations that were on full alert. Slightly further out was the main Chinese force. It consisted of a heavy cruiser, two more light cruisers and three destroyers. They were slowly heading away from the inhabited planet towards the shift passage back to Wi. The Chinese Commander was clearly waiting for the British ships to trip over one of his outer pickets and then he would pounce with his larger force. Taking the ships further into the system was like walking through a field of landmines. Worse, it was like walking through a field of landmines with an enemy force waiting for you to reach the other side while another force came along behind, forcing you to keep going. James was not enjoying the experience.

The last twelve hours had reminded James of the accounts he had read from submarine commanders during World War Two. Both the American and German commanders who had tried to sneak up on enemy convoys had had to endure hours of slowly overhauling their targets before they could attack. All the while surface patrol boats had been constantly searching for them, just waiting for a chance to blow them out of the water. The submariners often hadn't even known they had been detected until it was too late. So far Lightfoot had proven himself to have nerves of steel as he had led them onwards. James, on the other hand, was beginning to struggle. He didn't know how Lightfoot was doing it. He was beginning to feel himself fray around the edges. Knowing he needed to do something before his subordinates began to see past the confident front he had been projecting, he decided to retire to his quarters. Having spent the last fourteen hours on the bridge he needed to at least try and get some sleep.

When a COM channel on his command chair beeped, he almost jumped. Recovering quickly, he hit the accept button to bring up Lightfoot's face. The Captain of *Ghost* looked tired but his voice was still full of confidence and James could feel himself drawing strength from Lightfoot as he spoke. "Still awake Captain, I thought you would have retired for a nap by now? I guess you don't want to miss any of the action. This is definitely going to make a great story when we get back to Earth."

"Certainly sir," was all James could manage. He wasn't sure if Lightfoot was joking for the sake of his subordinates or if he really was enjoying himself.

"I think I've come up with a plan," Lightfoot continued. "We'll be lucky to make it out of here, never mind actually causing any damage so we need to adapt. You haven't been briefed on this but RSNI had received some intel that the next convoy going into the Void would be passing through New Shanghai in about four days. It was a secondary target for us to go after if we got a chance. The intel suggested that the convoy would be lightly guarded until it got to New Shanghai. That might be why there are so many more smaller ships in the system than we were expecting, some may be waiting for the convoy. Our best chance of intercepting the convoy is if we hit them here."

As James looked at his personal holo display an image of the shift passage connecting New Shanghai to Paracel appeared. The Paracel system didn't contain anything of importance but it did lead to the Anyang system which was as heavily developed as New Shanghai and it in turn led on through Chinese space to the Beta system and then back to Earth. The shift passage between New Shanghai and Paracel was a relatively straight one but it did have two very tight kinks in it. Ordinarily, it was deemed impossible to ambush a fleet as it travelled through shift space. Even though the ships had to make regular stops to realign when the shift passage twisted and turned the passages were so large it was impossible to predict accurately enough to plan an ambush where a ship might make its stop.

However, throughout known space there was five shift passages where it had been deemed just such an ambush was possible – at least by the RSN tactical planners. One of them was between New Shanghai and Paracel. There were two very severe turns in the shift passage that were also very narrow. Any ship hoping to pass through them in a timely fashion would have to exit shift space in a fairly small area of space. Provided the ships didn't suspect they would be ambushed and stuck to the least time route through the passage, the point at which they would come out of shift space was easily predictable.

As James studied the image Lightfoot continued, "This will only work, however, if we can convince the Chinese Commander of the system defenses here that we have gone somewhere else. If he suspects we are trying to ambush the convoy, all he'll have to do is send his ships to the twist in the shift passage and he'll have ambushed us.

"If we're going to convince him we're somewhere else we will have to be somewhere else, at least one of us will be. But first we need to get the Chinese Commander's attention. By now he'll have received a report from those ships that came into the system behind us on the damage we caused at Wi. Hopefully, we can give him some more incentive stop us attacking any other unprotected systems. Here are a couple of targets I've selected."

On his holo display James watched the image shift to show the New Shanghai system again. A series of dots appeared with scrolling text beside each one along with an ETA. As James looked closely, he could see they were all minor targets. Some small mining facilities and a freighter resupply hub, for freighters that wanted to pass through the system without going into the inner system. Their worth wasn't what made them important. Combined, their destruction would only cause a small headache to even a poorer Politburo member. Their importance was in where they led when the dots were joined. They didn't form a straight line but to anyone observing all the dots, it was clear that the British destroyers would be heading towards the Fujian passage. Theoretically the Fujian passage led all the way back to the Damang system, though it would take over a month to do so. Along the way it passed through four other Chinese systems. None had a habitable planet and so were poorly developed yet combined, they still had received a sizable amount of investment from the Chinese government. Given all the destruction *Ghost* and *Raptor* had dished out at Wi, no sane Chinese Commander would want the two British destroyers loose among the four unprotected systems.

"One of us is going down the Fujian passage to draw the Chinese off then?" James asked.

Nodding, Lightfoot fleshed out the details, "that's the plan. The greater risk will fall on the ship that does so I'll be taking *Ghost*. First, we'll hit all the targets I've sent you here in New Shanghai to convince the enemy we're working as a single unit. When I make the jump to Fujian, you will go to stealth and wait for whatever

Chinese ships are sent after us to make the jump. Then you can double back and head for the ambush site. As soon as I get to Fujian I'll begin stirring up a right hornets' nest. Hopefully in all the confusion it'll take the pursuing Chinese ships a while to figure out *Raptor* isn't there.

"If they do figure it out, things might get a bit hairy for you but it's two days to Fujian system along the shift passage. That'll give you at least four days to sneak out of New Shanghai and get to the ambush site before any message is sent back informing the Chinese Commander *Raptor* isn't at Fujian. The convoy is expected in four to five days, so, unless it is late you should be there before the Chinese have a chance to send any ships after you.

"Once it seems like there's no point hanging around the Fujian system I'll either jump on up the Fujian passage to draw as many ships away from you as possible or I'll try and sneak past them and back to New Shanghai. I'm sending you some coordinates for the Damang system. We'll meet back there when all this is done. Is there anything you want to add to the plan?"

James considered it for a moment. Obviously Lightfoot had been thinking it through for the last twelve hours. There was one flaw in his plan and James proceeded to point it out. "Wouldn't it be better if you were to take *Ghost* to attack the convoy? Even lightly defended the convoy will have some sort of escort. You have the last penetrator missile. If there is anything larger than a frigate escorting the convoy, you would need it to destroy the ship quickly before the rest of the convoy had a chance to jump away."

"You're right, it will be needed," Lightfoot began, "but it won't be on board *Ghost*. We're going to dock after we hit the last target here in New Shanghai and I'll be transferring it along with several other missiles over to you. We're both running low on missiles but, if you're going to take out as many of the convoy freighters as possible, you'll need more than I will to harass Fujian. I'll be giving you everything I can spare. Including the penetrator missile."

"But sir," James began to protest. *Ghost* was just as likely to need those missiles if she was going to draw half the Chinese fleet in this system with her to Fujian.

Lightfoot held up his hands to stop him saying anymore. "Listen James, I am the Senior Commander. The responsibility of making the command decisions falls on me. I'm not sending you to the Fujian system low on missiles with an angry Chinese fleet on your tail. I can, however, send myself. That will be the end of it. I want you to take the plan and run it over with your senior Lieutenants. See if there is anything I have missed. Then begin to plan for your ambush. I'll coordinate with your navigation officer. It'll be another six hours before we reach our first in system target."

"Aye sir," James said as he tried to hide his frustration at Lightfoot.

"Gupta, Romanov," James called over the two Lieutenants who were both on the bridge. "I want you both to go to my private office and begin to review a plan Captain Lightfoot has sent over. I'm going to retire for a nap and I'll join you presently."

"Sub Lieutenant Jackson, you have the bridge," James called as he followed the two Lieutenants out.

*

After his three hour nap James felt somewhat refreshed. The briefing with Gupta and Romanov had been disappointing. They had reviewed Lightfoot's plan and made a few minor suggestions, though they hadn't been able to give James any other viable alternatives. Splitting up was the best chance they had to cause the Chinese some serious damage. If both ships went up the Fujian passage, they would cause a lot of havoc but they would eventually be trapped. It was a much shorter route to go to the Damang system via Wi. Once the Chinese Commander was sure the British ships intended to go all the way up the Fujian passage, he could dispatch a blocking force to Damang via Wi. They could then travel down the other end of the Fujian passage and prevent *Ghost* and *Raptor* from doing too much damage. They would also likely trap the two ships and destroy them. The only other option was to turn around and run back to Damang via Wi now. Yet even that was all but impossible with the second Chinese squadron blocking their retreat.

After spending a couple of hours with both Lieutenants, James had come to agree with their conclusions. The best way forward was to split up and draw the Chinese ships into a wild goose chase. Resigned to the proposed course of action James also had to accept the fact he wasn't going to change Lightfoot's mind about which ship to send to ambush the Chinese convoy.

Instead he was back on the bridge preparing to attack the first target that would lead them to the Fujian passage. Both James and Lightfoot knew that as soon as they showed themselves the Chinese Commander would try to quickly close the net around them. Their attack would have to be swift.

As soon as they came into range of the asteroid mining facility both *Raptor* and *Ghost* opened up with their plasma cannons. Their first targets were the two freighters approaching the facility. If they could be destroyed before they could change their acceleration profile, it would take an hour or two for the electromagnetic radiation from the attack to be detected by the Chinese warships.

Someone on board one of the freighters must have been awake though, for as soon as *Raptor's* stealth field came down when she opened fire, the freighter began to accelerate wildly. To anyone in the system watching their gravimetric scanners it would be a large flashing beacon indicating that something was up. The acceleration only lasted a couple of seconds before three plasma bolts cut through the freighter, causing it to explode. The second one disappeared without ever even trying to evade. Even as another volley of plasma bolts drilled into the station, two Chinese picket ships that had been in close proximity to station powered up out of stealth and both began to accelerate towards where the station had been. Further away, both the squadron that had been following them into the system and the larger squadron waiting for them altered course and began to accelerate towards the station.

Soon the space around the station was filled with radar beams as every picket ship in the vicinity began to search for the destroyers. There was alarm on the bridge of both British ships as the amount of radar energy hitting them began to rise towards levels their absorbing tech could no longer handle. As they moved further and further away though the strength began to decrease. Eventually Lightfoot ordered a course change and once again both ships slipped back into the darkness of space.

James remained on the bridge for another half hour and then retired to his quarters, giving Gupta the watch. Five more times he returned to the bridge to watch target after target being hit. Three of the targets were destroyed without giving any immediate warning. He had been able to watch the Chinese' delayed response as the heat and light radiation from the explosions had made their way across the system. Twice more ships had managed to radically alter their acceleration profile, alerting the Chinese that they were under attack. Each time Lightfoot had managed to steer them around the net that kept threatening to close in on them. Two hours before they entered range of their last target, the two destroyers had closed with each other and, slowly and carefully, transferred ten missiles from *Ghost* to *Raptor*. It was a procedure every cadet at the naval academy had to train for but rarely was it actually ever carried out outside the simulators. Everyone had, therefore, been on their toes but thankfully, it had been carried off without a hitch.

After the last target had been hit, the whole system had suddenly come alive as if a loud siren had gone off. Every warship had boosted to its full acceleration profile. It was now obvious where the British ships were going. The first six targets had been selected to make it look like the British ships were either trying to work their way around to the Paracel passage or to get to a better point from which to launch an attack on the inner system. The last target had given their real objective away, just as it had been chosen to do. Now every Chinese ship was racing to get to the Fujian passage before the British ships could make it there themselves. As a result, and also a part of the plan, *Ghost* and *Raptor* had been forced to drop all pretense at remaining hidden and boost for the system's mass shadow and the opportunity to jump to Fujian.

As the counter ticked down, indicating when the two ships would reach their jump point, *Raptor* began to prepare to return to stealth mode. She powered down her engines, reactors and all non-essential equipment. Two minutes before the jump point James received a communication from *Ghost*. It was Captain Lightfoot. "Well, it's time to say our goodbyes. I hope everything works out as planned. All being well, I'll see you back at the Damang system. It may take us a week or two to work our way back around to meet you but I'm sure we'll both have some interesting stories to tell. Make sure you put our missiles to good use."

"Don't worry sir we will," James replied. "Just make sure you don't try to do too much without them. There's no need for you to take any unnecessary risks. Good luck sir"

"Good luck to you to Somerville, *Ghost* out."

James only had to watch the main holo display for a few seconds until he saw the brief flash that indicated *Ghost* had jumped to shift space. As she did *Raptor* immediately went into stealth mode, venting all the electromagnetic energy she could not contain away from the New Shanghai system and the Chinese warships. Then, slowly, she pivoted in space and brought her engines up to three percent thrust. It would take over four hours at that rate to come to a stop before she could then begin to work her way back into the New Shanghai system and towards the Paracel shift passage.

The slow acceleration meant James and the bridge crew had the best seats to watch as twelve Chinese warships made their way to the Fujian shift passage and, one by one, jumped out in pursuit of *Ghost*. The rest turned back towards the inner system and began to take up patrol positions. James was willing to bet he had not been the only one aboard *Raptor* who prayed a silent prayer for *Ghost* as the Chinese ships had jumped after her.

Chapter 27 – No Mercy

Before the discovery of the shift drive science fiction novels were filled with ideas and visions of what interstellar warfare in space would look like. No one had envisaged the impact shift passages would have both on strategic and tactical warfare.

-Excerpt from Empire Rising, 3002 AD.

20th May, 2465 AD, HMS Raptor

In total it had taken James and *Raptor* two days to secretly work their way past the Chinese warships patrolling the New Shanghai system after *Ghost* had jumped out. After that, it had taken another twenty hours to travel up the shift passage to the ambush point. Now *Raptor* was sitting, waiting for her prey. The Chinese convoy was expected to exit shift space within a sphere of space with a diameter measuring roughly one and a half light hours. James had placed his ship right in the center of the sphere. It was possible the ships of the convoy would come out somewhere where *Raptor* wouldn't detect them but the chances were low. Still, in the journey to the ambush point James had trouble sleeping, he didn't like leaving anything to chance.

Since Lightfoot had left, James had been comparing himself to the more senior Captain. He knew he had done well in the difficult situations he had found himself in as the commander of *Drake*. Yet the past week of operations as a Captain of a warship had begun to show he wasn't quite the invincible Captain he had thought himself to be. Lightfoot had handled the stress of being chased like sheep by a pack of wolves through the New Shanghai system without letting it influence his command ability. James had felt the pressure building and building until he knew he had been performing well below his optimal. He was beginning to realize there was a reason why the Admiralty had a slow process of promoting someone up the chain of command. It took time to develop true command capabilities, capabilities that only came after years of experience. Lightfoot had spent over six years as a Captain of a warship. James' two years as the Commander of a survey ship didn't even come close. Nevertheless, Rear Admiral Jensen saw something in him and Captain Lightfoot had entrusted this mission to him. That was something.

In the old style naval books he had been rereading, the Captain often took a tour of his ship before combat. Sitting in his command chair reflecting on the coming battle, James decided that he would do the same. "Romanov, you have the bridge. I'm going to carry out a quick tour of the ship. Please don't inform anyone I'm coming. I'd like it to be a surprise."

When Romanov nodded he strode out of the bridge. He chose to make his way to the engineering section first and then work his way back to the bridge. As he walked in Chief O'Neil had an access panel open on number three reactor and was tinkering with something inside. One of his officers tried to warn him about his Captain's approach but James waved the ensign off. When he got right behind the Chief, James shouted in his best command voice, "attention on deck."

Chief O'Neil swore as he immediately tried to straighten up and banged his head, dropping whatever tool he was holding. A few snickers escaped some lips and, as James looked around, he could see more than a few of the engineering crew trying to hold back smiles. The Chief continued a string of expletives as he picked up his tool and turned to see who had startled him. As soon as he saw it was the Captain he cut off mid-sentence. "Eh, Captain. Eh, I mean, my apologies Captain. I thought someone was playing a practical joke on me."

"Don't worry yourself Chief. I thought I would take a tour of the ship before the battle commences. I'm glad to find you so engrossed in your work."

"Yes sir, thank you sir. There has been a slight energy fluctuation in reactor two so I was taking this opportunity to make sure it wouldn't develop into something more serious once the fighting begins." Only once he had finished speaking did the Chief manage to look past his Captain to see many of his crew staring, some with open smiles on their faces. Glaring at them he continued, "I only hope my example will rub off on this useless lot of space vermin. Sometimes I despair at the men and women the Admiralty sees fit to recruit."

Turning to take in the men and women who were watching them, James saw that the Chief's outburst had actually managed to increase the number of people who were openly enjoying the Chief's discomfort. "Oh I don't know Chief," James said. "It looks like you have a fine group of engineers here. You might want to designate someone to give you a heads up the next time an important member of the command staff comes down to engineering though. It might save you a bit of bother."

That brought a couple of chuckles from the bystanders. The Chief dismissed them with an angry wave of his fist. "Is there anything else I can do for you sir?"

"No Chief, I just wanted to show my face before we go into battle. I trust you have everything under control." Turning to address the engineering crew directly James said, "We'll be counting on you all back up in the bridge. I know Chief O'Neil will make sure you all do your best. Good luck everyone." With that he shook the Chief's hand and turned to leave. As he walked out a couple of shouts followed him, wishing him good luck or welcoming him back to engineering any time, before Chief O'Neil's angry voice directed them all back to work.

As he toured through the various weapons stations, the marine barracks and the auxiliary bridge, James found very similar situations. Everyone was giving their equipment a once over in preparation for the approaching battle. Nerves were clearly high but James did the best he could to put people at ease and bring out a few chuckles. In the auxiliary bridge he had a quiet word with Lieutenant Gupta reminding her that if they managed to make contact with the Chinese convoy doing as much destruction as possible was paramount; more important than getting the ship home in one piece. If they could stop just one supply shipment from getting to V17 it would weaken the whole Chinese fleet there.

As he exited the auxiliary bridge his personal COM beeped. "Captain," Lieutenant Romanov began in an excited voice, "we have ships exiting shift space all around us." Without even bothering to reply, James sprinted down and around the corridor he was in to the nearest turbolift. Thirty seconds later he burst through the bridge doors and threw himself into the command chair. Looking at Romanov he half shouted, "Status report?"

The Lieutenant already had the sensor plot on the main holo display. Pointing to it he explained the situation. "We've picked up forty six ships that have excited shift space. So far we've identified five warships with a possible three more. The rest are all freighters."

From the plot James could see that *Raptor* was almost right in the middle of the formation. "That's way more ships than our intel suggested. This must be an important convoy. Have they spotted us yet?"

"No sir," Romanov answered, "the warships are just now beginning to scan local space with their secondary radar arrays. They'll pick us up in the next minute or so I believe."

"Very well, how many warships are in missile range?"

With a single command Romanov changed the holo display to only show the warships. "There is a destroyer off our port bow just outside plasma cannon range, a light cruiser off our starboard bow a little further out. One frigate is at the edge of our missile range. The other destroyer and three frigates we've detected are all further off."

"Ok, navigation, as soon as we open fire take us towards that destroyer at full speed. Romanov, on my mark fire a full spread of missiles from each broadside at the destroyer and the light cruiser. Then target the plasma cannons at the destroyer. We'll still get hits even though they are just outside our maximum range, we just won't be able to penetrate their armor. Hopefully we'll cause enough confusion to help our missiles get through. Target as many freighters as possible with our forward and stern tubes. After you have fired the first salvos I want you to hand over control of the starboard missiles tubes to the auxiliary bridge. They are to keep hitting that light cruiser as hard as possible. I want you focused on the port missiles tubes. As soon as we take out that destroyer I want you to switch everything towards hitting as many freighters as possible."

"Understood Captain," Romanov acknowledged.

"Everybody else know what they're doing?" James asked the bridge at large. After a chorus of, "yes sir," James looked back to Romanov. "Fire."

Instantly, fourteen missiles erupted from *Raptor*, announcing her presence to the Chinese convoy. They were closely followed by a rain of plasma bolts that pierced their way through space towards the Chinese destroyer. Accelerated to almost the speed of light, the first plasma bolts reached it only a handful of seconds after the ship's sensors had detected the British ship. The bridge crew hadn't had time to react before damage reports started coming in. Unable to penetrate the valstronium armor the plasma bolts were still able to damage the point defense weapons and sensors that bristled on the hull of the ship.

James wanted to cross his fingers as the seconds ticked by without any response from the Chinese ships. Every moment of delay greatly increased his chances of doing some serious damage to the convoy. Even as they watched a freighter exploded. It had been close enough for *Raptor's* point defense plasma canons to reach. Checking to see what happened James saw Romanov had the foresight to designate the freighters as secondary targets for the point defense weapons to engage if there was no in incoming missiles. Realizing what the Second Lieutenant had done James called to the navigation officer, "Keep us heading for that destroyer but if you can get us close enough to another freighter for the point defense weapons to take it out do so."

"Yes sir," Sub Lieutenant Jackson said.

A full minute after the first plasma cannon bolts had begun to pepper the hull of the destroyer it finally opened fire. James was alerted by the new beeps that came from the gravimetric sensors, announcing five new contacts heading their way. This was closely followed by another set of contacts as the light cruiser also fired eight missiles at *Raptor*.

Ignoring those threats for the moment, James watched his six missiles close with the destroyer. They had loaded their final penetrator missile in one of the port tubes and so the first salvo was going to do the destroyer a lot of damage. James didn't know whether to thank his lucky stars that they had the penetrator missile already aimed at the closest threat or not. A part of him would have liked to be able to fire it at the light cruiser in the hope it would have kept it off his back for a while.

He could only play with the cards he was dealt however and, as he watched, the Chinese point defenses began to try and pick off his missiles. As they entered range of the AM missiles there were three remaining. Only one was destroyed, the other two closed in for the kill. One scored a proximity hit along the destroyer's stern while the second ploughed right into the midsection of the destroyer and exploded. On the visuals James could see a gaping wound where two of the destroyer's missile tubes had been. As he switched the display to zoom in on the stern of the destroyer where the second missile had scored a proximity hit, he saw a volley of plasma bolts rip through the ship's engine compartments. The proximity hit had burnt off enough of the valstronium armor to allow the plasma cannons to penetrate what remained. Once they began to punch through the destroyer's armor, they tore through the innards of the ship, causing a number of secondary explosions. The fourth plasma bolt actually blew through the rear of the ship, taking out one of the engines and immediately sending the destroyer into a sharp roll. The ship desperately fired off its maneuvering thrusters to try and arrest the roll and bring its weapons to bear but they barely made a difference. Without being able to stabilize itself the destroyer no longer posed a threat to *Raptor*.

With the demise of the destroyer, Romanov fired off another missile salvo from the port missile tubes. He had been holding back from firing another broadside at the destroyer until he saw the effects of the first. Now the six missiles raced off, each one in pursuit of a freighter. Already the freighters were doing their best to flee from the British warship. On the main holo display it looked like someone had thrown a stone into a 3D lake. The freighters formed what looked like ripples heading off in all directions emanating from *Raptor's* central position on the plot. As James watched, two of the closest freighters disappeared even before the latest missiles began to close with their targets. Romanov had begun to pick off those in range of the heavy plasma cannons.

Raptor's free rein had come to an end though as James was alerted to the fact that the first Chinese missiles were approaching by the sound of the flak cannon firing. The distinctive whirring noise of the electromagnets rapidly accelerating flak rounds brought his attention back to *Raptor's* survival. "Romanov, pass control of the heavy plasma cannons to me. You focus on taking out the incoming missiles," James shouted over all the alarms that were going off on the bridge.

Confident that Romanov could handle the first five missiles coming in from the now incapacitated destroyer, James focused on taking out the two freighters that were coming into range of his plasma cannons. He spared the occasional glance to see how the duel with the light cruiser was going. There were now two volleys of missiles from the light cruiser approaching his ship. In turn, there were three on their way towards the Chinese warship.

Having dealt with the five from the destroyer, Romanov quickly took out four of the first eight from the cruiser with the flak cannon. Three more fell to the short-range point defense weapons. The fourth scored a proximity hit. Everyone on the bridge was thrown around but before James could ask, Gupta called over the open COM channel to the auxiliary bridge. "No major damage sir, we've lost a fair bit of our armor but it's reshaping itself to fill in the gaps now."

There was too much going on for James to double check Gupta's report. He had to focus on taking out as many freighters as he could. When the second salvo from the Chinese light cruiser got into point defense range, James handed over command of the heavy plasma cannons to Romanov. The chance they could hit any of the dodging missiles with them was slim but combined with the other point defense weapons they allowed Romanov to fill a larger area of space with explosive energy.

The eight missiles reduced to four as the flak cannon did its work. Next the smaller point defense plasma cannons took out two more. To James' amazement the AM missiles *Raptor* launched to intercept the larger Chinese missiles all failed to hit their targets. The final two missiles then closed with *Raptor*. Sub Lieutenant Jackson, who was manning the navigation console, launched *Raptor* into a series of evasive maneuvers. They succeeded in preventing either missile from getting a direct hit but both exploded less than five hundred meters from the hull. As the explosive power crashed into *Raptor*, large sections of valstronium armor were torn off along with vital point defense plasma cannons and anti-missile launchers. Once the inertial dampeners had compensated for the high g-forces from the concussive force of the explosions, James was able to review the damage. *Raptor's* point defense network was seriously compromised. Looking over at one of the secondary holo displays, he reviewed the list of confirmed kills. Thirteen freighters were gone. The destroyer they had initially crippled had also been finished off with a missile Romanov had sent after it as he waited for more targets to get into range. Still, they hadn't done enough to seriously disrupt the convoy, another twenty freighters were trying to get away from the charging *Raptor*.

"Navigation, work up a micro jump to get us out of here," James ordered. "Stand by for my mark. We'll have to take another salvo from that light cruiser but as soon as we've taken out enough freighters, we're out of here." The same thing that trapped the Chinese convoy in the shift passage meant that *Raptor* could escape when she wanted to. Having jumped into the area hours before her jump capacitors were fully charged. The Chinese ships would still be charging theirs and so couldn't escape *Raptor's* missiles nor give chase when she decided to jump out.

With one eye, James watched the steady approach of the second salvo from the light cruiser. Already three salvos from *Raptor* had crashed into it but without any penetrator missiles the light cruiser was shrugging *Raptor's* attacks off. James judged they had maybe scored two proximity hits but the thicker armor on the light cruiser enabled it to weather them much better.

With his other eye, he watched the main holo display and the fleeing freighters. The computer was predicting they would be in range of another four before the Chinese missiles made themselves felt. After that *Raptor* could get in range of another nine before the fourth spread of missiles came crashing home. James was under no illusions. *Raptor* might not survive the next missiles coming in, never mind a fourth salvo. Still, they had a mission to complete. Both Jensen and Lightfoot had entrusted him with this responsibility. As much as he wanted to run to safety the weight of their expectations held him in a firm grip. Besides, it was the job of a King's warship to put itself in harm's way, James said to himself with irony. After the attack on the Swedish colony ship he had hoped never to be facing a similar situation again.

A shout broke his concentration as Romanov pumped his fists, "I nailed him."

James checked the feed from the tactical console to see a replay of one of the frigates getting too close to *Raptor* and being shredded by her heavy plasma cannons. That was one less threat to worry about.

Almost as soon as the last missile streaked off after another freighter, the third salvo of eight Chinese missiles came accelerating into range of *Raptor's* point defenses. This time the anti-missiles fared a lot better and only one missile survived to try and make contact with *Raptor*. Again Sub Lieutenant Jackson threw the ship into a series of evasive maneuvers but to no avail. The single missile managed to get a glancing blow amidships. The angle of the contact meant much of its explosive force was projected out into space. Yet even the fraction of the force that was directed against the hull was devastating. The valstronium armor was blown away as if it was made of steel. Four point defense plasma cannons and three anti-missile launchers were vaporized. The force of the thermonuclear blast blew its way into the ship, crumpling reinforced bulkheads and taking out two missiles tubes along with the twenty men and women who manned them. The force continued into the ship, taking out almost half of the starboard crew quarters. Thankfully, no hands were lost as everyone was at their battle stations. The concussive force momentarily overloaded the inertial dampeners, throwing many of the crew around the ship like rag dolls.

"Damage report," James shouted over the din of all the alarms.

Gupta was the first to reply over the inter bridge COM channel, "we've taken a major hit to our starboard mid sections. Missile tube three is down and I can't raise tube two. Outer sections three through five are all venting atmosphere. As far as I can tell our point defense network is completely shot up along those sections as well."

"What about our weapons, can we still hit those freighters?"

Romanov answered this time, "the remaining missile tubes are all reporting full functionality. We're coming into range of the first freighter in thirty seconds."

"Navigation, can we still make our jump out?" was James' next question.

"We've lost some of our capacitors to an overload sir. I've already got the Chief rerouting some power couplings. I think we can make up the needed deficit by drawing directly from the reactors. The Chief will have to run them up to one hundred percent to meet the power need but we should be able to jump out in two to three minutes."

"Good enough," James responded, after he had checked the timing of the fourth salvo from the light cruiser. The next set of missiles wouldn't get to *Raptor* for another four minutes. Already the light cruiser had another eight missiles coming in behind them. It seemed like overkill to James, if the jump didn't work they wouldn't even last long enough for the last salvo to have anything to target. As he looked again at the ever-growing list of damaged or destroyed freighters, James could maybe understand the fifth salvo. The Chinese Commander was no doubt acting from rage rather than rational thought. He wanted to see *Raptor* blown out of existence!

"Navigation, as soon as Romanov fires his last missile get us out of here," James ordered. Once the officer had replied James opened up a COM channel to the auxiliary bridge and the Fourth Lieutenant who had been overseeing the attacks on the light cruiser. "Good job Jones, switch your fire to any freighters in range. There's no point throwing another four missiles at that light cruiser. Take out as many freighters as you can before we jump."

Less than two minutes later the last missile launched from *Raptor's* tubes and then the ship disappeared back into the darkness of space. Behind her she left twenty-one wrecks and five doomed freighters still trying to outrun the missiles that pursued them. All had once been carrying vital supplies to the Void that would be sorely missed.

Chapter 28 – The Cost of Peace

Few, if any events can be as strongly identified as contributing to the rise of the Empire, as the peace treaty between China and Britain at the end of the Void War.

-Excerpt from Empire Rising, 3002 AD

20th June 2465 AD, HMS Raptor, Excalibur

Thirty one days after the fateful ambush of the convoy, *Raptor* limped into the Excalibur system. She had spent ten full days in the Paracel shift passage effecting repairs. Only once James was happy the ship was stealthy enough to pass through the New Shanghai system, had he returned to the site of the ambush. There they spent a few hours confirming the last five missiles fired before jumping out had all hit their targets. The still expanding balls of wreckage confirmed that even with severely reduced targeting scanners, Romanov and Jones had managed to get all of their missiles on target.

Satisfied that he would be able to bring a complete report of the ambush back to the Admiralty, James had cautiously headed onto the New Shanghai system. Instead of the regulated one point five light hours he had dropped back into normal space three light hours from the system's mass shadow. Then he had very slowly taken *Raptor* into the outer system. What should have taken a slow freighter a day took James four, as he skirted around the edge of the system, carefully avoiding the system's picket ships. Once or twice there had been a few hairy moments, as James was sure the radar beams being sent out into space by the Chinese warships had penetrated the makeshift repairs they had done to the starboard amidships sections. Without having enough spare stealth covering they had only been able to seal up the damaged sections to stop them leaking atmosphere. All the way through the system James had kept the damaged sections of *Raptor* facing away from the known picket ships in the hope they wouldn't detect her. Even so, he hadn't been confident they would make it.

Once at the Damang system, he had finally been able to relax. The crew had been able stand down from battle stations and had begun to focus on the various minor repairs that were still waiting. When they had made it to the coordinates Lightfoot had given them, they sent out the prearranged signal. There had been no response. James then waited half an hour before sending out another. Still, there had been no response. For the next two days *Raptor* patiently waited for *Ghost* to join her. Just as James was about to head back to Excalibur, the sensor officer on the bridge had contacted him. A ship had been detected rapidly accelerating into the system from the shift passage that led back to Wi. A few moments later it had been confirmed as *Ghost*. She was making a direct line for the shift passage out of Damang and back towards the Void. Given the impossibility of real time communication due to the distances between them, James guessed that it was been Lightfoot's way of telling him to make a run for it. He wasted no time and *Raptor* rapidly begun to accelerate towards the shift passage to the Void herself.

Sure enough, forty minutes after *Ghost* had appeared at the edge of the system, four new contacts appeared. They immediately began accelerating along an intercept course towards *Ghost*. Over the next several hours it became apparent that *Ghost* had picked up some minor damage as the Chinese ships slowly gained on her. Soon a stern chase developed with the four Chinese ships firing missiles from their forward missile tubes. Between them they could only fire a total of five missiles yet they threatened to overload *Ghost's* weakened defenses and cause her more damage, slowing her even further. James dropped *Raptor* back to add her point defense to

Ghost's and together they made it to the mass shadow and safety. But only just, *Ghost* had picked up more damage as they hadn't been able to stop all the incoming missiles.

Presently, James sat on the bridge watching the hive of activity around Excalibur as *Raptor* and *Ghost* cruised into the system. In orbit there were a number of freighters unloading all sorts of equipment to the slowly developing colony. There was another group of freighters surrounding the repair station that had been enlarged since James had seen it last. He had looked to see if *Drake* was still docked at the station. It was unlikely; *Raptor* and *Ghost* had been away for sixty one days. *Drake* was likely already well on her way to Earth. Still, James had hoped to see his old command again. In addition to the freighters, Commodore West's heavy cruiser, *Avenger*, orbited the planet accompanied by a light cruiser and destroyer. Lightfoot already sent their mission report to the Commodore's ship as soon as they entered the system. As James waited for a reply, he stood all the crew down from their typical watch duties, leaving only the essential functions of the ship manned. They all deserved a time of rest and relaxation.

The mood of the crew was mixed and James felt the same. In total they had lost thirty-three personnel with the losses at New Shanghai and then at the ambush site. Some were faces James had only seen once or twice. Others he had started to come to know, while still others were hands that had transferred over from *Drake*. The victory had been an astounding one. The Chinese convoy had been decimated. Yet, to the crew, the losses still put a dampener on their achievements. In addition, the last thirty one days had been rough on everyone. The workload to get the repairs done had been enormous. Then they all had been forced to endure four days of nerve-racking shifts at their battle stations as they passed through the New Shanghai system. All the time, everyone had been wondering if the next moment would reveal a Chinese warship bearing down on them.

Now, at last, they were home, back in British space at least. If the new repair station could see to their needs James suspected *Raptor* would be joining the fleet around V17. It would take a fully tooled yard at least a month to make good the hole in *Raptor's* side and to replace the lost missile tubes. That was not likely to matter though. *Raptor's* main role in a large fleet engagement was to beef up the larger ships' point defenses. If her flak gun and point defense plasma cannons could be repaired, *Raptor* was likely to be sent to V17 to join one of the squadrons blockading the Chinese fleet.

"Sir," Sub Lieutenant Graham at the COM station called out, "I've got an incoming message from the Commodore. She's requested it to be broadcast across both our ships."

Slightly concerned James had no choice. "Ok Lieutenant, put it over the ship wide COM."

Seconds later Commodore West's voice could be heard across the ship. "Crew members of *Ghost* and *Raptor*, this is Commodore West. Welcome back to Excalibur. I have read over your Captains' initial reports and I wish to send you my congratulations. Each of you performed admirably." James was able to watch the visual of the Commodore and as she paused she allowed a small smile to creep onto her otherwise stern expression. "I also wish to inform you that as a direct result of your actions and the other raiders that went into Chinese territory a cease fire has been declared."

Immediately, a chorus of cheers erupted across both ships. They had been so loud on the bridge of *Raptor* that James hadn't been able to hear the rest of the Commodore's message. He waited patiently until everyone had settled down and finished exchanging handshakes and hugs. Once they had, he replayed the message on the main holo display.

"..a cease fire has been declared. A popular movement broke out on Earth and across many of the Chinese colonies demanding an end to the war. The Politburo tried to repress the demonstrations with force. When that failed a junior member of the Politburo launched a coup to oust the members he felt were responsible for the war. There is still fighting between the various factions on the Chinese colonial worlds but on Earth, Minister Na has officially been accepted as the interim president of the Communist Party. His first act was to request a cease-fire. At the moment discussions for a peace treaty are ongoing. You have done us all proud. Commodore West out."

James could only sit back in relief. He had known the PR battle back on Earth hadn't been going well for the Chinese government. His uncle's ploy to make it look to the rest of mankind that the Chinese had discovered the Void second and then were trying to steal it all for themselves, had worked perfectly. Even many of the Chinese populace hadn't believed their government's claims to have gotten there first. Those who did, then had to deal with the fact that their government had broken the UN Interplanetary Act. To make matters worse, on the same day news of the unprovoked attack on the British convoy had hit. RSNI had ensured that the recordings of the battle from the only surviving ship had been uploaded to the datanet. The Chinese government had tried to block their populace from seeing it but RSNI had made sure it was available. As the war had progressed, news of the nuclear bombardment of the colony on Excalibur had infuriated everyone. Only the officers involved in the first battle of Excalibur knew it had been a fake colony and they were all sworn to secrecy. James had no doubt that the visuals from *Drake's* encounter with the Chinese destroyers at New Stockholm had also been made available to the Chinese populace. The images of a warship firing on a fully loaded and undefended colony ship was sure to have had an effect on the war spirit of the Chinese people. If the other raiders had been as successful as *Ghost* and *Raptor*, things would have been getting very difficult for the senior

Politburo members before the end.

After he allowed the message to play throughout the ship a third time, James noticed he had also received orders to dock *Raptor* at the repair station. After that he was to appear on board Commodore West's ship. He passed on the information to Gupta and Romanov and then ordered Gupta to open communications with the station to inform them of *Raptor's* needs. Once that was done James called his steward. It would take another four hours to dock with the repair station. He wanted to prepare a celebratory meal for his Lieutenants before they got there.

*

Two hours after docking with the repair station, James sat in the reception area of Commodore West's office aboard *Avenger*. Lightfoot had already been in with the Commodore for almost an hour. No doubt she wanted to go over everything with him first and then get James' perspective separately to make sure she had covered every angle. She would be expected to send her own report back to the Admiralty with those of Lightfoot and James.

Coming out Lightfoot grinned at James and came over to shake his hand. "It's good to see you in person again Captain. There were a few moments back there I wasn't sure either of us would be seeing home again!"

"I know the feeling sir," James replied. "Maybe you'll take me up on the offer of a drink this time once I'm done with the Commodore?"

"I think I can do that but you better go on into the Commodore, she doesn't like to be kept waiting. Contact me when you are finished with her," Lightfoot said as he pushed James towards the entrance to Commodore West's office.

For the next forty-five minutes James went over every detail of the mission with the Commodore. She made him go over the ambush on the convoy twice as Lightfoot hadn't been able to tell her anything about that. After she was satisfied, she turned to the subject of *Raptor's* repairs.

"We lost a third of our starboard crew quarters. Missile tubes three and four are also completely destroyed. New tubes will have to be installed. We've sealed the damaged sections of the hull but if we take another missile hit in the same place it will likely split us in two. Having spoken with the Commander of the repair station I think our point defenses can be brought back to near enough ninety five percent efficiency. Our offensive capabilities will need the work of a repair yard back at Britannia or Earth though."

As she considered her options, West tapped her fingers on her desk. Her long blonde hair had been tied up tight at the back and her face seemed to almost always be set in a scowl. James knew she could smile but her default expression was one of somber seriousness. She reminded him of one of the dorm superintendents he had had back at boarding school. Her expression ensured that he and his friends had always known their place and were aware that crossing her would bring swift punishment. Everyone had been afraid of being caught up to no good by the superintendent. James felt the same way with West.

Finally, she came to a decision. "News of the ceasefire reached us three days ago. Admiral Cunningham has informed Admiral Zheng of the ceasefire although he has withheld the news about the change in government. Admiral Zheng is fiercely loyal to former Chinese Defense Minister Quin and if he knew there was still fighting going on he would be likely to break orbit immediately and head back to Chinese space. If he couldn't re-establish the now defunct Politburo members back into power, he might try to set himself up as a dictator. He now has almost thirty percent of the Chinese fleet under his command.

"Whilst we might be under cease fire conditions the Admiralty also sent orders that we are not allowed to let the Admiral return to Chinese space, at least not unless he relinquishes command of the fleet. Admiral Cunningham has already sent back to Earth requesting an official Chinese representative be sent to the Void to relieve Zheng of command. Yet that could take weeks. In the meantime we're not even sure if Zheng believes there really is a cease-fire. He may think it is just a ploy.

"In light of all this I'm afraid I can't send you out of the Void yet. We will need every ship we can get if Zheng tries to make a break out. The Admiralty is already dispatching reinforcements as they become available but they will be coming in drips and drabs. I want you to go back to *Raptor* and make every effort to speed up the repairs. I'll be taking *Avenger* to join up with Admiral Cunningham in two days. *Ghost* will be joining me and I want you to follow as soon as you are able. Understood?"

"Yes sir," James said as he stood, recognizing that the interview had come to an end.

Before he could turn to leave though West reached into a drawer and removed something. "This came for you. I was asked to deliver it to you personally," she said.

It was a message packet. The standard packet used by the RSN to transport personal items to ships in space. James occasionally received ones from his mother as she sent him items she thought would be useful on board a ship. Though they had never come via a Commodore before. Taking it, James saw it required a DNA scan in order to open. Another safety precaution he hadn't seen before. "I suggest you wait until you return to *Raptor* to open it, it looks important."

"Aye sir," James said as he saluted and walked out of the Commodore's office.

*

Once outside, James contacted Lightfoot and arranged to stop by *Ghost* for a drink before returned to *Raptor*. He enjoyed getting to know the Captain in a more informal setting but all the while his mind was on the message packet. Having spent just enough time with Lightfoot so as not to appear rude, James excused himself and retuned to *Raptor*.

Making his way to his personal quarters, he informed his steward that he didn't want to be disturbed. Sitting down at his desk James set the package in front of him. Slowly he pressed his finger to the scanner and it took a small skin sample to confirm his DNA. A few seconds later it opened to reveal an old style paper envelope. It was something James hadn't seen in person before but he easily recognized it from the holovids he had seen back on Earth. As he lifted it out, he could see his name written on the front of the envelope. The handwriting was unmistakable. It was Christine's.

James heart began to beat faster. He hadn't received a single communication from her since he last left Earth. He had hoped for one when he had returned to Excalibur from New Stockholm but nothing had been waiting for him. When one hadn't been sent to *Raptor* when they had returned from the raid into Chinese space he had begun to worry. He had feared the King had finally managed to talk Christine out of their relationship.

Carefully he opened the letter. It faintly smelt of her perfume and before he began to read it, he held it up to his nose. Then he looked down and began to read.

My dearest James,

Even as I write to you, tears roll down my cheeks. Since the day we met almost five years ago, you have been the only love of my heart. I still remember our walk through the rose gardens like it was yesterday. You know I don't care about your family history or your wealth or political power. My dream, our dream, has always been about more than that.

I write to you now because I have to tell you our dream is over. You've been on the front lines of this war since it started. You know what it has cost, the lives that have been lost.

Since childhood, I have been raised to be a princess. My life has never been my own. Every move has been watched. Everything I have ever done has been planned. My purpose is to help my family and to strengthen and protect Britain. I now see it was foolish of me to think I could forget about all that when it came to love. I want you to know, no, I need you to know that you weren't just a rebellious phase. I love you and I will continue to love you. But my love and my marriage aren't just mine to give. No matter how much both of us want that to be true.

By now you know of the ceasefire that has been called. What you don't know is that my father, your uncle and the prime minister have been in contact with Minister Na for the last couple of months. Together, they plan to end the war in a way that will bring lasting peace, in a way that will bind our nations closer together. There's going to be a marriage. Na is single. Father has arranged that as part of the peace deal, we will marry.

Na is planning a dramatic change in the government of China. He will be making the presidency independent from the Politburo and with longer terms. The idea is to provide a system of oversight for the Politburo. If I, a princess, become his wife, it will give legitimacy to his changes. The changes we need to secure a lasting relationship with China. It will also give me a real influence in the running of the country. You know how the Chinese populace loves our monarchy; we have fascinated them since the twenty first century. I won't allow myself to just be a figurehead; I can have a real impact.

I have to do this. I love you but I cannot be with you. I can only hope that you will understand. You have your duty. I have watched you fall in love with the RSN and that has made me love you all the more. But I have my duty too. If my marriage can help stop this war, if it can help prevent a future one, then I cannot put myself first. My duty, my people, must come first.

You will always be my first love, my true love, but we cannot have a future. Along with this letter I have included the rose you gave me on the first night we met. I have kept it ever since. You promised me then you would marry me. I'm sorry I am making you break your promise.

As I'm sure you know, we cannot be seen together again. I would ask you not to contact me and to avoid me if we happen to cross paths in the future. There cannot be any hint of a scandal. The official story will be that you were just a childish fling. It will be my official story too but I could not bear you not knowing the truth.

I hope in time this letter will bring you some comfort. Goodbye James.

In sadness and heartbreak

Christine

James could hardly take it in; it was as if time had slowed down to a standstill. He reread the letter twice. His hands were shaking so much that he scarcely managed to finish it the second time. As a tear began to run down his cheek, he reached into the packet and removed the case that was inside. He opened it to reveal a pressed rose, preserved between two vacuum-sealed pieces of glass. Below the rose was an inscription Christine had made on the glass along with the date. It was the date of the day they first met and read, 'James' promise.'

In anger, he vigorously shut the case and threw it across the room to smash into the steel bulkhead. With a sob he buried his head in his hands and began to cry uncontrollably. *Raptor*, her repairs, the war and everything else were forgotten. His future had just disappeared in front of his eyes.

Chapter 29 - The Burden of Duty

It is strange how we expect the biggest sacrifices from our armed forces and yet never cut them any slack. They are always expected to perform above their best, if they fall short, rather than helping them, we cut them loose.

-Excerpt from Empire Rising, 3002 AD

29th June, 2465 AD, HMS *Raptor*, Excalibur

Lieutenant Gupta sat in a corner of *Raptor's* canteen with Lieutenant Romanov. They both had their heads close together and they were speaking in whispers. "It has been over a week," Gupta complained. "The Captain has only been out of his quarters a handful of times. He should be overseeing the repairs. We're struggling to cover for him. I don't know how long we can keep this up. The crew know something is going on. Eventually the engineers on the repair station will figure something is wrong and word will spread."

"What else can we do? We don't even know what's wrong with him," Romanov said. "Peace is one the horizon but *Raptor* will be declared battle worthy in two more days, something needs to change and fast."

"I have an idea about what's wrong, but I don't know how we can solve it," Gupta informed Romanov.

"You do?" he asked surprised.

"Yes, but you must promise to tell no one," she said in an even quieter whisper. As Romanov nodded she continued, "You know about the Captain's affair with Princess Christine?"

"Of course," Romanov said, "everyone saw the news vids."

"Well, James received a messenger packet when we arrived back in Excalibur. I suspect it carried some news about Christine. The King has been doing everything he can to end their relationship. He may have succeeded."

"Well, we all have our personal problems. Everyone has to deal with such things. We need our Captain back. In two days we'll be heading back to a war zone. James can't be in command in his current state. What are you going to do about it?" Romanov asked.

"Me?" Gupta said, slightly louder than she wanted. Her shock was evident.

"Yes, you," Romanov said forcefully. "I will back whatever you do but you are the First Lieutenant. You need to find a way to get through to him or you need to declare him unfit for command. We have to think about the rest of the ship, not just the Captain."

"You're right," Gupta conceded. "But what am I going to do, I can't just confront him about it? We don't even know for sure what is wrong with him.

"We don't, but maybe there is a way we can find out. We need to talk to the Captain's steward. I know Fox fairly well. We have both been on *Raptor* since she was commissioned. I think we need to pay him a visit."

*

Two hours later and Gupta was sitting at James' desk in his private office. She was fidgeting nervously. Only a short time ago she and

Romanov had cornered Fox. He had been reluctant to speak at first but eventually they had convinced him that they were trying to help the Captain. It seemed that James had received a letter in the message packet. Fox hadn't been able to say any more except that it had been hand written on paper and that it had had a faint smell of expensive perfume. That had been enough to confirm Gupta's suspicions. The letter could only have come from one person and judging from James' response it could only have said one thing.

Now she sat waiting for the Captain to emerge from his quarters. He wasn't expecting her but she knew if she had requested a meeting he would have denied it. She still hadn't decided how to approach the subject but with every passing hour *Raptor* got closer to being ready to depart.

She continued to tap her fingers nervously for another thirty minutes. Still, she hadn't come up with a strategy. Eventually she gave up waiting and opened James' personal computer and keyed it to send him a message saying a high priority communication was awaiting him in his office. It still took him another ten minutes to appear.

When he did, Gupta was horrified by his appearance. His hair was all over the place, as if he hadn't tried to straighten it out for days. He clearly hadn't shaved since he had received the letter a week ago. He had his Captain's trousers on but his feet were bare and he was wearing nothing above his waist. In his hand he clutched a once crumpled letter, he had obviously tried to straighten out. Gupta assumed it was the letter in question. His eyes were bloodshot, either from a lack of sleep or tears or likely both.

When James saw the Lieutenant a look of anger came across his face. He clutched the letter tighter and moved his hand down to his side slightly hiding it behind his leg and the angle of his body. "What are you doing here?" he demanded.

James' anger flipped a switch in Gupta. She had given up the chance of a ship of her own to remain under his command and help him get *Raptor* fit for battle when he had been promoted to her Captain. She had worked tirelessly over the last month on the repairs to the ship. It had been even worse over the last week as she had tried to do his job and hers. Now, when he was failing the men and women who had put their trust in him, he had the audacity to get angry at her!

"I am here because I still know what it means to do my duty," she retorted. "I'm here because you need to be reminded of yours."

"How dare you talk to me like that," James said raising his voice to match hers, "I am your Captain."

"Wrong," Gupta shouted back, "you were my Captain. A man I happily followed into the face of danger at New Stockholm and at Wi and at New Shanghai and in the Paracel shift passage. Have you looked at yourself lately?" Gupta paused for effect and let her gaze wonder over James. In response he unconsciously looked down at his attire.

"That man I followed isn't standing before me now," she continued. Before he could respond, Gupta pointed to the letter he was trying to hide. "Is that the source of your misconduct? A Dear John letter from your princess? You're not the first person to go through a break up and you're not the first person to suffer a loss."

She started to list off names of crew members who had died under James' command. She began with those from *Drake* who had died at New Stockholm and then moved on to *Raptor* before pausing for breath. "Each of those people had wives and husbands, parents and children. They all suffered a greater loss than you have. And what about the men and women still under your command? Do they mean nothing to you? Do you even care if they die because they have an incompetent Captain?"

As she said that last sentence, Gupta saw something inside James break. His anger turned to despair and he slumped down into the chair behind his desk. His head fell into his hands and he began to sob quietly.

"You don't think I care about my crew?" he said between sobs.

With compassion, she reached across and placed her hand on his forearm, "I know you do. I've seen you care for them. I've seen you shed a tear over the losses we have suffered. Why are you letting them down now?"

"You don't understand, you can't understand. It's not about them," James mumbled before going back to sobbing.

"You're wrong. It is about them. You have a duty to them," Gupta said as she squeezed his forearm

"Duty? Don't speak to me about duty!" James said, flicking away Gupta's hand as his earlier anger threatened to rise up again.

"I will," Gupta broke in before James could say anymore. "I will because you swore an oath to your King and country. I will because you have taught me what it means, what it looks like. I will because you have a duty to the two hundred and sixty six men and women under your command. I don't know what has happened between you and the princess but it hasn't changed your duty."

In disgust James thrust the letter in front of Gupta, "here, this is what happened. Your duty be dammed."

As Gupta read the letter she began to understand the depths of

James' hurt. "You were going to marry her?" she asked.

"Yes," he replied, "even if it cost me my career."

"That's not true," Gupta said seeing an opening. "I know you. I know your love for the navy. You wouldn't abandon those relying on you. Not really. If you didn't care about us then why are you still here? You have risked your life in battle for the navy, for those under your command, for those in harm's way. Each time you took your future in your hands and risked your hope of a life with Christine because you knew, as a RSN Captain, you had a responsibility, a duty.

"Did Christine ever begrudge the sense of duty she knew you had when it took you away from her?" Not waiting for a reply Gupta continued. "She didn't. But now she has a duty. A duty she has had all her life. You cannot expect her to abandon it. No more than she ever expected you to abandon yours. If she had said no to this marriage, she wouldn't have been the woman you fell in love with. If you truly loved her, if you truly knew her, you would know that she didn't abandon you. She was caught between doing what she must and what she wanted. If she had chosen you, how do you think she would have lived with herself? She would have been miserable, wracked with guilt.

"I cannot take this pain away," she told him. "No one can. But it does get easier. Christine wouldn't want you to let this destroy you. She would want you to be the man she loved, to do your duty just as she has had to do hers."

"And how am I supposed to do that," James asked. "I'm a mess."

Gupta recognized his question for what it was, a plea for help. He wanted to get out of his depression but he didn't know how. "One step at a time James, one step at a time," she said using his given name for the first time since she had entered his office. "First we need to get you washed and dressed. I'm going to call your steward. Come on, up you get," she said as she walked around and lifted James to his feet.

Reluctantly, he followed her lead as she walked him back into his quarters. His steward was already waiting there, a look of concern on his face. "Take him into the washroom and get him showered and shaved. Then we'll get him into his uniform," Gupta ordered.

Turning back to James she said, "that's the first step. The second is a tour of the ship. The crew has been working tirelessly over the last week to complete all the repairs they hadn't been able to do without the help of the repair station. You're going to do a tour of the ship and see what they have done for you. They need to see your face and you need to see theirs. You need to remember who you are, the responsibilities you have."

As Fox led James into the washroom Gupta activated her personal COM, "Romanov, report to the Captain's quarters in twenty minutes. We're going to be taking the Captain on a tour of the ship to show him how the repairs are going."

"Yes sir," Romanov replied with more than a hint of relief and pleasure on his voice.

*

Two days later James strode onto the bridge of *Raptor*. He still felt tired and drained. His eyes were still raw and he knew he could do with several more nights of sleep. On the inside he felt hollow. The man he had once thought of as James Somerville didn't seem to exist anymore. At least he had hidden himself deep down away from where James could get to him. Now he just felt numb. Gupta's words had gotten through to him. Or at least she had made him see Christine's words in her letter. He had a duty to do. She had understood that. Gupta had reminded him of it, he couldn't let his crew down. However, the last two days had almost been worse than the previous week. It had taken all the inner strength he could find, just to get out of bed. He had tried his best to put on a brave face, to let the crew see him happy and confident. He knew he had failed. No doubt many of them knew something was deeply wrong with him.

Still, there had been no sign of any complaints and the work rate had actually increased since his tour of the ship. Deep down James knew that it meant they trusted him. They were willing to follow him, even though he wasn't at his best. At another time it would have been a great encouragement to him. Now he barely registered it.

As he sat down, Romanov announced to the bridge for his benefit, "the station's docking clamps will be released in five minutes."

"Very good Lieutenant, clear us of the station using maneuvering thrusters once the station releases us. When we're five kilometers clear take us out of orbit and plot a course for V17. We're going to re-join the fleet."

"COMS," James continued, "open a ship wide channel for me."

"Channel open sir," came the reply.

"*Raptor*," James began, "this is your Captain speaking. You've all worked hard and our repairs are complete. We'll be heading to the V17 system. There we'll be joining the blockade under Admiral Cunningham. Hopefully Admiral Zheng will surrender peacefully but, if not, we need to be ready to fight. Make sure you get some rest over the next few hours. Once we get to V17 we'll be on permanent standby. Somerville out."

As he finished his short speech, James looked over the Gupta. She nodded to him before going back to her duties. James knew he owed her a great debt. She could easily have reported him and relieved him of command. Instead she had risked his anger to help him. She would make a good Captain someday, he only hoped she would live to get the opportunity.

*

It took *Raptor* seven hours to break orbit and then a further four to jump to the fleet's coordinates at V17. Admiral Cunningham had most of his heavy ships split into two squadrons. Each squadron was at an opposite end of the system, three light days from the mass shadow. The smaller frigates and survey ships of the fleet were patrolling the edge of V17's mass shadow, watching the Chinese fleet. Splitting his fleet gave the Admiral the greatest degree of flexibility. No matter which way the Chinese Admiral tried to take his fleet out of the system both elements of the British fleet could jump into a blocking position. Usually splitting up a fleet could spell disaster but this strategy also gave the blockading fleet a chance to intercept any ships that tried to enter the system.

James had set course for the nearest section of the fleet. Rear Admiral Jensen was in charge and he expected to either be slotted into her squadron or have orders waiting for him to join the second squadron under Admiral Cunningham.

When his ship had been detected, he had been immediately requested to repair on board Jensen's battlecruiser *Valkyrie*. As he had been flown across, James had been able to get a good look at all the ships under Jensen's command. She had a total of two battlecruisers, four heavy cruisers, five medium and another six light cruisers. There were also thirteen destroyers, one of which was

Ghost, and James had spotted at least ten point defense frigates and corvettes also backing up the heavier ships.

Once on board, he was immediately shown into Rear Admirals' office. She stood to greet him and shook his hand. "It's good to see you again Captain. I was glad to see that my decision to put you in charge of *Raptor* proved to have been justified." As she sat down and motioned for James to do likewise, she studied him for several moments. "Is everything alright? You don't look too well."

"Everything is fine sir, I have just had some personal issues to deal with. Nothing I can't handle," James lied.

"In that case let me bring you up to speed. In total the Chinese now have two battleships, three battlecruisers, seven heavy, ten medium and twelve light cruisers. They also have almost twenty destroyers and twenty-five frigates. They outnumber us on the larger scale of things but all the skirmishes we have had over the last months have bled them dry when it came to destroyers and frigates. If it comes to a shooting match, they'll outgun us in terms of sheer numbers but our better point defense should more than even the odds. We're expecting more reinforcements to trickle in as ships can be spared from other sectors as they stand down because of the cease-fire.

"We've also been promised a delegation from China to come out and make sure Zheng keeps the cease fire. As yet he still won't believe us that his government has called an end to the war. Of course they didn't, the provisional government has, though he doesn't need to know that. The bottom line is that if he tries to make a break for it, we are to stop him at all costs. If he manages to get back to Chinese space, he will upset the peace process and possibly throw us back into a full-scale war. Do you have any questions?"

"No sir," James answered, "I'm just eager to get our orders and to begin to integrate into the fleet. The crew of *Raptor* is raring to go sir."

"Very well Captain. You're being assigned to my *Valkyrie's* covering flotilla. It'll be your job to watch my rear. You'll be joining the point defense corvette *Hope*, the flak frigate *Defiance* and a ship you are well familiar with, HMS *Ghost*. You can report to my Flag Captain after we are done here. He will take you through some of the finer details he has worked out with Captain Lightfoot regarding the defense of my flagship. For now, let us go over Admiral Cunningham's plans if it comes to a large-scale fleet action."

When James was finished with the Rear Admiral, he spent another hour with the Flag Captain going over the specific positions of the various ships protecting the flagship. He was also advised to make contact with the other Captains and commanders of the ships in his flotilla to introduce himself.

It was standard practice in the RSN that larger capital ships, such as heavy cruisers and battlecruisers, also have their own flotillas of smaller ships protecting them. Typically, two heavy cruisers would form a flotilla that would be filled with other ships ranging from corvettes to destroyers. A single battlecruiser was thought worthy of a flotilla of smaller warships all to herself. If it came to a larger fleet action, the remaining light and medium cruisers were all paired off, with each pair fighting together.

With the addition of the flak cannon technology to British tactics, Admiral Cunningham had altered the standard RSN battle formations. The idea was that as all the various flotillas joined together to form one combined fleet they would be able to overlap their flak cannon fire, to create a giant wall of shrapnel to fend off incoming missiles. To James, as both Rear Admiral Jensen went over the wider ideas of the various fleet formations and then as her Flag Captain went over the specifics for their flotilla, it look liked it should work. Though he didn't know how anyone could command so many ships once the actual fighting broke out and the nice formations began to break up.

When he finally got back on board *Raptor* he sent all the data to Gupta for her and Romanov to review. He then went to lie down for a while before he had to go over it for a third time with them.

Chapter 30 - Blockade Runner

In the era of near instantaneous galactic communications, we forget that it once took weeks and months for orders to be sent from one planet to another. As in the days of sail, this communications lag often meant wars continued to be fought on the frontiers even after peace treaties had been signed.

-Excerpt from Empire Rising, 3002 AD

31st July, 2465 AD, HMS *Raptor*, outer edge of V17 system

James woke with a start. The COM unit built into his bed was beeping furiously, demanding his attention. He had been struggling to adjust his sleeping pattern over the last month. His dreams had been haunting him with what he had or could have had with Christine. They were taking a toll on him. Each morning he had to pull himself together before he could go out and face his crew. Fox was the only one who knew just how much he was still struggling but James was confident he could trust his steward.

Still a bit groggy, he tapped the COM unit, "What is it?"

"Captain. A frigate has just jumped to the fleet from V17." Romanov informed him. "She's reporting that a freighter, escorted by a number of small warships, has just jumped into the system. Jensen has ordered us to prepare to jump. She's taking *Valkyrie* and her flotilla into the system in pursuit."

"I'll be on the bridge presently," James replied. "When is the micro jump?

"Twenty seconds sir."

"Very well, carry on without me until I get there."

As James half sprinted from his quarters to the bridge, he felt the subtle shift in the inertial dampeners indicating that *Raptor* had entered shift space. By the time he had sat down another subtle shift signaled they had reached the edge of the V17 system. With *Valkyrie* at the center of her flotilla, the ships all began to accelerate along the intercept course *Valkyrie's* navigation officer had plotted based on the data from the scouts.

It only took a matter of seconds for *Raptor's* sensors to begin to update the main holo plot of the system. The gravimetric data indicated that there were a number of Chinese ships maneuvering around in the inner system. There were too many to really make heads or tails of. Further out it was a different story. All the British scout ships were hiding in stealth and so couldn't be detected. This meant the freighter and its escorts were the only ships moving. They had obviously altered course slightly from when the scout had detected them. As soon as *Valkyrie's* navigation officer spotted the course change, an updated heading was sent to the flotilla and they turned in pursuit.

It only took the freighter a few seconds to react. Immediately it doubled its acceleration. James was impressed. He hadn't seen a freighter that could come anywhere close to the acceleration this one was doing. Obviously someone had upgraded it substantially. As the two escorts accelerated to match its speed the sensor officer was able to get a better read on them.

"I estimate those two warships to be destroyers sir."

"Stranger and stranger," James said to the bridge. An upgraded freighter being escorted by two destroyers, whatever or whoever was on board that freighter was obviously important.

As if by magic, the inner system suddenly came alive with activity. Every ship even remotely close to the incoming freighter began to rapidly accelerate towards it, coming to its aid. "I guess they must have recognized their friend," Romanov said. "A freighter with such acceleration has to be very rare. It must be known to someone in the Chinese fleet."

"Indeed," James said. As he continued to watch, the two destroyers escorting the freighter began to decelerate. It seemed they wanted to cross swords with *Valkyrie* and her escorts. They probably hoped to slow *Valkyrie* down enough to let the freighter escape. They had made a mistake though, potentially a fatal one.

Rear Admiral Jensen saw the flaw in their plan as well as James, for his command chair beeped to alert him that she was requesting a COM link. When he approved the link he saw Captain Lightfoot had been included as well. "Gentlemen," she began, "it seems our targets have forgotten about your extra acceleration. When I give the order, I want you two to take off all the safeties and boost to your maximum acceleration. Get your gaseous shields on too and run that freighter down. Whatever they are carrying it must be important. We can't let them make contact with the Chinese fleet."

"Aye sir," both James and Lightfoot said in unison. Jensen only nodded and then cut the transmission.

"COM, get me the Chief," James requested. Moments later the Chief appeared on his command chair holo display. "Chief, we're going to need everything you can give us from the engines and the reactors. In less than five minutes I'm going to ask you to boost us up to one hundred and ten percent military power. We'll keep holding that acceleration until we reach our maximum velocity.

The Chief looked a little nervous, "We can certainly configure the engines to do that but *Raptor* hasn't been taken to one hundred and ten percent since her space trials. Even then it was only for a very short burn to stress test everything. I can't guarantee what will happen."

"I know the risks Chief," James replied, "I have every confidence in you. If it looks like there is going to be an overload in the engines you have my permission to reduce power without waiting for authorization."

"Yes sir, I'll begin making the preparations now then," the Chief said as he closed the COM channel.

With the rate the two Chinese destroyers were decelerating, it only took them fifteen minutes to reach the point of no return. As *Valkyrie* and her flotilla were accelerating hard after the freighter, which itself was still accelerating to get to its top speed, the destroyers, having lost a great deal of momentum, couldn't hope to make it back to the freighter. As they crossed the line where they couldn't reverse course, both *Ghost* and *Raptor* shot forward from the flotilla. They both angled away from the approaching Chinese warships to remain out of their missile range. Immediately, the two Chinese ships tried to alter course to intercept the two British destroyers but it was easy for James and Lightfoot to keep altering their course to keep them at arm's length. The differing velocities meant that the Chinese ships had no chance of catching them.

Whoever was commanding the freighter quickly realized their mistake, for the freighter increased its acceleration again. They must have taken the safeties off their engines for the freighter shot forward with another five percent increase in its acceleration. When the plot updated, it was clear to James the freighter still wasn't going to make it to the ships coming up out of the inner system in time. What did concern James was that both *Ghost* and *Raptor* were close to getting into trouble themselves. After catching the freighter, they would have to decelerate hard if they were to get back out of the system before the Chinese warships coming out to greet them got into range. If either ship encountered a problem with their engines they might not be able to escape.

Over the next ten minutes, slowly but surely *Ghost* and *Raptor* began to overhaul the freighter. James had been analyzing the freighter closely on the visual images they were now getting. He was looking for any other surprises the upgraded freighter might have. It was clearly armed with a lot more point defense weapons than the typical freighter.

As Romanov reported that *Valkyrie* had opened fire James switched his attention back to the battle with the two Chinese destroyers. They were both accelerating hard, right for the battlecruiser. The commanders had clearly accepted their failure to protect the freighter and were trying to get into plasma cannon range of the battlecruiser to at least do some damage to her. It seemed they were unlikely to succeed, as twenty-three missiles from *Valkyrie* and the rest of her flotilla homed in on the two destroyers. In response, they fired off ten missiles of their own. James knew the point defenses of *Valkyrie* alone could handle that many, with the flak frigate and the point defense corvette cruising along beside her, they would pose no threat.

The closing speed of the two groups of ships ensured that the missiles from *Valkyrie* reached the Chinese ships before they could fire off another salvo. Their point defenses put up a good fight destroying fifteen of the incoming missiles, but the rest enveloped both ships in a shroud of nuclear explosions. James couldn't make out if any of the missiles got a direct hit but as the sensors cleared it didn't matter. Both destroyers were drifting wrecks. As James watched, a secondary explosion aboard one ripped what was left of the ship in two. The other one was clearly trying to arrest its erratic spin with its maneuvering thrusters but there weren't enough of them left to succeed. Suddenly a number of escape pods began to launch from it. James guessed the Captain had given up saving the ship and was getting his crew off before the British ships came into plasma range.

"Sir," Romanov said to get his attention, "Captain Lightfoot has sent over a firing plan for your approval."

"Thank you," James acknowledged. He then brought up the plan. Lightfoot wanted both *Ghost* and *Raptor* to turn broadside onto the freighter once they got into range and fire four missiles each. Cutting their acceleration would let the freighter get away but there was no way it could survive a salvo of eight missiles.

"Tell him I approve," James ordered. The he turned to the navigation officer, "Jackson, make the turn when *Ghost* gives the order. Romanov, be ready to fire."

Less than a minute later, eight missiles streaked out after the frigate. *Ghost* and *Raptor* then began to decelerate to allow themselves to escape the approaching Chinese warships that would be out for revenge. The flight time of the missiles was going to be over twenty five minutes as the freighter was continuing to pile on speed. As the time passed, James continued to watch the freighter on the visual feed. A number of compartments opened to reveal extra point defense plasma cannons. In total, the freighter seemed to have the defenses of a frigate. Still it would have real difficulty dealing with eight missiles.

Sure enough, as the freighter's point defenses began to engage the missiles they weren't able to destroy them quick enough. Five missiles made it through its defenses and two scored direct hits. As the sensor feeds cleared up after the explosions there was no sign of the freighter or of any escape pods.

"Sir," the COM officer called out. "I'm picking up a transmission from the freighter. It must have sent it out just seconds before being destroyed. It contains a visual feed and a large data packet. Neither has been encrypted."

James wasn't surprised. It would have been very hard for a civilian to get a Chinese military data encrypter, even for someone who was obviously able to get their hands on military grade plasma cannons. "Put the visual on screen, then give me a rundown of the data packet," James commanded.

An image of a young Chinese man appeared. James reckoned he couldn't be more than mid-twenties. He spoke in Chinese but the computer's translation program put sub titles onto the visual image. "Father," he began, "I've tried to contact you but all my attempts were intercepted. This was the last thing I could think of. There has been a coup. Minister Na has overthrown the Politburo and is trying to make peace with the British. He has arrested many of the senior military officers loyal to Chang for war crimes and has confiscated most of our wealth. I couldn't stop him. I'm sorry for failing you. I have shamed our family, I only hope you can use this information to undo my shame."

This wasn't good, James knew. The young man must have been Admiral Zheng's son. The Admiral wasn't going to take his death well. What would he do now that he knew about the coup? There was no chance he would surrender, not if the only thing that awaited him was prison. "How long until the message reaches the Admiral's battleship in orbit." James asked the COM officer.

"It will take the transmission another three hours sir," she replied.

"I guess we better get ready then. I think things are about get interesting."

When the message reached *Valkyrie* Jensen came to the same conclusion. She immediately sent a transmission to the courier ships that had jumped in with her flotilla. One was to inform Admiral Cunningham of the development. The other was to inform the rest of her squadron back at their position outside the V17 system and then to go on to Excalibur to order any ships that had arrived there to come straight to V17. A battle was surely approaching.

*

Back at the squadron's rendezvous point the next four hours were frantic. Every ship was taking its turn to come alongside the resupply freighters as they topped up their fuel and weapons. Regular updates kept coming from the scouts in the system as the Chinese fleet gathered itself, clearly intending to try and break out of the blockade.

At last the message came through. The Chinese fleet was taking a direct line for the shift passage back to Chinese space. Admirals Cunningham and Jensen had worked out plans for every eventuality. In this case, each section of the fleet would jump to a prearranged point and get into formation before jumping into the system to confront the Chinese fleet.

The number of ships forming up overawed James when they jumped to the fleet assembly area. Admiral Cunningham had four battlecruisers under his command; combined with their flotillas they constituted more ships than James had ever seen in one place. The smaller cruisers and destroyers that were taking up position along the outer edge of the fleet further bolstered the numbers. Jensen's squadron slotted in at the back of the fleet to inflate its numbers to an even more impressive level. In total six battlecruisers prepared to jump into the V17 system. Whatever happened, James knew this was going to be the biggest space battle in human history.

His role was likely to be rather small. The battle computers aboard *Valkyrie* would direct the fire of the point defenses of the flagship's flotilla. Jensen would also be designating targets for her ships to attack together. Only if the flagship were damaged would James have to step in and take direct control of how his ship was fought.

There was a moment of silence as the fleet waited for another scout ship to jump in and give them the latest flight vectors of the Chinese ships. When it did, every ship was updated with new jump coordinates from Admiral Cunningham's flagship. A timer appeared on the main holo display. They would be jumping in two minutes.

Before they did, Admiral Cunningham made a fleet wide transmission. His face appeared on the main holo display above the countdown. "Men and women of the fleet. We already have a cease-fire with the Chinese but you all know the situation before us. If this Chinese fleet gets back to their home space, they will reverse the changes taking place in China. Full-scale war will resume. That means that the real peace must be won here, today. I cannot guarantee we all will make it home safely. But that is not why we signed up to the Royal Space Navy. We signed up to protect our families, our homes and our country. That's what we are here to do today. Britain expects every man and woman to do their duty. I know you will give of your best. For King and Country," Admiral Cunningham closed with a salute.

Despite everything that had happened James found himself saluting and repeating the Admiral's last phrase with everyone else on board *Raptor*. No one could miss the historical reference to Britain's greatest Admiral. They had a tradition to live up too.

Thirty seconds after the Admiral's speech, the fleet jumped into shift space. The jump itself only lasted a handful of seconds. Then, once again, James found himself accelerating into the V17 system. The Chinese fleet had already been heading out of the system for the last two hours. They had reached the maximum speed of their battleships and were clearly still hoping they would be able to fight their way past whatever British ships appeared to engage them.

Admiral Cunningham had come into the system in a way that would allow his ships to loop around the advancing Chinese ships and come up alongside them. That way the two fleets wouldn't pass one another but would instead slowly converge. As a result, the Chinese fleet would be within missile range of the British ships for an hour before they would reach the system's mass shadow. The Chinese Admiral could try and veer away from the British fleet but doing so would take him away from the shortest route to the mass shadow. In turn, Admiral Cunningham could alter course and keep with the Chinese fleet, actually prolonging the time they would be in missile range. Admiral Zheng had no choice. If he wanted to try and get back to Chinese space he had to fight his way out. This was the British philosophy drilled into all her officers from the academy. When an enemy needed to be stopped, it was the duty of His Majesty's ships to lay alongside the enemy and hold them in their sights for as long as possible. One way or another the battle would end in a decisive outcome.

For the next two hours, James had to sit back and watch the two fleets slowly converge. He had read about many famous navel battles in the past and the firsthand accounts always mentioned the waiting. Both fleets knew they now had to destroy the other to live. Neither Admiral planned to back off. Yet everyone on board each ship of the fleet had to sit and wait. There was nothing that could be done until they got within range of each other. James tried to keep his crew busy. He ran a few firing drills to make sure everyone was on their toes. Then an hour before the battle he made sure everyone got a chance to go to the canteen and eat and take a five minute break from their battle stations.

Finally, the firing orders began to come in. Cunningham had decided that the first two salvos would be aimed at the smaller Chinese ships. Then, once the point defenses of the Chinese fleet had been weakened, the battleships and battlecruisers would be targeted until they surrendered or were destroyed. If they could take out the main ships of the Chinese fleet, with their senior commanders, it was likely the rest might give up and surrender.

It was the British ships that broke the silence first. Six hundred missiles poured out of their missile tubes and began to accelerate towards the Chinese fleet. A couple of minutes later the Chinese responded. James couldn't count all the missiles the gravimetric plot was showing but the computer estimated there to be at least seven hundred and twenty. The battle had begun.

Chapter 31 - Sacrifice

In the end history has taught us that all wars boil down to one simple thing, kill the enemy before he kills you. If you cannot achieve this, do the next best thing..

-Excerpt from Empire Rising, 3002 AD

31st July, 2465 AD, HMS *Raptor*, outer edge of V17 system

As James watched the first missile salvo crash into the Chinese fleet, he knew they had used their time since the first battle of Excalibur well. All the smaller British ships had fired at least one of their penetrator missiles, while the larger ships were keeping theirs for the third salvo. Even so, a lot less British missiles managed to get through the Chinese ships' point defenses than expected. Only one medium cruiser and three destroyers were destroyed. A light cruiser had also been damaged enough to cause it to begin to fall behind its comrades. As it did, it disappeared from *Raptor's* targeting priorities. Any ships that dropped out of the Chinese fleet could be ignored and picked off later. The objective was to stop any of them reaching the edge of the system's mass shadow.

Next it was the turn of the Chinese missiles to get their chance at causing damage. Their seven hundred and twenty missiles were first reduced to less than two hundred by the flak guns. Only fifteen actually managed to break through the inner point defense fire to lock onto targets. ECM jamming confused three more but the final twelve found targets. Three destroyers disappeared as they each took a direct hit, one, hit twice, left no trace of itself after the explosions cleared. A heavy cruiser was rocked by two proximity hits but continued on, shrugging off the damage. Two light cruisers weren't so lucky; as each took a proximity hit, they began to register some serious damage on the fleet status screen. Further explosions among the fleet took out four frigates and a corvette.

Immediately, the smaller ships of the fleet began to reposition themselves to best fill the gaps in the point defense fire that had been opened up by the losses. Once in position, every ship fired as one and the third salvo of British missiles, now reduced by over forty compared to the first, began to tear their way across the gap between the two fleets. The second salvo, fired before the Chinese missiles began to explode among them, was already getting into range of the Chinese fleet.

Again the Chinese point defenses served them well. Of the initial six hundred, only twenty managed to get close enough to detonate against a target. This time, three light cruisers and two destroyers were destroyed or severely damaged. Crucially, eight frigates were taken out as direct or even proximity hits ensured the fragile ships disintegrated. James had to pump his fists. The Chinese point defense fire was being whittled away.

His jubilation was short lived when the next Chinese salvo came crashing into the British fleet. One medium cruiser was destroyed and one of Admiral Cunningham's battlecruisers took two proximity hits from what appeared to be the heavier battleship missiles. With almost a third more explosive firepower than the smaller cruiser missiles the British battlecruiser lost five of her missile tubes and was struggling to stay in formation.

For another twenty minutes the two fleets continued to pound each other. After each salvo more and more ships dropped out of formation from each fleet. *Raptor* barely managed to dodge a missile that had beaten her point defenses and *Valkyrie* had taken at least one proximity hit. Their flotilla had also lost its flak frigate to a direct hit.

James already felt himself losing tactical awareness of the battle. It was hard to determine how it was going. Ships were constantly changing positions to fill in gaps and present the most effective defense. At other times ships he had thought had survived the latest salvo, were simply gone the next time he looked at the plot. It was likely they had brushed off a hit only to find their damaged systems had overloaded. Still, as far as he could tell they were beginning to get the upper hand. He had seen each of the two battleships take proximity hits and the whole Chinese fleet had been forced to reduce their speed to allow one of the battleships to stay in formation. One of the battlecruisers had also pulled out of formation. It had taken a number of proximity hits and then, when the first heavy cruiser of the battle had exploded, a part of its nose section had collided with the battlecruiser.

"New orders coming in," shouted the COM officer. "The fleet is to adjust course to heading five four two point three."

James checked the new heading. Admiral Cunningham was veering away from the Chinese fleet to keep the range open. He clearly thought the British ships were getting the better of the missile engagement. He didn't want to give the Chinese a chance to closing to plasma range.

Just moments after the British fleet came onto a new heading and fired another salvo of missiles, the Chinese reacted. Their speed told James that it was a prearranged maneuver. Almost all of the Chinese fleet came onto a new heading that didn't just compensate for the British change in course but actually meant the Chinese ships were closing the gap to the British. Three ships didn't follow the course change though. A battleship accompanied by two heavy cruisers turned away from the British fleet. James guessed Admiral Zheng was on board the battleship. He was sacrificing the remainder of his fleet in order to escape back to China.

That left Admiral Cunningham an almost impossible decision to make. If he turned his ships after the fleeing Chinese battleship, he would be presenting his bow to the main Chinese force. They would be able to fire missile salvos and soon plasma bolts at the British fleet while Cunningham's ships could only respond with their bow weapons. Typically, only half of a RSN navy's plasma cannons could actually target forward threats and even the battlecruisers only had four bow missile tubes each.

That meant that if Cunningham wanted to stop Zheng from escaping, his fleet would have to go through the main Chinese force, and fast. He could stand off and hammer them to pieces. Certainly they now had the numerical advantage. Yet as James did the calculations it was clear that unless they got some lucky hits and took out the Chinese ships quickly it would take too long. Admiral Zheng would be able to escape. The only other option was to close to plasma range. Yet there was no guarantee that any of the British ships would come out of a plasma duel undamaged. They would certainly take heavy losses and even then the survivors may not be in a position to catch the fleeing Chinese ships.

It seemed like Cunningham had to choose between keeping his fleet and protecting the Chinese reforms being made under Na. He couldn't do both. James certainly didn't know how he would make the decision, if he were in charge.

Before Cunningham made a move, Rear Admiral Jensen reacted. "Sir," Romanov called worriedly. "*Valkyrie* is breaking formation. She's turning towards the fleeing Chinese ships! Wait, *Ghost* is following."

Immediately, James knew what she was doing. Being at the back of the fleet *Valkyrie* could risk turning her bow to the Chinese fleet. On her new heading they wouldn't be able to get into plasma range before Jensen could bypass them.

"Take us after them," James ordered. It was a suicide mission. There was no doubt about it. If the main Chinese fleet didn't bother sending any missiles their way, the battleship and two heavy cruisers would probably finish them off anyway.

"Signal from *Churchill*," Sub Lieutenant Beckford at the COM station called. "*Valkyrie* and her escorts are to return to formation."

"Sir, what shall I do?" the navigation officer asked.

"Keep station with *Valkyrie*, we're only turning back if she does," James answered.

It only took a few moments for Jensen herself to contact James. When he opened the COM link he saw Lightfoot had been included in the discussion. "This is my fight, I have unfinished business with Zheng. I'm ordering both of you to return to the fleet immediately," she said as crossly as she could.

Lightfoot was the first to respond, "sorry sir, you're breaking up." Before Jensen could say anything more, Lightfoot cut the transmission from *Ghost*. Jensen was left staring at James. She tried to say something further but James cut his own transmission as well.

"Sir," the COM officer said as she waved him towards the main holo display. "A message is coming in from *Ghost*. It's text only."

Across the main screen came the message from *Lightfoot*.

She's planning to close to plasma range. Our smaller guns won't be effective but without our flak cannons she won't get close enough to do any damage. It's our job to screen the flagship, so let's make sure Jensen gets to where she wants to go.

"Send an acknowledgement," James ordered. The gravity of the situation suddenly hit him. Jensen had nothing to gain and everything to lose. There wasn't much chance *Valkyrie* would survive once she got into plasma range of the battleship's heavy guns. Why was she so willing to sacrifice her life to stop this Chinese Commander? Even if he got away what damage could he actually do with a battleship and two heavy cruisers? Then he realized. Duty. It was her sense of duty that drove her. She had seen the impossible situation Admiral Cunningham had been placed in. He had to choose between losing most of his fleet and letting Zheng escape. Jensen had taken the choice away from him and, in doing so, protected the rest of the fleet. He was reminded of an old navy saying, if you can't kill your enemy before he kills you, do the next best thing, take him down with you.

Suddenly, James realized that he had only been playing at being a naval officer before. All his life he had always had other things that were his priority, his family, his reputation, his future, and Christine. The common factor was that they all revolved around him. Even when he had made command decisions that everyone had applauded him for, he had still been acting to win approval, to further his career, his standing. Now he saw what a true sense of duty looked like, what true valor looked like. Jensen was going to sacrifice herself to save the fleet. Momentarily his thoughts turned to Christine. She had chosen her duty, to put herself second and others first. Now he understood.

"Captain," Romanov called breaking into his thoughts, "we have another message from Admiral Cunningham. He's threatening us all with a court martial if we don't turn back. What shall I do?"

James realized he too now had a decision to make. Did he simply follow orders or did he do what his sense of duty dictated. He was about to take his crew to almost certain death against orders. Yet he knew it was the right choice.

"Keep us steady Lieutenant Romanov," James said calmly. "This is what we came here to do. Let's be about it."

"Yes sir," Romanov said. "We'll give them hell." He was grinning as he shouted.

James couldn't help but get caught up in his enthusiasm, "that we will Lieutenant."

Over the next few minutes Jensen tried repeatedly to raise either James or Lightfoot on a COM channel. Both refused to acknowledge her call. Eventually she gave up; the next communication from *Valkyrie* was a set of targeting data. Charging straight after the fleeing Chinese ships meant that neither group could fire their broadside missile tubes. Jensen wanted to target one of the heavy cruisers with all their bow missile tubes. *Valkyrie* had four while *Raptor* and *Ghost* had one each. The battleship would shrug off salvos of six missiles all day but the heavy cruiser Jensen had targeted had already taken a couple of hits. It was possible they could sneak a missile or two in through its defenses.

Even though it would obviously indicate that there was nothing wrong with his communication array, James acknowledged the orders. When the timer to fire counted down to zero, six missiles shot off from the three British ships towards one of the heavy cruisers. In return, the Chinese ships fired ten missiles back from their stern tubes. Both sets of ships managed to destroy the missiles before they did any harm. Neither was deterred though, for as soon as they were ready more missiles came pouring out of the British and Chinese ships.

After the second round of missile salvos was destroyed, the navigation officer on board *Raptor* called out, "Captain, *Valkyrie* is increasing her speed, she must be giving her engines everything she has got."

"Contact Chief O'Neil, tell him we need to match speeds with the flagship. Increase our acceleration as soon as you can," James ordered.

As James watched, the flagship slowly edged ahead of the two destroyers. Lightfoot had obviously anticipated Jensen's idea for *Ghost* was soon catching her. Impatiently, James had to wait another thirty seconds before *Raptor's* acceleration increased enough to match the other two ships. When she slotted back into formation both destroyers received a text message from the flagship.

"You are both too stubborn for your own good."

Alongside that message James had also received a message from the Chief Engineer. *Valkyrie* was the newest battlecruiser to have left the *Vulcan* shipyards. Her acceleration was impressive indeed. Chief O'Neil estimated that the destroyer's engines wouldn't last more than twenty minutes at the current rate. *Raptor* simply couldn't keep up with the flagship for long. Quickly James sent a message back informing the chief that they would get into plasma cannon range in thirty minutes, the engines could blow up after that for all for al he cared but they had to last that long.

Five minutes later, as the fourth salvo crashed into the Chinese ships, a cheer went up on the bridge of *Raptor*. A single missile had punched through their defenses and scored a proximity hit on the Chinese heavy cruiser. Its speed didn't falter but when the Chinese fired their next salvo it had clearly lost one of its stern missile tubes, for only nine missiles streaked towards the pursuing British ships.

Ten more minutes passed as the two groups of ships continued to exchange missile salvos. *Valkyrie* brushed off another proximity hit and they managed to get another hit on the heavy cruiser. It visibly wobbled as James watched and then began to lose speed.

Just then the data on the holo screen began to change. "Captain, the Chinese ships are slowing. They're turning sir!" Romanov shouted.

Immediately, James knew what Admiral Zheng planned. He had accepted they couldn't drive off the pursuing *Valkyrie* before she got into plasma cannon range. He couldn't risk that so he was slowing and turning to present his broadside missiles tubes towards *Valkyrie*. Given the current speed of *Valkyrie*, the Chinese would be able to get off one and maybe even two broadsides before the range closed enough to allow the plasma cannons to join the fight. To confirm his suspicions, seventy four missiles erupted from the Chinese ships and began to accelerate towards *Valkyrie*.

A notification told him Lightfoot had opened a COM channel. "It looks like we're going to have to earn our pay today," he began. "*Valkyrie* needs to get through this storm or else we have wasted ourselves. I'm taking *Ghost* as close as I can to the flagship. She's a good ship I'm sure she can handle a hit or two."

James knew his talk was all bravado. Even a proximity hit from the battleship's large missiles would likely end either *Ghost* or *Raptor*.

Without a hint that he didn't believe what he was saying Lightfoot continued, "You've studied the trick Villeneuve used at the second battle of New France? I've suggested to Jensen we do the same; it might buy us a little time. I'll send you the targeting data now."

"Yes," James agreed, "I'll bring *Raptor* in to join you. If we survive this, it's my turn to buy the drinks. *Raptor* over."

As *Valkyrie*, *Ghost* and *Raptor* continued to accelerate towards the Chinese ships, the closing speed of the incoming missiles didn't give them long to prepare. When the missiles were only four minutes out, the British ships fired their bow missile tubes for the last time. The six missiles accelerated for only a minute before they exploded just in front of the approaching Chinese missiles. Of the seventy four, five were destroyed in the blast, six more had their targeting sensors fried and lost lock on the British ships. Sixty three raced on into a hail of explosions as the flak cannons threw up a wall of shrapnel to fend them off. As all the missiles were targeted at *Valkyrie,* they came in as a tight cluster allowing the flak rounds to tear through them, taking out over thirty. The closer in point defenses filled space with plasma bolts and then AM missiles. Still six got through. At that moment *Ghost* and *Raptor* turned their ECM up to full. As all three British ships were in such close proximity, two missiles were momentarily confused. It was long enough for them to fly past the ships and explode. The remaining four didn't lose their targeting lock and came crashing in. *Ghost* took a direct hit that was meant for *Valkyrie*. The missile penetrated her valstronium armor and detonated in *Ghost's* stern, knocking out her engines and sending her into a spin, luckily it took her away from *Valkyrie*. It must have been a missile from one of the heavy cruisers, for a battleship missile would have obliterated the whole ship.

A single proximity hit wracked *Raptor*; thankfully it was far enough away that the blast didn't get though her armor. Most of her starboard point defense weapons were burnt off the hull and alarms began to squeal from multiple terminals on the bridge, indicating the concussive force of the explosions had still caused some severe internal damage.

Valkyrie took a direct hit on her port side amidships. Six missile tubes were knocked out and large sections of the ship began to vent atmosphere. The last Chinese missile also got proximity hits on the battlecruiser but her thick valstronium armor managed to hold, preventing any serious damage.

As James was surveying the damage to his ship, he missed Jensen's next move. It was Romanov who was the first to spot it, "Captain, *Valkyrie* is accelerating again, she can't possibly hold that acceleration for long, she'll blow her engines."

Looking at the holo display, James saw Romanov was right. *Valkyrie* was pulling away from *Raptor* again. As the projected course updated he saw that Jensen would get into plasma range before another missile salvo from the Chinese could reach her. They would never have survived another one. Jensen had to take the risk of either overloading her engines or causing a reactor meltdown.

"What shall we do sir?" Romanov called, "we can't match her speed now."

Before James could answer, he received a communication from the Rear Admiral. "Turn back immediately, protect *Ghost*, that's an order Somerville. She's a sitting duck without any defenses. Get her crew off before something else happens to her. You can't help me now; your plasma cannons won't be able to penetrate the battleship's armor at the range mine can. My crew has sent their last messages for home across to you. Tell your uncle I hope I made him proud. Now go, don't let our sacrifice be in vain!" she shouted before switching off the COM channel.

James was momentarily frozen. He had already consigned himself to dying. Their mad dash after the battleship hadn't seemed like it would end any other way. Now he had been offered a lifeline. But did he want to take it? Dying would be so much easier than going on, what had he to live for? But if he let his ship be destroyed, it would be a mockery to Jensen's sacrifice. *Valkyrie* was dying for a purpose. How could he let his ship die for nothing? Yet he still needed something to live for. For a few desperate seconds he hesitated.

As his conflicting thoughts tugged at him, finally one side won out. Jensen had shown him what real valor, what a real sense of duty looked like. That was what he had to live for, to honor her sacrifice by living for what she exemplified, what he wanted to have in himself.

As he ordered *Raptor* to turn and decelerate to come alongside *Ghost* James couldn't help smiling. His uncle had obviously gotten to Jensen too. He was sure it wasn't through old style books but whatever method he had used, it had been just as effective. After the first book he had read almost two years ago now, he had laughed at the idealized view of a naval officer the book had presented. By the end of the books, he had hoped it could be true. Now he knew, he had seen it in Jensen. He only hoped he could live up to her example one day too.

After he made sure the navigation officer had put *Raptor* on the right course towards *Ghost* and Gupta had the damage under control, James set himself to watch Jensen's last moments. He willed himself to take in every last detail; this was something he didn't want to forget.

In vain the Chinese ships fired another volley of missiles. For a moment James was worried that some had been targeted at the two damaged destroyers but as *Raptor's* computers projected their trajectories it was clear they were all heading for *Valkyrie*.

Twenty seconds before the battlecruiser got into plasma cannon range escape pods began streaking away from the ship. Somehow James didn't think Jensen was aboard them. She had likely ordered everyone who wasn't necessary for the operation of the plasma cannons to abandon ship. Once they were clear *Valkyrie* opened fire. She carried four twin turrets of heavy plasma cannons. Four bolts streaked out towards the Chinese battleship. They all struck its stern, driving through the valstronium armor and ripping apart its engines and power transfer couplings. Each heavy cruiser also had two bolts targeted at it. One, already damaged, exploded as one of the plasma bolts hit something vital. The other cruiser immediately began to lose acceleration, indicating that the bolts aimed at its engines had found their mark.

For a few moments James feared the battleship would still get away as it seemed to continue on its course unfazed by the hits. Then one and then another secondary explosion tore through the stern of the ship and immediately its acceleration dropped to zero. It wasn't going anywhere soon.

Looking at the Chinese ships James had missed *Valkyrie's* fate but with a tap of his fingers he replayed the visuals. The Chinese ships had fired their plasma cannons less than a second after *Valkyrie's*. The bolts had passed each other in space before more than twenty collided with *Valkyrie*. On the visual she seemed to simply fall apart. At least five of the bolts tore right through the ship and appeared out the other side. The others caused so much damage that *Valkyrie* lost all structural integrity. The acceleration from her engines immediately caused her to break apart. The engines themselves actually accelerated through the ship until they collided with the reactor compartment. The resulting destruction from four fission reactors exploding blinded *Raptor's* sensors. When the feed came back on there was nothing of *Valkyrie* to be seen.

As he stopped the playback of the recording, James bowed his head. You *did it*, he thought to himself. *Now we just have to make sure your sacrifice was worth it.*

"Sir," the sensor officer called. "I'm picking up a transmission from Admiral Cunningham's flagship. He's calling for the immediate surrender of all Chinese ships."

Quickly, James looked at the wider sensor feed from the rest of the system. Admiral Cunningham's flagship had just burst out of the middle of the Chinese fleet and was heading towards the now stricken Chinese battleship. The computer estimated that they would reach it in less than twenty minutes. Relieved that he wouldn't have to deal with the damaged battleship, James replayed the sensor feed to see how the rest of the battle had unfolded.

Initially Cunningham had stood his fleet off from the approaching Chinese ships. They had then hammered the Chinese with four more missile salvos heavily damaging the battleship and remaining battlecruisers. With the risk from entering plasma cannon range reduced, he had left his smaller ships to continue hammering the Chinese with missiles, while he had taken the British battlecruisers and heavy cruisers into the teeth of the Chinese fleet. Even before the first plasma bolts had been fired a number of the more damaged Chinese ships had surrendered, including the battleship. Those that hadn't surrendered had been quickly crippled or destroyed as plasma bolts had rained down on them.

Returning to watch the Admiral's fleet in real time, it was clear that the British ships hadn't escaped unscathed. Two of the battlecruisers were already dropping behind, indicating they had suffered serious damage and one of the heavy cruisers that had accompanied the Admiral into the Chinese fleet was nowhere to be seen.

"Captain," the COM officer called, "the two Chinese heavy cruisers have surrendered, there is still no word from the battleship though."

James brought up the sensor feed on the battleship. Admiral Cunningham would be in missile range soon. It would have to surrender or face destruction. Part of the data the holo display was showing him seemed confusing. "Sensors, why does there seem to be a power fluctuation coming from that battleship?" James asked.

"Hold on sir," came the reply, "I've got the computer working on it now." James watched the display as the fluctuations continued to osculate getting stronger and stronger. "Sir," the Sub Lieutenant began again, this time with a lot more concern in his voice. "The computer has identified the readings as the early stage of an intentional fission reactor overload. Someone over there is trying to cause a meltdown."

Even as the Lieutenant spoke, James saw escape pods begin to launch from the battleship. The computer estimated that at least one of the battleship's fission reactors would reach a critical energy flow rate in twenty seconds. James hoped that whoever had ordered the evacuation had given their people enough of a warning. As the twenty seconds elapsed it became clear they hadn't. Even as the blinding light from a nuclear explosion burst forth from within the battleship itself, escape pods were still launching from the ship.

Admiral Zheng had known defeat would mean facing charges of war crimes. Either of his attacks on the Damang convoy, the Excalibur colony or the colony ship at New Stockholm on their own would get him life imprisonment. Knowing Chinese culture, James knew the shame he would have brought on his country and family would have been even worse than the actual jail sentence. To avoid all that, James had no doubt the Admiral hadn't even tried to leave the battleship.

"Captain, we're picking up a signal from one of the escape pods from the battleship. It's from the ship's Third Lieutenant. He says he's the senior surviving officer from the battleship and would like to formally offer the surrender of his crew," Lieutenant Romanov said.

"Very good Lieutenant," James replied.

"May I ask sir," the Lieutenant continued, "what does this mean?"

"It means," James said to the bridge at large, "it's over."

Epilogue - HMS Endeavor

14th January 2466 AD, Westminster Abby, England

Princess Christine Anne Elizabeth Windsor stood in a side room adjacent to the entrance to Westminster Abby, making some final adjustments to her dress. The walk from Buckingham Palace to the carriage and then the carriage ride through London had left her attire a little out of place. On this day that would not do, everything had to be perfect. The plans for what was about to happen had been settled months ago but the peace negations had strung out longer than had been expected.

Five months ago, news had reached Earth of what the news broadcasters were calling the Battle of the Void. When she had heard, her first thought had been to check the status of a small destroyer called *Raptor*, only then had she concerned herself with how the rest of the British fleet had fared. With the astounding victory, the British had secured the Void and the Chinese fleet had been decimated. Not one of the warships China had sent into the Void had made it back to Chinese space. Christine knew her father and the Prime Minister had been trying to thrash out as fair a deal for her husband to be as possible. In the end, they had settled on the original boundaries for the Void that had been laid out by the UN Interplanetary Committee. The British would keep Excalibur and Camelot, the Swedish would be able to try a second time at establishing a colony on New Stockholm and the Chinese would keep V17, the system they called Xi Wang.

That wasn't all though. Even if her father had wanted to let the Chinese off lightly, public opinion had made it impossible. The Void was now declared a demilitarized zone, at least as far as

Chinese warships went. In addition, all ships passing through the shift passage into the Void from Chinese space would have to go through a UN led customs inspection to ensure the Chinese would not be able to bring in weapons of any kind. Much more importantly, the one point Prime Minister Fairfax had not backed down on was that the Chinese government would have to open their borders to British shipping, removing all transit fees and opening all their markets to British traders. On the face of it this was the biggest cost the Chinese had to pay for peace. In reality it was necessary, the damage their economy, infrastructure and, specifically, their freighter fleet had taken meant many of their colonies were in dire straits, even on the brink of starvation. Those same problems meant the British shipping companies would quickly come to dominate the Chinese intersystem trade. However, over time this would begin to reverse. As the Chinese economy began to recover, the open border and open market policy between Britain and China would allow Chinese companies to begin to make inroads into the British economy. In time, the British government hoped this would further bind the two powers together, with Britain as the dominant force of course.

Even so, there had been public outcry when the official peace settlement had been announced four days ago. The British public had seen China as its main competitor for nearly a century. Now they had the Chinese beaten. It seemed to them that now was the time to make sure the Chinese government and its colonies could no longer try to expand or threaten British interests. Of course, even Christine with her limited study of history knew how such harsh peace settlements usually turned out. If the British tried to strangle China, they would only be guaranteeing another war as soon as the Chinese felt they were strong enough to throw off the British shackles. She knew her father's approach was the right one.

With a final tug on her dress, she was happy with how she looked. It had been tradition, for as far back as she knew, for British royalty to travel to Westminster Abby in the gold encrusted Royal State Coach. Having never been in it before, let alone any contraption pulled by eight quarter horses, she hadn't been ready for the uncomfortable ride. The suspension had been non-existent; she had been in space yacht races through the rings of Saturn that had been more comfortable. Still, at least the ordeal was over. Now all she had to do was face what was coming next.

As she looked at herself in the mirror one last time, she pictured James beside her in her mind's eye. He was dressed in the same exquisite suit his father had made him wear to the reception where they had first met. In her vision they were both smiling and holding hands. As feelings of despair threatened to well up, she quickly banished the image. She berated herself for being so foolish. She could not afford any thoughts of him today. That was a previous life. In this life, she was about to get married.

The door behind her opened and closed quietly. Quickly she reached up and wiped away the tear that had escaped and was making its way down her cheek. In the mirror her father came up behind her and placed his hands on her shoulders. "It's time," he said.

As he turned her around, he reached up to her other check and wiped away another tear. "I know this is hard for you, you're giving up your own happiness for the good of your people. This is the price we pay for our position. But think of the opportunity you have. The Chinese people love you. You can shape their culture, their future. From your new position you can help our people. Na is a good man; you may even grow to love him over time. Certainly you can work together. But I want you to know this. You will always have your mother and me to come to your aid. Don't ever think you are alone, we'll be here for you."

"Thank you father," Christine said, as she embraced him in a hug.

"I know this is what I'm supposed to do." After she continued to hold him for a minute or so he gently pushed her away.

"Let's go, everyone is waiting," King Edward XI said as he took his daughter's hand.

*

Vows complete, Na and Christine turned to face the assembled congregation. The Archbishop spread his hands as he presented the newly married couple. "Ladies and gentlemen, I now present to you Emperor Na Zhong the First and Empress Na Christine."

Christine almost let go of Na's hand in shock. Empress? As she looked around the room she saw that almost everyone else had the same look of shock that was no doubt on her face. When she looked over to Na, he was smiling at her. He leaned in and whispered to her, "impressive isn't it? I made a few last minute changes to our new constitution after the marriage was publicly announced. Don't worry, I still have a fixed term of twenty years, then I have to be re-elected, but I thought Emperor and Empress had a better ring to it. Plus, it puts the old ways of a president who was just the puppet of the Politburo behind us. Smile my dear, you're the first Chinese Empress in over five hundred years." With a snap she closed her gaping mouth and produced her best smile, all the while thinking she would have to keep a close eye on her new husband.

*

At the reception Admiral Somerville watched as King Edward mingled with all his guests. There were dignitaries from every nation state on Earth and representatives from all the human colonial worlds. For his part Somerville was happy to sit on the sidelines. If it served the men and women of the RSN he was happy to dive into the politics of such gatherings but if he could avoid it, he did. A tap on his shoulder revealed the Prime Minister who was standing beside him. "We need to talk about Chang, do you have any more information?" he asked.

"I do," Somerville began, "but I think we should include the King in this."

"Agreed," Fairfax said. He lifted his hand towards the King and waved at him slightly. The King looked over for only a second and nodded, then resumed his conversation with the Governor of the Utah system without even breaking sentence.

Five minutes later King Edward joined them in the shadows of a corner of the reception room.

"You daughter looked beautiful today," Somerville said by way of greeting when he arrived.

"Thank you, she reminds me of her mother when she was that age," Edward replied. "What is it you two want to talk about? I can only spare a minute or two."

"I'll come right to it then," Fairfax said. "We need to do something about Minister Chang. The public are outraged that he escaped from Beijing and are even more cross that we can't locate him. All of our approval ratings are slipping, we need to bring him to justice."

"Of course, I agree," Edward said, "but we don't know where he fled too, do we?"

Fairfax looked expectantly at Somerville who paused before answering. "We do have a lead. One of our contacts in the Indian colonies has recovered some files that suggest someone from China has taken up residence there. He managed to get his hands on some financial information that indicates a large amount of Chinese currency was transferred out of China to a shipping company based in the Indian Colonies. They have holdings on their two main colonies as well as on some of the smaller bases across the territory. It's possible Chang has paid them to hide him somewhere."

"Ok, so what do we do about it?" Edward asked.

"We need to send a ship in to investigate, and to get him back if he is there." Fairfax demanded.

"We can't just send a warship into Indian territory," Edward said, "The Indians already hate us. We don't need to give them any more reasons to do so."

"You are right your Highness," Somerville agreed, "but maybe we could send in a ship, if they never found out about it. We could investigate quietly, then if we find him, we grab him. A ship stealthy enough should be able to come and go in the Indian colonies without being spotted. Even if we have to use a bit more force and reveal ourselves when it comes to grabbing him, the Indians can't make too much of a fuss. If they do they will be admitting to harboring a war criminal."

"Ok, so we send in a ship with orders to quietly investigate things. Who do we send?" Edward asked.

"Well," Somerville answered, "My nephew has just returned from the Void. His ship *Raptor* is in need of a lengthy refit. I was planning on giving him HMS *Endeavour*. He has proven himself to be a wily commander and his First Lieutenant is of Indian origin. Plus, sending him has the added benefit of keeping him away from British space for the next few months. I'm sure none of us want any more drama where he is concerned?"

Somerville felt quietly devious as he spoke that last sentence. He had understood the King's desire to hold back his nephew but he hadn't agreed with the King's actions. Now he was getting a chance to use the King's fears to James' advantage.

Edward eyed Somerville for a few seconds before agreeing, "Ok, I'm on board. After today I will rain down hell on that boy if he causes any more trouble. I hope he has enough sense to realize he has lost as far as my daughter is concerned. But just in case he hasn't, sending him away for a while suits me. Just make sure he has very clear instructions on how far he can go. We don't need him provoking a shooting incident with another naval power."

"I will," Somerville said. "I'll give him another couple of days R and R while we set things up and then I'll pass on our instructions personally."

"Very good," Edward said. "I have guests to get back to. You two finalize the plans and I'll leave it in your hands." As he strode away back into the crowd of dignitaries Somerville and Fairfax left to find a quieter room to plan out how they were going to deal with Chang.

*

18th January, 2466 AD, HMS *Vulcan*, Earth

James stood outside his uncle's office waiting to be called in. *Raptor* had returned to Earth five days ago. She had spent almost six months in the Void after the final battle with Admiral Zheng. All the heavier ships had been sent home immediately, either to Britannia or to Earth. Their repairs took precedence. As a result, *Raptor* had spent a couple of weeks at the repair station in Excalibur and then been sent back out on patrol. That had been fine for James. He had needed something to do to keep him distracted.

For the last five days he had tried his best to avoid all the news broadcasts but it had proved impossible. Britain was filled with a new spirit of confidence. The peace was lasting and business was booming. Already people were flooding to Excalibur and Camelot. The public had become fixated on Christine. She was portrayed on every news broadcast as the British heroine who had stepped into the lion's den to tame the lions before they escaped and devoured the British nation. Of course, with the lion being so closely associated with the British monarchy the imagery was often replaced with fiery dragons but the idea was the same. Every step she took and every obstacle she faced made the headlines. If her life had been under scrutiny before it was now under a microscope. Yet for James every image of her was a reminder of his loss. In the end he hadn't been able to take it. After meeting with his mother and then André Clements to review his finances - finances that were flourishing thanks to her, he had spent three days relaxing on a remote south pacific island with nothing but the ocean and some new 18th Century war novels he had bought for himself. He'd also sent a message to his uncle requesting an update on his next assignment. *Raptor* had been handed over to the engineers aboard *Vulcan*. Her repairs were estimated to take upwards of six months for, on top of having to replace entire sections of her superstructure; there were a number of tech advances that had come out of the war that they wanted to install. Lieutenant Romanov had been left in charge but after they had docked with *Vulcan,* both Gupta and himself had received orders to prepare for a transfer.

Just then the doors to his uncle's office opened and Lieutenant Gupta walked out. James was surprised to see her. He had assumed that she would be spending at least another week on shore leave with her family. "Lieutenant, it's good to see you," he said warmly as he shook her hand.

After returning his handshake she released him and waved her finger in his face. "I'm afraid not Captain." Reaching into her pocket she pulled out a single gold star, the rank insignia for a

Commander. "It's no longer Lieutenant," she said grinning.

"Congratulations," James said with genuine pleasure, "You deserve it more than anyone else I know." He wanted to give her a hug but he wasn't sure their relationship had developed that far.

"Thank you sir, that means a lot to me," Gupta replied. She looked like she was debating something for a few seconds and then she pulled him into a hug herself, "I couldn't have done it without your example and your recommendation."

"Nonsense," James said as they broke apart, "you were ready for promotion even before I took command of *Drake*. We'll have to go out for a drink to celebrate. Can you wait until I am done with my uncle?"

"I'm sorry sir, my family already have a celebration planned. The Admiralty has put me on special assignment. I have two days to myself and then I have to report back to Vulcan to take charge of my new command – though I am still being kept in the dark as to what ship I'm getting. Until then my family wants to get as much time with me as possible. You should come though. We're meeting for dinner at Bishop's in London, it's on Regent Street."

"Well, I wouldn't want to intrude," James said not feeling up to having to deal with a crowd.

"Nonsense, Gupta insisted, "you'll be more than welcome. My family will love to meet you. You can tell them all stories about how I'm such a brave and courageous naval officer. I'll tell them you're coming so they'll be expecting you. If you don't show they will all be deeply offended."

James felt trapped but he was genuinely pleased for Gupta. She deserved her promotion and command of a warship. "Ok, I'll see you later," he conceded. "But I better go see my uncle now."

"Good luck then," Gupta said as she saluted and then watched James turn and enter his uncle's office.

As he entered, his uncle stood to receive him. "Welcome James, it's good to see you," he said as he came around his desk and shook James' hand. "I must say you have done us all proud. Your reports have been impressive. Both Lightfoot and Jensen spoke very highly of you. You have certainly exceeded my expectations and I think your ambush in the Paracel passage will become a set engagement to be studied at the naval academy."

"Thank you sir," was all James could find to say. He hadn't been expecting such praise.

"There has been one problem though," his uncle said sitting down and looking more serious. "The official reports of the Battle of the Void have you, Rear Admiral Jensen and Captain Lightfoot disobeying a direct order from Admiral Cunningham. Further, analysis of the COM chatter also indicates that you and Lightfoot disobeyed a series of orders from the Rear Admiral as well."

"Yes sir," James replied. He had been worried his actions would come back to haunt him. "We had been assigned to *Valkyrie's* flotilla sir. Lightfoot and I both felt it was our duty to protect our flagship. I've had the last six months to think about the battle. I don't think I would do anything different."

Somerville visibly relaxed, "That is what I was hoping to hear," he said. "As you know Jensen has posthumously received the Victoria Cross. Admiral Cunningham has also officially endorsed her course of action even though it was against his orders. We could hardly punish you or Captain Lightfoot for simply following her example. I wanted to make sure you were willing to take responsibility for your actions though.

"Now," the older Somerville said as his expression changed again, becoming more excited. "Let's talk about your future. You've distinguished yourself in independent command. I don't want you to be wasted being assigned to a picket squadron to spend the next few years going back and forth in Britannia or Cook. Tell me what you think of her," he said as he brought up a ship in his holo display.

James took several minutes to take the image in and read the text that scrolled along its side. The ship was four hundred and twenty meters long, more than a third larger than *Raptor*. She had two more missile ports on each broadside than his previous command and her three plasma cannon turrets were a caliber larger than *Raptor's*. Unlike the streamlined destroyer, or even the light cruisers of the RSN, however, her middle sections bowed out, giving her the impression that she was a light cruiser that had put on a lot of weight. As her technical details continued to scroll past, her operational range jumped out at him. His first command, the survey ship *Drake* had been designed to operate for up to seven months without having to return to port to refuel. Yet that had only been in extreme cases with every non-essential piece of equipment turned off. This ship boasted a maximum operational range of two years. It was astounding.

"She's certainly impressive sir, is this just a concept design or has construction on one already started?"

"Actually the first one has just finished her space trials and passed with flying colors. She's designed to be a deep reconnaissance ship. In times of war she can spend months behind enemy lines observing fleet movements and occasionally ambushing shipping. In times of peace she is designed to be able to carry out extensive survey patrols. She was due for completion about a month after the war broke out but we put her construction on hold when we shifted over to a war footing. It was deemed we needed to finish construction of the hulls meant to join a battle fleet first. After the war ended she was finished off and has spent the last month completing her space trials. Essentially, she is a light cruiser with some of her armaments stripped off and extra fuel tanks incorporated, she's yours if you want her."

James almost missed his uncle's last statement he had been so focused on taking in the new ship. "Mine?" he asked.

"Yes. You've earned the right to refuse. I'm sure we can find you another destroyer or light cruiser but I think you would be perfectly suited to command her. She's called the *Endeavour* by the way."

James took a moment to think. He had spent the first two years of his command on *Drake* cursing the day he had been forced to take command of her. Now he was being given another survey ship. Albeit it with a lot more prestige and a lot more firepower. If another war did break out commanding *Endeavour* meant he would be in the thick of it. Until then a long cruise away from Earth and the other British colonies might be exactly what he needed.

"I accept," he said. "When am I to take command?"

"Tomorrow if you are ready. She will be returning from a run in from the outer system by then."

"What is to be my first mission?" James asked.

Somerville paused and looked James over as if assessing him for the first time. "This stays between the two of us understood?"

"Yes sir," James replied, already intrigued.

*

It took his uncle another hour to fill James in on all the information regarding his upcoming mission. Eventually his uncle stood and shook his hand again to congratulate him on his new command. James was jumping at the bit to get out of his uncle's office. He wanted to go read up on his new ship

As he was leaving James suddenly remembered, "Oh by the way," he said as he turned back to his uncle. "Before she died Rear Admiral Jensen gave me a message for you. She said she hoped she had done you proud."

His uncle looked taken aback. For a moment his mask disappeared and James saw the grief he had obviously been hiding. "Thank you for telling me," he said.

"Was she close to you?" James asked.

"Yes," his uncle answered after a moment's hesitation, "she served under me as a Lieutenant aboard *Achilles* and then as a Captain when I was in command of the Britannia fleet. I always thought of myself as her mentor of sorts, I had hoped she saw me that way too."

"I'm sure she did uncle," James began, "I just hope I can live up to her example."

"That's a noble goal Captain, enjoy your next command."

"Thank you Admiral," James said as he saluted and left.

The End

You can follow James, Gupta and all the others in the next book in the Empire Rising series – Return to Haven, coming soon!

If you enjoyed the book don't forget to leave a review with some stars. As this is my first self-published novel every review helps to get my work noticed.

https://www.facebook.com/Author.D.J.Holmes

d.j.holmess@hotmail.com

Comments welcome!

Thank you to my fiancé-

Natalie Johnson